© **2026 Nayampalli House LLC**

All rights reserved.
No part of this publication may be reproduced, distributed, or transmitted in any form or by any means, including photocopying, recording, or other electronic or mechanical methods, without the prior written permission of the publisher, except in the case of brief quotations embodied in critical reviews and certain other noncommercial uses permitted by copyright law.
This is a work of fiction. Names, characters, places, and incidents are the product of the author's imagination or used fictitiously. Any resemblance to actual events, locales, or persons, living or dead, is entirely coincidental.

Publisher:
The Nayampalli House

Artwork By:
Kumari Talisman – Alana McCarthy

Editing Services Provided By:
Ian Harper
Casey Houseworth

Formatting & Chapter Illustrations:
K.A. Nayampalli

ISBN
979-89895020-3-5

Library of Congress Control Number
2025923340

First Edition
Printed in the United States of America
with global print distribution.

A JOURNEY TO THE HEART OF KUMARI

BLOODLINES & BETRAYALS

K.A. NAYAMPALLI

DEDICATED TO AMMA & PAPPA

Whose lives and love remind me
that every bloodline is a story,
and every story is a legacy.

Acknowledgments
आभार

With every new step in this journey, I am reminded that writing is never a solitary act. Every book carries a community. To those who walked beside me during the shaping of this one—thank you. Your presence, your wisdom, your light: it's all woven in.

To my mother, who still listens patiently and always speaks the truth, your voice continues to steady mine.

To Ravi, whose faith in me remains unwavering. Your willingness to carry so much so that I may write is a gift I never take for granted. I could never have fulfilled this dream of becoming an author without your steady presence, and your ability to challenge me to be fully, fiercely myself.

To my amazing children Harrison, Kiran, Cyrus, and Gabriel. Thank you for your honesty, humor, and sharp eyes. You remind me daily why my story telling maters.

To Ian Harper. Thank you for once again bringing your discerning insight and steady guidance to this manuscript. Your clarity, instincts, and attention to structure helped me shape this book into something stronger and more precise. You ask the right questions, and you push when it matters. I trust your judgment completely, and I'm grateful to have you on this journey.

To Casey Houseworth. Thank you for your thoughtful edits. Your attention to pacing, clarity, and emotional tone helped bring this story into better focus.

Special thanks to my Aunt Sally, who graciously served as one of my beta readers. Your patience, your eye for detail, and your encouragement helped shape these pages into what they are now.

To Kathy Stillwagon, whose efforts in spreading the word on Long Island breathed new life into this work. Your support in marketing and promotion reached further than I ever could have dreamed, and I am grateful for your energy and generosity.

To my sister Paula Walters. Thank you for your belief in me, and for setting the example that anything is possible.

To my sister Debbie Knakal, thank you for your steadfast help and support. You have been a pillar throughout this process, and your encouragement has meant more than words can express.

To my brother, Andrew Knakal, and his wife, Tammy. Thank you for the many unseen ways you've helped create space for this work to live and grow. Your quiet generosity and willingness to support this vision behind the scenes mean more than I can say.

To My sister Sarah Kistner. Thank you for your courage, your tenderness, and the way you keep going. You remind me what service looks like. I'm grateful for you, always.

I remain deeply grateful to the friends, family, and readers who continue to walk this path with me. Each of you has left an imprint on these pages, whether through your time, your insight, or your belief that this story is worth telling.

To Nepal. Thank you for your silence, your ache, your mountain breath. You held me through the unraveling. The land whispered things I didn't know I needed to hear. Your sky opened something in me that had been shut for too long. I return to your memory often, and each time, it stills me.

To the Kumari. You are not a character. You are not a symbol. You are living breath beneath this work, the resonance I was entrusted to follow. I approach you not with claim, but with awe. Thank you for letting me glimpse what cannot be explained, only carried. This offering is placed at your feet. May it serve.

Every word in this book is a vow—of gratitude, of memory, of spirit. I release it into the world as a quiet blessing, carried on breath and intention. May it resonate with those who need it. May it stir something deep and ancient. Writing this story was not simply an act of craft—it was an act of devotion. Of returning what I've been given. This is simply my way of giving back.

Introduction

प्रस्तावना

November 10th
Himalayan Mountains
160 miles northeast of Kathmandu, Nepal

The wind howled, biting at Harrison Sharma's skin as it whipped across the mountaintop. The cold was bone-deep, cutting through his jacket, and the thin air made each breath a struggle. Around him, the peaks of the Himalayas stood vast and ancient, as if guarding secrets older than time. Snow swirled through the gusts, and the jagged mountains pierced the sky like sentinels of forgotten ages.

Harrison stood, rooted as the wind tore past him. The gale rose, testing his balance, but he held firm. He stared into the endless horizon, the weight of destiny pressing upon his chest with a relentless force.

It wasn't the altitude that made his heart pound—it was the path he and his family had already walked and the journey ahead. The power calling to him was more than just a whisper; it was a shout pulling him toward something greater than he had ever imagined.

Nepal was meant to be a holiday—a simple family trip, a break from their everyday lives. But something had shifted the moment their plane touched down. He couldn't explain it, not in words his family would understand. It wasn't the air, though the weight of it felt older here. It wasn't the mountains, though their jagged silhouettes stirred something familiar. It was deeper, almost like a fading memory pressing against the inside of his skin. Before the visions. Before the silence in the ancient temple in Chitwan. Before the goddess's gaze had met his own.

Even then, the Spirit of Kumari had already begun to stir.

Some say the Spirit of Kumari is real. Others say she is an illusion. A myth. A figment of the imagination. They speak of her in whispers—sensing her in wisps of temple dust that settle strangely and wind that moves against itself through narrow passes. She is said to slip along forgotten paths, into the stillness that lives between one breath and the next.

They say she waits.

Not a goddess. Not a ghost. She was something older—something that had listened when the first stars turned and had watched as the first fire caught.

The monks gave her names. The priests left offerings. The children…they simply felt her—in the tremble before dreams, in the scent before rain.

And now, she was stirring again.

Calling to Harrison.

Harrison hadn't expected the child—the living goddess Kumari, the physical embodiment of the Spirit—to notice him. But she had. Her gaze had somehow been drawn to his, and when their eyes had locked, it had awakened something deep inside, something ancient that felt beyond his control.

He hadn't been able to explain this new sensation to his family, but now, standing there, with the wind roaring around him, he could feel the truth settling in his bones. Ancient. Unfamiliar.

The stories would have named him the Seeker.

They whispered of how the Heart of Kumari had been a red diamond bound to balance. It had been thought to exert its pull when the world drifted too far in one direction or another, calling to what the old tales named the Seeker. What it corrected in one place was known to unmake elsewhere. That had been how it had always been told.

What no one could ever agree on was the cost.

The journey had already begun: the Kumari Mandala, the cryptic symbol that seemed to follow them; the prophecy they had uncovered in the jungles of Chitwan; and the ancient parchment that named him as the one meant to find the Heart. The last revelation had struck him like lightning. He hadn't asked for this role, hadn't sought it out—but now, there was no denying it.

The Heart wasn't just a gemstone; it was something far more dangerous. Its power tugged at him, straining the limits of what he believed himself to be. This wasn't just a physical quest to find the diamond; whatever awaited him would reach into the places where belief and self were not yet separate.

Without warning, shadows crept over the landscape. The mountain vanished. Harrison was no longer standing on the peak. He was somewhere else, a place darker, colder. Ahead of him, suspended in the void, was the Heart of Kumari. It glowed faintly, pulsating like a dying star.

There was something wrong.

Dark tendrils crawled toward the Heart, coiling around the diamond, choking its light. Figures emerged from the shadows—faceless and silent, their eyes gleaming with a hunger for the Heart. They reached, desperate to claim its power.

One of the wraiths turned toward him, towering, menacing. The voice came in three fragments, each colder than the last.

"Many are searching for the Heart, Seeker. But only the strongest will endure. Claim it...or be swallowed."

The words landed across seven hammering heartbeats. The message delivered, the vision shattered.

Harrison gasped as the mountain snapped back into place around him. The wind surged again, sharp and unrelenting, as if nothing had happened at all. Snow stung his face. The sky remained unchanged. He waited. For the pressure to lift. For understanding to settle. For something—anything—to confirm what he had just seen. Nothing came. Only the wind. Only the cold. Only the thin, merciless air pressed into his lungs.

The warning lingered without shape or instruction, its weight unresolved. Whatever had spoken to him had already withdrawn, leaving no assurance in its wake. Harrison swallowed and made the choice himself. This wasn't just about finding the Heart of Kumari. It felt like it was about reaching it before anyone else could.

He didn't turn back.

***

He jolted awake, his mind racing. The mountain was gone.

The soft hum of the vehicle's engine brought him back to reality. They were on the road to Pokhara, the van rattling along as the peaks of the Himalayas loomed in the distance.

He glanced around at his family, all asleep, unaware of what he had just seen. They didn't know. They couldn't. Harrison lay there with the knowledge, unable to set it down.

The road ahead was filled with danger.

And time was running out.

When Wonder Fails
यदा वस्मियः क्षीयते

Walk as before, with open eyes,
Through trusted doors where comfort lies.
Not knowing what the path will take,
Where light will bend—and truth will break.

Beyond the glow where answers sleep,
Where vows were sworn and secrets keep,
The Heart still waits, its fire the same,
It calls you forward. It knows your name.

Reach for the truth and hold it tight—
It will not mend the coming night.
For those who seek with love unguarded,
The ledger holds. The debt stands.

PART I

THE ONWARD JOURNEY
अग्रयात्रा

"...When the Time..."
— Doctrine of Balance, Fragment 9

"The Greatest Secrets Are Hidden in the unlikeliest of places."

—Roald Dahl

-PROLOGUE-
A Crack in the Pattern

सूत्रभेदः

KATHMANDU, NEPAL
TWENTY YEARS AGO

The night draped Kathmandu in a pall of secrecy, the city's ancient streets veiled in moonlit shadows. The scent of sandalwood and guggul curled through the air, winding into the labyrinthine halls of the Shatranj Ke Sipahi's stronghold, where a clandestine assembly convened. The chamber, tapestried with relics that whispered of a forgotten age, bore witness to a clash of wills brimming with power and ambition.

Within the vaulted sanctuary, the Path Lords stood at the four corners, unmoving as carved sentinels. Each bore the mantle of a cardinal point—the Watcher of Stillness to the North, the Kindler of Flame to the South, the Weaver of Flow to the East, and the Binder of Stone to the West. Their ceremonial sashes shimmered faintly in the torchlight, embodying the sacred balance of the Pattern.

Seated around the center table, the Council of Bishops gathered. Cloaked and hooded, their faces unreadable, they held the spiritual authority to interpret the Pattern and guard the mysteries of the Heart of Kumari.

Anchoring the chamber, Bhaskar Bhattarai commanded the room, his eyes ablaze as he surveyed the gathered elite. Opposite him sat Manav Bhattarai, the younger brother of Bhaskar's father—the venerable Vikrant Bhattarai, Chancellor of the Order—his countenance weighted with tradition and foreboding. Between them simmered an unspoken rift, heavy with the anticipation of conflict.

Bhaskar's authoritative voice cut through the silence. "We were once the custodians of the Heart of Kumari, placed upon the Board by divine design, entrusted not with ownership, but with balance. Yet, our ancestors, in their ignorance and fear, failed to grasp the Pattern's true intent. They mistook duty for sovereignty. Blind to the deeper current, they defiled the Flame, burning within the diamond. They tried to control what was never theirs to command. The monks hid the Heart—not out of malice, but because the Board was cracked. We were deemed unworthy. And so, the Pattern was veiled."

A low murmur rippled through the Council of Bishops. Some nodded, their eyes bright with fierce agreement; others exchanged wary glances, unsettled by Bhaskar's blunt condemnation.

A stern bishop spoke up, his voice cracking through the chamber. "Are we to believe our ancestors were so blind as to forfeit their sacred duty?"

Another answered, more measured than sharp. "Blind, perhaps—but not without cause. The Board was cracked. And cracks do not form without pressure. We cannot claim innocence when alignment with the Pattern collapsed."

Whispers rose and fell like a restless tide.

The first bishop's gaze fixed on Manav. "If redemption remains possible," he asked carefully, "what does the Pattern require of us now?"

A third bishop inclined his head. "Through service, we must set right what our failure fractured."

The second bishop's voice returned, tighter now. "Service, yes—but what if waiting is only another form of defiance?"

Manav's response was measured, his gaze unwavering upon Bhaskar, though his words carried past the bishop and to every corner of the chamber. "The Pattern requires restraint," Manav said at last. "We were cast aside, but not by thieves. We were cast aside by consequence. It was not their treachery that undid us. It was our own undoing. The Pattern remembers. The Law corrects. The monks did not seize the Heart; they were called to guard it. Not forever. Only until we are found worthy again. Redemption is not claimed through force. It is answered when we are ready to serve, not command."

A few bishops nodded; slowly, exchanging knowing glances. Others tightened their lips in silent disagreement.

"That day is upon us," Bhaskar said with resolve. "We are worthy and shall reclaim what is rightfully ours. The Heart of Kumari must return to the protection of the Shatranj Ke Sipahi."

Manav's rebuttal came swiftly. "The Heart is not a prize for our ambitions, Bhaskar. We were its guardians, bound by duty, by the Pattern. We were never meant to control it through dominion. We must realign ourselves through humility, recognizing the folly of our past."

A murmur of agreement spread among the more cautious bishops, while a few voices challenged quietly from the back rows.

Among the guild members, Bhaskar's nephews Raju and Siddharth watched with bated breath. Behind them stood King Arjun Bhattarai and Queen Reena, silent among the elders, watching as their sons learned what power looked like.

The twins' hearts were torn between the allure of glory and the warnings of caution—Bhaskar's fervor igniting a spark of longing, Manav's wisdom tempering it with apprehension.

"My son is right," said Vikrant Bhattarai, the eldest living member of the Order. "The time has come to retake what is ours."

The chamber erupted in cheers.

Manav's gaze shifted to Vikrant, his expression unyielding yet filled with a sorrowful understanding. "Vikrant, you, of all people, should remember the lessons of our downfall. The pursuit of power led us to this very fate. It was our arrogance and hubris that brought about our banishment. The monks who were entrusted with the diamond hid it not out of malice but out of necessity—to protect the world from our unchecked ambition."

A murmur of disapproval rippled through the gathering as Manav's words struck a nerve, revealing the uncomfortable truth that many were reluctant to confront.

Manav turned back to Bhaskar, his voice resolute. "The Heart of Kumari is a sacred artifact, meant to be kept and guarded, not wielded as a tool for dominance. Our ancestors' failure was not in losing the diamond but in losing their way. Redemption does not come from forcefully reclaiming what was lost. It comes from proving that we have learned—that we are only worthy through humility, compassion, wisdom, and true guardianship. To act otherwise is to repeat past mistakes and doom ourselves to the same fate."

Bhaskar's patience waned, his frustration mounting. "Your timidity has tethered us to the shadows for too long. It is time for action, not idle contemplation!" Bhaskar swiftly unsheathed his dagger, the blade's glint punctuating his threat.

A sharp gasp rose from the Council of Bishops.

One elder stood. "This council does not tolerate violence within these halls!"

At the chamber's corners, the Path Lords exchanged cold,

measured glances. The Watcher of Stillness tightened his grip on the carved staff. The Binder of Stone's jaw clenched, his silence heavier than thunder.

The room stilled—the fragile balance of the Board trembling on the edge of chaos.

Manav rose to meet Bhaskar's challenge, drawing his own blade with a heavy heart. "Bhaskar, this is not the path."

"Your path ends here," Bhaskar snarled.

The chamber held its breath as the two leaders faced each other, the weight of their conflict playing out in the flickering torchlight. The clash of steel reverberated through the chamber—a bright, relentless sound. Raju and Siddharth stood frozen, their eyes wide with terror.

Bhaskar and Manav engaged in a deadly battle, each strike and parry imbued with the weight of conviction. Their daggers sparked in the half-light, the metallic clangs echoing against the stone. The sounds of the conflict blended with the heavy breaths and murmured prayers of the onlookers.

Raju and Siddharth's hearts pounded in unison, torn between the fiery temptation of Bhaskar's ambition and the grave wisdom of Manav's restraint. The air thickened with tension—every swing of the blades a harbinger of fate—as the young men witnessed a struggle that would shape their destiny.

Bhaskar's onslaught was relentless, fueled by the lust for power. Manav, weathered by time but fortified by wisdom, evaded each blow with precision. Yet as the fight wore on, the prudence of age could not contend with the passion of youth, and Bhaskar's strength began to tip the scales in his favor.

With a final, decisive strike, Bhaskar's dagger found its mark. Manav's eyes widened in disbelief as the steel pierced his heart, the weight of betrayal stealing his last breath.

Bhaskar stood over Manav's fallen form, his chest heaving with the exertion of battle. His gaze swept over the assembled members. "I am your leader now," he announced. "We shall reclaim the Heart of Kumari and restore our honor."

For a moment, no one moved.

Then Vikrant stepped forward. He touched two fingers to his lips, then he raised his hand skyward. A vow without words. A sign as old as the Order itself. "To my son, the new Chancellor of the Shatranj Ke Sipahi!"

The hall erupted—some fierce and jubilant, others cautious, eyes shadowed. Whispers rose, gathered, and swelled into one voice. "To the Heart of Kumari!" Again, it came. Louder this time. "To the Heart of Kumari!" Their pledge was solemn. And uneasy.

Raju and Siddharth exchanged a glance as they processed the unfolding events. Bhaskar's words beckoned them toward glory, yet Manav's sacrifice lingered like a phantom in their minds.

Raju, his resolve ignited, stepped toward Bhaskar's cause. Siddharth, unsettled by Manav's warning, hesitated. As the Order ventured into the unknown, the brothers' destinies braided with the echoes of a dark past…and the shadows of an ambitious future.

***

Far from Kathmandu, deep within the bowels of the Earth, in a hidden enclave awaiting discovery, a candle guttered. A crack appeared in the Mandala. The Pattern had shifted…and not toward light.

— 1 —
JOURNEY TO POKHARA

पोखरायात्रा

PRESENT DAY
NOVEMBER 10ᵀᴴ
MUL KHOLA, NEPAL
(170 KILOMETERS WEST OF KATHMANDU)
2:00 P.M.

Beneath the van's tires, the gravel crunched as Raju, Siddharth, and the Sharma family ventured forward. In the second row, Harrison—sixteen—studied the trail through the front windshield from his middle seat. To his right sat Ravi, his father, one arm slung over his son with a quiet grin. On the opposite side, Sophie, his mother, watched the shifting landscape with a quiet attentiveness, something between wonder and warning rising in her chest.

Just behind them sat his grandparents, Hema and Ray. Known to the family as 'Amma' and 'Pappa,' they sat hand in hand, enjoying every moment of the experience. In the back, Cyrus and Kiran, his younger brothers—six and five, respectively—had claimed the last row as their fort. Having wrapped the space in blankets and backpacks, their laughter rose and faded with the climb into the hills.

Up ahead, billows of mist shrouded the road, blurring the line between the visible and the unseen. Raju kept his hands on the wheel as the jungle thinned, guiding the Sharma family through the changing scenery. The dense foliage gave way to the ascending Himalayan foothills. A sharp wind rose from the hills, bright with pine. It scattered the humidity, but the mist held its ground, curling low across the asphalt as if unwilling to yield.

The road before them was narrow and winding—a stretch of challenges at every bend. Oncoming trucks darted past at reckless speeds, often overtaking carts drawn by oxen. No one spoke. Even the children had stopped whispering.

Villages blurred into view—bright saris strung between doorways, prayer flags snapping above corrugated roofs, engines grinding through dust. Horns called out in uneven bursts. A radio crackled from somewhere unseen. The van moved through it all without slowing.

Harrison gazed out the front window. The hills rose and folded back into mist. A thought had followed him since morning, refusing to settle.

He opened his mouth—then closed it. A horn blared, too near. The van shuddered as a truck cut across their lane. Harrison blinked. The thought sharpened.

"It's strange, Raju," Harrison finally said, the words rolling awkwardly off his tongue. He shifted, taking a swig from his water bottle. "The last time we rode in this van, you shared the legend of the Heart of Kumari with us."

Raju's eyes met Harrison's in the rearview mirror.

"Do you know," Harrison asked. "About me? About me being the Seeker?"

The van entered another blind curve.

"No, I had no idea. This legend is unraveling for all of us in real time." Raju's eyes remained in the mirror a moment longer than necessary before returning to the road.

Harrison sank into his seat, his mind trying to untangle what had just been said.

From the back, Cyrus shifted in his sleep. His stuffed lamb slipped to the floor. Amma reached and tucked it beneath his arm.

Leaning forward, "Raju, Siddharth," he began again, his words steady despite the van's movement, "we're not only on a trip." He paused to clarify. "Well, I mean, we are, but as you've seen, we're on a quest that could change everything."

The engine strained as the road steepened.

"We know the goatskin revealed my name as the Seeker. We need your help. Your family knows the legends better than anyone. Maybe you're meant to help us?"

Raju kept his eyes on the road ahead while Siddharth, seated beside him, surprised by how the conversation was unfolding, turned to give Harrison his attention.

"This journey…it's more than just finding an object," Harrison said. "It's about figuring out our place in something way bigger. We're not after this gem just because it's a treasure—it's the key to something else, something I can't yet understand."

Raju's eyes again caught Harrison's in the rearview mirror, a flicker of contemplation giving way to a slow, deliberate nod.

The door had been opened. He felt it shift. The trust settled easily in the air. Too easily.

His grip tightened on the wheel.

"Will you help us?" Harrison asked.

Silence gathered—a breath, a measure, something unspoken passing between the brothers.

"Your trust honors us," Raju replied, the warmth in his voice contrasting with a steadiness that did not waver. "My brother and I will guide you. We'll take you as far as the legend goes and maybe to the Heart itself."

Raju was already charting the course, one that would lead back to what his bloodline had once been entrusted to guard. His expression stayed open, earnest. A calm he wore easily—because he believed it had always been his. The innocence of the Sharma family was the key he needed to unlock the path to the diamond. It felt clean, almost simple.

Sophie's voice rose, light against the hum of the engine. "Your knowledge—it might be what leads us to the gem."

"Our knowledge of the legends may indeed help," Raju said. "How you all fit into them is as much a mystery to us as it is to you."

Siddharth, contemplative, added his perspective. "The Heart works in mysterious ways. It's not about finding it; it's about the journey of faith."

Harrison leaned in, pressing. "Like what we're doing now? My dream showed Pokhara ahead of us. As if it were waiting. And here we are, en route, not knowing what comes next."

Siddharth gave a nod. "Faith isn't certainty," Siddharth said. "It's movement."

"We'll help," Raju said.

From the back seat, Kiran laughed in his sleep.

***

An hour passed with the vehicle's steady hum providing the only sound amidst their collective introspection. Eventually, Pappa broke the quiet; his voice was filled with the fatigue of their long journey. He leaned forward, one eyebrow lifting.

"Ravi," Pappa began, "do we have our accommodations arranged for tonight?"

Sophie nudged her husband. "Based on past experience," she teased, "Ravi hardly ever has those things figured out in advance."

Ravi groaned and rolled his eyes in mock annoyance. "Okay, okay," he said, pulling out his phone. "I'll find us a place."

"I'll help," Sophie offered, taking out her phone with a smirk. "Just want to make sure we end up somewhere with a gorgeous view...and not the first place that shows up on Google."

Amma rested her hand on the seatback. "It would be so nice to find a place with a spa. A hot shower and a foot massage would be nice, too."

Pappa winced as he shifted his back. "I second that idea! A back massage wouldn't be too bad either."

Amma gave him a look that conveyed half amusement, half exhaustion. "Oh, please, Ray. You'll fall asleep halfway through yours and start snoring before the poor masseuse even begins."

"That's the sign of a job well done."

Amma shook her head. "You're impossible."

"After all these years, you're only realizing that now, Hema?"

Among their banter, Sophie announced with triumph, "Got it! There's a hotel close to the city center. It looks luxurious from the photos."

"Perfect," Ravi replied, relieved. He rubbed his temples and closed his eyes. "Book it!"

The van climbed. The signal bars flickered and vanished.

Sophie fiddled with her phone, her frustration mounting as she battled a weak cellular signal. She turned to her husband. "Can you check your connection?"

Ravi, already half-asleep, groggily murmured a response

without opening his eyes. "Ask Siddharth to help. He's got better internet than we do."

Sitting behind Siddharth, Sophie extended her phone. "Siddharth, could you please help me make the reservation? This is the hotel we would like to stay at tonight. My connection is poor."

Siddharth smiled. "No worries, madam. I'll use my handy. The local SIM card usually gives a better connection," he said, taking the phone from her hand. Their fingers touched for a second before he looked down at the screen. "Let me see the hotel you had in mind."

Pappa turned, his brows knitting. "Handy? I thought only the Germans said that. They say that here now?"

"I picked it up in Thermal years ago," Raju explained. "It just…fit."

Siddharth agreed. "Makes sense, doesn't it? It's always in your hand. We've used it ever since."

Amma grinned. "The way you explained it to Kiran at Pashupatinath, I really thought it was a Nepali thing. Goes to show how much I know."

Pappa chuckled, shaking his head. "Hmm. Handy. I might start using that myself. Sounds oddly right."

Sophie sat back, sinking into her seat, letting the exhaustion of the trip catch up to her. She watched the scenery outside the window, the villages and fields blurring into streaks of color as the van rumbled forward. The lowering sun cast the world in a strange light.

Her thoughts drifted back to the past week. *The diamond. Where could it be hidden?* The idea of it, gleaming and powerful, tugged at something deep inside her. She turned her gaze toward her family. Ravi, half-asleep beside her; Pappa, gazing out the window in quiet reflection; and Amma, softly humming. In the back seat, Cyrus and Kiran were sound asleep, their peaceful faces unaware of the weight pressing on her.

A pang of guilt tightened in her chest.

What if I'm dragging them into something dangerous?

She shifted, the thought gnawing at her. But then she reassured herself. *Pappa and Ravi believed it was safe. If they were at ease, surely, I could be too. They wouldn't let anything bad happen. And there was Raju and Siddharth; they would be with us the whole time. They knew the land, the risks. They wouldn't lead us into harm, would they?*

She took a deep breath, pushing the uneasy thoughts aside as her gaze found Siddharth's reflection in the windshield—calm, composed, exactly in place. His long dark hair had come loose from its tie, falling over his shoulder.

The pull remained—quiet, persistent, unplaced.

Meanwhile, Siddharth worked quietly, the faint tapping on the phone a steady beat in the background. There was a long moment where the only other sounds were the tires rolling over the uneven road and the wind rushing through the open window.

Then, suddenly, Siddharth broke through her meditative trance. "You're all set," he explained, handing her cell phone back.

Sophie blinked, pulled from her thoughts. "Thank you, Siddharth," she murmured as she took the device from him.

"It's no trouble at all, madam. I'm here to assist."

The van did not slow.

Sophie hesitated for a moment, then she asked, "And where will you stay?"

Siddharth glanced back at her with a slight smile. "I've just made arrangements to stay at the same hotel. That way, we're at your beck and call, should you need anything."

"Oh," Sophie said, a little taken aback by his formality but amused by his choice of words. "I didn't realize I'd have my own personal attendants," she said softly. "I'll try not to be too demanding."

"You could never be too demanding, madam," he said with a smile. "As I mentioned, we're here to assist."

Sophie let out a small breath and settled back into her seat. It was only exhaustion, she told herself. The thought did not quite settle.

As the road narrowed, Raju glanced at Siddharth. He hadn't expected it to be this simple.

***

5:00 P.M.

Two hours later, the van pulled up to a hotel that contrasted starkly with the grand establishment Sophie thought she had asked Siddharth to book. She had expected towering columns, manicured gardens with flowing fountains, and an imposing façade edged with golden trim that exuded luxury. Instead, they found themselves outside a humble, old-fashioned inn. The exterior featured faded wooden signboards and exuded rustic charm. Contrary to their expectations of luxury, the inn's quaint simplicity caused the Sharma family to exchange puzzled looks.

Sophie looked down at her cell phone and then at the inn. "This isn't the hotel I booked," she remarked.

"This is where the GPS led us," Raju said. "There must have been some confusion in the listing. It will do."

Sophie turned to Siddharth. "Could you check the booking for me?"

She watched as Siddharth pulled up the reservation details. A moment later, he paused, his expression shifting to confusion. "That's strange. It still looks like the reservation is for this hotel."

Sophie processed this unexpected twist. She exhaled a weary sigh.

"No worries, Siddharth. We're all tired."

Ravi looked around, pausing at the faded sign that hung above the inn's entrance.

SURYA CHANDRA INN—ESTABLISHED 1890.

Ravi smiled. "At least we're not missing out on history!"

Upon stepping into the lobby, the weight of centuries settled around them. It was as if they had entered another world entirely, one much different from the impression given by the building's exterior. Every corner held its history close. Weathered wooden beams—relics of a bygone era—stretched across the ceiling, their presence imposing. The rough-hewn stone walls held the day's cool. Dark wood paneling lined the lower half, rising to the height of a man. Carved doors stood closed along the corridor. Nestled in arched recesses, sconces cast a warm radiance that did not quite reach the corners. Sofas faced one another near the window, arranged with deliberate symmetry.

The chime of a grandfather clock resonated through the space, Each note landed cleanly, as if marking more than the hour.

Along the back wall, a grand bookcase dominated the room, its base set deep into the stone, as though it had been built with the room rather than placed inside it. The surrounding panels met its edges without seam. It rose from floor to ceiling, narrowing the space. Antiquated books filled its shelves, which bowed under the weight, though the frame remained rigid. Among them were manuscripts in Sanskrit, their spines marked with dense, unfamiliar characters

Mirrors mounted in gold were fixed to the walls, reflecting the room at uneven angles. Their glass caught the light, refracting it just enough that no single pane returned the room exactly as it was.

Between them hung paintings of terraced fields, women carrying woven baskets, elders seated before ancient temples. The varnish had darkened at the edges. One frame hung slightly askew.

Beneath their feet, the floorboards creaked, then yielded to black and white marble laid in a strict checkered pattern. Every step fell somewhere chosen.

Within its blend of age and polish, the inn held a deliberate composure. From the flicker of the sconces to the weight of the wood, nothing appeared out of place—at least not at first glance. The light along the stone pooled unevenly, gathering where it should have thinned and thinning where it should have gathered, as if reluctant to settle. And yet, something in it held.

The inn's proprietor approached the Sharma family with a measured smile. Tall and slender, her raven-black hair cascaded in soft waves down her back, a striking contrast to her fair complexion. Her features were fine and symmetrical, her gaze steady as she took them in.

After the briefest pause, she reached out her hand to Ravi. "I'm Priya Chandra, the inn's owner. Please follow me so we can get you checked in."

The Sharma family trailed behind Priya to the front desk.

As she began to pull up the reservation, Ravi hesitated. "I'm not sure if we have a reservation here. We thought we had booked another hotel. Could you please check to confirm we are in the right place?"

Priya's smile didn't falter. "Of course. May I see your passports, please?"

Ravi glanced at Sophie. She had already reached into her bag. One by one, she placed the passports on the counter—hers, Ravi's, the children's, then Pappa's and Amma's—aligning the small navy booklets into a neat stack. Priya gathered them in both hands and turned toward the computer, their covers briefly catching the light before disappearing from view.

Priya looked up and nodded. "Yes, your reservation is right here. You are expected." She returned the passports across the counter, one by one. "Welcome to the Surya Chandra Inn."

Her smile widened slightly. "Our humble abode has its unique charm and plenty of stories to tell. It's one of the oldest establishments in Pokhara." She rested her hand lightly on the desk. "Built within the bones of the old fort. It was never torn down. Only… repurposed."

The chandelier light shifted as she spoke.

The family exchanged a look.

Priya noticed their interest and continued, "In fact, many believe the spirits of warriors who once protected the fort haunt this inn. There's a hidden room in the basement, inaccessible for years, where some say the soldiers hid their treasures."

Harrison straightened.

Pappa's brow lifted.

Sophie's fingers tightened around her bag.

"And don't worry," Priya added, her tone light, "we do have a spa and sauna. Not quite the marble columns and fountains you may have expected… but restorative, all the same." She paused, then slid a brass key attached to a tiny charm across the counter. "Your suite is on the third floor."

Amma blinked. "Suite?"

"A three-bedroom," Priya said smoothly. "We've given you an upgrade for the inconvenience. Breakfast begins at six."

Her smile returned, perfectly measured. "If you'll excuse me."

She turned—and in that turn caught sight of Raju and Siddharth entering with the luggage. A flicker—too precise to be surprise. Then it was gone.

A thin draft trailed in behind them, stirring the curtain by the front window.

Sophie's gaze followed the movement. Through the shifting fabric, she caught a glimpse of something pale beyond the glass. She stepped away from the counter, drawn toward it.

With a swift, almost involuntary movement, she darted through the front door for a clearer view.

The obscuring fog had lifted like a theatrical curtain revealing the awe-inspiring sight of a towering mountain. It seemed to float above a layer of clouds in the sky, like an ethereal island suspended between Heaven and Earth.

A shiver of reverence ran through Sophie as she recalled the words of the mysterious woman at the chai hut they had passed a few days earlier on their journey to Chitwan. *"People climb these mountains to get closer to the gods, but sometimes, the gods come down to visit us."*

The rest of the Sharma family followed her outside. There, they gasped with astonishment as they gazed upon this unexpected reveal. The inn, though simple, had the perfect vantage point for this magical view. The mountain, surrounded by an ethereal mist, evoked a sense of spiritual wonder.

"So, that's Machapuchare," Ravi marveled.

"It's incredible," Cyrus uttered, smiling as he beheld the grandeur before them.

Sophie turned to him. "See? Sometimes, the universe moves faster than our plans."

"'In the land where the scales touch the sky,'" Pappa repeated excitedly. "This is it! We're closer than we thought!"

"What do you mean, Pappa?" Sophie asked.

"Don't you see? Machapuchare is also known as Fish Tail Mountain! Fish have scales! The goatskin we found in Chitwan! It referred to 'the land where the scales touch the sky!'" Pappa explained.

"You're right, Dad," Ravi praised, his eyes widening with realization. "I think you've cracked the first part of the clue!" He turned to Harrison, his excitement contagious. "Isn't this amazing? It's all coming together! We're meant to be here!"

Harrison stared at the mountain, hoping his father was right.

"Phew, I'm glad it's not dragon scales," Kiran said.

"Me too, Kiran," Sophie replied with a light laugh, already turning toward the door.

They had almost gone inside when the air shifted—nothing dramatic, just a sudden pull through the courtyard that stirred the prayer flags along the stone wall. The movement caught them off guard, enough to make them glance back once more toward the mountain. It looked the same as it had a moment before. Clean. Still. Unmoved.

The moment passed.

They stepped into the Surya Chandra Inn, welcomed by warmth and the low murmur of voices. What had begun as an ordinary booking mistake settled quietly into place, stripped of explanation. The inn asked nothing of them. It simply received them—and that, without their knowing, was where things first began to come undone.

***

7:00 P.M.

With a fire roaring in the hearth that evening, the Sharma family gathered in one of the inn's comfortable sitting areas. The grandfather clock chimed seven times, each stroke a deep thrum that reverberated through the bones of the old building, a resonant echo that spoke of passing time with grave certainty. Above the pendulum, a small brass plate gleamed: WHEN THE TIME... (DOCTRINE OF BALANCE, FRAGMENT IX). They couldn't help but feel the twist of fate that had brought them to the Surya seemed to settle into place around them, whether they noticed it or not.

Pappa unfolded the map he had acquired from the Jungle Lodge Camp library and placed it on the coffee table. He pointed at a spot near their current location. "Look here. I think this is where the fort used to stand, where we are now." His finger tapped the same area he had just indicated, pausing as his brow furrowed in concentration. "And this..." He hesitated, removing his reading glasses. He rubbed them against his shirt before placing them back on his face.

A faint symbol was etched beneath his finger—a rook, like the chess piece, but stylized in a way that hinted at something older.

He peered closer at the mysterious mark. "Hmm... I'm not quite sure what this is."

"May I?" Raju asked, peering over Pappa's shoulder to take a closer look.

Sensing Raju's interest, Pappa gestured toward an empty space beside him. "Come, have a closer look," he encouraged, sliding the map across for better viewing.

"Fascinating," Raju whispered, a spark of enthusiasm igniting as he studied the intricate lines and symbols.

Siddharth, observing from a distance, approached with

a questioning look. "What's the latest?" he inquired, folding his arms.

Harrison eyed the map, then looked back at Siddharth. "The clue from the goatskin hints at caves, and the dream pointed us toward Pokhara," he explained, trying to hide his uncertainty. "Beyond that, we're piecing it together."

"The caves around Pokhara are quite numerous," Raju interjected, "creating a labyrinth within the mountains."

Siddharth's interest was piqued. "May I see the goatskin?"

"Of course," Harrison replied, reaching into his backpack. With care, he extracted the parchment and handed it to Siddharth.

Siddharth's fingers trembled as they traced over the material. The Sanskrit characters seemed to dance before him, revealing secrets only the chosen could perceive. The goatskin felt alive, a conduit of energy and history. "Incredible," Siddharth murmured, almost to himself. He felt an inexplicable magnetic pull, as though the Heart of Kumari had assigned him a distinct role to fulfill. The feeling left Siddharth with a growing sense of purpose.

"I believe I might know which cave we should explore. It's closer than it appears." Siddharth proclaimed.

"Which one is it?" Raju asked, his gaze fixed on the map.

"It's the bat cave near Phewa Lake," Siddharth said. "I'll make the arrangements to go there."

"How do you know that's where we should look?" Harrison asked.

"Well, I don't know for sure," Siddharth said, rubbing the back of his head as he searched for the right words. "It fits," he concluded.

His statement was met with nods and murmurs of approval. The family's trust in him solidified. All except for Harrison.

For Harrison, Siddharth's words hadn't landed quite right.

They felt like a note slightly out of tune—almost correct, but just enough off-key to make his nerves cringe.

Harrison watched Siddharth for a beat longer than the rest, his eyes narrowing. "If you say so…"

Raju sensed Harrison's doubt and leaned closer to the map, drawing the family's focus with him. His finger traced the contours of the area housing the bat cave that Siddharth had mentioned. He then followed the faded lines that branched across the parchment, reminiscent of the sprawling roots of an age-old tree. "You see these?" His voice lowered as though sharing a secret. "They're said to be old tunnels, remnants from a time when the Shatranj occupied the land."

"The Shatranj?" Sophie asked, looking up.

Raju nodded. "Yes. As I mentioned back in Chitwan, they were a secretive order, active centuries ago. Obsessive, some say." He traced the root-like lines again. "They searched for religious artifacts—not for wealth, but for what they believed was spiritual power. The Heart of Kumari was one of their most sought-after relics."

The family leaned in, captivated.

"Legend has it," Raju continued, "these tunnels were lifelines during sieges, escape routes for royals, and pathways for silent armies. But not all led to safety. Some spiraled down into the depths of the earth, into caves shrouded by mysterious old tales."

Sophie tilted her head, intrigued. "What kind of tales?"

Raju shifted, eager to elaborate. "Tales of hidden treasures and perilous traps," he began. "Of one tunnel, in particular, that led to a cavern where the Heart of Kumari was thought to be hidden. The cavern is known to few, its entrance sealed by an ancient force."

Harrison drew nearer. "Is it possible these tunnels still exist? Could they lead us to the diamond?"

Raju gave a slow nod. "Yes, they could. But navigating them is treacherous. We would have to be absolutely certain before entering. The few who tried either never returned or came back...changed. They spoke of whispering shadows and walls that breathed, of darkness so thick it could swallow the light."

"I'm not afraid," Harrison declared emphatically.

Raju's gaze locked onto Harrison's. "You're not afraid now. But you will be," he warned.

A subtle yet noticeable shiver of fear rippled through Harrison's expression, and he quickly shifted his focus past Raju and into the hypnotic dance of the fire blazing in the hearth. The world seemed to fade into the background. Raju's words echoed in his mind, awakening deep feelings. As the flames danced and twisted, they seemed to take on sinister shapes. Malevolent creatures and demons emerged from them, their warped visages contorted in torment, foreshadowing the depths of darkness yet to unfold. One shape lingered. A silhouette—a girl with a blade held low, her hair tangled by wind, her face unreadable in the flicker. Then gone. As if memory had coughed, then swallowed it whole.

A sudden crackle from the firewood snapped Harrison out of his trance—one sharp pop, then three smaller snaps, followed by a scatter of sparks that seemed to stutter through seven quick clicks, dispelling the dread Raju's revelation had sown. His pulse had quickened, and both fear and determination surged through him.

Still pondering Raju's story, Pappa looked up and was drawn to each family member. With heightened emotion, he spoke. "The inn could be more than a place to rest; it might be the starting point for our quest. We can't predict what secrets or clues may be hidden within its historic walls, guiding us on our journey." He then turned to Raju and Siddharth. "I'm glad you've joined us."

Raju exchanged a quick look with Siddharth before responding. "Thank you, Ray. We're glad to be here," he said, shifting to mask his discomfort.

Filled with youthful wonder, Kiran stared at the map. His imagination transported him to a world of cinematic splendor. "When do we find this treasure?" he blurted out.

Cyrus, clutching his beloved stuffed animal, Sheepy, looked up with a curious gaze. "Does this mean we're treasure hunters now?"

Ravi laughed. "It appears so, son."

"Take a look at this," Raju said. His index finger glided over the contours, pausing at the outlines that represented landmarks. "You notice these curves? They might show a concealed route leading from our location. It follows the Seti River. In theory, it could be an underground passage that bypasses the harsh Himalayas."

Cyrus's excitement surged. "I want to explore a secret tunnel!"

"Me too!" Kiran added, his eyes wide.

"But shouldn't we check out the caves first?" Sophie asked, glancing up at Siddharth. "Do you think we could go tomorrow?"

Siddharth met her gaze, pausing briefly before replying. "I don't see why not." He glanced at Raju for confirmation, who gave a quick nod.

Sophie beamed. "Oh, that would be wonderful!" She looked at Ravi. "Right, honey?"

"Yeah," Ravi said, "sounds great."

Raju stood up and walked over to the bookshelf, scanning the spines before selecting a worn, leather-bound book with Sanskrit writing along its binding. "This is it," he said. He brought the book over to Pappa and flipped it open to a page marked by an intricate symbol.

"Here's the legend," Raju continued, pointing to the page written in Sanskrit.

Pappa leaned in, eyes narrowing as he examined the page. The image of the Kumari Mandala was unmistakable, etched at the top of the ancient text.

Raju tapped the symbol with his finger. "See this? This mark—the Kumari Mandala—I think this is what's guiding you. And look here; it says a secret chamber is hidden deep in Nepal. This is what we need to find." He paused, glancing at Siddharth before continuing. "And according to what you saw on the goatskin, the next clue is in the bat cave?"

"That's right," Siddharth confirmed.

Raju studied the map closely then glanced back at the book. He returned to the map, searching intently. "Wait," he murmured. "Look at this." He pointed to a faint mark on the map. "Here's the cave Siddharth thinks the clue is in—and just as I suspected, it's marked. But it's almost invisible."

He traced the faded lines with his fingertip. "See this broken ring? The mark itself shows a fracture—like something was split here long ago. That's why the symbol is faint. Places like this were sealed to keep their secrets hidden."

He went back to the book, comparing the designs. "See this?" Raju continued, tapping a similar symbol in the book. "It matches the mandala. That's how we know it's the right cave."

"Let me see that," Harrison said, reaching for the map. His voice was sharper than he meant it to be.

Pappa leaned closer to the map, his eyes widening. "No, Harrison, Raju is right—it's the Kumari Mandala, the same design. How did I miss that?"

"It's subtle, Pappa," Sophie added comfortingly, leaning over to examine the map herself. She turned to Raju and nodded in agreement. "The mandala marks the cave."

Harrison didn't respond. Instead, he reached for the goatskin, the script inked in a language he couldn't read—but one he could feel. The letters shimmered faintly as his fingers brushed them, the words quivering like something alive. The goatskin never lay still—it bent toward resonance as it slipped between hands like a mirror unwilling to settle.

The words were meant for him. He knew it. Something was off. "If I'm the Seeker," he muttered, more to himself than the group, "why did the goatskin speak to Siddharth?"

Sophie's hand found his arm. She pulled him gently aside, just out of earshot. Her gaze lingered on Siddharth before she spoke. "We asked them to join us for a reason," she said. "They know this land. Its silence. Its signs."

He looked past her at the twins, then back at the goatskin. "Yeah. You're right."

Still holding the goatskin, he handed it to Pappa. "Does it say the name of the cave?"

Pappa scratched his head, squinting at the markings. "No. Just the clue. Doesn't name it."

Siddharth stepped forward, the book pressed to his chest. "Harrison, listen. The goatskin didn't *tell* me," he said. "I just… put the pieces together." He then opened the book, turning it toward Harrison. "Look. The mandalas—they match. Same broken ring, same central glyph. I thought if you saw it, it would make sense."

"Yeah," Harrison murmured, eyes tracing the worn patterns. "I guess you're right. Just wish I'd figured it out first." He looked up. "No hard feelings?"

"Never," Siddharth said, shaking his head. "You'll have your share of puzzles to solve."

At that moment, Priya slipped into the room, her bright smile catching everyone's attention. "If you're chasing hidden corridors and forgotten tales, it seems fortune brought you to just the right place," she said with a playful lilt.

Raju looked up, snapping the book shut. "We can pick this up later." He walked to the bookshelf and carefully slid the book back into place.

"Am I interrupting something?" Priya said, setting an appetizer platter on the table. Local cheeses and ripe fruit lay beside warm bread. The offering was generous. Almost disarming.

"No, just planning our next adventure," Ravi quipped, chewing on a cracker.

Pappa reached for a piece of cheese. His smile brightened as the rich flavor melted on his tongue. With a satisfied nod, he followed Raju's lead, carefully folding the map and tucking it out of sight. He cast a quick glance at Priya, not wanting her to catch on to what they were up to.

Aware of his cautious actions, Priya continued, "How about I arrange a brief tour tomorrow? The older, forgotten parts of this inn have remained untouched for ages, holding secrets of their own."

"Sounds wonderful," Sophie remarked. She took a bite of a cracker.

"Thank you, Priya. That would be lovely," Ravi said, smiling as she poured the wine.

There was a brief pause in the room before Harrison spoke up. "I'd say our change of plans looks more like serendipity than a mistake," he mused, spreading a dollop of plum jelly onto a heel of bread and popping it into his mouth with satisfaction.

As the wine flowed and the conversation carried on into the evening, Priya excused herself, quietly leaving the room. Raju and Siddharth took the opportunity to settle beside Sophie and Harrison, while Amma and Pappa relaxed on an adjacent couch. The kids were happily immersed in their Nintendo Switch devices, their giggles and laughter a clear indication of their amusement. Ravi, enjoying his drink, settled across from his wife. His smile widened as the group relaxed, a warm camaraderie filling the air.

Ravi sat back with a mischievous grin. "Hey, Siddharth, did I tell you about Sophie's little elephant bath adventure?"

Sophie groaned, laughing as she buried her face in her hands. "Not that story again."

But Ravi was relentless. "We were at the elephant nursery, and Raju had this brilliant idea to get Sophie up on the elephant alone, just for fun. So, we led the elephant out to the river, and the next thing you know—splash! It sprays her with its trunk! She was completely drenched."

The room erupted in laughter, and Siddharth turned to Sophie with a grin. "I wish I could've seen that."

"It was epic!" Harrison chimed in.

Sophie chuckled, shaking her head at the memory. "Trust me, it wasn't as fun as it sounds."

"Oh, come on, it was hilarious," Ravi said, still laughing. "I've got the picture to prove it."

Raju smiled. "One of many great stories your family will have to tell again and again."

Harrison leaned forward. "Dad—tell the one from when you were deployed in Afghanistan. The one where you got stopped at the checkpoint."

Ravi hesitated, his tone shifting. "That one?" He set his glass down, the weight of his experiences with the U.S. military softening his posture. "That was years ago. Different world."

"Go on," Amma urged. "You can't stop there."

Pappa turned to her. "Hema, maybe he doesn't want to tell it."

Ravi's gaze shifted to Sophie.

She nodded. "Tell it."

The room drew inward as if to listen.

"I still remember the mountain road in Kunar," Ravi began. "It cut through the rock like a scar. I was assigned to move classified cargo—no escort, no convoy, just a white Toyota Hilux pickup truck. My superiors said it would draw less attention than a military rig. Beside me sat my sergeant—American, young, by-the-book. He knew the protocols; I knew the terrain. That's why they put us together."

"I never heard this one," Cyrus said, looking up from his game.

"That's because it happened before you were born," Harrison explained.

"Oh, I want to hear, too," Kiran piped up. His brow furrowed. "A sergeant? That's like Ms. Malik? You had to do what he said? Even you?"

Ravi laughed. "That was his job—to make sure I did what kept us alive."

Kiran wrinkled his nose. "Did he make you eat your vegetables, too?"

"He didn't have to," Ravi said with a grin. "Smart soldiers eat their vegetables before every mission."

Laughter stirred around the room.

The old inn seemed to exhale with them.

"We came around a bend near Asadabad." Ravi's voice deepened and steadied as the memory drew him in. "The road was narrow, carved into the cliffside, just wide enough for one truck. At the edge, the drop-off fell away into certain death. Ahead, a line of men stood across the path—faces hidden behind scarves, rifles slung low. Their clothes were a patchwork of American uniforms and local fabric, the colors of every side of the conflict. A makeshift barricade blocked the way—barrels, sandbags, a flag that belonged to no one. On the ridge above them, another Hilux crouched with a rocket launcher mounted in its bed, the tube pointed down at the road. It was there for the ones who tried to run."

Cyrus stared in amazement. "What happened next?"

"My sergeant said what he'd been trained to say—'Drive. Barrel through. Don't stop.' But I pointed to the ridge. 'If we move, they'll fire.'"

Ravi's voice grew quiet. "The engine idled. Dust drifted through the open window. The men stared. The one in front raised his rifle, and in that silence, I knew—we were already caught."

Amma's hand flew to her mouth.

"The men tensed," Ravi said. "Rifles lifted, safeties clicked off. I could feel the air tighten—I thought we were dead men. My sergeant's hand went for his rifle, but I caught his arm. 'Trust me,' I said. I turned to the man staring me down. His weapon steady."

As he continued, Ravi's tone grew more animated. "The soldier shouted in Pashto—'Americans!'—and the others closed in. I could see the tremor in my sergeant's hand. I told him again, 'Trust me.' Then I spoke—slow, careful. 'As-salaam alaikum,' I said. Peace be upon you."

Kiran leaned closer, captivated by his father's storytelling.

Ravi's tone lowered. "He hesitated. My face didn't fit the word. In his own tongue, he asked, 'Where are you from?' I told him, 'India.' The rifle dipped, just a little. Then he said he needed something for his leaders—money, weapons, anything to show that he had stopped us."

"What did you do?" Amma asked.

"I said I had American chocolate from the PX and a six-pack of Gatorade," Ravi said. "I told him that in Pashto. It caught him off guard. He said when he was a boy, his father would bring home American candy from the markets. Then, he smiled—said he used to listen to Bollywood songs before the bans. His favorite was from Sholay."

Ravi allowed himself a brief smile. "He hummed the 'Mehbooba Mehbooba' theme from the movie. I sang the next line, and before we knew it, we'd broken into song. The men behind him started laughing—quiet at first, then louder, until the tension dissipated. I handed him the drinks and candy, and he waved us through. On the ridge, the Hilux with the launcher never moved. It didn't need to."

Pappa exhaled. "That took a lot of courage. And wit."

Ravi laughed. "My sergeant still talks about it. Says he's never seen anyone sing their way out of a firefight."

Sophie's expression softened. "God was with you that day."

Ravi looked at her. "Maybe. Or maybe death just changed its mind."

Pappa grinned. "If I ever tried that, I would be buried before sunrise."

Amma smirked. "Ray, you would've eaten all the chocolates before they stopped you."

Laughter rippled through the room.

"Wow, Dad," Cyrus said, eyes wide.

"I still can't believe you made it out alive," Harrison added. "That's luck."

"That's your father—Mr. Luck." Sophie winked.

Raju leaned forward, his voice low. "You looked a man in the eye while his rifle was on you. You faced death and didn't look away." His tone held no judgment—only a dark curiosity. "How did that feel?"

Ravi studied him. "Back then, it simply felt like survival. But looking at it now, I don't think it was about me. In that moment, we all found the courage to do the right thing. It wasn't about facing death; it was about accepting our humanity."

"Well said," Siddharth replied. His gaze flicked briefly to his brother, then away. "Perspective matters."

Silence stretched. The fire hissed.

Raju's smile lingered, his eyes unreadable. He wondered what it might feel like—to stand at the edge of death and feel power, not fear.

Sensing the heaviness, Sophie moved closer to her husband and gave him a playful nudge. "Oh, but you should've seen the time Ravi tried to feed a monkey at the temple," she said, her eyes gleaming with amusement. "He held out a banana, thinking he'd make a new friend. The monkey grabbed the banana so fast, Ravi barely had time to react. Then it started chasing him—cornered him against a wall with this crazy look in its eyes!"

Everyone burst into laughter again, with Ravi shaking his head, grinning. "That monkey was after more than just a snack. I swear it had revenge on its mind!"

"It was definitely out to get you!" Harrison added, barely holding back his laughter. "You were backing away like it was some sort of showdown."

"Hey, I was just defending our snacks!" Ravi joked. "I wasn't about to let that thing steal our whole lunch."

As the laughter faded, Ravi grinned. "We've all had our moments, haven't we? But seriously, I don't know how I got so lucky with this one." He pulled Sophie close with a playful wink.

Sophie chuckled, shaking her head. "Maybe it's because you always make things interesting." With that, she slid onto his lap, wrapping an arm around his shoulders.

"I'll drink to that," Pappa offered, lifting his glass.

"Cheers!" the group answered.

Ravi exhaled, leaning back comfortably. "Well, whatever it is, you're right. I'm the lucky one. Don't know what I'd do without you."

Sophie's smile deepened. "You make it easy to stick around." Her gaze held his for a lingering moment before she stifled a yawn. "I think that's my cue to get the kids to bed. I'm exhausted."

Ravi nodded. "You're right. Big day tomorrow."

Sophie stood, stretching. "Goodnight, everyone. We'll see you in the morning."

Ravi followed her lead, standing as well. "Yep, let's all get some rest. Tomorrow's going to be something."

Siddharth got up from the couch. "I'll check with the inn's management to secure a visit to the caves for tomorrow."

"That'd be great," Ravi replied, nodding in appreciation.

Raju grinned, glancing at Harrison. "At this rate, you'll have that diamond in no time."

"With you leading us, Raju, I have no doubt," Harrison said, returning the smile.

"Priya mentioned something about a tour. I think that's first, but I could be wrong," Sophie said, glancing at the kids sprawled out on the floor, their eyes glued to their Nintendo Switches. "Boys, it's time to head back to the room."

"You might be right," Siddharth chimed in. "She did mention that, didn't she?" He paused. "Maybe the tour won't take too long."

Kiran jumped up from his game, darted over to Siddharth, and wrapped his arms around his leg. "Goodnight, Siddharth!" he said brightly.

Siddharth smiled, ruffling Kiran's hair. "Goodnight, little guy. Sleep well."

Cyrus stood up, gave a little wave, and added, "Yeah, goodnight."

Amma and Pappa rose from their seats, with Amma stretching while Pappa gave Siddharth a hearty pat on the back.

"Glad you decided to come along with us," Pappa said. "Your knowledge is invaluable."

"I wouldn't miss it," Siddharth replied.

As they made their way toward the stairs, they crossed

the checkered floor that separated the sitting area from the lobby in neat black-and-white symmetry. Cyrus slowed for half a step, frowning faintly, as if his foot had landed wrong. He adjusted without comment and continued on.

Pappa paused beside a small display table crowded with postcards, brochures, and a folded newspaper. "Ah, The Kathmandu Herald," he murmured, picking it up with idle curiosity. "Even this place keeps its pulse on the world." He tucked it under his arm, meaning to glance at it later.

Ahead, Sophie gathered the kids and started up the stairs, reaching for Ravi's hand. Their fingers intertwined effortlessly.

Ravi grinned. With a playful bow, he gestured ahead. "After you, my lady."

Sophie laughed, giving him a soft nudge before they began to ascend the stairs. She glanced over her shoulder and gave Raju and Siddharth a warm smile.

Siddharth returned it and called out, "Goodnight, Sharmas! See you in the morning."

Harrison trailed behind the rest of his family, his mind wandering, caught up in his own thoughts.

10:00 P.M.

The Sharma family made their way to their accommodations, a spacious three-bedroom suite anchored by a central sitting area with a wide, stone hearth. Above the mantel hung a large oil painting of the fort that had once stood where the inn now rose. It was depicted at twilight—its ramparts dark with age, the light behind it low and smoldering. Mist curled around the foothills, half-concealing the outline of Machapuchare in the distance. The brushwork was delicate but fractured, with hairline cracks tracing across the canvas like veins. Something about the scene felt paused—not still, but waiting.

Across from the hearth, a woven tapestry stretched the length of the far wall. Threads of red, indigo, and gold showed Sherpas scaling icy cliffs, villagers in mid-dance, stupas circled by wind-blown prayer flags. But the faces were indistinct. All celebration, no joy. Motion, but no warmth. In the shifting light of the room, the figures seemed to blur at the edges, as if not meant to be seen too long.

The stucco walls, painted in an earthen orange, peeled back in places to reveal the original stonework beneath—sections left exposed, like something remembered by the building itself. The timber beams overhead were heavy and timeworn, echoing those in the lobby, their presence solid but strangely close. The room held its warmth, but not all of it felt welcoming.

They stood for a moment in the quiet, each sensing something they couldn't name.

Cyrus wandered toward the nearest door. "Can this one be ours?" he asked, already peeking inside.

Kiran darted past him. "I get the bed by the window!"

Sophie exchanged a glance with Ravi. "We'll take the one closest to them," she said softly. "Just in case."

"That leaves the corner room," Amma noted, setting down her bag with a decisive thump.

"Which I'll gladly claim, unless anyone objects."

"No objections," Ravi said, managing a tired smile.

Sophie walked Kiran and Cyrus toward their room, brushing a hand over their hair as they passed.

"Goodnight, explorers," she said—not with excitement now, but something quieter. Protective. Wary.

"Goodnight, fellow Seekers," Amma added with a grin, though her eyes lingered on the painting above the fire a moment longer.

Ravi paused near the hearth, his eyes on the cracked canvas. "Strange piece," he murmured. But he didn't elaborate.

The others drifted into their rooms, doors creaking closed one by one.

Harrison lingered. He stood before the hearth, studying the painting. In the lighting, the mist seemed to shift—no, just flicker. But something in the shadows near the ramparts held his gaze. Not a figure. Not quite. Just a darker shape where the stone met the trees. He leaned in, then blinked, and it was gone.

He stepped back, unsettled without knowing why.

Then, slowly, he turned and followed the others.

Behind him, the room settled. The beams overhead creaked once. And above the hearth, the fort watched on.

***

After Sophie put Kiran and Cyrus to bed, thoughts of what the next day would bring churned in her mind—ancient treasures, hidden passages, and the lure of the diamond. She felt its pull sharpening, its promise of power filling her thoughts. It wasn't the journey she had planned, but it was shaping up to be an adventure she could have never foreseen.

"Sophie, can you call down and see if they can bring some water to the room?" Ravi's voice interrupted her reverie, cutting through her thoughts.

Sophie glanced at the phone next to the bed but shook her head. "I'll go down and get it," she said, standing up. "I've got a second wind, and I need to stretch my legs anyway."

Ravi looked at her for a moment, then nodded. "All right, just don't be long."

"I won't," she promised, grabbing the metal keychain from the table. The weight of it in her hand was grounding, but her mind kept drifting back to the diamond—the way it called to her, the way it made everything else seem so distant, so insignificant.

As she locked the door behind her and started down the dim hallway, she couldn't help but think about what the morning might bring. The diamond felt close enough to disturb her thoughts, teasing her with possibilities. Her pulse quickened. They had come here seeking a respite from their daily lives, yet it was the diamond that now occupied her mind, like a shadow she couldn't shake.

And then, there was Siddharth.

Morning couldn't come soon enough.

— 2 —
Secrets in the Shadows

छायासु रहस्यानि

November 11th
12:01 A.M.

Locked within a sitting room at the Surya Chandra Inn, the air held, suspended. In the shadowy parlor, the flicker of a lone candle caught the earnest faces of Raju, Siddharth, Priya, and Anil. Bound by blood—cousins and heirs to a legacy marred by darkness—Priya and Anil served as the stewards of the inn, its purpose not entirely what it seemed.

Many centuries ago, a guild bound by blood once took a vow to guard the Heart of Kumari, a red diamond burning with an emerald fire. The Order of the Shatranj Ke Sipahi was strategically named after chess pieces, meant to evoke intricate strategy. Its members came to be regarded as custodians of secrets as old as the legends themselves—described as keepers not of power, but of balance, charged with safeguarding what could not be owned. Over time, those who remained formed a lineage, bound less by blood than by what they carried forward as duty.

The candle dipped, then steadied.

However, as time eroded its original foundations, the Order became corrupt, its responsibilities and privileges gradually stripped away. Once regarded as guardians of balance, the Shatranj Ke Sipahi became ensnared in the world's dark underbelly, engaging in illicit activities to fuel the corruption that had overtaken an Order meant to be a beacon of protection. What had remained was not honor, but its repetition—performed long enough to resemble virtue.

The Heart of Kumari was never meant to bestow dominion. It was understood as a mirror, veined with divine resonance. When the Shatranj ceased to listen—when power replaced stillness—the Pattern withdrew. What remained was theater. An Order hollowed from within.

Over time, the Order had splintered into two factions. One group held fast to what they believed was the Order's original purpose, convinced that finding the Heart of Kumari would restore it to former glory. The other faction dismissed the Heart as a fool's errand, focusing instead on the more tangible gains of power and influence, maintaining the appearance of protectors while pursuing darker ends. The divide between these two groups deepened, with one chasing ancient prophecies and the other consolidating control through more pragmatic means.

Raju, Siddharth, Priya, and Anil had been born into this paradox, offspring of a legacy that had wandered far from its original purpose, yet bound by blood to a cause that had once sworn itself pure. Now, the torchbearers of both Surya Chandra Inn and the Order's covert endeavors were a mix of willing and reluctant participants in this inherited saga.

Priya's desire for autonomy was no longer a quiet longing; it had grown into a fierce, consuming fire. She couldn't endure another day under Uncle Bhaskar's suffocating grip, trapped by his ambition and control. She didn't just want to escape. She wanted to surpass him, to carve out a power, one he could never touch. But as the years had passed, her faith in the Heart's existence had begun to crumble. She had witnessed too many quests ending in death, too many promises of power dissolving into nothing.

Raju rarely doubted the Heart's existence, having been raised with the certainty that it would one day be found. To him, the Heart was not a symbol of conquest, but what he believed could restore an order he felt had lost its way. In his mind, the call was not guaranteed, but it was something he had been preparing for all his life.

Siddharth wasn't after power—he sought redemption. He believed that finding the Heart could cleanse the Shatranj Ke Sipahi of its corruption and return it to what he understood as its original purpose. For Siddharth, the Heart wasn't a symbol of conquest, but a chance to atone for the sins of the Order.

Anil's motives were simpler, more personal. He didn't share Priya or Raju's ambitions; he was content to stay in the background, driven by loyalty to his sister. All he wanted was to prove himself to Priya, to gain her approval, and to show he was more than just a follower in her shadow.

Raju scanned the room, absorbing the timeworn wooden beams and cherished artifacts passed down through generations. As he took a deep breath, the space seemed to pulse with memories, and a knowing smile tugged at his lips. "There's a reason I brought the Sharma family here—especially Harrison." He paused, looking first at Priya and then at Anil. "I believe the two of you have pivotal roles in our shared mission.

This inn is no coincidence; it matters more than it appears. Together, we're closer to the Heart of Kumari than ever before."

Priya crossed her arms, her eyes narrowing with defiance. "Cut the crap, Raju. You know damn well this inn is a front for the Shatranj Ke Sipahi's dealings. Uncle Bhaskar watches over it with a hawk's eye. He sent you here with the Sharmas. This was his plan, not yours."

"Yes, the Chancellor knows we are here."

A shiver passed through her at the mention of the word 'Chancellor.' She faltered, her gaze dropping for a fraction of a second before she forced herself to meet Raju's eyes again. "And when you speak of him, you'll call him Uncle Bhaskar. I detest having to call him 'the Chancellor.'" She lifted her chin, trying to mask the fear, but it lingered in her eyes. "Understood?" The challenge in her voice was thinner now, the defiance beginning to crack.

Raju acknowledged her correction with a nod. "Understood, Priya. Just making sure we're all on the same page," he said, a knowing glint in his eyes. "Let's start again. The Chancellor…" He cleared his throat. "Uncle Bhaskar has sent me here. He's sanctioned this operation and is ready to supply us with everything we need, but only if we retrieve the diamond for the Shatranj." He lifted his arm, revealing the seared emblem of the rook on his skin. "We're bound by it, in pursuit and in purpose."

Priya touched her neck, feeling the seared mark of a higher rank hidden beneath her hair. "I know all too well," she said tersely, her fingers lingering there. Her usual self-assured demeanor shifted, but only slightly. "Yes, Uncle Bhaskar believes the diamond will bring power back to the Order," she continued, her voice regaining its sharp edge. She looked at Raju with a piercing gaze. "But let's make one thing clear. Uncle Bhaskar sent you here to babysit the family while we figure out a plan and gather more information. Don't act like you're running the show." She let her fingers fall. "Rooks hold."

Raju's lips tightened, and a muscle in his jaw twitched. He leaned back in his chair. "Watch your tone, Priya. We're in this together, whether you like it or not. I'm not here to argue doctrine. We have a mission, and I intend to see it through. So, drop the attitude and focus on what's important."

Priya scoffed. "Spare me the lecture, Raju. Let's cut to the chase. Uncle Bhaskar laid it all out for me on the flight from Kathmandu. He's convinced the red crescent moon is a sign the Seeker will be revealed."

The candle sputtered, sending a thin curl of smoke toward the ceiling.

She turned to Siddharth. "Your vision has shaken Bhaskar to the core. It was after my mother told him about your dream on the eve of Eid that he went to the archives and found your prophecy. She's convinced him it's true." Her mouth curved, just barely. "He's a believer now, and I have to admit, it's… intriguing."

Siddharth met her without retreat. "Maybe you should listen to your mother, Priya."

He didn't look away.

Priya's expression hardened. "Let's be clear—I don't believe in your prophecy."

Siddharth leaned back slightly.

Priya's gaze shifted from Siddharth to Raju.

Raju's expression was unreadable. "Well, I guess it's my job to convince you otherwise."

She stared him down, her heart racing, but kept her expression cold and controlled. The prophecy unsettled her—not because she dismissed it entirely, but because of what it suggested. "Convince me?" She scoffed. "You'd have better luck coaxing truth from a stone lion."

Raju said nothing at first. He lifted his tumbler, took a slow pull, and studied her over the rim. "The diamond is real."

Her jaw tightened, but she didn't speak.

"I can help you find it," Raju went on. "Not for Bhaskar. But for you. Maybe it's you and me," he said evenly. "Maybe I'm the piece that's been missing."

"Don't flatter yourself. If it weren't for Uncle Bhaskar, you'd be irrelevant. So, let's not pretend we're equals in this."

Raju shot to his feet, the sharp grate of his chair cutting through the room. A muscle jumped once in his jaw. "If Bhaskar wants us to work together, fine. But don't mistake my cooperation for submission."

Priya met his stare. She was about to retort when a vivid memory flashed in her mind, pulling her back to a different time—the sight of Raju sprawled out on the stone floor back in Kathmandu. She had stood there, a faint smirk on her face, as Uncle Bhaskar had thrown him against the wall without mercy, his hand closing around Raju's throat until he gasped for air. After Bhaskar had left, she had leaned down and whispered in his ear. She had believed then that Raju's spirit had been shattered.

Seeing him there, standing defiant, was unsettling. But she buried the discomfort, her practiced veneer unbroken. The memory just strengthened her resolve to keep the balance of power where it belonged. She couldn't afford to let him gain any ground. "Don't mistake standing for rising, Raju. You're still where I left you."

Raju didn't flinch. "Strange," he said. "From where I'm standing, it's you who's looking up."

Her eyes flashed.

"I am a queen. You will show respect." She turned away for a moment—then back to him, colder than before. "Now tell me the truth. The boy—Harrison. Is he the Seeker the legends speak of?"

Raju sat back down, responding without hesitation, his resolve firm. "Yes. I'm as sure as the signs allow. I glimpsed the goatskin before the script shifted to that confounding riddle. His name was written there, as I read it."

Siddharth cut in. "I can vouch for that. It unmistakably spelled out 'Harrison Sharma.' Unless, of course, there's another by the same name lurking around here."

Anil frowned, his brow creased with doubt. "But the writing—it was in Sanskrit. Are we absolutely certain it deciphered to 'Harrison'?"

Color rose in Raju's cheeks. He slammed his fist onto the table, echoing the depth of his frustration. "Yes! I'm well-versed in Sanskrit."

Anil shifted in his chair uneasily, avoiding Raju's fiery gaze. "It's just…what if they're just here to experience the beauty and wonders of Nepal? Not everything might be as it seems."

"I'm telling you—Harrison is the Seeker!" Raju held Anil's gaze, jaw tight, as if daring him to disagree.

Anil leaned back in his chair, a sly smile playing on his lips. "All right, Raju. If you're so certain, tomorrow, I'll introduce myself to the Sharma family as the event coordinator for the inn. That way, we can subtly maneuver them exactly where we need them to be."

Priya's smile barely touched her lips, a subtle, dismissive tilt of her head accompanying her words. "That's perfect, Anil. They haven't the faintest clue—oblivious to our family ties and the legacy they've wandered into."

She turned her gaze to Raju. "So, you say the Sharmas are the chosen ones?" Her voice dropped as if humoring him. "The goatskin alone isn't enough for me. Prove the diamond exists."

Raju paused, fingers tapping lightly on the table as if to

gather his thoughts, then he leaned forward. "You've seen the signs, Priya. The Kumari, the prophecy, the goatskin—it all points to the Heart. You've felt it. It's real. And we're closer than anyone has been in centuries." He straightened, his gaze meeting hers. "You're not just a queen in the Shatranj Ke Sipahi; you're part of this, whether you want to admit it or not. The Heart is as real as the legacy we carry."

The room stilled. Siddharth sat upright, brow furrowed, while Anil, lounging in his chair, shot Raju a curious glance.

They waited.

Priya crossed her arms again, her expression skeptical. "Spare me the drama, Raju. Stories and prophecies don't prove anything. I've heard the legends just as much as you have."

Raju shook his head, undeterred. "I'm not talking about myths, Priya. Think back to when we were kids. Remember, you found that book in the library—The Vākya Sādhanā. Our last names, Chandra and Bhattarai, were referenced in the text. You read it night after night, memorizing every word, reciting the incantations. It wasn't just some bedtime story to you. You believed our family might be tied to the diamond. The book suggested our bloodline had a role to play—that the Shatranj were meant to guard something others were never meant to touch. We were raised to believe we were the guardians of a secret legacy, Priya. The Heart was entrusted to our ancestors—and it was you who found that scripture of sacred utterance. That wasn't coincidence. It doesn't reveal the Pattern," he said quietly. "It shows how the Pattern responds. And you know the spells, Priya. You've always known how to use them."

He held her gaze. "You could choose to step into that." He paused, letting the silence stretch between them.

"It was our Order's charge to safeguard the Heart, before it was taken from us. It's our right to reclaim it." He didn't look away. He didn't even blink. "You've lived with this longer than you admit."

Priya raised an eyebrow. "You sound just like Uncle Bhaskar before he killed Manav."

Raju nodded once. "That's right.... You were there. We were just children."

Priya's gaze flickered, looking away as the memory resurfaced.

Raju leaned forward. "But the Heart was meant to be guarded by us. I'm not saying what Uncle Bhaskar did was right." He held her gaze again, more insistent now. "But finding it was never meant to fall to strangers. No one can deny that. It's written in the Pattern."

Priya scoffed, a dismissive sound escaping her lips. "Hmph!"

Raju did not back down. "Look at what's happening now. You think it's a coincidence that the Sharmas are here? That Harrison—of all people—was chosen by the Kumari? You think Bhaskar sent us here just for old times' sake? No. This is real, Priya. It's unfolding. And the Sharmas are the key."

"The Sharmas are tourists, Raju. Caught up in something they can't possibly comprehend."

Raju's eyes locked onto hers. "Exactly. And yet, they're here. Do you think that's by chance? Harrison's interaction with the Kumari didn't feel accidental. The signs are there. The red crescent moon, the prophecy—everything we've studied. The Sharmas are connected to the Heart. I'm sure of that."

"Uncle Bhaskar brought them here, not the diamond," she retorted.

Raju leaned in. "Exactly. He believes."

A flicker of doubt crossed Priya's face. She bit her lip, the tension in her shoulders slowly melting away as she absorbed his words.

He leaned closer. "You don't want to believe because of what it would demand. Because if everything we've been told—everything we've trained for—isn't just some ancient tale, then none of us gets to walk away untouched. It's time to face what this might mean, Priya. The Heart is real, and everything seems to be pointing in their direction."

Priya stared at him, her arms still crossed, but the skepticism in her eyes was giving way to something else—something she refused to name.

Raju leaned back. "You've felt it too—whether you want to admit it or not. The Sharmas are part of this. And it's our job—your job—to see it through."

For a moment, there was silence. Priya's gaze remained sharp, but her posture had shifted—less defiant, more guarded. A faint smile tugged at her lips, gone almost as quickly as it appeared.

"Careful, Raju," she said. "You're starting to sound convincing."

Raju lifted his glass. "That's all I'm asking."

Across the table, Anil shifted in his chair, while Siddharth went still.

Priya eyed Raju's raised glass for a moment before lifting her own, her smile turning icy. "Don't get too comfortable, Raju," she said, bringing her glass to meet his. "Agreeing on one thing doesn't mean you're suddenly competent. Keep that in mind."

Raju brought his glass to his mouth—but paused. He did not drink.

Priya noticed. "We let the Sharmas lead us to the diamond," she said. "Just as Uncle Bhaskar intended."

Siddharth's fingers tightened around his glass. He did not lift it.

The candle flame at the center of the table guttered, throwing the wall into brief distortion. No one commented.

Anil shifted in his chair, the wood creaking too loud in the stillness.

Siddharth opened his mouth—then stopped.

Raju finally drank. The clink never came.

Anil frowned, glancing between them. "We're really betting everything on the Sharmas? What's the backup plan if they screw it up?"

"The Sharmas are just a piece on the board," Raju said coolly. "If something goes wrong, we adapt. For now, we let them move first."

Siddharth spoke up quietly. "There's something you should know. The bat cave near Phewa Lake is where the latest clue leads us. The goatskin revealed this location to me this evening while Raju and I were in the lounge with the family. This message reinforces we are part of the Heart's calling. I will lead Harrison to the cave, and I believe he will uncover the final clue."

Priya turned to her cousin. "Very well, Siddharth. Yes, if the script is changing, then it is a good sign."

Siddharth slowly turned his glass in his hand. "But we must remain vigilant—we must keep them safe."

He hesitated, just long enough to be noticed. "We don't know what this will demand of them," he added quietly.

Priya rolled her eyes, cutting him off. "Always about caution with you, isn't it? We're on the cusp of something extraordinary!"

Siddharth met her gaze. "Extraordinary things still exact a cost. And it's rarely paid by the ones reaching for them."

Priya's expression hardened. "Careful, cousin. You're starting to sound sentimental."

"No," Siddharth said evenly. "I'm being precise."

"Enough of this!" Raju countered. "Let's stay focused. We need to maintain the family's trust in us. That is our top priority. Our play is simple—we craft the problem, wait for their reaction, and then step in. They trust us, and we will use that—creating situations only we can resolve." He leaned closer, his whisper almost a hiss. "They have no idea. Their trust will pave the way to our triumph."

No one spoke.

Anil took a measured sip of gin, the clear liquid catching the light as he raised it to his lips. "'Probléma. Reakció. Megoldás.' The classic strategy," he mused with a nod. "Clever indeed."

Priya's eyes sparkled with intrigue as she listened to Raju's scheme, her mind quickly grasping the potential of their plan. A slow smile spread across her lips. "Raju, I must admit, this is a brilliant strategy," she praised. "Uncle Bhaskar has outdone himself with this plan. The family's trust is our most powerful weapon."

Raju nodded, irked she had given Uncle Bhaskar the acclaim. "Now that we're all on the same page, let's move on to another crucial matter." His tone grew more serious. "The sealed door in the tunnel under the inn—we need to see if the Sharma family can open it. I've already enticed them with the possibility the gem may be down there."

"The rebels carved deeper than the visible walls," Siddharth murmured. "They never trusted a single door."

Anil's interest was piqued, and he set down his glass. "The Heart? You think it's really there?"

"It's possible," Raju replied. "The markings on the door indicate it's connected to the Heart of Kumari. It's never been opened to my knowledge."

Priya leaned in. "I sent the last Seeker down there. He couldn't open it. Said it was sealed with some kind of magic."

"Khan?" Raju asked, the image of his corpse still fresh in his mind.

"Yes—he mentioned needing a key," Priya replied.

"Sounds about right," Raju said. "The door is sealed. I'm not sure if it's magic, but a key is needed. That I am sure of."

"Bhaskar tried to blow it up about a month back," Priya recounted. "He used high-end explosives and advanced techniques. The door didn't budge—not even a scratch. It might not be magic, but there's definitely some kind of invisible force field protecting it."

Siddharth's brow furrowed. "Maybe it isn't sealed by magic at all. Maybe it's resonance." He reached back absently, tightening the cord at his nape. The gesture was instinctive—old habit, older vow.

Raju turned to him. "You mean a sound unlocks it? Explain."

"Not a sound, per se, but a frequency—one the Pattern feels. The legend says the Heart chooses its Seeker," Siddharth said quietly. "Not by title. By alignment. The old rites would've followed that law. When the Seeker stands before the seal, it stirs—but it will not yield unless the Pattern knows him fully. Khan failed. The Pattern saw through him."

"What, like some kind of moral test?" Anil scoffed.

Siddharth shook his head. "Not moral. Resonant. The Pattern doesn't reward good behavior. It has responded to something like truth. Maybe it can sense the frequency of the Seeker's soul, an unseen, unquantifiable impulse that only the Pattern responds to."

Priya dropped her head. "Then the Pattern saw weakness. And Khan died."

A silence followed. None of them broke it.

Siddharth lowered his eyes.

Finally, Raju spoke, his voice low and contemplative. "Unless there's a way to bypass resonance entirely."

"The lamb," Siddharth cut in. "That's where the lamb comes into play."

"What lamb?" Anil questioned, taking another sip from his glass.

"The stuffed toy Cyrus always clings to," Siddharth answered.

"Yes, Siddharth, the lamb," Raju affirmed. "We believe the Kumari Talisman is inside its belly, pointing to the Heart of Kumari. Perhaps that's the key Khan referenced."

"Too bad he's dead," Raju muttered, more to himself. "He might've helped us. I think Uncle Bhaskar had him killed… But I'm not sure."

Across the table, Priya flinched, just for a moment—but Raju caught it.

He turned to her, his eyes narrowing. "Do you know how he died?"

Priya hesitated, her gaze dropping briefly before she met his eyes again. "As I said, the Heart didn't choose him."

Siddharth's brow furrowed. "That's what scares me."

Raju moved closer. "But what if the 'key' in the lamb wasn't meant to be found by the chosen?" He looked at each of them. "What if it was built as a bypass—hidden in the rites, not to honor the Pattern, but to override it? A way in, even for those the Heart would reject."

Siddharth stared at him. "Then it wasn't meant for the Seeker," he said. "It was meant for a thief."

Raju didn't look away. "Not a thief, but a safeguard. Maybe our forebears left it—those who lived through the Kali Raatri, when the Shatranj faced silence from the Heart. Perhaps they feared being locked out and created this as another way through. Not a key of worthiness, but a key of necessity."

Siddharth's gaze flickered once—brief and involuntary.

Goa surfaced without permission.

A stillness tightened around the table. Even Anil stopped shifting. Because a safeguard meant origin. It meant hands that had touched the Pattern and dared to leave behind a back-door. And that kind of heresy never lived only in rumor—it lived in ink.

Raju's gaze drifted to the candle, then to the shadow behind it, as if he could see the shelves of the Shatranj archives through the wall.

"There's an older name in the archives," Raju said. "One Bhaskar keeps sealed."

Priya's hand stilled.

Siddharth's eyes lifted.

"Don't say it," Priya murmured.

Raju didn't smile. "Padmé."

Anil blinked once—as if the name meant nothing at all. Then he leaned forward, already moving on. "We need to get them to enter the tunnel and open the door."

Raju grinned, appreciating Anil's cunning. "Exactly. We play on their curiosity. If they succeed, we gain access. If they fail, it's their resources and effort wasted, not ours."

Anil raised a finger and announced, "We could call it 'Operation Pawn's Gate.'"

"I guess that works," Siddharth replied. "If it needs a name, that's as good as any."

Priya shrugged. "Sure, whatever." Then, leaning in, she added, "What matters is we keep the pressure on them—keep them eager to uncover the mystery. Meanwhile, we stay in the shadows, pulling the strings."

Siddharth's hand brushed his chin, a thoughtful gesture as he considered the implications. "Should we inform the family the Talisman might be the key, and it's in the lamb?" he mused, the chair's wood groaning under his weight.

Raju's response was immediate, a firm shake of his head. "No, that would reveal too much. They mustn't learn we've been aware of the Talisman since Kathmandu. It could shatter their trust in us. Besides, if the Heart has chosen Harrison, the key is irrelevant."

"But we'll still need it," Priya murmured.

Anil didn't look up. "Not if Harrison opens it for us."

"And if he can't?" Priya said.

The space between them closed.

"Then we will need the key," Siddharth said, cutting through the quiet.

"My point exactly." Priya let the silence stretch a moment longer, long enough to feel its pressure. Her hand stilled on the table. "So tell me—what does this key even look like?"

Raju delved into his pocket and extracted a neatly folded piece of paper. He opened it, revealing an edge with a precise tear, indicating it had been removed from a book. He placed it in front of Priya. "I believe this is what we need to access the door. This is what Siddharth saw the boy conceal inside the lamb."

As he held the parchment under the flame, the image of the necklace caught the light, making it appear to shimmer as though filled with a life of its own. Along the trimmed footer, a printer's ghost-line surfaced in heat: ...*BLOODLINES*... (DOCTRINE OF BALANCE, FRAGMENT IX). It passed without pause.

Anil's jaw dropped in amazement as he marveled at the brilliance before him. The necklace exuded a hypnotizing fascination that was impossible to ignore.

"It's incredible," Priya exclaimed as she gazed upon the image. Though it was just a picture, it radiated an undeniable beauty, captivating her. Her features sharpened as she looked up and leaned closer to the others. "That lamb, and whatever it holds within, is paramount." Her eyes gleamed with calculation. "If the boy is that attached to it," Priya said carefully, "then timing will matter."

Siddharth rocked back, the chair's movement deliberate. "That's the real trick, isn't it?"

Raju cut in sharply. "Yes, Siddharth, that's the problem! The boy seems to have an unyielding bond with that thing. He never puts it down, not even for a moment."

They turned to Priya, a silent plea in the half-light of the candle's flame.

Priya raised an eyebrow, shaking her head. "Don't look at me. Anil's the one with all the bright ideas."

Anil nodded. "Let's stick with my plan. If they're the chosen ones, they'll uncover the secrets themselves. We won't need the lamb, and we'll keep their trust."

Priya's expression took on a shrewd glint as she considered this. "Brilliant," she praised, "but how will we know if they succeed?"

Raju met her gaze steadily. "We'll be with them, of course."

She wasn't convinced. "And if they go without you?"

"Nonsense," Raju replied with a hint of impatience. "They'll call on us. We're their guides, after all."

Priya's brow furrowed. "Are you certain? They might not."

"They trust us," Raju said firmly.

"And if they don't ask?"

"We will have to follow them."

Siddharth frowned, weighing the risks. "What if they don't take the bait?"

With a sly smile curling her lips, Priya offered, "I might know someone who can assist us with stealing the lamb." Her words dripped with intrigue, promising a new twist in their nefarious plot.

"But only if they don't take the bait, Priya," Anil insisted.

"Of course," Priya conceded, her sincerity dubious.

Quiet enveloped the room as they each mulled over the plan.

Anil straightened, meeting each person's eyes. The candle flame flickered between them as he spoke, his voice low and deliberate. "If we are to embark on this quest, we walk this treacherous path together, bound not only by the Heart of Kumari but by the unbreakable ties of family."

Priya folded her arms. "We keep the Sharmas in the dark about our bloodline and the Order. They stay close, but our true agenda remains hidden. Agreed?"

Raju and Priya exchanged a glance before turning toward Anil and Siddharth.

Anil spoke first. "Agreed."

A breath later, Raju echoed him, lifting his glass. "By our blood, we are bound."

Siddharth did not raise his glass.

No one noticed.

The candle burned lower, folding in on itself.

No one reached to steady it.

— 3 —
SURPRISES IN POKHARA

पोखरायाम् आश्चर्याणि

7:00 A.M.

On the far side of the dining room, sunlight filtered through the lace curtains, breaking unevenly across the room. The aroma of brewed coffee hung in the air, unmoving. The atmosphere in the Surya Chandra Inn still carried traces of the previous night's activities—a lingering residue.

As the Sharma family gathered in the hotel's dining area, a buffet had been set out. Steam rose faintly from platters. Masala tea, coffee, and hot chocolate were set out beside chilled mango lassi. Condensation clung to the glass.

Pappa was the first to arrive, as he liked to get up early and chronicle his thoughts. By the time the family joined him, he was already deeply absorbed in his journal, the pen scratching across the pages with quiet intent. A steaming cup of coffee sat beside him, sending wisps curling upwards. His brow furrowed in concentration as he documented their journey, each word penned with deliberate care. Lost in the rhythm of his thoughts, he barely noticed the bustle of activity around him.

Amma slipped into the seat beside him, her plate piled high with fresh fruit and golden parathas, a flaky, layered flatbread. "Up early again, I see?"

Pappa didn't look up but smiled, still focused on his writing. "Oh yes, Hema, lots to jot down. You know I don't want to forget a single thing."

"Well, just don't forget to eat something, too," she said, glancing at his notes.

Pappa chuckled, finally pausing to take a sip of his coffee—pen still poised.

Sophie walked by with a smile. "Did you both sleep well?"

"Yes, dear. And you?" Amma asked.

Sophie nodded as she sat down, cradling her cup of coffee. "I slept like a baby, thanks. Last night was something special. I had such a great time."

Ravi strolled over, giving her a quick kiss on the cheek. "It was, wasn't it?" He winked as he slid into the seat beside her. "I enjoyed every bit of it."

Sophie smiled and added, "I mean, all of us hanging out together. It was fun, just being with everyone and telling stories."

"I enjoyed it, too," Amma chimed in. "This is turning into quite the vacation."

Pappa looked up from his journal, smiling. "Definitely one for the books."

Harrison strode in, eyes wide with excitement. Ignoring the spread of food, he went straight to the table, gently pushing aside a few plates and glasses with a soft clatter to make room. "Check this out," he said, sliding a large, map across the table. "I found this in the bookcase in the lobby." His voice brimmed with enthusiasm as he unfolded the paper, revealing trails and markings, hidden routes through the local forests, and secret spots along the riverbank. He glanced up, his eyes alight. "So, what's the plan for today? Are we going to the caves?"

Before anyone could answer, the door swung open, and Priya walked into the room with purposeful strides. Everyone looked up; her youthful demeanor contrasted with a striking sense of authority. She smiled warmly, yet there was an undeniable command in her presence.

"I've scheduled a guided tour of our historic inn for you all right after breakfast," Priya declared, her words exuding the same warmth as the spices that infused the surrounding air. "Afterward, you can spend the rest of your day relaxing by the beautiful Phewa Lake."

"What about going to the bat caves?" Sophie asked.

As her questioning gaze met Priya's, her smile held for a beat, then shifted. "Ah yes, your guide did mention you were interested in exploring the caves." She inclined her head slightly. "Unfortunately, the bat cave is currently inaccessible due to a film production. However, there might be a possibility for a private tour, thanks to my uncle who oversees the local police department. I'll explore our options and keep you updated."

Sophie's face fell at the news. "That's unfortunate," she murmured, her disappointment unmistakable.

Ravi placed a hand on her shoulder. "Let's not lose faith."

Sophie didn't answer right away. Her fingers rested on the edge of the table, still. Her thumb traced the grain of the wood once. Then she gestured to the map. "In the meantime, let's look at where this Phewa Lake is. It might give us a clearer picture of where we're headed." She glanced around the room. *Where are Raju and Siddharth?*

Ravi hunched over the map, his gaze skimming past the image of Phewa Lake to the surrounding foothills. While he nodded along to Priya's suggestions, his mind was already focusing on the tunnels hinted at by the map's contours. Yet, he kept his musings discreet.

Ravi looked up at Priya. "That sounds like a splendid plan," he said, offering her a smile of gratitude. "A tour to understand the history of the inn, followed by downtime beside Phewa Lake, would be most welcome. We appreciate you arranging this for us." Ravi took another sip of his coffee and addressed the family, his voice ringing with convincing ease. "Spending a day on the water offers us a unique perspective of Nepal's scenic beauty from a boat. It's an opportunity not to be missed."

Sophie stared past the table, toward the mountains beyond the window. Above the roofs, a darker shape cut the morning haze—stone on stone, watching. The locals called it Tal Knot. The inn sat below it like a polite mask.

She shifted slightly, drawn by the slant of light across the tablecloth. Sitting by a lake felt like waiting. She didn't know why it bothered her—only that it did.

Just then, a man unfamiliar to the Sharma family entered the dining area. He moved with confidence, his tall and lean frame dressed in a well-tailored suit. His jet-black hair was cut close at the sides and combed back with deliberate precision. His features were sharply set, his skin sun-warmed rather than softened. The resemblance to Priya was immediate — not warmth, but structure. The same unyielding line of the jaw. The same steady, appraising gaze.

Priya gestured with a welcoming smile. "This is my brother, Anil Chandra. He's the event coordinator for the inn."

"Good morning, everyone," Anil said. "Priya tells me

you are interested in history. If you could please meet me in the lobby after breakfast, I have a tour planned for you."

"I see you've got this," Priya said to Anil with a smile. She placed a reassuring hand on his shoulder.

"Thank you, Priya," Anil responded, appreciating her introduction to the group.

"Enjoy your tour, everyone." With those words, Priya turned to walk away. As she did, she unconsciously pulled her hair aside, revealing a seared mark akin to a queen chess piece located on the nape of her neck.

Sophie, who had observed the image, responded with a thoughtful *hmm*.

Kiran, directing his question to Anil, asked, "Are there ghosts on this tour?"

Cyrus couldn't hide his grin. "Ghosts? Awesome! I want to see some!"

Anil chuckled at their fervor, shaking his head. "We don't plan for ghosts, but who knows? The history here is rich enough to stir some tales."

Cyrus leaned forward eagerly, while Kiran glanced down the hallway as if expecting something to move.

"Priya mentioned something about a secret room with treasure. Is that part of the tour?" Harrison asked.

"Maybe…" Anil said with a wink. "You'll have to wait and see."

Ravi and Sophie exchanged a glance. Neither of them looked away first.

Sophie felt the pull of it despite herself.

Pappa leaned in slightly. "I'm sure you've got some fascinating folklore to share with us on this tour?"

"Absolutely," Anil assured. "The walls here whisper many stories." He gave them a nod. "Let's meet by the front desk in an hour." With that, he excused himself.

In the lobby, the grandfather clock's three-quarter chime carried softly through the inn.

* * *

9:00 A.M.

Gathering in the lobby, the Sharma family waited for Anil. The grandfather clock ticked softly. Harrison stood near the bookcase, his fingers trailing along the worn spines without really reading them.

Sophie lingered near the window, studying the courtyard beyond the glass. Ravi crossed the room slowly, pausing beneath one of the paintings as if trying to place it.

Kiran stepped from white tile to white tile, avoiding the black.

"You'll lose if you touch the dark," Cyrus called, hopping behind him.

Kiran lunged for the next square and slipped. He caught himself with a palm against the marble and looked up. In the angled glass, his reflection stood a fraction straighter than he did—composed, almost expectant.

Harrison glanced up at the same mirror. For a second, he thought he had missed something—but the corridor reflected only what it was given.

"Careful," Sophie said, turning at the sound of the slip.

Ravi stepped forward instinctively, then relaxed when Kiran laughed it off.

A warm flicker appeared at the edge of the glass before the sound of footsteps reached them. "Ready for the tour?" Anil asked, the corners of his mouth curled into a smile. He was carrying an old-fashioned lantern.

"Yes, we are," Ravi responded. His gaze lingered on the

flame behind the glass.

"If you would please follow me."

Anil led them through the maze-like corridors of the inn, pointing out the various locations of historical relevance. An ancient painting framed by worn wood depicted a king dressed in a red robe, hung slanted on the wall. The fabric of the robe was faded by time. Gold jewelry caught the lantern light. The man's smile matched the angle of the frame.

Anil gestured toward the portrait and explained, "This is Mahendra Malla, a king of the Malla dynasty. His reign coincided with a period of significant artistic and architectural expansion in the Kathmandu Valley. He commissioned the construction of the original fort here, consolidating control over the region."

"Eighteenth century? Wasn't that during the Kali Raatri… when the Shatranj were in power?" Sophie asked, recalling her visit to the historical archives back in Kathmandu.

Anil's expression tightened. The lantern made a small, nervous sway.

"The Kali Raatri began long before the eighteenth century," he said carefully.

"People confuse its first wound with its loudest one." He glanced at the portrait again. "The Order had already taken root by then. But in 1769, they made it visible. That's when the valley learned what it had been living under." He gestured to the walls around them. "It was one of their bastions. From here, they pressed their will across the region—down the trade roads, into the borderlands."

Pappa's brows knit. "The Shatranj were here in Pokhara…at this very fort?"

"Yes," Anil admitted, lowering his voice as if wary of being overheard. "They ruled by fear. Some believed they chased relics of great power; others claimed it was only a tale spread by monks to turn the people against them. Either way, the Order left scars. The Kali Raatri did not pass cleanly."

He cleared his throat, the moment passing as quickly as it had come. "The museum in town has more detailed records. I can arrange a visit."

Amma nodded.

"All right," Anil said, gesturing toward a smaller portrait. "Shall we move on? This painting shows the jewels worn during that period."

Sophie's attention lingered on the painting. "That's something," she murmured.

Ravi, standing beside her, said, "People knew where they stood."

Harrison interjected with a grim note. "It doesn't look like it was peaceful."

Sophie nodded, her gaze never leaving the jewels. "They were careful—"

Anil cut in. "This way."

As they continued down the stone corridor, images of Nepali royalty lined the walls. Handwoven tapestries depicted mountain palaces, while faded paintings captured regal processions—kings and queens in flowing robes, flanked by loyal courtiers. They passed one mural, half lost to soot and age, that seemed to stir with its own breath—a queen lifting her torch toward encroaching dark. Beneath her feet, a bronze plaque glinted faintly through the grime. The letters were small, almost worn to nothing: '*THE TORCH REVEALS THE FIRST, NOT THE WHOLE. WHAT THE FLAME TOUCHES FIRST SHALL LIGHT THE WAY.*' (DOCTRINE OF BALANCE, FRAGMENT XI-B)

The lantern light shifted, the queen's torch seeming to dim as they walked on. At the corridor's end, the family reached a narrow wooden staircase that creaked underfoot, leading them up four flights to the attic.

"Mind your heads," Anil cautioned, holding the lantern high to illuminate the space. It was crowded with trunks, old books, porcelain dolls, and unfamiliar objects.

Anil glanced around the space. "Some of this dates back to when the inn was part of the fort."

In the half-light of the room, a guard's armor stood sentinel against the wall. Its surface caught the lantern light and let it go.

A chill traced Sophie's spine. She didn't move back.

In the corner, one trunk sat apart from the others—longer, narrower, shaped more like a travel chest than attic storage. Its wood was darker than the rest, the grain tight and glossy in places as if it had once been oiled by salt air.

Sophie took a step toward it without meaning to.

A clasp—bronze, dulled—curled across its mouth like a serpent biting its own tail. Not decorative. Not playful. The kind of detail someone chose because it meant something.

"That one's old," Anil said quickly, as though her attention had drifted somewhere it shouldn't. He lifted the lantern higher—light skimming the chest and then sliding away. "Was found sealed when we restored the upper beams. No one opens it now. Superstition."

"What's inside?" Harrison asked.

Anil's smile tightened. "Dust. Broken cloth. Things that belonged to people who never came back for them."

Sophie stared a moment longer. The room smelled faintly of cedar and something else—sharp, brined, like the ghost of a coastline. Then the lantern swung, shadows moved, and the chest returned to being only a chest.

But it felt…kept.

Anil raised the lantern slightly higher. The light caught his face and held there. His voice dropped to a whisper. "Have you heard about the woman who once lived here?"

He paused. The atmosphere shifted, and even the dust seemed suspended in time.

Anil leaned in closer. "Legend says she was a noblewoman, a 'mohi,' dressed in the finest patuka and gunyu," he said, referring to the traditional clothing worn by Nepali women in the eighteenth century. "She lived in this fort when it stood tall, long before it became an inn."

He paused, letting the tension thicken before continuing. "She was betrothed to a king much older than she, and the marriage was arranged. But she had a secret—she had fallen in love with a young soldier stationed at the fort."

Sophie leaned in, captivated. "What happened?"

"They would meet in secret by the old banyan tree near the edge of the river, where no one could see them. Under its branches, they spoke of leaving, but not yet. There was always one more night."

Anil drew the lantern closer. "Before they could escape, her betrothed discovered their secret. In a rage, he ordered the soldier to be executed right before her eyes. Her love was slain, his blood staining the ground beneath the banyan tree. She was left heartbroken and alone, forced to marry the man she hated." Anil's voice dropped lower, taking on a chilling edge. "Unable to bear the grief and the cruel fate forced upon her, she was found here… right here, in this very attic. The rope was still warm."

A cold silence gripped the room as Anil's words lingered like a thick fog. Even the old guard's armor seemed to shift.

"She wanders these halls now, searching endlessly for her lost love," Anil stated matter-of-factly. "Guests have claimed to see her, dressed in her flowing gunyu, her face pale and tear-streaked. Sometimes, she appears at night, her presence foretold by the wind gathering strength, swirling around the room in a silent vortex. The temperature plummets, and some have seen her standing at the foot of the bed, waiting…. Waiting for her lover to return."

Sophie reached for Ravi's arm. She didn't realize she had moved closer until she was already there. Harrison raised an eyebrow, half-amused but unable to shake the eerie feeling that had settled over the attic. Kiran clutched his arms to his chest, his face pale as he glanced nervously around, while Cyrus's eyes grew wide.

Anil wasn't done. He leaned in closer. "And sometimes, if you listen closely, you can hear the creak of the rope swinging from the rafters. They say if she calls your name in the dead of night, she believes you're her lost love—and she'll draw you across the threshold where the living cannot follow."

Kiran's eyes mirrored his brother's. "No way…"

Sophie's grip tightened as her gaze instinctively lifted toward the ceiling. Pappa chuckled, trying to brush off the peculiar sensation, but his eyes flickered toward the corners of the attic, as if half-expecting a shadow to emerge.

Kiran stepped back. "Do you think she's still here?"

Ravi forced a smile, squeezing Sophie's hand. "We should head back."

Anil grinned, lowering the lantern and allowing the shadows to settle back into their places. "Some stories don't stay upstairs."

With a shiver, the group turned to leave.

Making their way back to the lobby, Anil guided them to an area located behind the front desk. A stone staircase descended, its egress blocked midway by an imposing iron gate. It stood as a formidable barrier, separating the activity of the lobby from the world below.

"The basement," Anil declared, his voice echoing as they walked down a few steps and stood before the gate. Producing a key from his pocket, he unlocked it with a definitive click.

They passed through, descending further down a spiral staircase. The lantern swayed with the rhythm of their footsteps, its flame bent toward a hidden current of air.

Upon reaching the bottom, Anil flicked a switch, and light flickered three times, then steadied. The space opened wide, its walls washed pale with age. Rows of khukuris and curved talwars hung beside seven brass-rimmed shields, their surfaces tarnished by centuries. Between them, faded thangka scrolls showed deities half-devoured by mildew.

The air smelled of iron and damp cedar. Dust glittered in the light like stirred ash.

"These stones came from the old fortworks," Anil said softly. "Outer walls. Storage corridors. The true fort still sits above us." He let the lantern light settle along the seams. "Some say the passages run beneath the hill—though no one has found them in centuries."

"This is incredible," Pappa murmured, his tone carrying wonder. He stepped closer to a khukuri mounted on the wall. "These are Gurkha blades—true khukuris. I've read about them, but I've never seen one in person."

Anil was pleased by the recognition. "Yes. The Gurkhas carried them into every battle. A man's khukuri was more than a weapon—it was his honor. When the blade left its sheath, it had to taste blood before it returned. Some even say the curve was shaped after the crescent moon, to strike in harmony with it."

A faint metallic glint caught the lantern light—too clean, too precise to belong with the rest.

Pappa's gaze snagged on it.

It hung slightly apart from the others, not mounted like a museum piece but fixed with an odd care, as if whoever placed it had wanted it seen…yet not named. The blade was narrower than a khukuri, straighter, with a darkened edge that drank the light instead of reflecting it. The hilt was wrapped in worn leather, the grip flattened where a hand had held it too long.

Pappa stepped closer. Something tightened behind his ribs—small, irrational. The lantern's flame bent again, just slightly, and the air seemed to thin.

There was a mark near the guard. Not a decorative etching—more like a burn scar in the metal. A shape that looked almost accidental until you stared long enough. A tower.

Harrison stepped closer. The air pressed differently here—cool, but not cold. The blade seemed to watch, not gleam. His fingertips itched, and a whisper brushed the back of his mind. Not a voice. A weight. A presence behind the metal. Behind the mark. One that remembered its bearer too well.

Then, a scent rose, faint and wrong. Clove oil. Leather. Burned thread. Not strong enough to name. Not recent. But it hadn't faded. Harrison didn't know why it caught him the way it did. Only that it stirred something he couldn't name. Not memory. Not déjà vu. Just—presence.

Pappa didn't say it out loud. He didn't even know why his mouth went dry. Only that this blade did not belong to the fort's story the way the others did. It belonged to something else. Something that had not finished happening.

Cyrus leaned in. "So, they were like knights? Did they wear armor?"

"Not like in the West," Anil replied. "They fought in the mountains—speed mattered more than weight. Their strength was in precision and endurance, not steel. Still, when you see one of these blades, you know why whole armies feared them."

Kiran's eyes darted from sword to shield, his imagination catching flame. "I bet they fought dragons," Kiran said, completely certain.

Anil humored him with a small nod. "Perhaps they did, in their own way. The old kings called their enemies *rakshasa*—

demons in human form. So yes, Kiran…they fought dragons."

The boys grinned, satisfied.

Sophie turned to Ravi. "Priya mentioned a hidden room. I hope he shows it to us."

"Let's see what Anil has planned. There might be more than meets the eye," Ravi replied.

Catching snippets of Sophie and Ravi's conversation, Anil paused the tour. With a subtle glance toward them, he pursed his lips. "Is there something you wish to ask?"

Sophie spoke up. "Priya mentioned a secret room. We were curious about that."

Meeting Sophie's gaze, Anil responded with a sly grin. "Well, if it were a secret, I wouldn't know of it, would I?" He let out a laugh that didn't quite reach his eyes. "But I'll admit, this place has more whispers than walls. You hear them if you stay long enough."

He started walking again, the heel of his shoe striking sharply against the stone. "People love their ghost stories. Hidden doors, buried treasure, spirits that guard what was never meant to be found—it's good for the inn's reputation."

Pappa chuckled, trying to ease the tension. "Every old building has its tales."

Anil's reply came quick, almost clipped. "Yes. Tales." He stopped near a darker stretch of wall, the light trembling in his hand. There was a noticeable moment of hesitation.

Harrison stepped closer, drawn by something he couldn't name. He reached out, his fingertips brushing the stone. "Did you feel that?"

"Old walls remember," Anil said. He knelt and ran his hands through the air, searching for the faint draft emanating from below. As he did, his sleeve rode up, and the seared mark of a knight resembling a chess piece came into view.

Amma looked on, curious about its meaning.

"Here we are," Anil announced. Confidently, he lifted a loose floorboard to display a hidden latch. He ensured the family's attention was fixed on him. "This, dear guests, is no ordinary wall."

Ravi thought of Priya's words. *This must be what she meant.*

With expertise, Anil released the latch. A low, hollow moan rose. The wall swung open like a door, unveiling a narrow tunnel that went on indefinitely.

For a moment, Sophie thought of the shadow she'd seen above the inn at breakfast—the higher stone, the real crown of this hill. If passages still ran beneath the ground, they did not belong to the inn alone.

The tunnel emitted a blast of cool air, akin to an exhale. The breath carried the musty scent of earth and aged stone. The stale air filled their nostrils, a reminder of the passage's age and mystery.

Sophie stepped closer. "It's real," she said, almost as a breath.

Ravi leaned forward, peering into the shadowy expanse.

Amma clasped her hands together, her gaze transfixed by the opening. "Such mysteries these old walls hide!"

Usually reserved, Pappa allowed a rare smile to cross his face, nodding in approval at Anil's revelation. "Incredible," he said quietly, the word echoing in the enclosed space.

Experiencing a subtle magnetic tug, Harrison approached the entrance of the tunnel and peered inside. "What do you think lies ahead?"

The darkness stirred—not moving, not breathing, but attentive. Like something waiting to be seen. Not monstrous. Not welcoming. Something in-between.

"Legend has it," Anil began, the light of his lantern creating strange shadows on his face, "that the fort's soldiers used this tunnel for secret movement or escape during sieges. Its destination remains unknown, as its route became impassable long ago."

"Why?" Kiran asked, his curiosity driving his gaze to the forgotten passage before them. His attempt to peer into its depths was thwarted by the impenetrable shroud of darkness that consumed it.

Anil cast a cautious glance down at Kiran. "You see," he explained, his volume lowering as though sharing a well-guarded secret, "there exists a legend—a tale passed down through generations. It speaks of a vast treasure of unimaginable power hidden somewhere within this labyrinth. This tunnel was blocked off and sealed as though by magic to keep its secrets safe."

"Wow!" Cyrus called out. "Can we go in?"

Anil's smile faltered for a moment before he spoke. "Local folklore also speaks of a creature of unimaginable dread that guards the treasure within. Its fearsome roar has been known to echo through these passages, frightening away all who dare to venture inside." He glanced at his watch, forcing a smile. "Besides, we don't want to be late for our boat ride on Phewa Lake, do we?"

Cyrus took a step toward the opening before Ravi's hand closed gently around his shoulder.

"Easy," Ravi said quietly. "Not yet."

"But I want to see the monster," Cyrus protested, craning his neck toward the dark.

"Me too," Kiran said, looking up at his father.

Ravi hesitated, then shook his head once. "Another time."

Anil glanced at his watch, then at the opening, as if weighing whether it was worth mentioning at all. "It's usually best not to linger down here," he said mildly. "These old passages have a way of…distracting people."

The lantern swayed, then stilled.

No one argued.

Sophie leaned forward, peering into the opening, then drew back just as quietly. She whispered, almost to Ravi, "This is incredible. It's like the inn is part of the legend we're chasing."

Anil, overhearing Sophie's remark, let out a soft reply. "Interesting." His volume was low, almost to himself, yet it carried through the stillness.

Sophie studied him. "You talk about legends like they're still breathing."

Anil smiled. "Perhaps they are. Every legend waits for its time. When the time comes…well, the world ends now for someone."

She tilted her head, perplexed.

Without another word, Anil moved to close the hidden door. The stone hesitated, grinding softly before settling into place.

"As you can see," Anil said lightly, "the Surya Chandra Inn is more than it appears to be."

His words lingered.

The family followed him back toward the lobby. Footsteps echoed, then softened as the familiar sounds of the inn returned around them.

"Thank you, Anil," Sophie said. It was all she could think to say.

Anil nodded, then walked away.

— 4 —
A Day on Phewa Lake

फेवायां एकः दिवसः

12:00 P.M.

Only twenty minutes had passed before the family regrouped in the lobby, waiting for Anil to take them to Phewa Lake. The uncertainty of their next steps lingered, thick and unrelenting, like a mist that refused to lift.

Cyrus and Kiran fidgeted on the couch near the entrance while Pappa stood at the front desk, his thoughts miles away. He considered saying something—about the tunnel, the way the day had unfolded—but let it pass. Sophie scrolled through her phone, her brow furrowed as if the screen might hold the answer they needed. Harrison paced restlessly, each step sharper than the last. Ravi sat by the window, fingers tapping rhythmically on the arm of his chair, his gaze distant. Amma sat silent, organizing her purse, though her eyes betrayed the storm of thoughts churning beneath her composed exterior.

Just then, Raju and Siddharth entered, immediately catching the family's attention.

Sophie was the first to speak. "Raju, we've got a problem. Priya told us the bat caves are off-limits because they're filming some big-budget movie. I don't know what we're going to do." She turned to Siddharth. "The next clue is in the cave, right? We can't just wait for the police to give us the go-ahead. What if they say no? Then what?"

Harrison, who had stopped pacing, jumped in. "We can't wait forever. The cave is key. We have to get in somehow."

Ravi, leaning back in his chair, spoke calmly. "I get it, Harrison, but if it's meant to happen, it will."

Harrison frowned, frustration bubbling beneath the surface. "But we're just supposed to wait?"

"Yes," his father replied firmly, his tone leaving no room for argument.

Harrison, clearly unhappy with the answer, crossed his arms and turned away with a frustrated huff. "Hmph."

Siddharth, watching the boy, let the silence stretch before he spoke. His voice was quiet, deliberate. "How was your tour with Anil?"

"Eh, it was all right." Harrison stopped mid-breath, remembering the heavy door and the tunnel yawning behind it.

Sophie looked up from her phone, a smile flickering across her face. "Our tour was wonderful. Anil has a way of turning history into ghost stories."

Before she could say more, Cyrus slid down from the couch, Sheepy dangling from his hand. His small voice cut through the air. "He showed us a tunnel in the basement."

No one corrected him. No one dismissed it, either.

For a heartbeat, the Surya Chandra Inn didn't feel welcoming. It felt like a throat closing.

Siddharth's eyes darted toward Raju before settling his gaze upon Cyrus. "A tunnel?" His tone carried weight. "What did he say?"

Kiran jumped in. "That a monster lives down there."

Siddharth let the words hang in the lobby like smoke. His mouth tightened—not quite a refusal, not quite a warning. Both boys began to plead at once. "Can you take us? Please? We want to see!"

Harrison straightened, his sulk forgotten. His voice came low, urgent. "Cyrus and Kiran are right! You told us there are tunnels all through Nepal, Raju. Some could lead to the diamond. Will you take us?"

The room's atmosphere shifted. The children giggled at the possibilities, Sophie's smile brimmed with rising interest, even Amma looked up, intrigued. The inn waited, as if the question had already been asked before.

Then, Siddharth spoke. His words landed like a stone in still water. "Some paths are not traveled in haste. They wait. They test." His gaze swept the family, steady and unreadable. "Today, we go to the lake. Tonight—if the way is open—we'll see."

The children groaned in unison.

Before protests could build, Harrison spoke, his tone edged with thought. "I think the bat cave matters more anyway. The goatskin mentioned a cave, not a tunnel. Maybe there's something we need in that cave. I'd vote we check that out first, then we explore the tunnel."

Siddharth studied him with quiet intensity before offering a single nod. "You may be right, Harrison. The Kumari does not reveal her pattern all at once. Sometimes, the first step is hidden in another."

"Yeah, but the cave's closed. The lady said people can't go," Cyrus interjected, scrambling back onto the couch.

Sophie pressed her lips together, her excitement dimmed. Ravi exhaled through his nose, resignation etched across his face. Even the boys fell silent, the lure of the tunnel dulled by the reminder of the cave that was just out of reach.

Pappa glanced down the hall again, as if expecting someone to arrive with the answer.

Just then, the STAFF ONLY door swung open and Anil sauntered into the lobby.

He leaned against the front desk, smiling. "You know, Priya's uncle is my uncle, too. He's got...pull. Sometimes." Anil's smile widened just a fraction. "If there's a way in, he might know who to ask."

Sophie frowned, casting a sideways glance at Siddharth. "Can we trust Anil?" she whispered. "He seems...a little too eager."

Siddharth exchanged a brief look with Raju, a silent understanding passing between them. He leaned in closer to Sophie. "We don't have much of a choice," he murmured. "Anil's the one with access. If we want to get where we need to go, we'll have to trust him. For now..."

Sophie exhaled. "Fine," she said. "We wait."

Anil pushed himself off the desk and shoved his hands into his pockets. "All right, I just need to make a quick phone call, and then we can leave." With that, he turned and walked out of the lobby.

The moment he was gone, Harrison turned to Raju, his impatience flaring again. "What about the caves? We can't wait for Anil's uncle to pull some strings."

Raju's expression shifted, a plan already forming in his mind. "I've been looking at maps of the area. There might be another way in—a back route that's not as well known. But it'll be tricky. We'll have to do some spelunking. It's not ideal, but we'll have to take that route if the official way doesn't work."

Ravi straightened up. "I'm game. No way we came all this way just to be stopped by some movie set."

Raju gave a half-smile. "Good. If we have to go that route, I'll take you, Harrison, and Pappa with me. Sophie, Amma, and the kids can stay behind."

Sophie shook her head. "Spelunking? That sounds dangerous. Are you sure that's a good idea?"

"We'll be careful," Raju assured. "But let's give Priya and Anil's uncle a chance to come through first. If that falls through, we'll move on to Plan B."

"When would we go?" Harrison asked, cutting in.

Raju thought for a moment. "Tomorrow, I'd say. That should give us enough time to get things together."

Siddharth chimed in. "I'll stay behind today and go into town. I'll see what strings I can pull for official access. And I'll make sure we've got everything—ropes, harnesses, lights—everything we'll need in case we have to take the back way."

Sophie looked between them. "I don't like it. But I know we have to keep moving forward. Just...be careful, okay?"

Raju gave her a reassuring smile. "We will. We're just covering all our bases."

Before anyone could say more, Anil strolled back into the lobby, his confidence on full display. "Everything's set for our trip to the lake. We can leave now."

As if on cue, Priya appeared with a large picnic basket in hand. "The hotel packed lunch for you to take," she said, handing the basket to Ravi.

"Thank you," Ravi said, giving her a grateful smile. "We'll definitely need it."

With nothing left to discuss, the family gathered their things and piled into the van, leaving behind the warmth of the inn for the cool lake air. Raju took the driver's seat, chatting away about the day's plans, while the others settled in, quiet—each of them carrying something unspoken as the road pulled them away.

***

12:45 P.M.

The van hummed steadily down the winding road toward the lake, and a silence had settled over the passengers. Their earlier conversation lingered, and each family member was lost in thought. Anil's comments about his uncle's influence had sparked something, but there was still unease—Siddharth's words about the bat cave hung there, unanswered.

Sophie stared out the window as she mulled over the possibilities. Priya's warning about the cave being closed for a movie set played over in her mind, casting doubt on their next move. *Could the chief of police really help, or are we about to risk a far more dangerous route into the cave?*

Beside her, Harrison shifted impatiently in his seat. His earlier frustration simmered, but his father's words repeated in his mind. '*If it's meant to be, it'll happen.*' It wasn't enough to quiet the urgency he felt, though. *The clue was there—it had to be, just out of reach.* He couldn't shake the feeling that time was no longer waiting.

Raju sat quietly in the driver's seat, his eyes on the winding road ahead, his mind elsewhere. He had told them about the alternative entrance, weaving the tale with ease. The maps, the spelunking—it was all part of the narrative they needed to hear.

He glanced in the rearview mirror, watching the family. Kiran sat on his grandmother's lap, tiny fingers playing with her bangles, sliding them back and forth as if counting each one with meticulous curiosity. Ravi leaned back, calm and collected, while Harrison fidgeted restlessly. Sophie stared out the window, deep in thought.

The tunnel had done its work. The boys had begged; Harrison had pressed. *Perfect. Let them believe the tunnel was another prize waiting to be earned. The more they want it, the easier it will be to guide them where we need them.* No one questioned him. Ravi deferred without realizing he had. Even Harrison waited for Raju to speak first. Raju didn't correct them.

His fingers gripped the wheel a little tighter. For now, he had to focus on the present—the lake. The afternoon offered a brief respite from the mounting tension, a chance to recenter before the next challenge. "I hope you can enjoy the lake today," Raju said aloud, breaking the silence. "The caves will still be there tomorrow."

Sophie nodded. "You're right. Let's make the most of this afternoon."

The tension went quiet as the van rolled toward the lake, and the cave mystery was momentarily set aside as they prepared for an afternoon on the water.

***

1:22 P.M.

Upon their arrival at the lake, the family was greeted by a clear view framed by the majestic Annapurna range—a backdrop offering a pause from their adventure-fueled musings. The lake's calm waters shimmered under the intensity of the early afternoon sun, drawing the Sharmas to bask in the beauty of the moment.

The Sharma family exited the vehicle, each allowing a smile at the thought of what awaited. The natural splendor around them contrasted with the dark passages they had just glimpsed.

Anil gestured toward the sailboat docked at the lake's edge. "Your adventure awaits," he said with a flourish, stepping aside as if presenting a grand gift.

Sophie raised an eyebrow and smiled. "Oh, you're not coming with us?"

Anil chuckled. "No, no. I have to get back to the inn. The crew from Lake Breeze Tours will take care of everything. You'll be in good hands."

Amma glanced over at the boat, taking in the scene. "It's such a beautiful day for a sail. I can already feel the peace of the water."

The sailboat rocked gently at the dock, its mast rising white against the sky. The cockpit held benches on either side of the tiller, space enough for the family to sit together while the captain steered. Forward, on the deck, the mate checked the rigging, his movements steady and sure.

Ravi looked from the boat to Raju. "How about you, Raju? You joining us?"

Raju shook his head. "I'll stay back and let you enjoy yourselves for the afternoon. Maybe I'll meet up with Siddharth and see how he is progressing with our plans for tomorrow. I'll be here when you're finished. You still have my handy number, right?"

Ravi patted his pocket. "Got it. We'll let you know if anything comes up."

"Take your time," Raju said. "Have a wonderful day out on the lake."

As he spoke, a man came up from the dock. He walked with a confident stride and wore a white cap with gold trim. "Namaste," he said as he extended his hand. "I'm Sujan, and I'll be your captain for the afternoon." He nodded toward a man moving along the deck. "This is Daha, my mate. He'll see to the sails."

The family offered polite nods and a wave in Daha's direction, acknowledging him. He returned the gesture with a brief smile.

Sujan then looked at the younger children, his pleasant smile beaming. "Is everyone ready to set sail?"

"You bet!" Cyrus answered.

"Let's go!" Kiran shouted, echoing his brother's excitement.

"Okay then," Sujan replied. "Please, follow me!"

***

2:30 P.M.

As the sailboat ventured farther from land, its white sail billowed against the pristine blue sky. The hull, cutting through the lake's still waters, created ripples that shimmered with the mirrored reflections of the majestic foothills.

Ravi allowed himself a moment to sit back and drink in his surroundings. The stillness of the lake and the beauty of the peaks looming in the distance gave him a rare feeling of peace, a calm he seldom allowed himself to experience. For a moment, the weight of their quest shifted, and he was simply a man adrift on the water. The world paused just for him, and he found a measure of serenity in that pause.

"Isn't it breathtaking?" Sophie exclaimed, breaking Ravi's reverie, her eyes alight as she took in the stunning landscape— the cool air and the vast lake stretching out before them.

Ravi, however, wasn't looking at the view. He was looking at her. "It is," he said softly, his gaze lingering on his wife.

Sophie caught his meaning and gave him a playful nudge. "Not me, Ravi. I meant the lake. Pokhara. Nepal.

Look around—it's incredible!"

Ravi grinned, unbothered. "Yeah, well, you're the best part of the scenery."

Sophie shook her head, a laugh escaping her lips as she scooted closer to him on the bench. "You're hopeless," she teased, sliding her hand into his. With a soft smile, she leaned in and kissed him.

From the other side, Harrison groaned dramatically. "Ugh, seriously, guys? We're in public! Get a room!"

Ravi glanced over at Harrison, chuckling. "Hey, kiddo, we're on a chartered sailboat with its own captain and crew. This is about as private as it gets."

Sujan tipped his hat in acknowledgement.

Ravi winked at Sophie, who laughed softly and squeezed his hand, the two of them sharing a moment of quiet amusement.

Harrison rolled his eyes, barely suppressing a grin. "Just keep it PG, okay? There are children here."

Before Ravi could respond, Cyrus, who had been leaning over the side, suddenly spoke up. "The water's so clear. You think we can see the fish?"

Ravi shifted his gaze to Cyrus, smiling. "Maybe. With water this still, you might just catch a glimpse of something."

Kiran, sitting beside him, looked up. "Why is the water so clear?"

Sujan turned toward the towering, snow-capped peaks of the Annapurna range. They loomed over the lake, ethereal and majestic, like ancient sentinels. "That's because this lake gets its water from the melting snow of those mountains," he said, pointing to the distant peaks. "The snow melts, flows down, and fills this lake."

The mountains stood unmoving around the lake, their presence heavy and watchful.

Holding his stuffed lamb close, Cyrus noticed the reflection of the range in the water. His smile lifted, unguarded and bright. "Look," he said. "The mountains are in the water, too."

The reflection wavered.

Not shattered—only bent, as if something unseen had passed through it. A single bird lifted from the far reeds, wings breaking the image. Then the water settled again, smoother than before, the peaks returning to their place as though nothing needed to remain.

Pappa shifted beside them, drawn by the quiet more than the sound. For an instant, he felt the absence of something he could not place—no threat, no warning—only the faint awareness that whatever had passed was already gone.

A thin unease settled in the quiet that followed—light as breath, easy to ignore. The lake lay calm once more, unchanged, as if it had absorbed something and given nothing back.

Sophie turned, meaning to answer him. But the moment had already closed.

3:15 P.M.

As the sun passed its zenith and the day wore on, gratitude brimmed in Sophie's heart as she eagerly opened the picnic lunch provided by the inn for their lake excursion. She unfastened the woven basket, revealing an arrangement of culinary delights. The inviting aroma of *aloo parathas*, with its golden, buttery layers, and the rich and spicy scent of *chana masala*, filled with chickpeas and fragrant spices, wafted from the compartments, mingling with the irresistible fragrance of vegetable *pakoras*, crispy fritters bursting with a medley of flavors.

Along with this thoughtful lunch, thermoses of steaming masala chai awaited. Ginger cookies added a hint of zing. The lunch presentation and its attention to detail left a lasting impression. It was a feast for the senses and the soul, reflecting the inn's commitment to providing an experience extending past mere sustenance. Wrapped in cozy blankets provided by the tour company, the lake's embrace became even more enchanting as they savored the flavors of a meal surpassing all expectations.

Daha moved along the deck, tightening a line and glancing across the water with a sailor's instinct. His expression gave nothing away, yet Sophie caught the way his eyes lingered on an unassuming boat.

His belly full, Kiran nestled comfortably on Sophie's lap. She allowed herself to become immersed in the beauty surrounding the lake. The rippling water, the distant mountains—it was all peaceful, a moment of calm she accepted. Yet despite the serenity, she couldn't calm her thoughts. They drifted back to the riddle on the goatskin, its cryptic message a puzzle she couldn't shake. The diamond and its legendary power…it all felt near, weaving itself into her mind.

Within this meditative trance, her gaze rested on the tiny boat that had drawn Daha's attention. It was floating with an eerie stillness, the water lapping at its sides. Its occupants motionless, as if lulled. A fishing pole extended haphazardly, infusing the scene with a sense of effortless leisure. The image looked like a canvas painted with the hues of peaceful calm.

Sophie's reverie was shattered by a sudden splash. She scanned the disturbed surface, where the ripples hinted at a cause unseen and left her mind grappling for explanations. The previously undisturbed, mirror-like surface of Phewa

Lake now seemed like an enigma.

Sophie's uneasiness grew; the splash was an anomaly in the stillness, and the boat in the distance seemed suspect to her. The men aboard created a tableau of relaxation, yet Sophie's instincts screamed this was a façade. There was an element in this idyllic scene that didn't seem to fit, a puzzle her intuition needed to solve.

The tranquility of the surrounding mountains offered little comfort to Sophie as her gaze lingered on the boat. The laughter and conversations around her faded into the background as her senses heightened. The splash was more than a mere disturbance—it was a mark, a crack in the picture-perfect scenery, hinting at underlying currents she couldn't ignore.

Sophie leaned toward Harrison and whispered, "Can you sense we're being watched?"

Harrison's brow furrowed, his gaze shifting to meet hers. "You know what? I've been noticing them, too." His tone matched her quiet demeanor. "Those men over there seem out of place, don't they?"

The two exchanged a knowing glance, united in their unspoken thoughts. There was a sense of camaraderie between them. As they continued to observe the distant figures, their suspicion deepened, and the mystery of the unfamiliar onlookers added a layer of intrigue to their lakeside adventure.

As if in response to Sophie's suspicions, the men fishing on the nearby boat reeled in their fishing lines with slow precision, their movements deliberate.

As one man turned his head, his gaze briefly met Sophie's, and a chill ran down her spine. *Were they indeed watching us?* she asked herself.

Ravi's voice broke through her trance. "I see them, too," he offered, sensing her concern.

"They are watching us, right?" Her gaze fixed on the men.

"Not sure. But they're not catching any fish, and I don't think there is any lure on their lines."

Harrison chimed in, adding to the suspicion as he shared his observation. "They're not dressed like fishermen either; what's up with the suits?"

Perched on Sophie's lap, Kiran pointed at a cluster of colorful boats dotting the lake. "Look, Mom, like a rainbow on the water!"

Smiling, Sophie allowed herself to be drawn into Kiran's enthusiasm. She reminded herself that sometimes, the simplest and most beautiful moments could quiet troubling doubts. As her family continued to soak in the picturesque scene, the mysteries and uncertainties of their journey to Nepal took a back seat, if only for a little while.

3:55 P.M.

The island temple rose from the center of the lake, its pagoda roof dark against the sky.

Sophie's breath caught. "I did not know there was a temple out here."

"The lake keeps her secrets," Sujan said softly. "Tal Barahi—protector and destroyer. Travelers ask her blessing before they venture on anyway."

Sophie's eyes lingered on the temple. "Oh… Maybe we should ask for a blessing," she said, turning to Harrison.

He shifted, uncertain but willing. "If you think it will help."

Pappa leaned forward, his gaze fixed on the shrine. "Can we stop and take a look around, Sujan?"

Sujan glanced from the tiller to the family and gave a slow nod. "As you wish. Tal Barahi receives all who come with respect."

At the bow, Daha was already moving. He hauled the sail down in steady folds, dropped the fenders, and coiled the line for docking. Sujan shifted the tiller, angling the hull toward the stone landing.

The boat glided closer, ripples breaking in widening rings until the vessel kissed the steps with a hollow knock. Daha leapt ashore, rope in hand, and tied the line fast.

One by one, the family stepped onto the stone landing, the air heavy with the scent of incense drifting across the water. Pigeons lifted from the roof, circling the pagoda before settling again along its eaves. Bells trembled faintly, stirred by the breeze.

A narrow path rose from the steps, leading beneath low branches toward the temple courtyard. The shrine itself stood dark and solemn, a two-tiered pagoda of timber and brick, its carved struts worn smooth. Butter lamps flickered at the doorway, their glow painting the threshold gold.

Sujan lingered at the edge of the path. "Tal Barahi waits. Ask, and she may witness your journey."

Sophie looked from the lamps to her family. "Shall we?"

Ravi bent down and scooped up Kiran, nodding. Pappa placed his hand in Amma's. Together, they began the slow climb toward the entrance of the temple.

***

4:25 P.M.

As they entered, a priest in saffron robes stood at the threshold. He raised his hand, directing them toward the altar. Sophie stepped forward and pressed her palms together, then knelt. Ravi bowed beside her with Kiran in his arms, while Pappa drew Cyrus close and helped him scatter rice. The white grains fell sharp against the dark stone. Overhead, pigeons startled from the beams, their wings beating through the silence.

Harrison lingered. His gaze fixed on the bronze figure within: Barahi, tusked and fierce, her eyes unblinking. For an instant, the lamplight caught her face, and he thought the bronze burned. He blinked—only metal. Yet the weight of being measured clung to him.

The priest carried a dish of vermilion in his hand. One by one, he pressed the red mark to their foreheads, thumb sure, marking each with quiet solemnity. When he reached Harrison, his touch faltered. The silence stretched, heavy, unbroken. Then he bent close, his whisper meant for him alone. "It remembers you."

The hush did not lift. It pressed deeper, as though the temple walls themselves had registered it.

Behind him, Pappa bent toward the wall, brushing soot with his fingers. "Look," he murmured.

Carved lines hid in the smoke-dark surface, a lattice older than the beams themselves.

Sophie's breath trembled. "The Kumari Mandala. It's here."

Pappa nodded. "We're on track."

The bells overhead rang once, hollow and clear, though no hand had touched them. Cyrus held tight against Amma's side, wide-eyed.

Sophie turned, her lamp wavering, gaze drawn past the shrine to the lake beyond. Through the carved doorway the lowering sun spread crimson across the water. A boat floated just outside the temple's reflection, two men within, their oars at rest. They did not fish. They watched.

Sophie turned back to her family quickly, her voice thin. "We should go."

As they turned to leave, the priest's voice followed them. "When the time comes, the world will remember its own blood."

Harrison glanced back—but the priest had already turned away, his eyes closed in prayer.

***

5:12 P.M.

Back on the sailboat, the sun slipped behind the mountains, and twilight gathered over the lake. The day's wandering loosened its grip on the family, leaving them quieter, lighter. Beauty did what it always did—it asked nothing and gave relief. Sujan loosened his hold on the tiller, letting the boat find its own line. The sail caught the last breath of evening and the water folded around the hull, smoothing itself as they passed.

At the bow, Daha paused. He did not rush the sail. He let it fall, measured the wind with a glance toward the far shore, then gathered the canvas. When the lines were coiled, he did not move away. He stood still, watching the lake as if waiting for something to finish crossing.

Sophie's attention drifted back to the distant boat. Nothing about it had changed—yet the sense remained. Not threat. Not certainty. Only the quiet impression that something had been seen and not answered.

Again, a sudden splash erupted from the water, causing her heart to skip a beat. Her gaze darted in the direction of the commotion, only to glimpse a shimmering tail disappearing beneath the surface, a fish slipping away.

Harrison pointed at the ripples left by the fish's tail. "Did you see that, Mom? The fishtail! It's like Machapuchare is showing us a sign."

"I did," Sophie said, her pulse slowing. The brief flash of the fishtail breaking the surface had jolted her. The water stilled. Machapuchare's silhouette settled back into the reflection, filling the space where the fish had been.

Nothing pressed forward. Nothing pulled back. Time drew in around her.

The distant shore sharpened as the sailboat glided across the lake. Wind filled the sail, and the soft creak of the boat's rigging set a calming rhythm as they neared their destination. The vessel cut through the water, bringing them closer to the lush greenery and rugged terrain. With a final shift of the sail, Sujan guided the boat toward the dock. The hull bumped gently against the wooden planks, marking their arrival with a quiet thud.

"And with that, I'm afraid our ride has come to its end," Sujan announced. "I hope you've had the day you needed."

"Absolutely," Amma replied.

"Thank you, Sujan," Pappa offered. "It's been a pleasure."

"Thank you," the rest of the family echoed.

"The pleasure has been all mine," Sujan assured them. With that, he lithely stepped over the side of the boat and began tying it to the dock.

One by one, they stood up, steadying themselves against the boat's sway. Ravi extended his hand to Sophie, offering support as they stepped out onto the solid ground. Their movements were cautious, mindful of the boat's rhythmic bobbing. Following them, Kiran and Cyrus leaped out with youthful agility, though their sudden movements caused the vessel to rock unsteadily for a moment. They laughed, steadying themselves, their smiles bright with the thrill of adventure.

Amma and Pappa were next, their movements more measured. Harrison stood by, ready to assist. He reached out, offering a guiding hand as they disembarked. With his help, they navigated their way out of the boat, ensuring they were safely ashore before he stepped out, grounding himself. The earth felt surprisingly firm under their feet, a notable contrast to the fluid motion of the boat.

The air grew chilly as the Sharma family gathered their belongings. As the light of day turned to the darkness of night, the cheerful adventures of the day also turned toward the uncertain mysteries. Back on shore, the reality of their journey's next chapter set in. The day's interlude had been restorative, and now the mysterious path ahead remained, waiting.

* * *

5:25 P.M.

The figures of Anil and Raju were almost indistinguishable from the shadows in the dimming light. They stood beside a humble hut that sold local trinkets, lingering as the Sharma family returned from the lake.

Anil peered down the path. When he finally spoke, his low, conspiratorial whisper blended with the evening air. "Do you think they suspect anything?"

Raju, his back casually pressed against the hut, replied, "I don't think so. Best not to test it." His eyes betrayed a cunning gleam.

Anil's lips curled into a sly smile. "Exactly. It was brilliant you brought them to our inn, guiding them toward uncovering the diamond for us."

With a casual shrug, Raju responded nonchalantly, "Oh, it was nothing. It was a simple maneuver to keep them moving. But I must admit, it's working better than expected. By the way, Operation Pawn's Gate is proceeding as planned. The tunnel did what it was meant to."

"They sure seemed intrigued," Anil replied, projecting a hint of confidence. "I bet they would have gone in if I didn't bring them back upstairs. I won't lock anything tonight. I wouldn't be surprised if they go exploring."

Raju nodded his head slightly. "They already asked Siddharth and me to take them."

Anil's grin widened. "Perfect. Then our plan is working."

Raju's tone cooled. "Not everyone shares your confidence. Priya's already arranged for the street boys from the Mahendrapal Bazaar to approach them." He paused, remembering their conversation. "We need to get them there around three."

Anil scowled. "I hate how she undermines me."

"She doesn't think you can hold the pieces together," Raju said flatly. "Don't take it personal—that's simply how she is."

"I do everything for her, and still, she doubts me," Anil muttered, bitterness tightening his jaw. He hesitated, then lowered his voice. "What about Siddharth? He's so intent on safeguarding the Heart of Kumari. Will he be a problem?"

A dismissive smirk played on Raju's lips. "There's no need to worry about Siddharth. His devotion lies with the Shatranj Ke Sipahi and the Heart, and his loyalty to me is unshakable. He's as entangled in this quest as we are. Rest assured, he will not be a problem." Raju glanced up at Anil, his expression darkening slightly. "I am more concerned about Priya. Your sister is a force to be reckoned with—relentless and unwavering in her pursuits."

"You're right. Priya is a formidable adversary, unyielding and shrewd." Anil's face cracked into a smile. "I believe Priya will prove invaluable to our endeavor."

Anil's phone buzzed, pulling his attention away for a moment. "Speaking of Priya…" As he read the message aloud, a wry smile crept across his face. "Bat cave in the morning, then the bazaar."

"You're right about her getting things done."

Their malevolent plotting was interrupted as they noticed the Sharma family approaching in the distance. Instantly, their expressions shifted to ones of innocence, and their conversation ceased. As they prepared to greet the family with feigned warmth, the night air suddenly seemed heavier, laden with secrets and unspoken schemes.

* * *

5:45 P.M.

Harrison was the first to spot their ride. "Look, Anil and Raju are waiting for us," Harrison called out, waving his arm, drawing their attention.

On their way down the path, the Sharma family passed an appealing row of stalls set up by the lake's edge, a showcase of local craftsmanship. Handwoven blankets draped over the sides were decorated with images of Nepal's picturesque landscapes, their stunning patterns and vivid colors catching the eye. Paintings of the majestic mountains stood on display, each canvas a tribute to the towering peaks surrounding them. Among these artistic expressions, gleaming copper relics rested on makeshift tables, their sheen catching the ambient light around them.

Nestled within the serene setting, two women caught their attention. The older of the pair sat quietly beside a small flame that flickered in the evening breeze, her figure forming a gentle silhouette against the backdrop of her stall. Her face bore the lines of many years, and her eyes held a depth that hinted at untold stories and wisdom. The younger woman, seated beside her, tended to the fire with skill. Upon the flames rested a pot of masala tea, its inviting aroma mingling with the scents of tandoori and fried street food.

"Mom, can we get a blanket? They're amazing," Harrison asked, captivated by the detailed handiwork.

His mother smiled, her eyes also scanning the woven patterns. "Those are called *dhaka* blankets. They're handwoven."

Harrison nodded, impressed. "They're beautiful."

Pappa, who had been examining the fabrics alongside him, stepped closer. "I'll buy one as well."

Meanwhile, Amma's discerning eye caught sight of the simmering masala tea, the flame beneath it enticing her to indulge in its comforting warmth. "Would anyone be interested in a cup of hot chai?"

Unanimous agreement met her question—save for Cyrus, who had his eye on a classic glass bottle of Coke.

Harrison wrapped himself in the new blanket and took slow sips of the flavorful chai. As he drank, a calm washed over him—but it did not hold. The faint fizz of Cyrus's soda sounded sharp in the stillness, the bubbles popping too fast, too close, like breath breaking at the wrong moment.

In that moment, the younger woman tending the chai turned her gaze toward Harrison. Then she whispered, "Remember, appearances can deceive. Be cautious of those who are bound by blood." With a knowing look, she passed him a crumpled note.

Upon unfolding it, Harrison's eyes widened as he recognized the markings from the Monkey Temple and the goatskin. This familiar Kumari Mandala was the symbol woven into their journey's fabric.

Harrison's mind spun, taken aback by her mysterious words and the crumpled paper. He thanked the woman with a nod, his thoughts swirling as he pondered the cryptic message. The exchange left him astonished and curious, and the echoes of the woman's warning lingered in the still night air as they moved away from the fire.

They approached the van, and Raju opened the side door. "I trust you enjoyed your day?" His gaze flicked to the tika pressed on their foreheads. "Ah, you went to the temple."

Sophie touched her brow. "Oh—this. Yes, we thought to ask for a blessing."

"That was wise," Raju said.

Amma smiled. "It was beautiful. We lit a lamp for the goddess."

From the passenger's seat, Anil called out, "Tal Barahi Temple, isn't it? They say the goddess rose from the lake to protect the valley."

Sophie nodded. "Yes, that was the name."

Pappa hesitated, lowering his voice. "Raju, we saw the Kumari Mandala there. Do you think it's a clue?"

Sophie added, "Siddharth said it was guiding us. Should we go back?"

For a moment, Raju said nothing. The evening light sharpened the angles of his face, turning his expression into something unreadable. "I don't think it's a clue, per se," he said at last. "It's a confirmation—from the Kumari herself—that you are where you're meant to be."

The words did not settle, yet the family hung on to them. There was a certainty about him that drew them in, the kind of quiet conviction that made doubt feel foolish.

A faint smile touched his lips. "You thought the lake would slow your steps," he added softly, "but perhaps it was meant to give them direction."

No one spoke.

Pappa considered this as he offered his hand to Amma while she stepped into the van.

Cyrus, barely containing his bubbling excitement, brushed past his grandmother and leapt into the vehicle. "Sorry, Amma,

I want to sit in the back seat!"

"Oh, you can have it, sweetheart," she said, steadying herself before settling in behind him.

Raju stepped aside to let them climb in. Then, with a quick grin, he added, "By the way, you'll be happy to know that tomorrow morning, we're headed to the bat cave."

Sophie lit up with excitement. "That's wonderful! Siddharth did it!"

"Awesome!" Cyrus cheered from the back row.

"Mama, are we going to see the bats?" Kiran asked as Sophie lifted him into the van.

"Looks like it!" she affirmed, kissing his forehead before nudging him toward his brother in the back row.

Ravi turned to Sophie with a lighthearted smirk. "See, I told you to have faith."

"You're right, my love," she agreed. With a fleeting kiss, she slid into the seat beside him and placed her hand in his.

Pappa turned toward his eldest grandson as he approached the van. "Did you hear that, Harrison? We are going to the bat cave tomorrow."

"That's good news, Pappa." Harrison's face brightened at the prospect, yet he couldn't help but ponder the development. *Had fate conspired to lead us to the Heart of Kumari? Could Siddharth know its whereabouts? Is there any connection to the cryptic words written by the woman from the lake?* He unfolded the crumpled paper in his hand and peered at it.

The intricate Kumari Mandala, along with the woman's warning, stared back at him. For a moment, they shimmered, as if the paper itself exhaled the warning.

Bound by Blood.

Startled, Harrison caught his breath and slid the paper in his pocket, hiding the words before anyone could see. *'Bound by blood.' Did she mean not to trust his own family?*

The thought slid beneath his skin like a shard of ice. He wanted to shake it off—dismiss it as nonsense.

Slowly, he drew the paper halfway free and glanced down again, just to be certain. The word pulsed faintly, steady and insistent.

BOUND BY BLOOD.

The words carried weight—cold, final, and unrelenting. They didn't explain. They accused.

Who? The question coiled inside him. Pappa? Amma? Mom?

No. He couldn't believe that.

But the mandala seemed to shimmer with knowing.

"What do you have there, Harrison?" Pappa inquired, his attention caught by the peculiar light.

"It's nothing, Pappa. Just something I picked up by the lake," Harrison replied, a hint of nervousness betraying his casual tone. He shoved the paper back into his pocket, his secrecy a silent handshake with fate. He wasn't prepared to divulge this enigma to his family—not yet.

As they began their trip back to the city, Harrison couldn't help but notice how the clouds had reappeared, draping the landscape in a mist. The weight of his calling pressed against his chest, as heavy as the fog closing in.

7:00 P.M.

Upon returning to the Surya Chandra Inn, the Sharma family was greeted by a mesmerizing sight. The garden lanterns' glow intertwined with the mist swirling above the ground, creating an ethereal radiance. This gentle illumination cast enchanting shadows along the paths. The Raat Ki Rani, or 'Night Queen,' opened its petals, releasing a heady, sweet fragrance that intensified under the moon's light. Embraced by this tranquil ambiance and the peacefulness of the evening, the family felt a comforting sense of well-being.

"We couldn't have asked for a more fulfilling day," Sophie said, her smile reflecting the contentment that filled the air.

Ravi cast a lingering glance at the mountain silhouette framed by the mist. Gratitude overwhelmed him. "We've got to give it to Surya Chandra Inn; its humble setting has delivered an unforgettable experience."

Anil walked a few steps ahead, eager to be back inside the inn. His eyes focused ahead of him, he lifted a hand in parting and tilted his head to speak over his shoulder. "Have a good evening, Sharmas—and Raju. Tomorrow, breakfast will be out on the back patio."

"Good night," they all called after him, their voices rising in unison.

As they walked down the garden path, Siddharth stepped out from the shadows. His hair, tied low with a leather cord, brushed the back of his shirt as he moved. His voice carried the weight of suggestion. "The day's still young. Why don't we get something to eat, and then…" He leaned in, his words almost a whisper. "We go explore that tunnel."

"Food sounds good. We could all use it." Sophie's glance flicked toward Siddharth, though her words were meant for everyone.

Harrison muttered, frustrated. "Always waiting…"

"Patience," Ravi said firmly, his hand resting on his son's shoulder. "One step at a time."

"I'm not hungry!" Cyrus announced, leaping down the path, Sheepy dangling in his grip. "I want to see the monster."

"Me too!" Kiran echoed, tugging at Amma's sleeve.

Amma gave a soft laugh. "Dinner first, boys. There will be plenty of time for the tunnel later."

Raju gestured toward a lantern-lit path that curved around the inn. "I think the dining hall is this way."

Together, they followed him, the night air rich with the scent of blossoms.

A few steps later, the path opened onto a carved wooden sign that read CHANDNI LOUNGE, the letters glinting faintly in the light.

The family entered, with Raju and Siddharth leading the way. Inside, the space glowed with a soft, amber hue. Brass oil lamps swung gently above a bar hand-carved from indigenous wood. Along the mirrored back wall, bottles stood in formation like soldiers. The air carried the pungent scent of cumin and fried garlic drifting in from the kitchen. Beneath it lingered the faint edge of local spirits.

The room hummed with quiet life—low conversations, the clinking of glasses, the shuffle of feet across worn floorboards. Shadows pooled in the corners while the lamps cast a wavering gold across polished wood.

The Sharma family was cheerful but weary. Their chatter blended into the din as they found a table tucked into the corner. Before they sat, Raju offered to fetch their drinks.

"I'll have a red wine," Amma said, settling into her chair.

"That sounds perfect," Sophie echoed, a faint smile tugging at her lips. "Make it a local wine, if they have it."

Raju turned to the children. "Mango lassis for the boys?"

"Yes! Yes!" Cyrus and Kiran cheered in unison.

Raju nodded, then glanced at Ravi and Pappa. "For the rest of us, a round of Gorkha beers—it's the pride of Nepal."

Pappa gave a small, approving grunt. "Strong choice."

Ravi leaned back, his expression weary but amused. "All right, let's try it. When in Pokhara…"

Raju smiled as he stepped away to place their order.

Behind the counter, the bartender polished glasses with a

well-worn cloth. His movements were deliberate, practiced, as though he had been repeating the same gestures for years. He looked up when Raju approached, recognition flickering for only an instant before his face settled into studied neutrality.

"I'll have two red wines, one masala tea, two mango lassis, and three Gorkha beers. Chicken momos and sel roti to the table." Raju called out. As the order was noted, he leaned in, lowering his voice so only the bartender could hear. "Keshav," Raju murmured, "Bhaskar's still got you working the bar?"

Keshav was no stranger. He was a distant cousin, a companion from the days when he and Raju had grown up working in these halls. Now, he was a pawn still trapped in service—exactly where Bhaskar had placed him.

The bartender set down a glass. His sleeve slipped as he did, revealing a faint scar seared into his wrist—a sigil in the shape of a pawn. "Good to see you, Raju," Keshav said, tugging the sleeve back down. "Been a while since you've been in Pokhara. Business?"

"You could say that." Raju's words carried the weight of warning. "I'm to pretend I don't know you, so you'd better do the same."

Keshav's eyes glinted, betraying the hunger he tried to hide. "It's that family, isn't it?" He reached for a bottle, tilting it so a thin stream of wine filled the waiting glasses. "Bhaskar said to treat them as if they were the royal court." His voice dropped, almost reverent. "The diamond is close. I can feel it."

"Careful, Keshav. We all have our role to play." Raju allowed the faintest smirk. "And it's Bhaskar who decides whether you're worth keeping on the board."

For a beat, silence bristled between them, their faces unreadable. Raju slid a folded note across the counter, their eyes locking for a breath—both men bound by their marks. The paper lay between them like a blade sheathed in silence. Then,

Keshav palmed it away.

The mask returned. His smile spread easily as he lifted his head to the room. "Your food will be right out."

"Good," Raju said. Their eyes lingered one last moment before he lifted the tray and carried the drinks back.

The Sharmas saw only a friendly bartender. They hadn't noticed the scar. They hadn't seen the note disappear.

Raju dragged a chair beside Siddharth, took a long swallow of his beer, and leaned forward to address the family. "So…you think that tunnel Anil showed you could lead to the diamond?"

Sophie jumped in before Ravi could. "Yes. But we don't know for certain—that's why we need you and Siddharth to take us."

"It wasn't just a door," Ravi added quickly, as though to anchor her excitement. "It was hidden in the wall. Anil had to use a lever to open it."

Raju leaned back, eyes flicking to his brother. "What do you think?"

Siddharth shrugged, feigning ignorance.

They both did their best to portray casual interest, but their hearts secretly raced at the possibilities.

Harrison's voice cut through the pause—quiet, but sure. "The tunnel. It felt…" His voice trailed off, unsure of itself.

Raju turned toward him. "The tunnel felt what?"

Harrison shifted, doubtful how to put it into words.

The others watched him, waiting.

"The air changed when Anil opened the door. Like the tunnel had been asleep for a long time…and it came to life when it noticed us."

Raju studied him for a beat, his brow creasing. "Places don't usually notice people."

Harrison met his eyes. "This one did."

Raju straightened, then he turned toward Pappa. "Do you

still have the map from last night?"

"Yes." Pappa reached into his coat and drew it out, smoothing the creased parchment across the table. Its folds spoke of long hours in his hands, studied and hidden again.

They bent close, lantern-light washing over the faded ink.

"These lines," Raju said, tracing with his finger, "they're different. See here." Raju angled the parchment so they could get a better look. "They're lighter than the original ink."

"So, they were added later?" Harrison asked.

"That, or someone tried to erase them," Siddharth said.

"Erase them? Who would do that?" Cyrus leaned forward, wide-eyed.

"Someone who wants to hide them," Kiran blurted. He huffed, as if it should have been obvious all along.

Ravi glanced up. Kiran had made a sharp point.

Sophie dismissed Kiran's show of exasperation and turned back to Raju. "So, what do you think they represent?"

"They could be the outlines of old passageways under Pokhara. And here…" He tapped a jagged scrawl. "It says '*Tal knot.*' This was the name of the fort before it fell—it's written right over the symbol of the stronghold."

As his finger passed over the ink, the lamplight trembled. For an instant, beneath the overlapping lines, a hidden inscription surfaced—so faint it might have been part of the paper's grain: *The torchlight reveals the Pattern: follow what is first to catch the flame.* (Doctrine of Balance, Fragment P-II)

The shimmer faded. No one noticed. The words sank again into the parchment.

Harrison leaned closer, inspecting both the writing and the glyph. The script meant nothing to him, just curling strokes and broken lines. "So, this is the fort? Where we are now?"

"Yes," Raju said, lifting his beer.

Harrison's eyes burned with eagerness. "Then the basement really does lead somewhere?"

Sophie's words came too fast, her voice sharpened by hope. "And if it links to the caves, it could take us straight to the diamond."

"It may…" Siddharth replied. His hand pressed the parchment flat. His gaze met hers, steady and unyielding. "Or it may not. Old maps mislead as often as they guide. Better not to mistake every line for a promise."

Sophie refused to look away. "And if we doubt every step, we'll never take one."

The silence between them bristled, taut as wire, until Ravi cut across, steady and practical. "We don't go now. Too many eyes. We wait until the inn sleeps, right?"

Raju gave a single nod. "Midnight."

"Midnight," Ravi repeated, raising his cup.

The others echoed him, even Kiran and Cyrus, their small voices bright with excitement at the thought of sneaking through forbidden halls.

But Harrison did not lift his cup. His eyes had drifted toward the bar. For an instant, he caught the bartender watching him—not with the genial smile he'd worn for the family, but with something else. A flicker too sharp, too knowing, gone as quickly as it came.

A chill needled through Harrison's chest. His fingers tightened around the table's edge. "No," he said, sudden and strained. "We shouldn't go tonight."

The table stilled.

Sophie blinked, startled. "Harrison—"

He shook his head, pushing back his chair. The scrape of the legs rang loud in the hush. "I can't. Something's wrong. I don't know what, but we shouldn't go down there tonight."

Ravi leaned forward. "Son—"

But Harrison was already moving, stepping away from

the table. His gaze flicked once more to the bar, where Keshav polished a glass as if nothing had passed. The man didn't look up, but his aura drove a splinter of concern deep into Harrison's senses.

Without another word, Harrison turned and walked out of the Chandni Lounge, his footsteps swallowed quickly by the inn's silence.

* * *

Retreating to the sanctuary of his room, Harrison found himself relentlessly pursued by the woman's cryptic message. The words echoed in his mind, clear and resonant—*a prophetic nod from the Spirit of Kumari?*

At first, the words had made him recoil, dragging his thoughts to Pappa and Amma, to his family. But that didn't hold. They had been his anchor in all of this—steady, unshaken. *If betrayal lurked nearby, it wasn't in them. It couldn't be.* The bond they shared wasn't the kind that broke in silence.

So, what did the woman mean?

His thoughts churned. Reluctantly, he moved on to the others.

Raju and Siddharth? They weren't his family—not by any stretch—but the brothers were twins. Close. Inseparable. Bound by blood in the truest sense of the phrase. *Maybe that was the warning. Not about my own family, but about them.*

His skepticism about Raju and Siddharth lingered beneath the surface. *Why had Raju not alerted the rangers after their jeep breakdown?* Yet against his better judgment, Harrison wanted to extend his trust to the twin brothers, as though compelled by an unspoken covenant.

He thought of his family who, beguiled by his younger brothers' enthusiasm for the two men, sang their praises, especially grateful for their guidance through this foreign land and the murky waters of his calling. *But the lake woman—could her warning really involve these brothers, men who have helped us time and time again?* Conflicting memories of the safari tugged at Harrison: the laughter, the close calls, the shared triumphs—all clouded now by a haze of doubt.

And then there was the bartender. Harrison couldn't shake the way the man had looked at him across the lounge—just a flicker, sharp as a blade before it disappeared behind a smile. No one else had seen it, but Harrison had. It wasn't a stranger's glance. It was recognition. It was intent.

In the quiet of his room, he stilled for a moment, listening to his own breathing. His reflection watched him from the narrow mirror above the dresser—pale, unsettled, not quite finished with the night.

A strange pressure settled between his shoulders, as if a presence had once stood just behind him—close enough to guard, close enough to strike.

He turned slightly, eyes lifting to the mirror. Nothing shifted. The room remained unchanged.

And yet the sensation lingered: the memory of stillness before violence, of breath held not in fear but in resolve. Someone—older, sharper—had known this moment. Had stood at the edge of a choice and not looked away.

The feeling slipped beneath his thoughts before he could name it.

He needed time to think, to unravel it, before stepping into the tunnel.

Is someone watching? The questions resurfaced in his mind, each one too important to cast aside. In the labyrinth of his thoughts, one echo was loudest: *'Be cautious.'* With guarded tenacity, Harrison kept his questions to himself, letting the mystery simmer quietly in his mind.

— 5 —
WHISPERS IN THE NIGHT

निशानिनादाः

10:45 P.M.

Dread surged through Harrison as he jolted awake, drenched in a cold sweat, his heart racing. In the dream, a voice had found him, haunting yet alluring. It wasn't a command or a plea—just a quiet presence, urging him forward. And its nearness left him certain he had woken too late.

He slipped out of bed careful not to wake his brothers and slowly opened his door. The suite was still. He padded across the darkened sitting room. The hearth sat cold and empty. But above it, the painting loomed. The old fort in twilight. The amber light. The mist. Machapuchare rising in the haze behind. And there—a figure.

He stopped.

A woman now stood in the painting's lower courtyard. Just

inside the outer wall. Her face half-turned. The paint cracked with age, but her shape was sharp, recent. Wrong.

He stared, heart thudding. She was back. But clearer. A chill slid over his skin. He stepped back without meaning to. Then, quietly, he turned and continued down the hall.

He knocked once before entering his mother's room.

"Mom, I had this dream." He hesitated, then went on. "Kumari, or someone, called me from the tunnel entrance in the basement. Not talking exactly. Just...there." He searched his mother's face not for disbelief, but for the moment something in her might give itself away.

Sophie looked at her son, a sliver of moonlight filtering through the curtains to outline his form. Her eyes slowly adjusted to the darkness as her maternal intuition picked up on the worries shadowing his features. She reached out and drew him closer, the way she had when he was small, as if proximity alone might almost steady him. "Dreams can be powerful. Sometimes, they can linger."

Harrison hesitated, waiting for something else she didn't say.

Her breath caught.

"Mom, maybe the dream is telling me we should have explored the tunnel."

"You want to explore the tunnel, now?" She glanced at the bedside clock. "It's only ten forty-five. Raju and Siddharth are probably still awake."

Harrison looked at his mom intently. "We can't tell them about this, Mom."

Sophie tilted her head. "Why not?"

The pause stretched.

"Does this have something to do with dinner?" she asked.

"Yeah...sort of. I just got cold feet. The bartender—he felt off to me."

"The bartender?"

"Yeah. I can't explain it, but something didn't feel right."

Sophie's eyes narrowed. "What's going on, Harrison? Explain."

Harrison studied her face before speaking. "Today, where we got tea by the lake—you know, where we bought the blankets?" He paused.

"Yes, Harrison. What happened?" Sophie urged her son to continue.

"A woman handed me a piece of paper with a message on it. It said, 'don't trust anyone.'" He shifted uneasily, clearly troubled by what he had to say next. "She used the words 'bound by blood.'" He then presented the crumpled paper he had been carrying and unfolded it before her.

She looked at the paper a fraction too long. "Why didn't you mention this earlier?"

"I was still piecing things together, Mom, and then this dream happened. It felt like a nudge, a warning of sorts."

He looked at her, barely visible in the shadows of the room. His fingers tightened around the paper. For a fleeting moment, doubt crept in where it never had before. *Should I even be telling her this?* The woman's words pulsed in his memory. *Bound by blood.* The thought chilled him. He hated it. But it came all the same. He remembered falling asleep to the sound of her voice on long drives, trusting she would know when to wake him. She had always been his compass—her calm presence, her quiet strength. And yet, here in the dark, with truth and dreams beginning to blur, even she seemed just out of reach.

Sophie caught the hesitation in his face. She shifted, propping herself up in bed. Her voice was calm, but her eyes searched his—still shadowed, still trying to find him. "You're scared. I get that. But don't let fear turn you against the people who love you."

Harrison exhaled, guilt threading through the tightness in his chest. "Yeah. I know. I'm sorry, Mom." He rubbed the back of his neck, the words coming slower, heavier. He hesitated, then continued. "I keep thinking about the note," he said. Maybe it's about Raju and Siddharth. They're not family—not mine. But they are family to each other. And as twins… aren't they literally bound by blood?"

He stopped there. The thought didn't settle the way he'd hoped. It lingered, unfinished. It wasn't proof—just a shape his fear kept returning to. Raju with his easy charm. Siddharth with his silence like stone. Something beneath the surface—something watching.

And now, Harrison was watching, too.

Sophie's gaze flitted from the paper to her son's worried face. "Harrison, Raju and Siddharth haven't done anything to suggest we shouldn't trust them."

She paused, searching her thoughts.

"The jeep safari, for one," he replied. "Raju was too eager to leave us in the jeep and never told the rangers about us."

Sophie scratched her head, bringing up the memory. "Yeah, I remember, that was a little odd."

"Odd? Mom, he should have sent the rangers to get us," Harrison argued.

"It's not like we were alone," Sophie countered.

"Well…then there's this inn. What if coming here was a setup, not a random accident?"

Sophie shook her head firmly. "Could've happened to anyone."

"But, Mom, think about it. They lied to us."

As Sophie listened to Harrison's concerns, her instinct was to defend Raju and Siddharth. She looked toward the window, where the moonlight filtered through the curtains. She let the silence stretch.

"Mom."

Sophie blinked, clearing her mind and forcing herself back into the present. "No, Harrison," she said more firmly. "I don't think Raju and Siddharth would do that to us. They're on our side."

Silence settled on the room, broken only by the distant hoot of an owl.

"Now, let's focus on your dream," Sophie finally said. "What did the angel say?"

"It wasn't an angel, Mom," he exhaled deeply, clearly frustrated. "I think it was the Spirit of Kumari. She was standing in front of the door Anil showed us."

Not facing him. Not speaking at first. Just there—like someone who had once stood watch over the same stone.

She carried no torch, yet light gathered near her, the way a body might hold warmth in winter.

In the dream, he hadn't questioned her presence. Only now did he wonder: Why had she been waiting at the gate—and not beyond it?

Harrison's voice quickened. "Remember what Anil said about the secret passageway and this inn? He mentioned a sealed door in the tunnel protecting a treasure. This inn might have something to do with finding the diamond."

She paused. "We're in the right place."

Harrison shifted uneasily, wrestling with his doubts. "Mom, do you think they brought us here because they knew about the tunnel in the basement?"

"I hear you," Sophie said quietly. "And I know you're trying to make sense of it." She reached for his hand, not looking at the paper. "But we can't let fear decide who we trust," she continued. "Not yet."

"Mom, why don't you get it? I don't think we can trust them."

Sophie did not answer right away. "Harrison, I'm not ignoring your feelings," she said. "But you need to consider that the warning from the woman at the lake may not be about who you think."

"You're thinking about those suited men on the boat. They seemed so out of place—as if they were there to watch us."

"Maybe, I forgot about them."

Harrison's brow furrowed. "But then…how do they fit into the message on the note?"

Bound by blood, bound by blood. He kept circling the words as if they were a fence, never thinking to look beyond it.

Sophie paused, the silence between them thick. "I don't know, Harrison," she admitted. "We just have to trust the process."

Harrison nodded, though he wasn't sure what the process was supposed to be. "Then what should we do now?" Harrison asked.

"Why don't you get some rest," Sophie said softly. Her fingers brushed the hair from his eyes. The gesture was automatic, practiced—the same one she'd used since before he could remember. She then glanced over at her husband, who was asleep. "We'll let everyone know in the morning, before we head to the caves. Perhaps there, something else will come to light."

Harrison stood up, kissed his mother good night, and returned to his room.

* * *

11:45 P.M.

His mother's words lingered in Harrison's mind as he lay in bed, refusing to settle. Caught between his mother's calm and the sense that something was already slipping past him, Harrison wrestled with indecision. He wondered if he should venture alone into the tunnel—or wait until morning to speak with his father, though the word wait sat wrong in his chest. As he flipped his pillow over to find a more comfortable side, he couldn't escape the feeling that time was of the essence.

Then came the knock at the door.

Startled, Harrison froze, his heart pounding. He yanked the covers over his head, trying to convince himself it was just his imagination. But the knocking persisted.

"The ghost," he whispered, breathless beneath the sheets.

A muffled sigh answered him.

"Harrison, it's me. It's Mom. Open the door."

In a rush of adrenaline, he threw off the covers and hurried to unlock the door. His parents entered, closing the door behind them, their faces tense.

"What's wrong?" Harrison asked.

"I woke your father because I couldn't shake the feeling from the dream you had. We need to investigate the tunnel tonight."

"Tonight? Now?" Harrison asked.

Ravi nodded. "We'll go quietly. We won't wake Raju and Siddharth."

"But why not? If they're helping us, shouldn't they know? I thought you trusted them, Mom."

Ravi exchanged a glance with Sophie before speaking. "If we wake them," he said, "we explain. And if we explain, they decide. If they decide 'not now'—we miss it entirely."

Sophie nodded once. "Your father's right."

Ravi patted the map in his pocket, the faint rustle sharp in the silence. "I've got the map. They talked us through the route."

No one answered right away.

"All right. But we need to be careful," Harrison said quietly.

"Come on, get dressed," Ravi encouraged.

As Harrison slipped on his pants, he hesitated. "Cyrus and Kiran—they're not coming?" He glanced toward the second bed. Cyrus and Kiran lay sprawled across the blankets, fast asleep, one small arm flung over the other.

"We've already woken Amma and Pappa," his father said. "They'll stay behind."

"But Amma and Pappa—we'll need them."

"We just need to see for ourselves," Sophie said. "If there's something there, we'll come back."

Remembering the iron gate separating the basement from the lobby, Harrison asked, "How are we going to get past the gate? We don't have the key."

A vivid memory from his boarding-school days flashed in Ravi's mind. He recalled how he had become adept at picking the lock of the "sweets cupboard," where confectioneries and treats from care packages sent by parents were stored. It was a skill he had honed late at night when the school prefects—often considered the headmaster's spies—had retired for the evening.

Ravi's gaze shifted from his son to Sophie. He scanned her outfit before his eyes settled on her hair.

Puzzled by his scrutinizing gaze, Sophie asked, "What are you looking at?"

Ravi, focusing on a solution, said decisively, "Your clips. Give me your hairpins."

Realization dawned on Sophie, and with a small, steadying breath, she began to unpin her hair. "Okay."

Harrison's brow furrowed. "What are you doing with those?"

Ravi held up the pins. "I'm going to use these to open the gate."

"But wait—" Harrison started.

Ravi cut him off. "Do you want to go, Harrison—or not?"

Harrison glanced at the door. He took a breath and held it. "I do want to go. It's just…"

Ravi gave him a look. "Then let's go."

Harrison exhaled sharply. "All right, I'm ready."

"Good. Now, move out," Ravi commanded, gesturing toward the door as he led the way.

They slipped into the hallway and down the stairs to the lobby. Their footsteps fell like hushed whispers on the tile floor as they retraced the path Anil had led them down earlier. The lobby was eerily dark and quiet; all the guests had retired, and no one was visible at the front desk. Descending the eleven steps that led to the iron gate, Ravi, Sophie, and Harrison moved carefully, Harrison counting them under his breath.

Ravi took out the hairpins. As his fingers brushed the cold metal, the gate creaked open—just enough.

They paused there, still believing the way back was theirs.

Ravi's hand went still. "It's open."

"What does that mean?" Harrison asked.

Ravi, now puzzled, turned toward his family. "I don't know," he admitted.

Sophie studied the gate, saying nothing.

Harrison's mouth went dry.

Silence settled between them.

Harrison's concern deepened. "Is it a trap?"

"I don't know," Ravi said. "Who would want to trap us?"

No one answered at first.

"Could it be Raju and Siddharth?" Harrison could not think of a better answer.

"How would they have access to this gate? They're guests here, just like we are," Ravi said.

"You're right." Harrison paused.

Sophie spoke quietly. "They don't run this place."

Harrison swallowed. A thought crept in—unbidden, unwelcome. "But the bartender would," Harrison reasoned. "This is where they keep supplies, right?"

"He has a point," Sophie said, turning to Ravi.

"The bartender?" Ravi frowned. "Where does he fit in?"

Harrison faltered. "Um, well—"

Sophie finished for him, her voice steady. "That's why Harrison left the restaurant at dinner. He said the bartender felt…off."

"Yeah," Harrison agreed quickly. "The way he looked at me—it spooked me."

They waited too long. Their conversation was interrupted as a door in the lobby swung open. They heard footsteps. Then, there were voices. Startled, the three scrambled to find cover. They slipped behind the gate; the air behind them went still. Then they hurriedly descended farther down the stairs leading to the basement. Pressed against the stone wall, they stilled their breathing, listening as the conversation unfolded above.

"One more thing. The Fishtail Corner Mart is behind on their payments this month. I might have to remind them of their obligations."

While concealed, Ravi could make out the profile of a tall man with a distinguished gray beard, clad in a police chief's uniform, who was speaking quietly with Priya.

"An example might be due to ensure promptness in the future." He paused. "And make sure those receipts for the inn's income are accounted for. I'll handle their disposal."

Priya discreetly handed a folder to the man in uniform.

The man's lips tightened as he examined the contents. "These records…they're a risk. We must ensure they're kept secure and away from prying eyes."

Priya nodded. She scanned the lobby to ensure they weren't being watched. "I've taken precautions, but we can't afford any mistakes."

The man in uniform agreed, his face reflecting the seriousness of the situation.

"Thank you, Bhaskar Mamaji," Priya responded calmly. She addressed her uncle in the tradition Nepali form, with his given name first, followed by his familial title. "Is there anything else you need from me?"

Bhaskar shook his head. "Not now. If there's anything, I'll let you know."

Priya leaned forward. "Good night, Mamaji," she spoke. Then, kneeling, she kissed her hand and touched his feet, bowing low—a gesture deeply rooted in Nepali and Hindi cultures to show respect.

"You too, my queen," Bhaskar said before turning and heading toward the exit of the inn. As he passed the stairs leading to the basement, a folder slipped from his hand. Bending down to retrieve it, his shirt sleeve rode up, briefly exposing a distinctive mark on his arm—an image of a crown entwined with a serpent, burned into his skin like a tattoo. It was a symbol of control and power, seared into his flesh long ago. The brand's intricate detail was visible, but only for a fleeting moment.

Harrison's eyes narrowed, capturing the image and filing it away in his mind as Bhaskar continued on, unaware of the watchful eyes on him.

As Bhaskar departed, Priya glanced down the stairwell that led to the basement and noticed that the iron gate was ajar. "Anil left the gate open." She shook her head, incredulous at his actions.

She couldn't suppress a snicker as she casually descended the steps and locked the gate, locking Harrison, Sophie, and Ravi in the basement. *He thinks they're going to fall for that*, she mused, walking back up toward her office.

"Did you hear that?" Harrison asked. "It was Anil who left the gate open. That means no one's down here," Harrison said.

"I hope you are right." She paused, her focus shifting. "But who's the man?"

Ravi's voice cut through the darkness of the stairwell. "That must be her uncle, the chief of police," he whispered with certainty. "Mamaji means 'uncle' in Hindi. Looks like the inn's involved in shady dealings with the local police," he muttered, his volume low.

Harrison leaned in. "Like espionage and secret agents?"

"More like extortion." Ravi answered.

"Do you really think the inn is involved in that kind of activity?" Harrison asked.

"I've seen this before," Ravi said quietly. "Enough to suspect it."

"What about the suited men from the boat?" Harrison asked. "How do they fit in?"

"Where did that come from?" Ravi asked.

"They could be surveilling us?"

Sophie's eyes lifted to her husband's.

"Look, right now, that's not our concern," Ravi said quietly. "We're together. That's what we have right now."

"But we haven't done anything to warrant this kind of attention," Sophie protested.

Ravi gave a rueful chuckle. "No, we haven't. But we are attempting to infiltrate a hotel basement's secret tunnel as we speak, so 'right' and 'wrong' might be a matter of perspective," he pointed out with a wry twist of his lips. "And don't forget, we are looking for a rare diamond. That may draw unwanted attention."

Sophie sighed, conceding the point. "I suppose you're right."

The silence settled thick between them.

Harrison glanced from one parent to the other, the woman's warning threading back through his thoughts.

Bound by blood.

He almost asked again.

Instead, he said quietly, "We should be careful."

Ravi met his eyes. "We will."

Sophie held his gaze a fraction too long. "Eyes open," she said.

Harrison swallowed. "C'mon. We have a tunnel to explore."

"You're right. Let's find out where this secret passage goes," Sophie said, stepping forward to lead the way.

Harrison's foot caught on something. Sophie reached back without looking and took his hand. He looked down. Along the lowest step, half buried beneath dust, a thin line of brass cut across the stone. Letters were etched into it—worn, fractured, difficult to make out in the half-light: WHEN THE TIME BEGINS TO TURN, BLOOD WILL OPEN THE WAY. He blinked. The words refused to hold.

-6-
THE ANCIENT DOOR

प्राचीनद्वारम्

NOVEMBER 12TH
12:45 A.M.

Looming before Harrison, the concealed door seemed to pulse with secrets as old as the stones around him. His hand trembled as he knelt, fingers searching along the floor until they brushed the loose floorboard. Lifting it carefully, he uncovered the hidden release lever. After a moment's hesitation, he pulled it up.

The door groaned—a deep, weary sigh, as if from the weight of centuries—and creaked open to reveal a long, shadowed passage. The sconces lining the walls stood cold and unlit, casting faint, skeletal shadows. The tunnel stretched before him, its depths swallowed in an impenetrable darkness that seemed to hum with forgotten whispers.

Harrison selected the flashlight option on his phone and

peered into the opening. The feeble light struggled to pierce the pitch-black void beyond.

Beside him, Ravi turned to the weapons, his gaze settling not on the khukuris but on a blade hung slightly apart—set higher than the others. The one Pappa noticed this morning on the tour.

He reached up and lifted it down. The metal did not shine the way the other weapons did. It drank the light. Longer than a khukuri. Narrower. Straighter.

Ravi's fingers tightened around it, not knowing why.

The air shifted—small, almost imperceptible—like the corridor had just recognized what had been taken.

"What are you doing, Dad?" Harrison asked, one eyebrow raised.

"We don't have any protection. Perhaps we should bring it along," Ravi replied, trying to sound nonchalant.

Sophie gave him a stern look.

"We'll return it when we're done," he said quickly.

"Dad?"

Ravi sighed, his bravado evaporating. "All right, all right. I suppose it's a bit over-the-top." He put the sword back on the wall, muttering, "Always wanted to be a knight, though."

Harrison laughed. "Maybe next time, Sir Ravi."

Sophie rolled her eyes but couldn't suppress a smile. "Let's get serious." She straightened up, taking a deep breath. "Here's the plan. We walk for one hour. If we don't find the door Anil spoke of—" She stopped herself. "—we reassess."

Sophie met Harrison's eyes. She didn't look away.

"That should get us back before the rest of the family wakes up," Harrison said.

No one answered right away.

"What if we find the door?" Ravi asked, eyeing the sword.

"Then we open it and see what's on the other side." Sophie's voice was firm, her eyes scanning their faces for any signs of hesitation.

Ravi exhaled slowly through his nose.

Harrison gave a thumbs up. "Sounds like a solid plan, Mom." He waited for someone to say something else. No one did.

Sophie looked at her husband. "Do you have *the* map?"

Ravi patted his pocket. "Got it right here." He reached in and pulled out the map—the one they had studied with Pappa in the lobby.

Sophie illuminated the paper with the light from her phone.

"According to this," Ravi began, "the tunnel extends for two miles, if not longer." He looked at both Sophie and Harrison. "That gets us to about an hour in. Are we ready?"

The question hovered like a specter, compelling each to face their fears. No one moved.

Harrison nodded. "Let's go."

As they took their first steps inside, cobwebs greeted them like the cold fingers of the past. Navigating through the darkness lit only by the faint glow of their phones' flashlights, Sophie, Ravi, and Harrison felt the weight of their breaths, each exhale cutting through the oppressive stillness. The air was damp and thick, almost physical in its presence, and it smelled of ancient earth and mildew. Their flashlight beams shook unsteadily over gnarled roots jutting from the walls, the cracked stone telling of eons past.

The farther they ventured, the more constrictive the tunnel became. Each one remembered Anil's words about the creature lurking in the depths. He had spoken only of fairy tales, yet they suddenly wondered if the beast might appear.

Just when the darkness seemed unbearable, they reached a crossroads. The passage split into three separate pathways, each shrouded in darkness and echoing with the distant sound of dripping water.

Ravi illuminated the map with his flashlight. He scanned the lines and markings, then looked up at the branching paths before them. "This intersection isn't on the map." A flicker of bewilderment crossed his face. He studied the map again, looking closer. "I don't think these lines indicate a tunnel after all." He folded the useless map and slid it back into his pocket. "We're officially off the grid, folks."

They hesitated, exchanging uneasy glances as they contemplated the choices before them. The wrong path could have dire consequences, and each possibility carried its own form of dread.

Harrison scanned each option. Then, as if guided by some unseen force, he pointed his flashlight down the center path. "This way," he declared, a newfound confidence filling his words. "I can't explain it," he said. "But I don't think we should choose the others."

And with that declaration, the trio pressed onward, leaving the other paths untouched—unchosen for reasons none of them could name.

* * *

After walking for what felt like an eternity in the seemingly endless tunnel, their journey was suddenly interrupted—a door stood in their path. But this was no ordinary door. It was a work of ancient craftsmanship, built from timeworn wood darkened with the passage of centuries. Decorative carvings were etched on its surface: an elaborate montage of mythical beasts, mysterious symbols, and inscriptions giving the impression that they belonged to a long-lost language. A heavy iron ring, rusted by time yet still imposing, served as the door handle, set into the wood like an ancient guard.

"The door Anil spoke of in his story! It's really here," Sophie whispered.

The door was framed by stone, meticulously cut into interlocking pieces. The whole doorway emanated an intense aura of dread and reverence, as though it were protecting something beyond human comprehension. Cobwebs clung to the corners, and a coating of dust veiled the door's details, but none of that could diminish its grandeur. It beckoned them forward while seemingly warning them at the same time.

Harrison, Ravi, and Sophie stood before it, captivated by its undeniable beauty. Here was a boundary between the world they knew and something unfathomable, something they felt was meant to protect secrets that were locked away. Their eyes met, an unspoken agreement passing between them. They were destined to uncover whatever mystery lay behind that door.

Ravi stepped up to the door first, his gaze fixated on the Sanskrit engravings that were highlighted under the flashlight's beam. A reverent whisper escaped his lips. "It's the Kumari Mandala."

As Sophie gazed at the mandala fixed to the door, recognition washed over her. She leaned closer. "Oh my." Her fingers traced the detailed patterns—the symbol that had been guiding them. "You're right. It's the Kumari Mandala. But something is off; it's not quite right," Sophie remarked, her memory flashing back to the familiar glyph.

The impressive design of the emblem, with its geometric circles and mystical symbols, resonated with a deeper meaning, suggesting a familiarity that unsettled her more than it comforted her.

"Yes, it's the same," Harrison confirmed. "But you're right; it's a little off."

Ravi placed his hands on the door, his anticipation mounting. Despite straining every muscle, the door remained stubbornly unyielding. "It won't budge," he grunted, his muscles tensing and flexing as he exerted himself.

"We need Pappa. We need him to decipher the Sanskrit inscriptions," Sophie stated.

"Let me take a picture to show Pappa," Harrison suggested. With a quick motion, he snapped a photo of the door, capturing its intricate details. "This should do," he added before changing the phone back to a flashlight.

Sophie sighed. "Why didn't I think of that?"

Harrison couldn't help but smile, appreciating the innocence of his youth. "Well," he replied, "that's because you're a bit older, Mom. Your thinking doesn't quite match up with the Gen-Z mindset."

"I must admit, he's right," Ravi said, with a wink at Sophie.

"You didn't think of it either," she retorted, acknowledging the truth in his statement.

As the trio turned to walk away, a slight pull drew Harrison back. His heart raced as an apparition materialized before him, a shimmering vision amidst the floating particles. Its presence was ethereal yet commanding, beckoning him forward with an otherworldly allure.

"I think—it's her," Harrison said, his voice unsteady. "The Spirit—"

Sophie's confusion formed on her brow as she looked around. "Where?" she cut him off, scanning the surroundings in vain. Sophie searched the darkness. Nothing stood where Harrison was staring.

He turned to his family. Their inability to see what he could disappointed him. "You can't see her?" he asked with frustration. "She's right there." He turned back to point at the apparition, but as quickly as the Spirit of Kumari had appeared, she dissolved into the surrounding air leaving it altered, in a way he couldn't name.

The experience left Harrison shaken, grappling with the profound encounter that seemed to extend beyond ordinary perception. "I feel like I need to follow her, but how?" he pondered, his thoughts racing as he surveyed the door, contemplating his next move. "Wait, I have an idea," Harrison exclaimed, the thought hitting him like a bolt of inspiration.

Ravi and Sophie watched Harrison with rapt attention.

The door loomed in the dark, its carvings alive with beasts and symbols no one could read. Harrison studied it, running his eyes along the seams. There was nothing to suggest it would open—no hinge, no lock—only the iron ring set deep into the wood. His father had already tugged at it until his hands hurt.

Maybe, Harrison thought.

As Harrison stepped forward, he reached for the door. The moment his skin met the wood, a faint hum shivered through the frame, and Sanskrit characters along the outer ring flickered faintly as if stirred awake.

Ravi and Sophie exchanged a knowing glance. *It only reacted when Harrison touched it,* Sophie thought.

"It's doing something!" Harrison shouted as his fingers traced the embossed pattern of the Kumari Mandala. Intrigued, he stumbled back for a wider view.

The glow winked out the instant his hand broke contact.

In the darkening silence, the tunnel pressed close.

"Maybe it means it'll open now," Ravi said. "Like you activated some hidden mechanism." His voice sounded too loud against the stone. He planted his palm on the wood and pushed.

Nothing. The carvings stayed dead, the Mandala cold.

When Harrison reached out again, the effect returned,

faint but steady, as though synced to the boy's breath.

Sophie paled. "It reacts to him," she whispered.

Harrison bent closer, his hands hovering over the center of the mandala, where the intricate lotus petals beckoned. Bathed in the illumination of his phone's light, specific Sanskrit characters on the ring began to glow subtly, as if to provide a code for unlocking the door.

"Look," Sophie murmured. "It's reacting."

Harrison twisted the lotus, trying to align it with the glowing word. Nothing budged. The pulsing light only quickened under his palm.

Ravi frowned. "Maybe it's not the center; it's the rings. Step aside. I'll try."

Harrison obeyed, and the light instantly died.

Ravi cracked his knuckles and squared his stance. "Stand back. Dad strength, coming through." He gripped the outer ring and hauled. Muscles corded in his neck. His teeth bared. The ring didn't so much as twitch. After a long, groaning attempt, he dropped his arms and blew out a breath. "Well. Clearly rusted shut."

Sophie folded her arms. "Well, clearly rusted shut."

Ravi wiped his palms on his jeans, trying to look dignified. "I loosened it for you, son. Go ahead."

"Loosened it?" Sophie arched an eyebrow.

Ravi nodded. "You'll see."

Harrison stepped forward. The second his fingers touched the door, the carvings stirred, vibrating with life. The glow came back—brighter this time, crawling across the Mandala like fire beneath the wood. "It's happening again, Mom!"

"I see it," Sophie said, her voice trembling.

Harrison drew in a breath. He expected it to fight him—after all, his father had failed—but the ring shifted under his grip, reluctant yet yielding. Slowly, painfully, the outer circle began to rotate around the still lotus.

The flashlight's beam caught the cascade of dust motes as each glowing symbol in the alignment was revealed. The chaff seemed alive, drifting with intent rather than chance.

Ravi leaned in, grinning through the unease. "Told you I loosened it."

Sophie shot him a look. "Really?"

"Absolutely." He grinned wider, but his eyes didn't leave the door.

Harrison ignored them. Breath quickening as the mandala inched toward alignment. His fingers worked with careful precision, aligning the symbol with the north mark. It was drawn toward a single inscription—कुमारी. Each incremental adjustment heightened their anticipation.

When the symbols finally aligned, the mandala resisted—then flared with an emerald light, forming strange shadows on the ancient stones. The low hum of gears grinding whispered through the tunnel—a sound that suggested something old adjusting, not yielding. They waited with bated breath and with nerves stretched taut as the tunnel became a nexus between the now and the ever-after.

A sudden thought flickered through him—not triumph, but exposure—as if the door were taking note of him rather than responding to him.

A subtle click echoed, and a small panel, cunningly hidden within the grand façade of the door, creaked open. It revealed a slender shaft—a secret passage cleverly masked by the false promise of the larger portal.

Curiosity pushed him forward, pressing down his fear rather than erasing it. Harrison crouched low and entered. Ravi and Sophie exchanged a quick glance of concern, but each knew that they had no choice. They had to follow.

The trio slipped into the dark confines of the narrow corridor, hearts thrumming with a surge of adrenaline. The panel swung shut behind them with a silent, decisive thud, cocooning them in darkness. Encased within the passageway's close quarters, they were left to the mercy of the unknown ahead.

***

2:00 A.M.

Raju crouched before the ancient door, the unsteady glow of his flashlight trembling as the beam traced the carvings. He couldn't shake the thoughts of the family—how eager they'd been at dinner to see the tunnel, how quickly they'd pulled back at the last moment. They'd looked to Siddharth and him for guidance, but then Harrison, uneasy, had shut it down altogether. *Why pursue their quest without us?* The question lingered, sour and insistent, no matter how he tried to bury it.

His voice came low, taut. "Why drag me down here, Anil? They wouldn't go without me."

"They were here. I can feel it," Anil murmured, his voice tinged with a thread of hope as he traced a finger over the time-smoothed carvings.

Raju's eyes were fixed unblinkingly on the door, the central mandala staring back almost as if mocking his doubts. Around him, the chamber's musty air seemed to thicken with his skepticism. "Anil," he said, "we're faced with nothing but this ancient relic—steadfast as history itself. They haven't passed this way. This door has not been opened."

Yet, Anil's resolve remained. "The door opened for them. They passed through—I'm sure of it." He glanced at the mandala. "Just as you said. Resonance."

Raju swept his flashlight over the door's frame and weathered hinges. There was no sign of disturbance, no break in the ancient seal. Cobwebs, intact and undisturbed, laced the door's corners. "Look, Anil," Raju urged, his light lingering on the dust and silken threads. "See for yourself. This door hasn't been opened." He shrugged. "I don't think Operation Pawn's Gate went according to plan."

"But the sounds, Raju. I heard them, as you did—whispers, feet shuffling." Anil pointed to the floor. "See, the dirt is disturbed. They were here."

Raju glanced about, a slight frown creasing his forehead as he considered the possibilities. "It doesn't make sense. Maybe it's just the echo of this old place, or our imaginations," he reasoned, trying to still the unease Anil's words had stirred within him.

Raju ran his light over the door, revealing the ancient Sanskrit inscriptions. The warning was clear. *Only the chosen are to seek the heart.* He paused, his light resting on a slot so seamlessly integrated into the design, it seemed to disappear at a glance. Memories of the photograph they'd found in the Chitwan library popped into his mind. *The Kumari Talisman. The key. The way to bypass the requirement of the chosen.*

"This is where the key goes," Raju murmured. He stepped closer and touched the slot. The wood was cool and unyielding. Untouched.

"I wonder if they know they have the key," Anil muttered.

"Doesn't matter. They don't need it," Raju replied, stepping into the light.

"Wait, so are you saying that they *did* pass through?"

"I don't know. If they did, the door would've been disturbed. So, no."

Anil remained unconvinced. "But if they didn't, we would have seen them. They would have passed us on their way back."

"Unless they ducked into one of the side passages we

passed," Raju countered. "Maybe they heard us and found a place to hide."

"Maybe." Anil's eyes narrowed. "But why keep it from you and Siddharth? I mean, I thought they asked you to go along."

"They did. Then they backed out at the last minute." *Harrison backed out*, he thought. *The others simply followed his lead.*

Anil let the silence hang. He tilted his head in contemplation. "Strange. I wonder why. Maybe…" He paused, his voice thinning into a whisper. "Maybe they suspect something."

"If he does, it's a little concerning."

"He?" Anil questioned.

"Harrison," Raju explained. "He's the one who called things off. He said something felt wrong."

The news of Harrison's comment forced Anil to reconsider. "Maybe you're right. Maybe the unlocked gate was not enough to entice them, and my plan did not work. Perhaps the boy became troubled by the Heart's lore and decided their actions aren't worth the risk." Anil's mind raced back to their earlier conversation with Priya regarding the security footage. "But Priya was certain she saw Ravi, Sophie, and Harrison. They left their room at midnight."

"Any footage from the lobby?"

"No, Priya had turned off the lobby cams because Uncle Bhaskar was coming for a visit. He insists on it."

Raju shook his head. "Doesn't surprise me. Anyway, if they were seen leaving their room, they must have turned back. Where else could they have gone? Were the younger children and grandparents with them?"

"No," Anil admitted. "But maybe it was past the kids' bedtime. Or past all of their bedtimes, for that matter."

Raju paused, brow furrowed. He shook his head, convinced. "They're not down here. They wouldn't leave the children. And they wouldn't come without me." His hand reached out, his fingers tracing the cold, unyielding surface of the door.

Despite his silent plea, the door remained a stubborn sentinel, guarding its secrets with a tight-lipped resolve. It was as though the Spirit of Kumari had cast a shroud of blindness over them, obscuring the way forward.

"Perhaps a simple evening stroll enticed them," Raju mused, his light casting about the surrounding darkness, searching for evidence in vain.

"Nonsense, Raju. This does not add up. I was certain my plan would work," Anil insisted.

Raju's eyes remained bound to the mandala. *What secrets do you know?*

The weight of their unmet expectations settled in the still that followed. They had gambled on the Sharma family's curiosity, believing them to be the chosen ones to unlock this very door. Yet as the silence remained unbroken, the reality of their failure became inescapable—cold and uninvited doubt rose unbidden into Anil's thoughts, as pervasive as the darkness itself.

"Let's go check those other passageways. Who knows, they could be hiding," Anil suggested again.

"Your plan failed," Raju countered. "Let's get back to the inn."

"There's always tomorrow night," Anil insisted.

Raju gave him a long look, the beam of his flashlight cutting across Anil's face. "Tomorrow night, then."

With a heavy heart, they turned from the door, its secrets remaining sealed, highlighting their folly. The Heart of Kumari lay beyond their reach, its silence a verdict they could not contest.

***

2:05 A.M.

Harrison, Ravi, and Sophie emerged from the tunnel's dark embrace and stood, their hands and knees marked by the arduous journey. They panned their flashlights around a vast underground chamber that opened all around them, defying the imagination in its grandeur. The expansive area had been meticulously cut from the stone—a silent watcher to ageless secrets—with architectural elements reminiscent of Gothic design. The room resembled a grand chapel crafted in the shape of a decahedron. Rows of stone tiers, akin to seating for esteemed council members, surrounded a central pedestal.

The seating fanned out in elegant terraces, lending the room a dignified air. Ten doors were fixed within the tiers, each one reminiscent of the entrance door that had brought them here. Each sealed door bore an identical mandala. Stone columns rose like spires, drawing their gaze upwards to a vaulted ceiling which opened into a natural atrium. The faint sound of twitching bat wings resonated from the higher recesses, intertwining with the echoes of the past.

"This seems to be a gathering place," Ravi contemplated, "possibly used by secret societies or cults."

Sophie directed the beam of her flashlight onto the altar. Intrigued, she approached with caution. Standing in front of the pedestal, a gasp caught in her throat, drawing the others to her side.

In the soft illumination, they discovered a pendant of exquisite craftsmanship. The chain was composed of tiny prayer beads, each reflecting the phones' light, creating a kaleidoscope of colors. But what truly held their rapt attention was its centerpiece: leaves cradled something within. As they drew closer, the light revealed a mesmerizing blue, S-shaped stone nestled among the petals.

The necklace contained no ordinary gem. Its depths swirled with miniature galaxies akin to an entire universe. The pendant wasn't just an ornament—it was a relic, a puzzle, and an adventure waiting to unfold. Its design only added to the object's intrigue. It appeared to be only one half of a whole, suggesting the existence of another piece.

Ravi picked it up cautiously, examining it in the subdued light. "What could this be? It looks like half a jewel attached to prayer beads."

Harrison nodded, trying to grasp the significance of their discovery. He was drawn to its sheer beauty.

Sophie's eyes fixed onto the pendant nestled in Ravi's palm. Its chain of prayer beads draped off his hand in an elegant cascade. "May I?" she asked. With reverence, she lifted the necklace, allowing it to catch the light. The lustrous, S-shaped gem at its center captivated her—its curves reminiscent of half a taijitu, the symbol of cosmic duality.

Sophie peered closer to get a better look. "A taijitu," she declared.

"You mean like a yin-yang, Mom?" Harrison chimed in. His attention fixed on the pendant as he watched his mother cradle the gem.

"Yes," Sophie replied, her voice filled with wonder. "It's technically known as a taijitu." The word lingered between them, ethereal and charged with meaning.

As if under a spell, Sophie draped the necklace around her neck. Her eyelids fluttered closed, and she inhaled a deep breath. In the quiet that wrapped around her, Sophie's lips moved in a silent, heartfelt invocation. The gem seemed to pulse with an ancient rhythm against her skin, as though answering her unvoiced prayer.

Harrison shattered the stillness. "Whatever this necklace represents, it's a crucial puzzle piece. I don't think this is coincidence," Harrison said. "Not anymore." Seeking validation, his gaze met his mother's. "I swear I saw her, Mom. She told me how to open the door."

"I know, Harrison. I believe you," she reassured him.

Just then, as the charm rested against her collarbone, a surge of energy pulsed through her. In that moment, Sophie had a stunning realization. "It has to be the Kumari Talisman!"

"What talisman?" Ravi asked.

"The Kumari Talisman! The one that Pappa and I saw in the book!"

"What book?" Ravi and Harrison asked in unison, their confusion tempered by intrigue.

Sophie paused, realizing her mistake. "Sorry, I guess we haven't mentioned that yet," she said sheepishly. "Anyway, Pappa and I stumbled upon this ancient, dusty book in the library in Chitwan. I'm pretty sure it's the book he's carrying now—or maybe it was the one with the diamond on it?" She scratched her head. "No, wait, that was the book about Pokhara. Maybe it was the last book he picked up right after he grabbed that letter opener…"

Ravi and Harrison exchanged a look as her words tumbled out in a jumbled mess.

"Mom, can we please focus?" Harrison interrupted, trying to suppress a groan.

"Right, right!" She gripped the necklace with newfound determination. "So, there was this page in the book that was partially ripped, but the caption was still visible."

"Mom, what did it say?"

"Oh, um…"

"Mom?"

"Okay. Okay. Don't rush me," she said, exasperated. "It said something about needing a talisman to find the Heart of Kumari. Unfortunately, there wasn't a picture, so we don't know what it looks like. But this—this must be it!"

Harrison's gaze focused on the gem resting around his mother's neck, his words taking on a burning intensity. "Then this…this *is* her doing. She beckoned us to find this."

"But how can we be sure it's the Talisman?" Ravi asked with skepticism.

"I can feel it!" Sophie said, her words cracking under the strain. She needed to make him believe it.

"What else could it be?" Harrison questioned.

"A beautiful necklace someone left behind?" Ravi offered.

She slipped the chain from around her neck and pressed it into Ravi's palm. "Feel it," she urged, her eyes pleading for his comprehension.

Ravi cradled the necklace. He turned it over once in his palm, the beads clicking softly against his skin. His thumb traced the curve of the blue stone. It was warmer than it should have been.

He closed his eyes—only for a second.

Something pressed at the edges of his thoughts. Not images exactly. More like impressions. Height. Wind. A vastness that made his chest tighten.

He opened his eyes immediately.

"This…" He hesitated, searching for something rational to anchor to. "This is…unusual."

He studied the stone again, as if expecting to find a seam, a battery, some mechanical explanation hidden beneath the polish. "It's only half," he said at last, the skepticism settling back into his voice. "Whatever it is."

The word hung there. Half.

No one said what they were all thinking. Halves meant something missing. And things missing had a way of asking to be found.

"Maybe we only need half," Harrison said—too quickly.

"Or maybe the other half is here, somewhere," Sophie murmured, scanning the room. Warmth pulsed from the gem as Ravi placed it back around her neck.

"Come on, let's spread out," Ravi said as he fastened the clasp. He turned and adjusted the beam on his flashlight.

Harrison took a few steps toward the nearest wall, inspecting the chamber's vast geometry. "It might be hidden. A compartment, maybe. Something built into the stone."

Ravi gave a faint nod and began to sweep his light across the chamber floor—slowly, with intention. He moved like someone searching a field for something fragile, afraid to step on it. The beam skimmed across dust-covered tiles, lingered on the base of a carved column, then climbed its length until it vanished into the dark overhead.

"Dust," Ravi murmured.

Something shifted above them. The sound was faint, just enough to make them stop breathing for a second. It was wings. Hundreds of them.

"Dust...and bats," Ravi corrected.

Harrison flinched and ducked, his light jerking upward. "They're everywhere."

"I don't like this," Sophie murmured, steadying her breath.

"Let's keep searching," Ravi said, lowering his beam. "We need to find the other half."

Sophie approached the pedestal in the center. Her footsteps were soft, yet they seemed deafening in the silence. She blew across the surface, and tiny particles lifted in lazy swirls, catching the beam of her light before drifting out of sight. She pressed her palm to the cold stone and held it there.

Nothing happened. No hum. No warmth. Just unyielding silence.

She ran her hands along the rim of the platform, searching for seams, hidden hinges, or tricks of the stone. She stepped back, clapping her hands together to shake off the grit. "It's not over here," she said.

Ravi didn't answer. His light was still moving, still slow and deliberate, like it might catch something if it didn't blink.

Harrison moved toward one of the sealed doors and gave it two sharp knocks. The sound thudded dully, then it was swallowed.

"Solid all the way through," he called. "No hollows. No seams. Nothing."

"Wait," Sophie said. She was crouched by the pedestal again, her fingers tracing a shallow groove—barely there, nearly worn smooth by time.

"There's something here," she murmured. "It could've been a symbol."

Ravi walked over and knelt beside her, squinting at the faint line. It wasn't writing—not anymore—just the outline of something once meaningful. "Pappa would've known," he said. "We're just…guessing."

Sophie sat back on her heels, still staring at the pedestal as if it might give up its secrets if she looked at it the right way. "He'd tell us we're looking at it wrong," she said. "That it's not what's here—it's what's missing."

"I hate that," Harrison muttered. "Philosophy. When what we need is the goddamn other half." He nudged a loose pebble with his boot. It bounced once, twice, then disappeared into the stillness.

"Harrison!" Sophie chastised.

The silence that followed tightened around them, suffocating. They all stood there, listening to nothing. The room didn't creak. It didn't whisper. It didn't help. It was as if the chamber had decided to ignore them.

Their flashlights drifted again, painting soft arcs on uncooperative stone.

No secret door. No whisper of magic. No half of the pendant lying forgotten in the dust.

"It's not here," Ravi finally concluded. "We've found what was meant for us. If the Spirit intended us to find the other half, it wouldn't be so difficult to find." A pause lingered before he continued, urgency quickening his tone. "Let's return before dawn breaks; the family mustn't worry."

"Okay." Sophie stood up. She brushed the dust from her hands and shifted her focus toward the ten doors encircling the chamber. "Now, we need to figure out how to get out of here." She looked around the chapel. "How are we supposed to know which door we came through?" She stepped closer to one of the doors, inspecting the frame and its edges for any kind of mechanism.

"What do you mean?" Harrison began. "The shaft is right—" He stopped. He walked toward the door he thought they'd entered through, frowning. "This isn't it."

He turned to the next door. Then the one after that. His movements slowed. "They all look the same," Harrison muttered.

Ravi stood next to him, scanning the chamber with his flashlight. The beam skimmed over the carved thresholds.

"The entrance to the shaft…it's gone," Ravi said. "It was right here. But now, there's no way to tell which door we came through."

"That's what I was trying to tell you," Harrison replied, his voice growing louder with concern. "The shaft we came through is gone!"

Ravi rubbed the back of his neck, squinting at the circle of identical doors. "It could be any of them."

Harrison's eyes flicked from one door to the next, circling them like numbers on a clock. "No symbols. No signposts. No way to know."

Frustration twisted in his gut.

"Spirit of Kumari!" he shouted, louder than he meant to. His voice cracked against the stone and came back smaller. "I need you to show me which door leads back to the inn! Please—just show me!"

His echo died, swallowed whole.

For a breath, there was nothing. No answer. Then, a faint vibration pulsed through the floor beneath their feet, barely noticeable. It rose like a hum, the kind that finds its way into your teeth before your ears catch on.

Sophie took a sharp breath. "The necklace." She reached for the pendant at her chest. It was warm again—warmer than before, as if it had been lying in sunlight instead of darkness. She turned slowly, the chain brushing against her knuckles, until the warmth intensified. Her eyes landed on a door just right of center. "This one," Sophie said hesitantly. "I think."

Ravi stared at it. "How do you know?"

"I don't," Sophie replied. "But I can feel it."

Harrison stepped forward, suddenly calm. "She's right. I feel it, too."

His hand rose. The instant his palm touched the door, the carvings pulsed with a green light. Sanskrit letters flickered awake as though recognizing him.

Sophie gasped, and tugged Ravi's sleeve. "It's turning…"

Beside her, Ravi let out a small laugh. "Guess it didn't need my muscles, after all."

No one reacted.

A narrow seam, no more than fissure, appeared to their right. The shaft yawned open. The tunnel looked the same—but it did not feel the same, as if the sameness were a disguise rather than a reassurance.

"Let's go," Ravi said, gripping Sophie's arm. Without waiting, he stepped toward the opening, pulling her gently with him.

Sophie paused. "Wait! Let's take photos of the doors for Pappa. He might decipher their secrets."

Harrison smiled. "That's wise, Mom."

"I learned from the best." Her hands were steady as she raised her phone, but the click of the camera shutter seemed unnatural in the still air.

With the documentation complete, they returned to the shaft's mouth—a dark maw that seemed to mock their attempts at bravado—and the moment of relief passed, replaced by the sobering reality of the dark path before them.

Harrison went first, crawling low through the tunnel, his phone's light bouncing ahead in steady arcs. He didn't look back. Ravi followed, moving fast despite the tight quarters—shoulders scraping stone, breath even, as if the darkness couldn't touch him.

Sophie hesitated. Her grip on the necklace was a lifeline, the cool metal pressing into her palm and whispering reassurance to her racing heart. Summoning her courage, she followed closely behind her husband, her breathing shallow in the cramped space.

A few moments later, they arrived back at the small door they had opened earlier. Harrison's hand lingered over the surface, his apprehension taking form in the quivering shadow of his fingers, which loomed against the tunnel walls. With a gentle nudge, the panel creaked open, its protest a sharp whisper in the hush. They peered through the gap—nothing but the emptiness of the tunnel greeted them. The quiet was almost a physical presence, thick with the unsaid and unseen, yet it offered them an unobstructed passage back to the perceived safety of the inn.

They stepped out into the tunnel and retraced their steps. As they neared the iron gate leading them back to the lobby, Ravi remembered Priya closing it. He retrieved the hairpins from his pocket, expecting the gate to be locked. But the gate, to their collective astonishment, was ajar; its solid bars stood open. An uneasy question gnawed at them, unspoken yet heavy with implication.

No one said the question aloud. Saying it felt like an invitation.

Ravi glanced at his phone. The glowing time of 3:33 A.M. stared back at him before the screen succumbed to the inky blackness of a drained battery. "My phone died," he announced.

"Mine, too," Harrison echoed.

"Looks like we're out in the nick of time," Sophie declared. "Let's get some rest and charge our phones." Sophie reached automatically for her phone—then stopped, her hand hovering, as if she'd forgotten what she meant to do with it.

With that, they navigated through the lobby's shadows, a silent parade of specters moving undetected. They were a family united in purpose yet troubled by the mysteries the chapel unveiled. The riddle was far from solved—if anything, it had deepened. However, they were determined to discover whatever lay beyond the unopened doors and figure out how the half-pendant fit into the equation. They needed Pappa—the historian, the translator, the missing link in their extraordinary journey.

***

4:10 A.M.

In the peaceful stillness of the predawn hours, Siddharth wandered alone in the gardens of the Surya Chandra Inn. The lanterns swaying in a gentle breeze cast dancing shadows on the garden's cobblestone path as Siddharth, a seeker of truth and a devotee to the divine, sought solace among the backdrop of this peaceful sanctuary. His life, a spiritual journey dedicated to pursuing enlightenment, had come to a crossroads between light and darkness, virtue and vice, and the divine and the profane. His twin brother Raju had already chosen the treacherous path shrouded in shadows. Siddharth wondered if he could avoid the same fate.

In a back corner, among the quiet rustling of leaves and the distant hoot of an owl, Siddharth knelt before a decorative stupa and lit an incense stick. Its fragrant smoke rose like whispers, ascending prayers to the heavens. Siddharth's heart burned with the flame of unknown destiny and unwavering sincerity. He bowed his head in supplication, the moment's weight pressing upon him like an ancient stone. The cord at his nape loosened. A few dark strands slipped forward over his shoulder.

Whispered pleas for guidance and the redemption of his twin flowed from Siddharth's lips, with each word being a sincere offering to the divine. The moisture from the dew on the grass clung to his knees, a physical reminder of the humility of his petition.

Siddharth's voice carried through the garden as he spoke, permeated with his devotion and the incense's sweet fragrance. Yet, his moral dilemma extended far beyond his brother's fate. The allure of the Heart of Kumari—promising worldly desires and power—and the responsibility Siddharth bore to protect the stone tugged at his soul in different directions. He ached to restore honor to the Shatranj Ke Sipahi and to fulfill the destiny that had been written in the ancient books long ago.

As Siddharth knelt in prayer, he pondered the enormity of his actions. "Will the Heart of Kumari absolve the stains on our souls? Can it purify the darkness that has seeped into our lives? I seek not only the power it offers but the chance for absolution, for both my brother and myself."

As Siddharth's fingers moved across the worn prayer beads, the rhythmic dance of the beads became a grounding cadence amidst the whirlwind of his thoughts—one bead for breath, three for mercy, seven for the burdens he carried. With each pass, they seemed to absorb a portion of his anxiety, a temporary balm to his restlessness.

"In seeking the Heart of Kumari, I strive to correct the missteps taken along the way. If this path leads to forgiveness," he whispered, "let it not mistake suffering for redemption." The beads were still warm when he reached the end of the prayer.

In the sacred solace of the Surya Chandra Inn's gardens, in this ritual, and in this moment of stillness and reflection, he sought the wisdom to navigate the intricate maze of destiny that lay before him. His prayers were for understanding, for the light to pierce through the impending darkness, and for the fortitude to honor his commitment to enlightenment—despite the shadowed paths his twin had taken.

Siddharth grappled with his monumental spiritual struggle. It was a moment of critical significance, where the destinies of two souls hung in the balance, awaiting cosmic guidance. He could only hope his earnest plea for divine intervention would reach the heavens, invoking a sacred grace that might redeem their souls and offer a chance at salvation he so desperately sought.

-7-
CAVES AND TREASURES

गुहानिधयः

8:22 A.M.

In the crisp morning air of Pokhara, excitement stirred among the Sharma family more easily than it should have. Their next adventure—a deliberate push toward the bat caves—promised to reveal the next clue in their search for the Heart of Kumari. After a quick breakfast at the inn's garden patio, their expectations grew as they discussed plans for the day ahead.

Still carrying the residue of the night, the discovery of the pendant went unmentioned; they opted to wait until the family was alone to reveal the secret.

Sophie automatically tucked the necklace under her sweater, its half charm resting close to her heart. The soft fabric brushed against her skin, a constant reminder of the secret she now carried, one that needed to stay hidden—at least for now.

With a hint of eagerness he didn't bother to temper, Harrison remarked, "I can't wait to explore the bat cave. Supposedly, such places contain treasure." He turned and winked at his father, the night before still close enough to touch.

Ravi smiled back a half-second late.

Pappa spoke up. "The goatskin mentioned a cave as the location of the next clue. Let's hope Siddharth is right about which cave it's in."

A spoon struck the cup rim with a sharp clink.

Raju nodded. "If there's anyone who can sort that out, it's Siddharth. He's good with places like that. Caves, trails—he's spent a lot of time exploring around here."

Sophie glanced up. "I thought you and Siddharth grew up in Chitwan. Your parents—Reena and Arjun—own the camp we stayed at?"

The table went still for one breath.

Raju paused for a measured beat, his hand stilled on the pack strap. "Yes. But we spent a fair bit of time in Pokhara when we were kids. Family friends, holidays, that sort of thing." He shrugged. "Enough to get into trouble."

No one laughed.

"So you were explorers even back then?" Cyrus asked.

Raju chuckled. "Something like that."

Harrison's gaze drifted to the gear Raju had been setting aside. "Do we really need all that—"

Raju answered before the question fully ended. "Caves have a way of taking more than they give." He smiled. "Better to be prepared."

Cyrus chimed in, a grin forming. "Oh yeah, just like in those adventure movies! They always discover secret passages and hidden treasures in bat caves."

"Treasure—that would be awesome!" Kiran said.

Raju's smile lingered a moment too long. "Sometimes,"

he said, "finding your way back out is the real prize."

For a moment, no one replied. The words sat between them, unnoticed—or deliberately left untouched.

Then Amma turned to Kiran. "Let's hope the bats won't mind a few visitors. It sounds quite thrilling, I must admit."

Kiran, wide-eyed and curious, looked up at her with wonder. "Bats? Are they like superheroes, Amma? Maybe we'll find Batman in there!"

"Oh, Kiran, you're thinking of superheroes guarding the secret treasures now? Well, who knows, there is a good chance those bats guard something special in their cave!"

Cyrus laughed, then hesitated. "Wait—do caves ever... not let people out?"

Ravi lifted his cup to his lips and paused long enough to be noticed.

"You know, Cyrus," Pappa said before Ravi took a sip, "exploring a bat cave can be an incredible opportunity for us. We could learn so much about those fascinating creatures by watching them up close."

"You're right," he said simply. "You wouldn't take us somewhere bad." The statement landed like a conclusion, not a question.

Pappa's laugh came a beat too late.

Sophie reacted when they did, then slipped her fingers beneath her sweater, pressing lightly against the pendant without breaking her smile.

Just then, a breeze moved through the patio, stirring the hanging prayer flags above them. One knot loosened; the cord slipped a fraction and held.

Raju gathered the last of the gear, then paused. He looked at Harrison, weighed something, and handed him a length of rope. "Carry this."

Harrison took it without arguing and slipped it into his

pack. The rope settled in his bag, heavier than he expected.

Sophie noticed the rope change hands but said nothing.

Just then, Siddharth's voice cut through the air. "The van's ready. We can head to the caves when you are."

Chairs scraped back. Bags were lifted. The conversation drifted forward, already elsewhere without circling back.

Sophie, her movements brisk, all-purpose, slung her bag over her shoulder. A playful gust of wind caught her hair as she turned to Siddharth, her features reflecting the morning's light. "Thank you for this, Siddharth. Your efforts haven't gone unnoticed."

Siddharth inclined his head. "I'll pass that along." His gaze lingered a fraction longer than he intended. He caught himself and looked away.

"You might be selling yourself short," Sophie said easily, a smile playing on her lips.

The group, already moving again, was about to board the van when Harrison slapped his pockets in a sudden pang of realization. "Wait, I've left my phone upstairs," he announced, turning on his heel. His words cut across the group's movement.

Ravi extended the room key to his son. "Here, you'll need this." The keychain, a metal pawn, clinked softly.

"Thanks," Harrison murmured, already moving away. "I got one."

Ravi watched him go, then slipped the key back into his pocket.

Harrison's heart raced as he ascended the stairs to the third floor. Turning the corner, he slowed. The corridor was quiet—too quiet. His footsteps sounded louder than they should have. The lights hummed faintly overhead, and for a moment he thought he was alone. Then he noticed the shadows. They stretched across the tile from farther down the hall, long and unmoving. Two of them. He counted them without meaning to. Harrison stopped. Something tightened in his chest. He didn't wait to understand it. Not here. Not yet. Alone.

Abandoning his quest for the phone, Harrison retreated. His pace quickened as he took the stairs two at a time. He hit the checker floor hard, his foot landing on the black-and-white tiles. For a split second, the pattern tilted beneath him, the sharp contrast pulling his balance sideways. He stumbled—not enough for anyone to notice, not enough to fall. Harrison shook it off and kept moving. He pushed through the front door and rejoined his family in the van, sliding the door closed behind him. His entrance was swift, his excuse for his empty hands swifter. "Phone's dead. Thought I'd just leave it," he said, his voice a half-step too nonchalant.

Ravi's brow furrowed, a light frown creasing his forehead. "That was fast," he said, his instincts telling him there was more to his son's sudden return.

Harrison slid into his seat, the shadows of the men in suits forming dark clouds across his thoughts. "Yeah, well," he started, his voice a quiet hush as he whispered to his father, "I think I saw them again—the men from the boat."

Ravi's concern was immediate, his fatherly protectiveness kicking in. "The same ones?" he pressed, matching his son's quiet demeanor.

Harrison's nod was almost imperceptible, yet it spoke volumes.

"Maybe it's time to mention something to Raju," Ravi said.

Sophie and Harrison exchanged a glance, their silent understanding clear.

She nodded at Harrison. "Show him."

Without a word, Harrison slipped a folded piece of paper into his father's hand under the cover of his jacket. "Look at this," he murmured. "We need to be careful."

Ravi discreetly unfolded the note in his lap, glancing down just long enough to take in the message: DON'T TRUST ANYONE WHO IS BOUND BY BLOOD. Below it, the familiar image of the Kumari Mandala stared back at him, the symbol seemingly heavy with warning.

His brow furrowed, and he leaned closer to Harrison. "What does it mean?" Ravi asked, as he folded the note smaller than it had been, then passed it back to his son.

"I don't know," Harrison admitted. "But we have to stay on guard."

Ravi's eyes narrowed as he glanced out the window, the image of the men in suits flashing in his mind. "The message feels oddly vague. Deliberately so. But you think it could be about them? The men in suits?"

Harrison shrugged slightly. "Maybe," he whispered. "But they aren't bound by blood."

Silence stretched, thin and held.

"How do you know?" Ravi finally asked, leaning in, his voice low. He suddenly understood who Harrison had in mind. "You mean—"

"We're not sure," Sophie answered.

There was another beat of silence.

"Whoever it's about," Harrison said, "it feels like a warning. And warnings don't come without reason."

Just then, the opposite side door slid open. Siddharth's voice carried a note of cheer that felt out of place. "All set?"

"Let's go!" Cyrus implored.

Siddharth took the seat beside Ravi. "I have a feeling about today," he offered, a smile on his lips.

No one answered him.

Raju jumped into the driver's seat while Anil slid in beside him, giving a brief nod.

"Let's get this show on the road, as you Americans say," Anil said with unmistakable enthusiasm.

Sophie glanced at Anil, eyebrows raised. "You're coming with us?"

"Wouldn't miss it. Besides, who else is going to get you in?"

Sophie exchanged a concerned look with Ravi.

He squeezed her hand gently. "Don't worry."

Still uneasy, Sophie's eyes caught Siddharth. He was laughing along with Anil and Raju, his relaxed demeanor at odds with the worry gnawing at her. For a moment, their eyes met, and he gave her a quick, reassuring smile—subtle, but not enough to ease her nerves.

She smiled back, though the tightness in her chest didn't subside. Uncertainty still pressed on her. As Pokhara slipped past the window, she couldn't remember the last time she'd felt sure she'd chosen any of it.

***

10:00 A.M.

Raju parked the van, and the group stepped into what felt like the makings of a movie set. The parking lot was crowded with equipment for the film Priya had mentioned—light stands, cables, cases stacked and unattended, as if left mid-thought. Harrison had the odd sense of arriving late to something already underway or finished.

For a moment, no one moved. It was as if they were waiting for a cue that never came.

Sophie walked over to her husband, stepping over a string of prayer flags tangled in the dirt. "It doesn't look how I imagined."

Ravi didn't look at her. "It never does," he said, stepping

forward.

Sophie hesitated, just long enough to notice she hadn't.

Harrison bent down and picked up an old top-hat that was half-covered in mud. "Like we missed the beginning or something," he said.

"I wonder how it ended?" Pappa mused, holding up the bottom half of a broken film slate.

Ravi gave the slate a glance and a half-smile. "Hopefully before lunch," he said, already walking.

Harrison turned to Raju, sidestepping a coil of cable. "What's the name of the movie they're making?"

"I'm not sure, but it's supposed to be a big Bollywood film. I think Shah Rukh Khan is in it," Raju answered, lifting a trunk so Amma could pass.

At the mention of Shah Rukh Khan, Ravi reached for his mother and gave her a gentle half-turn, a few notes from the movie *Om Shanti Om* slipped out as he did.

Amma laughed, steadying herself against him. "Is Deepika Padukone in it? They make the most beautiful couple."

"Perhaps," Raju responded, already following Anil.

"Will we see any of the actors?" Cyrus asked as he jumped over a low cable stretched across the ground.

"No, I think everyone is off set. That's why we're allowed to be here," Raju explained.

Anil gestured ahead. "This way."

The path narrowed.

"That means people got out," Cyrus said softly.

"Or nobody comes," Kiran whispered.

The others were already moving on.

Their footsteps kicked up dust on the dirt path as they approached a steep, uneven set of stairs. The descent revealed itself one step at a time, pulling them downward rather than inviting them. Below them, a river wound its way from the higher elevations, flowing to join Phewa Lake. The steps bent toward a waterfall cascading from a massive rock formation high above them. Mist from the falls kissed their faces, blurring the edges of the drop.

Siddharth pointed ahead and raised his voice over the roar of the water. "The cave is this way!"

Ravi squinted and asked, "Where? I don't see a cave."

"Come closer and look carefully," Siddharth urged.

"I see it!" Kiran shouted.

"I see it, too!" Cyrus chimed in, jumping up and down. His foot slipped. Sophie caught him.

A myna perched on a rock, cocked its head, then took off.

Amma leaned in. "Where is it?"

Kiran pointed. "Look over there, Amma."

As they approached the waterfall, the hidden cave entrance began to resolve itself—not all at once, but in fragments. First, a dark break in the rock, visible only when the curtain of water thinned. From certain angles it vanished again, leaving only stone and motion.

Pappa squinted, then nodded slowly. "'Find the cave hidden beyond the veil'—it's a waterfall!" His face lit up with childlike excitement, recalling the Sanskrit writing on the goatskin. "The next clue must be here."

Sophie stared past the falling water, her smile fading as she took in the narrowness of the opening, the way the rock seemed to fold inward. "I wouldn't have seen it," she said.

"Maybe this is what discovery feels like," Ravi teased, already slipping past her and into the narrow crack in the rock.

"Wait for me!" she said, following close behind.

Sophie moved ahead, then looked back—Cyrus paused at the opening, Kiran close, both of them briefly weighing the dark.

She held their gaze for a breath, then turned back, trusting them to follow.

As they stepped behind the 'veil' concealing the cave, they entered a mesmerizing subterranean world. Gradually, their eyes adjusted, revealing rock formations of stalactites and stalagmites, creating a maze-like labyrinth sculpted by nature over countless centuries. The air was cool and damp, heavy in the lungs. Water dripped somewhere deeper inside the cave, slow and deliberate. The path forward was visible only a few steps at a time.

Anil's flashlight cut through the darkness, catching on the ceiling above them. It wasn't rock alone. The surface shifted subtly—layered, uneven—until the light moved and the shapes resolved into bats clinging in dense clusters, their bodies pressed so close they blended into the stone.

"Be cautious here," Anil said, keeping his voice low as he handed out flashlights.

"These caves are home to thousands of bats, so we must stay alert," Siddharth added.

Amma paused, one hand resting briefly against the stone, as if weighing the choice that had brought them here—Kiran and Cyrus close at her side.

"That's a lot of bats," Kiran said, peering into the darkness. "Do they all sleep at the same time?"

Pappa glanced up toward the dark ceiling. "The bats mostly keep to themselves," he said. "They sleep during the day, hang high where they won't be disturbed." Then he lowered his voice slightly. "The spiders stay closer to the walls. Some of them can live for years without moving much at all—just waiting."

Kiran grimaced. "Waiting for what?"

Pappa gave a small shrug. "Whatever wanders too close."

Cyrus edged nearer to Amma, tightening his grip on Sheepy. "I don't like the waiting ones," he muttered.

No one spoke for a while after that.

The sound of dripping water mixed with the distant echoes of their footsteps, creating an eerie yet unnerving soundtrack. With every twist and turn, the family's senses sharpened, drawn forward by the feeling that something was hidden just beyond reach. It felt like stepping into a story already in motion—one that did not pause to explain itself.

The air shifted as they moved forward—cooler, mineral-heavy, carrying the same damp tang they'd breathed in the night before.

Harrison whispered to his dad, "Do you think this cave is connected to the one we explored last night?"

Ravi matched his tone. "If that's the case, it wouldn't be luck."

A dusting of grit fell from the ceiling.

Harrison brushed it off and took a step forward, his boot landing where the ground dipped and turned.

The path narrowed as it bent inward, the floor rising briefly before dropping away again. To the right, a thin stream threaded along the stone, water slipping over rock in a steady pull that seemed to guide the way forward. They followed it instinctively, boots finding purchase where the ground sloped and dipped, the sound of moving water drawing them deeper as the walls pressed closer. The main passage curved on, broad and shadowed—but the stream veered, disappearing into a tighter cut in the stone where the air felt cooler, more intent.

Harrison's light drifted as he lowered it, not searching so much as following a pull he didn't have words for. It felt less like discovery and more like recognition—like following a thread someone else had already pulled through this stone. The path didn't just call to him. It remembered him.

The beam caught on a narrow seam in the rock—too straight to be chance, too dark to be depthless. Air moved there, faint but steady, brushing his knuckles when he leaned closer.

He didn't call out. He just stood there, listening.

Siddharth noticed Harrison had stopped. He followed the line of his gaze, then the angle of his light, until the darkness there seemed less empty than it should have been. He knelt, set his hand against the stone, and felt the faint movement of air along his fingers. Then he straightened and turned to the others, who had gone quiet, watching him.

"There's a narrow tunnel here," he said quietly. "It's tight." His eyes settled on Harrison. "What does your instinct say?"

Harrison's heart quickened. The narrow cut in the stone felt less like an opening and more like an invitation. He glanced at his father first—then at his mother.

Ravi's eyes flicked to Sophie, concern crossing his face, before returning to Harrison. "Do you want me to come with you?"

Sophie held Harrison's gaze a moment longer than necessary. "Be careful."

A breath passed.

"I'll go," Harrison said. "With Siddharth." For a moment, a hint of uncertainty flickered as he looked at Siddharth. While his intuition urged him to explore the tunnel, a quiet doubt tugged at him. *'Remember, appearances can deceive. Be cautious of those who are bound by blood,'* the woman at the lake had warned. She hadn't spoken idly—he was almost sure of it now. Bound by blood.

He refused to let it be about his family—he'd convinced himself of that. No, it made more sense this way. He justified the thought quietly, as if reasoning with another part of himself that still resisted it. *She must have meant the twins. Raju and Siddharth. They were the ones bound by blood in the truest sense— shaped in the same womb, moving in silent accord, always just a step ahead of understanding.*

The possibility that they might not be what they seemed was a thought he couldn't shake. It lingered beneath the surface, a taut, invisible thread of tension running through the search for the diamond.

Harrison approached Siddharth. "I'll follow your lead."

"Come this way." They stepped into the smaller tunnel. Siddharth turned and offered a reassuring smile. "You're in capable hands, Harrison. Besides cave exploration, I've got a knack for solving riddles and puzzles. Back in my village, it's something I'm known for—and it's come in handy more than once."

They lowered onto their hands and knees to squeeze into the narrow passage, the rocks shifting beneath them.

"That could be helpful," Harrison said.

"Oh, definitely," Siddharth continued, his voice light, almost cheerful. "When I was twelve, the village priest got locked out of the inner sanctum—brass key snapped clean off in the lock. People were frantic. But I noticed these old carvings on the door—geometric, symmetrical. A code, really. The shrine was built during the Malla dynasty, and they used patterns to hide latches. I found the release behind a lotus motif no one had touched in decades. Pressed it, and the door opened like it was breathing."

He let out a quiet laugh. "After that, they called me for everything—missing and broken heirlooms, even a goat that vanished. That one turned out to be less about riddles and more about a jealous neighbor with a rope and a grudge."

Harrison managed a small smile despite the narrow walls closing in around them. *It was a good story—maybe true. We could've used his expertise last night*, he thought, remembering the sealed door deep in the tunnel.

Still, the woman's warning clung to the edges of his

thoughts like smoke.

As they continued through the tight passageway, Harrison wondered again whether he could trust Siddharth. *He could be instrumental in locating the Heart of Kumari.* For a brief moment, Harrison wanted to believe in Siddharth's sincerity, drawn to his seemingly trusting demeanor and the knowledge about the diamond's lore. That thought was quickly extinguished, like a shooting star streaking across the night sky, as the woman's warning echoed in his mind.

"I'm sorry, Siddharth," he whispered inadvertently as he followed him into the tunnel.

"What was that, Harrison?" Siddharth glanced back. "Did you say something?"

Realizing his voice had carried farther than he had intended, Harrison forced a quick smile. "Oh, nothing," he muttered. "I just said I'm sorry. I almost bumped into you."

"No worries," Siddharth replied.

Their flashlights cast beams ahead as they crawled forward. The passage was tighter than expected, forcing them to maneuver carefully to avoid the jagged walls threatening to scrape them.

As they ventured deeper, the air grew colder, and the distant fluttering and screeching of bats echoed through the cavern. Harrison found himself relying on Siddharth's expertise, a reminder that trust sometimes must be extended even after doubt has crept in.

A sudden scuttling sound cut across the stone.

Harrison froze as a large, hairy spider skittered into the beam of his light, its legs clicking softly against the rock. His breath snagged in his chest. The tunnel felt tighter, the air thinner.

For a split second, he was back in Mr. Jenkins's classroom—the tarantula heavy and alive in his hands, the room too bright, the other kids watching. He remembered the weight more than the fear. The way it had waited.

He swung the flashlight toward the wall. Webs stretched across the stone in layered sheets, glistening where the light caught them. Shapes clung to the threads, motionless.

His pulse hammered—but he didn't move. Didn't panic. One breath. Then another.

When he glanced over his shoulder, the webs and their spiders were gone. Bare stone. Nothing else.

"Siddharth," he whispered. "Did you see those spiders?"

Siddharth shrugged without turning. "Insects move quickly in places like this. You're a visitor in their home."

Harrison crawled on, unsettled. Mr. Jenkins's voice did not return. Neither did the spiders.

They continued forward on their hands and knees, the silence pressing so close it felt as though the tunnel were narrowing—yet the stone widened enough for them to stand.

"Harrison, look at this." Siddharth ran his fingers over images carved into the stone. "These markings were drawn hundreds, maybe thousands, of years ago, when indigenous groups lived in these caves."

The carvings depicted a man hunting a deer with a bow and arrow.

"That's incredible," Harrison replied, scanning the wall with his flashlight. He stepped closer without waiting, tracing the edge of the carvings until the beam drifted ahead of Siddharth.

Without realizing it, Harrison took the lead. Soon, they reached a fork. "Siddharth, which way should we go?"

"Why don't you choose?" Siddharth said from behind. "What does your instinct tell you?"

Harrison hesitated. He studied both passages—the left narrowing quickly, the right sloping downward into shadow.

Neither offered anything he could name or trust.

He opened his mouth to speak. The air felt thinner. Then he turned—only to find the space behind him empty. The place where Siddharth had stood moments before was vacant, his flashlight beam cutting across bare stone and darkness, as if no one had ever been there at all.

Panic gripped Harrison. *Where did Siddharth go?* The cave seemed to constrict around him. The absence of Siddharth sent shivers through him. He was alone. Siddharth had vanished.

***

Siddharth emerged from the shaft, a trace of relief crossing his face as he saw that Harrison had not followed. *He didn't see me slip away*, he thought, a clever smile playing on his lips. This was a crucial part of his plan to see if Harrison's destiny was to find the clue needed to seek the Heart of Kumari. Everything was falling into place.

His eyes rested on the Sharma family, who were anxiously awaiting his and Harrison's return. Their gazes fixed on Siddharth. He addressed the worried faces before him with a calm but concerned expression.

"It seems we've taken different paths within the tunnel," Siddharth explained, feigning reassurance. "Harrison must have taken a wrong turn or chosen an alternative route. These caves can be quite complicated."

"How could you let this happen! Where is he now?" Sophie's words quivered with anxiety as she asked.

"The tunnels can be disorienting. I'm sure he'll join us soon," Siddharth replied. "I'll give him a few more minutes to find his way back."

Sophie spoke, her words controlled as a tremor revealed

her true anxiety. She leaned closer to Ravi, ensuring Siddharth was out of earshot. "We need to do something quickly. Letting him go into the tunnel might have been a huge mistake." She searched Ravi's face for reassurance.

Sensing Sophie's anxiety, Anil walked over and added, "Siddharth's right. These caves have a way of leading us on unexpected paths. Let's give Harrison a little time to navigate through. He's a bright young man; I'm sure he'll return soon."

To the Sharma family, every moment felt crucial. Despite Siddharth's casual response, the weight of worry hung like a shroud. Ravi's grip on his flashlight tightened, his internal turmoil hidden beneath a mask of composure.

Amma stood very still, counting the seconds between drips of water, though she didn't realize it.

The cave's eerie atmosphere amplified the beating of their hearts, a rhythm punctuated by the uncertain passing of time. As they awaited Harrison's return, the cavernous darkness held its breath, just as the group did.

Undeterred by his unexpected solitude, Harrison pressed on through the tunnel. It was as if something was urging him on, regardless of whether Siddharth was with him. Squeezing through a tight passage on his belly, he emerged onto a ledge overlooking a vast, cavernous room. The walls glowed with shimmering rocks, casting a ghostly aura. The air was warm and resonated with an otherworldly energy carried on a gentle hum.

A pedestal stood resolute in the center of the chamber, illuminated by a concentrated beam of light from an indiscernible origin. A golden box was perched on top, its surface covered with gleaming patterns.

The chamber had already turned toward him. Not in welcome, not in warning—only in recognition. As if someone had once stood where he stood. As if the box had already learned the shape of a waiting hand. The sight was mesmerizing, and excitement surged through Harrison's veins. *Could the box contain the fabled Heart of Kumari that I've been destined to find?* As he paused to take in the space around him, a nagging thought crept into his mind. *Could it simply be a prop, part of the elaborate movie set?*

He grappled with whether he should take it.

Raju's ominous words from their drive to Chitwan came back to him, the tales of the terrible fates befalling those who sought the sacred stone. Harrison couldn't shake the feeling that this had all been too easy.

Without warning, a feeling of inevitability stirred within him. *This box somehow belongs to me.* Though he had never laid eyes on it before, he felt drawn toward it, as if the distance between them had already been measured.

The pedestal sat below, separated by a steep drop into shadow. Harrison scanned the chamber, then pulled a length of rope Raju had insisted he carry. He looped it around a jut of stone, testing the hold once, then again. The rope held.

He lowered himself carefully, boots scraping against the rock face, arms burning as the rope bit into his palms. When his feet finally touched the chamber floor, he didn't look back up.

With cautious steps, he approached the pedestal, his gaze fixed on the artifact. As he extended his hand to grasp the chest, the beam of light intensified, bathing the chamber in a radiant glow.

The golden box pulsed once with a subtle energy, responding to his presence. Every instinct told him this was a pivotal moment, a discovery holding the promise of untold secrets.

***

Meanwhile, the impact of Harrison's absence became increasingly distressing to the family. Each passing minute amplified their unease. Ravi's distress was now unmistakable—his brow creased in worry, glistening with beads of sweat.

"It's been a while. Shouldn't he be back by now?" Sophie's voice trembled with worry. She wanted to trust Siddharth, but doubt clung to her, tightening her chest.

Siddharth offered Sophie another reassuring glance. He stood at a crossroads of intent and trust. He needed to uphold his guise of concern, while letting the boy seek the clue alone. Raju was for intervention, but Siddharth held back, betting on Harrison's destiny to unfold naturally. Their credibility with the family hinged on Harrison's safety, and Siddharth was acutely aware that any misstep could shatter the fragile trust they had built. It was a thought-out plan of watchfulness and restraint, with Siddharth leading the tempo, ensuring Harrison's protection without disrupting the path the goatskin clue had set him on.

Raju's gaze lingered on Siddharth before gesturing discreetly for a private word. They stepped aside, their volume muted, careful not to echo within the cave.

Raju's voice, though low, carried a thread of urgency. "I think it's time to intervene. We can't let him wander aimlessly. Enough time has passed. If we go in now, we'll be the heroes."

Anil approached them, his presence adding tension to the whispered conference. "It's been too long," he interjected. "He could be lost or in trouble."

Raju glanced at the family, their worried faces revealing their growing doubts.

Siddharth's silhouette remained rigid against the rock wall. "Patience," he murmured, the steady cadence of his words conveying firmness. "The Pattern reveals itself to those who trust it. If the Heart of Kumari is truly his to find, then he must reach it by his own path." His voice shifted, gaining an edge of warning. "Besides, our intervention may do more harm than good."

"Maybe, but if something happens to him, the family will lose trust in us. They won't blame the Pattern. They'll blame *us*," Raju said through gritted teeth.

"Intervening risks undoing everything that's meant to unfold," Siddharth explained quietly. "You want the Heart, but not the path to earn it."

Raju's eyes flashed. "I want the Heart before someone else gets to it first. That's the only outcome that matters."

Anil shifted nervously, glancing over his shoulder. "Keep it down—what if they hear us?"

Raju watched the tunnel's entrance with a furrowed brow, a sense of unease gnawing at him. "He's been gone too long," he muttered to himself.

Disregarding his brother's words, Raju positioned himself at the entrance to the shaft. He shouted into the darkness. "Harrison!" As he yelled, rocks shifted and crumbled under his weight, an indication of the instability of his plan.

A hush fell over the group.

Moments later, a faint echo reached their ears—a distant, muffled voice calling out from somewhere deep within the tunnel. The words were indistinguishable, but the urgency was unmistakable.

Raju's expression changed abruptly. "That's Harrison!" Without a moment's hesitation, he continued into the entrance of the tunnel, his instincts guiding him to act. "I'll go get him. Wait here."

Five minutes later, the beam of Raju's flashlight re-emerged. He peered out of the dark space with a sly smile.

"He's fine," Raju announced. The tension in his voice dissipated into a relieved exhale.

Harrison made his way out of the tunnel. His clothes were smeared with bat droppings and mud, but beyond that, he was fine. And there was something else—he held a golden box in his hands.

"Look what I found!" Harrison exclaimed.

Sophie exhaled—relief first, then something sharper. She pulled him close, her fingers brushing the edge of the box between them. "I was so worried."

"I'm fine, Mom," he reassured her.

Pappa turned to Harrison. "My dear boy, what have you stumbled upon?"

"I'm not entirely sure. Let's take a closer look."

"Open it," Sophie said, too quickly.

Pappa's gaze lingered on the box. "It seems almost too easy, doesn't it?"

"I want to see!" both Kiran and Cyrus chimed in unison, bouncing up and down with excitement.

Raju and Anil leaned in. Siddharth did not move.

"Okay, here goes." Harrison lifted the lid of the box. As he did, his smile faltered. Inside, a flint arrowhead lay against the inner wall, its edge still sharp. Beneath it, a bundle wrapped in dark goatskin came apart in his hands, revealing fragments of broken pottery. At the bottom sat a lump of beeswax resin, pressed hard by a scatter of small stones... The Heart of Kumari was not there.

"It's not the diamond," he remarked dejectedly.

"But is this the clue the goatskin referenced?" Amma questioned, peering over Harrison's shoulder with curiosity.

"Hold up the parchment, Harrison. Maybe the clue will materialize like the last one," Ravi suggested.

Harrison took out the parchment and held it up, shining

his flashlight at it. Nothing happened.

"Humph," Sophie muttered. "Check the box again. Maybe we missed something."

Harrison examined the box once more, scrutinizing its every detail, turning it this way and that. He shifted the contents around, scanning every surface. At the bottom, his fingers brushed against a shallow, circular indentation carved into the interior. It felt made for something that wasn't there yet. After a moment of contemplation, his shoulders slumped. "I can't find any sign of the Kumari Mandala. It doesn't seem to connect to our search," he concluded.

"Well, it may not be the Heart or the clue, but it seems your detour was worth it. Hold it up, I'll snap a picture," Ravi said with a smile.

As Harrison held up the box, his family gathered around, eager to capture this moment. They took out their phones and cameras, snapping pictures of the remarkable find. Given its contents, the box appeared to be a treasure trove of history. Even if that turned out not to be the case, they still thought it would make a cool souvenir to take home.

Siddharth stood quietly as the family gathered around the mysterious box.

"Everyone look this way," Sophie called out, waving them together with a smile.

As they turned for the photo, Siddharth glanced at Sophie. "Here, give me your phone," he said, offering to take the picture. "You should be in it, too."

Sophie handed him the phone without comment. After posing with the rest of the family, she called out to Siddharth. "All right, you need to be in it as well. Raju, Anil, you two join in! Let's make it a group shot."

Siddharth hesitated briefly before stepping into the frame beside Raju.

Grinning, Ravi playfully jostled them into place before stepping out to set his camera on a nearby rock. He started the timer and dashed back into frame. "Okay, everyone—smile!"

The camera clicked, capturing the entire group. As the moment passed and the laughter settled, a quiet thought took hold in Siddharth's mind. *What if I could get my hands on those photos?*

The photographs weren't just ordinary family pictures. In the right hands, they could prove vital. Sunjata—the museum curator and eldest daughter of Police Chief Bhaskar—would need to see them. She was more than just a curator; she was the protector of their heritage, safeguarding the reputation of the Shatranj Ke Sipahi. These pictures could serve as an important link, leading them to the Heart of Kumari.

As he glanced at Sophie's phone in his hand, a plan began to form.

The excitement of the camera clicks waned, and Harrison found himself enveloped in a contemplative silence. The weight of the box was solid in his grasp. He mulled over his father's observation and realized that maybe, just maybe, his father was right.

The relic, though not the legendary diamond from Raju's story, still infused their adventure with a new layer of mystery, making it truly unforgettable.

Raju, visibly shaken by Harrison's discovery, turned to Siddharth and asked, "Is that boy lucky?"

Siddharth didn't look at him. "No," he whispered. "He has the blessing of the Kumari on him."

No one heard him.

Within the shadows of the cave, the pieces of the Sharma family's adventure seemed to be falling into place.

Sophie glanced at the others. "It feels like something's guiding Harrison. Leading him to all of this?"

Pappa nodded slowly.

Cyrus, quietly observing, chimed in with his childlike intuition. "Maybe the 'jungle magic' is helping Harrison find the way."

Harrison turned the idea over silently.

He had never believed in magic or mystical forces, but the pattern was hard to ignore. Perhaps "spirit" was simply the language people reached for when something resisted easy explanation—a way of naming a force that felt consistent, even if it wasn't yet understood.

Fragments of old sayings surfaced in his mind, not as answers but as echoes: that actions carried weight, that balance mattered, that what was set in motion did not vanish.

It didn't feel like revelation. More like adjustment—as if the aperture of his mind had opened just enough to let in a law he'd never been taught to measure.

That thought unsettled him.

-8-
A Day at the Bazaar

विपरायां दिवसः

2:00 P.M.

Noticing the time as he glanced at his watch while driving back to the Surya Chandra Inn, Raju proposed a detour. "Why don't we make a stop at the Mahendrapal Bazaar? It's still early, and it's the perfect place to unwind. Best street food in Pokhara. You'll love it."

The thought of fragrant spices and hot breads was enough to break the lingering silence in the van.

"Street food sounds perfect," Amma agreed.

The others quickly nodded along, hunger stirring at the promise. Cyrus perked up, clapping his hands. Kiran leaned forward eagerly. Even Sophie, wearied by the day, managed a smile—except for Harrison, who said nothing and went along with it.

Raju let the agreement settle before adding, almost casually, "And later tonight, we can finally explore the tunnel."

The van filled with eager voices—Amma chuckling, Cyrus and Kiran chanting, "The tunnel! The tunnel!"

Sophie smiled as she leaned toward Harrison, her words barely more than a breath. "Should we tell him we've already been down there?"

Harrison shook his head, his eyes fixed on the road. "No. His feelings would be hurt. Let's keep it between us…for now." The words lingered longer than he meant them to.

Sophie hesitated. She really wanted to let the others know, the half-pendant seemingly burning against her chest. But she nodded, her smile tightening as she turned to face the window.

* * *

They soon found themselves immersed in the vibrant chaos of Mahendrapal Bazaar. Harrison took it all in. This bazaar wasn't some tourist trap like the lakeside district; Mahendrapal was a living, breathing relic of Pokhara's diverse and layered past.

He recalled stories Siddharth had shared during their drive from Chitwan to Pokhara, how the Newari artisans had crafted the older buildings, with their detailed woodwork standing proud in tribute to ancient skill. Siddharth had mentioned vendors whose families had managed the same stalls for decades, each generation preserving traditions while selling an eclectic array of items.

Vibrant colors, exotic scents, and enthralling sounds surrounded the family. The marketplace was a cultural fusion awakening all the senses, selling everything from rich textiles to aromatic spices and time-honored medicinal herbs.

Pulling Harrison out of his amazed state, Ravi reminded him, "It's fascinating, but let's not forget why we're here. We're on a quest, not a shopping spree." He said it with a half-smile—less like a warning and more like someone reminding himself.

"You're right, Dad," Harrison acknowledged. "We need to stay focused and keep our eyes peeled for clues. Remember, Siddharth said it was the Kumari Mandala that is guiding us, so look for relics with symbols or markings emblazoned on them."

Ravi scanned the maze of stalls and nodded. "Yes. Eyes open. But," he added, glancing at a vendor selling hand-carved trinkets, "let's not forget to enjoy the journey. And if something can help us on the quest, maybe we can bend the rules a little."

"Like a compass that points to destiny," Pappa chimed in, clearly amused. "Or a blade that only cuts through lies."

Sophie gave him a look. "Let's try not to come home with a cursed knife, hmm?"

Cyrus pointed to a tiny brass bell dangling from a rack. "Can I get that for Sheepy?" he asked, his eyes wide. "So I can hear him if he gets lost."

Ravi laughed. "That's actually kind of brilliant."

Sophie looked around the long stretch of stalls. "There's too much to see in one pass. Let's spread out—see what we can find."

"One hour," Ravi said, checking his watch. "Meet back here, by the fruit stand. Don't get too adventurous."

"I'll take Cyrus and Kiran," Amma said, tightening her shawl. "We'll stick to the main road. There's a vendor with kids' clothes and another with prayer stones. And I'll get that little bell for Sheepy."

Amma started to turn, but Sophie called after her. "Oh—Amma! You just reminded me. Grab a few shirts for the boys if you see anything nice."

"Of course," Amma said, waving it off like it was done.

Pappa joined her, already scanning the nearby lanes. "Pretty sure I saw a bell shop just past the clay pots."

Cyrus clutched Sheepy to his chest. "He wants one that jingles loud…and maybe some snacks."

That got a laugh from the group.

"All right," Ravi said. "Let's move. One hour. No detours. No rescues. Our top mission: a bell and snacks for Sheepy!"

Sophie nodded. "All right. Harrison and I will go that way—antiques, anything that looks older than it should be."

"I'll catch up with you in a second. I saw something over here that caught my eye." Ravi waved as he crossed the street. "Call out if anything strange happens," he added with a wink.

"Everything here is strange," Harrison muttered under his breath.

"Exactly," Sophie replied.

And with that, they split—Amma and Pappa disappearing into the market with the little ones, the rest drawn into the chaos of color, spice, and sound.

"It's like stepping back in time," Sophie mused as she and Harrison passed a shop selling ritualistic items of Tibetan origin.

The narrow streets, the smell of incense lifting and mixing with the aroma of fried street food, and the chatter in multiple languages—Nepali, Hindi, Gurung, Tibetan, and English—gave Mahendrapal Bazaar a rich texture of complexity and charm.

Harrison couldn't tell how long they'd been walking. Just then, something ahead caught his eye—bright, then gone. He turned to his mother. "I saw something across the street. I'm just going to check it out real quick." He disappeared before Sophie could respond, swallowed by the flow of the crowd.

Mesmerized by the maze of vendors, Sophie found herself in front of a stall teeming with stunningly designed jewelry and exquisitely woven textiles. "These are truly one-of-a-kind," she remarked, her fingertips gliding over the swatches of the cloth.

Her purpose was more than admiration; she was searching for something specific. She meticulously scanned the array of beaded chains, hoping to find a piece like the mysterious necklace they had stumbled upon the night before. The pendant had seized her imagination—one half of a larger design, awaiting its missing counterpart. She wondered if she might discover the other half among these market wares. She hoped to find a clue, bringing them one step closer to solving the puzzle they were piecing together.

Harrison suddenly reappeared at her side, slightly winded and grinning, a small paper bag swinging from one hand. "Got what I needed," he said. "And maybe one or two things I didn't."

Sophie glanced at him, then back to the necklaces. "That seems to be the theme of the day."

"Speaking of," came Ravi's voice behind them. "We might need to make room for extra souvenirs in our luggage." He weaved through a pair of tourists carrying oversized drums, a fresh coconut in one hand, a folded paper bag in the other. He handed the coconut to Harrison. "Stay hydrated, Seeker." Then, lowering his voice, he leaned toward Sophie. "Find anything?"

She shook her head, her eyes drifting over the stall's display. "Not yet. But something's here. I just know it."

Ravi nodded toward the shop's exit. "Harrison, let's step outside for a minute. This place is starting to smell like incense and goat."

Harrison followed, sipping from the coconut. "Do you

think she'll actually find it here? The other half?"

Ravi didn't answer right away. The street outside had gotten busier—rickshaws weaving through foot traffic, children darting between stalls, and vendors shouting over one another in a dozen different tongues.

"Not sure," he finally replied.

They walked in silence for a bit, past a shop selling antique locks and another with rusty brass cookware stacked like armor. Harrison meandered a little ahead, taking it all in. The coconut was almost empty. As he tipped it to drain the last of the sweet water, his eyes caught something on the wall opposite—a smear of red vermilion forming three crooked letters: *W T T*. He blinked. A rickshaw rolled past, its wheel kicking up grit, and when the dust settled, the wall was clean.

"You know," Harrison finally said, tossing the drained shell into a nearby bin and turning to face his father, "this place feels like it's keeping secrets. Like every alley's daring us to look."

Ravi chuckled. "That's the bazaar. It hides what matters in plain sight."

Harrison nodded, then slowed. A vendor had laid out a rug covered in oddments—rusted keys, cracked figurines, weather-beaten toys. Something about the randomness of it sparked a thought.

"Dad, check this out!" Harrison shouted. He reached into the bag he was carrying, pulled out a baseball, and tossed it toward his father.

Ravi looked up, his eyes widening as he tracked the ball's arc. With a quick motion, he reached out and caught it cleanly. He grinned, inspecting the ball closely. "You've got a powerful arm, son," he said, turning the ball over in his hands. He smiled as he noticed the signature. "Wait a second—no way! Is this signed by…Babe Ruth?" He paused, squinting at the signature. "Yeah, sure. And I'm the King of England." He tossed it back to Harrison.

Harrison shrugged, catching the ball. "Yeah, I bought it at that antique shop." He tossed it back. "Thought it was a good buy."

"Come on, let's see what else we can find," Ravi said, slipping the baseball into his backpack.

Just then, Sophie stepped out of a nearby shop, brushing the dusty curtain aside. "I didn't see anything that looked like the half-pendant," she said, "but I found this." She held up a delicate silver ring. In the center was a tiny green stone surrounded by six red ones. They were only polished glass, but the piece had a captivating charm.

Ravi took it from her hand and turned it over, squinting. "Looks like something a priest might've worn," he said. "Or a street vendor with good taste."

Sophie raised an eyebrow. "Well, I'm both practical and stylish."

"Good choice, my love. It won't take up too much space."

"Thank you, dear," she said, slipping the ring onto her finger. She then leaned in and gave him a quick kiss on the lips. No fanfare, just familiar affection. The moment complete, she turned, already scanning the next row of stalls.

He followed, smiling to himself.

As they continued, Harrison's attention was caught by a vendor selling flashlights along with other random items. "Hey, Dad! Check this out!" he called eagerly. He picked one up, feeling its weight. "These are solid but not too heavy. Definitely an upgrade from our phones. Should we get them?"

Ravi took the flashlight, turning it over in his hands and testing the switch. The beam was strong and steady. He nodded approvingly. "Smart thinking, son. These could come in handy."

At the same time, Sophie's gaze fell upon an old roll of

35mm film covered in dust, a relic amidst the modern swag. She grinned, holding it aloft. "Can you believe this was once the height of technology? It's practically a historical artifact now."

Harrison took the film from his mother, dust particles dancing in the sunlight. "Twenty-four shots in one roll. That's it. I can't imagine capturing a whole trip on that."

Ravi's smile widened as he reminisced. "We had to make every shot count. Not so long ago, it was quite the skill."

As they continued through the bustling market, the family's pace slowed when Sophie caught sight of a beautiful temple ahead, its copper spire gleaming in the late afternoon sun.

"Look," Sophie said, stopping for a moment. "That's the Dharma Shanti Temple. I read about it in the guidebook. I'd love to go inside."

Ravi glanced at Harrison, clearly not interested, then back at Sophie. "You go ahead. We'll check out those antique shops down the street." He nodded toward a row of small, cluttered storefronts filled with brass trinkets and colorful textiles.

"Yeah, Mom, we'll catch up with you in a bit," Harrison added.

Sophie smiled. "All right, I'll meet you both back here in a little while," she said before turning toward the temple's grand entrance.

As Sophie disappeared into the temple, Ravi and Harrison exchanged a quick grin, veering toward the shops.

Just then, they spotted Amma and Pappa approaching with Kiran and Cyrus tagging along.

"Look who we ran into," Pappa said with a hearty laugh, clapping Ravi on the shoulder.

"Isn't this market wonderful?" Amma added, her eyes gleaming with excitement.

"Find anything interesting yet?" Ravi asked, glancing at

the stalls lining the path.

"Did we ever!" Amma replied. "And there's so much more to see."

As they passed a stall adorned with brass statues and gemstones, a gregarious shopkeeper caught sight of them. His broad smile and exuberant greeting broke through the noise of the market. "Namaste! Welcome, welcome! I am Laxman," the shopkeeper called out, his hands gesturing toward his display. "Come, take a look at the finest treasures in all of Pokhara!"

The group exchanged amused glances, drawn in by the shopkeeper's charm.

Engaging in lively conversations with Laxman, the family learned about the significance behind the items he presented. The shopkeeper's tales transformed the trinkets into tokens steeped in history and culture, enriching their appeal.

Amma's eyes caught the glint of the exquisite singing bowls, an ancient musical instrument. With an inquisitive gleam, she approached them, picking one up and examining the detailed designs etched into the copper sheen. She looked up and engaged Laxman in conversation. "Can you tell me about this?"

"Of course." Laxman was happy to have people interested in his culture. "Singing bowls hold a special place in our hearts and traditions, with a history dating back centuries. They are unique artifacts and powerful tools for healing and spirituality."

Amma looked at its design, fascinated, as she inquired, "How so?"

"You see," Laxman began, holding up a singing bowl, "each of these bowls carries its own unique sound and countless stories and experiences. Allow me to share one such tale, passed down through generations."

"Oh, there you are!" Sophie's voice rang out as she entered the shop, picking up a nearby bowl, the smooth metal cool against her fingers. "I was looking for you…" Her words trailed off as she realized the shopkeeper had been speaking. Her expression softened. "I'm so sorry. I didn't mean to interrupt."

Ravi smiled. "No worries. Laxman was just about to share a story with us."

Sophie, intrigued, turned to Laxman. "Please, Laxman, I'd love to hear the story, too."

The rest of the Sharma family also listened eagerly.

Laxman's words flowed in a melodic rhythm as he began his storytelling. "Years ago, a wise and revered monk named Dharma lived in a remote village in the Himalayan foothills. He possessed a singing bowl of exceptional beauty, known far and wide for its captivating tones."

Pappa was fascinated by the imagery Laxman was painting with his words. "What made Dharma's singing bowl so special?"

"Dharma's singing bowl was said to have been crafted by a master artisan who had poured his heart and soul into its creation. Its rich, resonating sound had the power to heal the wounded hearts and troubled minds of those who heard it. Dharma often used it during his meditations, creating an atmosphere of serenity and mindfulness, attracting seekers from far and wide."

Ravi's imagination soared as he envisioned this ancient monk and his mystical singing bowl. "What happened to Dharma and his remarkable bowl, Laxman? Did they continue to spread their wisdom and healing?"

Laxman's expression lit up, his smile reflecting the reverence for this tale. "Indeed, Dharma's legacy lived on through his teachings and the profound impact of his singing bowl.

It is said that after his passing, the bowl retained its healing properties, bringing solace to those who sought its soothing melodies."

Harrison couldn't help but be moved by the story. "That's a beautiful tale, Laxman. It's like they carry the spirits and wisdom of those who have used them."

"Exactly. And thank you. I want to give you this singing bowl as a gift." He presented the bowl to Amma.

Laxman then went behind the counter and returned with two traditional Nepali wooden spinning tops for Cyrus and Kiran. The toys were beautifully crafted, about the size of their palms, with vibrant, hand-painted designs depicting images of Nepali folklore decorating their surfaces.

Laxman handed the tops to the children. "These are a popular toy in Nepal. They are for you to keep."

"Wow, these are awesome! Thank you!" they cheered.

"We could easily spend hours here," Sophie confessed. Her face lit up with an insight. She leaned close to Harrison, her volume dropping to a whisper. "Should we tell Laxman about the pendant, arrowhead, and other artifacts we found? His knowledge could be important."

Harrison hesitated for a moment, his eyes sweeping over the bustling market. "I've been looking around, and nothing here remotely resembles what we found. I think we should keep it under wraps for now. No need to draw attention to it."

Sophie nodded. "All right, if you think that's best. Let's keep it between us for now and see what else we can find out ourselves."

"Thank you, Laxman," Ravi finally said, bringing the conversation to a close. He turned to the family. "I'm going to check out some street food. Anyone want to join me?"

"I'll go! I'll go!" Cyrus and Kiran cheered in unison.

Harrison, lost in thought, nodded. "Yeah, I'll come, too."

Pappa opted to keep browsing the market stalls with Amma, and Sophie waved them off. "I'll catch up in a bit. I want to look around a little more."

As they walked, Harrison's mind drifted back to the treasure box and the series of events that had led him to this remote corner of the world. His musings were cut short when his father thrust a steaming piece of spicy fried momo under his nose.

"Here, try this," Ravi insisted, grinning.

As they savored the flavors, a prickle crept up the backs of their necks—something wasn't right. Scanning the sea of shoppers, they spotted a hooded figure leaning against a crumbling wall, his eyes locked onto them.

"Who's that?" Harrison muttered.

Before Ravi could respond, Amma called out, drawing their attention. "Kiran, Sophie, Cyrus, over here! This shop has the most exquisite pashmina scarves in the entire bazaar!"

As the family members moved to meet Amma, the hooded figure surged through the multitude of people and snatched Cyrus's beloved toy lamb out of his tiny arms.

"My sheep!" Cyrus wailed, his words slicing through the commotion.

The toy—his battered plush lamb with the new brass bell Amma had just bought—was already vanishing into the crowd.

At that same moment, another cloaked figure darted behind Harrison. With a swift motion, the figure grabbed his backpack just as Harrison was about to sling it over his shoulder.

Reacting instantly, Harrison shouted, "They've got my backpack!" His scream rose above the surrounding noise, alerting everyone to the unfolding situation.

Pappa had been engrossed in haggling with a vendor over the price of a vintage dagger when he heard his grandsons' pleas. He turned to see two figures cutting through the crowd, one carrying Harrison's backpack, the other Cyrus's sheep. "Stop! Thieves!" Pappa bellowed, his words reverberating through the narrow lanes like the clap of thunder.

Springing into action, Kiran, Cyrus, and Sophie darted through the maze-like passageways of the market. They dodged women carrying baskets, avoided precarious stacks of clay pots, and narrowly escaped a collision with a cart full of mangoes. Trailing them, Ravi, Harrison, Amma, and Pappa screamed alerts and directions, their feet pounding against the cobblestones in a frantic rhythm.

Suddenly, amid the thundering footfalls and shouting vendors, a faint metallic chime rang out—soft, high, and impossibly out of place.

Sophie skidded to a halt. "Wait—did you hear that?"

Ravi, breathless beside her, strained to listen.

A delicate jingle rose above the noise, a whisper of direction.

Harrison's eyes widened. "It's the bell," he panted, the words barely making it past his breath. "The one Amma tied to Sheepy."

They desperately scanned in all directions, trying to locate the soft tinkle.

"There!" Harrison pointed, catching a glimpse of a hooded figure vanishing into a gap between stalls as Sheepy's bell faded into the throng.

The family surged forward in pursuit.

As they stormed through the vendors, their path twisted sharply, opening into a chaotic plaza choked with people—bodies pressing from all sides, colors blurring, sounds collapsing into cacophony. A rickshaw trundled by, blocking their line of sight. By the time they had cleared it, the hooded man was gone.

Ravi cursed under his breath, eyes scanning wildly. Harrison spun in circles. Cyrus called out for Sheepy.

Nothing. Then—

"Turn left, here!" came a loud shout. It was Raju, appearing out of nowhere. Siddharth was right behind him. "We can corner him down this alley!"

Without a second thought, the family charged into a narrow, shadowed alley, almost bowling over a merchant carrying a tray full of ceramic elephants. Amma stumbled, but Siddharth swiftly steadied her.

"Keep going!" he urged, his eyes ablaze.

"Up there!" Sophie cried out. The hooded thieves were at the alley's end, where it spilled into the open courtyard of the centuries-old temple.

His heart pounding like a drum, Harrison sensed a surge of adrenaline electrifying his limbs. "They're heading for the temple !"

Summoning reserves of speed they didn't know they had, Ravi, Kiran, and Harrison narrowed the gap. Just as one figure was about to turn the corner into the temple, Ravi lunged forward, seizing the culprit by the arm and yanking off the hood. A collective gasp caught in their throats as they stared into the eyes of a surprised teenager. The boy—no older than Harrison—dropped the stuffed animal to the ground.

"My lamb!" Cyrus squealed, darting forward to reclaim his treasured plush toy.

Realizing the jig was up, the second figure let go of Harrison's backpack and tried to run for it. But Siddharth was faster. In a flash, he lunged forward, his leg hooking around the thief's ankle, and sent them both sprawling onto the cobblestones.

"You're not going anywhere," Siddharth declared with an unwavering resolve. With a firm hand, he yanked the thief upright by a fistful of hair, forcing a strangled grunt to escape from the boy's lips. And as he stood, disheveled and subdued, Siddharth's fist found its mark, driving into the thief's gut with precision.

The impact left the boy folding in on himself, and he toppled back to the cobblestones. The air whooshed from his lungs as he hit the ground, forcing him to gasp for breath.

Harrison's eyes were sharp as he watched Raju snatch the abandoned backpack from the ground. With a fluid gesture, Raju handed it back to Harrison. As their hands met, Raju's sleeve slipped up, revealing a mark on his arm that Harrison had never noticed before. The skin was seared with the image of a rook, the scar raised and rough, resembling a chess piece. It stood out like a brand, momentarily sparking Harrison's curiosity.

Kiran, standing close at Harrison's side, didn't look at the mark. He looked past it. Past Raju. Past the place where the crowd had already closed. "Something stayed," he said, so quietly it almost didn't sound like speech.

No one answered.

Harrison shifted, the backpack suddenly heavier in his hands. "Thank you, guys. Really," he said, the words arriving a beat too late, as though they'd been waiting for the moment to pass before stepping in.

As Amma hugged Cyrus, his fingers clenched around his reclaimed lamb, the soft fabric bunching under his tight grip. She looked up at both her family and Raju and Siddharth. "We couldn't have done this without every one of you."

Raju grinned, his teeth flashing in the dappled sunlight.

For a split second, Harrison caught something in his demeanor. An unreadable flicker. A slight undertone that indicated Raju was not entirely on their side. The look vanished in the space of a breath.

Ravi sensed it, too, his eyes meeting Harrison's in a tacit acknowledgment of something more complex, something more profound. "Remember the woman at the lake," he whispered.

Harrison nodded. "'*Be cautious of those who are bound by blood,*'" he repeated.

Just then, a man in a police uniform, his movements authoritative and precise, stepped forward to secure the boys with zip ties. As he wrapped the ties around their slender wrists, the fabric of his uniform sleeve shifted up his forearm, exposing a mark that caught Harrison's eye.

It was a crown entwined with a serpent, burned into his skin—a symbol of control and authority.

Harrison's memory flashed back to the inn's basement stairwell. For an instant, it aligned with something he couldn't place.

As the officer straightened up, he gave the Sharma family a reassuring nod. "I'm Chief Bhaskar, the head of the local police." He introduced himself with a calm assertiveness. "You have nothing to worry about. My team and I will handle this situation."

Ravi, relieved and respectful, extended his hand to Chief Bhaskar. "We're grateful for your swift action. Thank you."

Chief Bhaskar accepted the handshake, his grip firm. "It's our duty to ensure the safety of both locals and visitors," he stated, leaving no room for doubt.

Bhaskar walked up to Raju and clapped him on the back, offering his hand in gratitude. "Outstanding work, Raju. We've been chasing these two for quite a while." He winked and flashed a knowing smile before turning to Siddharth, acknowledging his contribution to the situation.

Harrison couldn't help but contemplate the exchange between Raju and Bhaskar. *Odd. They seemed to know each other—like old friends.*

Bhaskar gave a final nod of assurance to the family, his team working efficiently in the background. Yet, the tension hadn't fully dissipated.

As Bhaskar's men secured the area, Ravi stepped closer to Harrison, his eyes narrowing as he scanned the scene. "We should move quickly," he murmured under his breath, just loud enough for Harrison to catch. "This isn't over."

Harrison looked from Raju to Bhaskar, unsettled by how easily the moment had resolved.

Siddharth stepped forward, his gaze steady but his movements tense. "Let's get back to the inn. We'll figure this out later."

Something felt off.

As the family turned away, a heavy, almost electric tension clung to the surrounding air. Everyone sensed it. Something had been set in motion, though no one yet knew its shape.

-9-
SECRETS STITCHED IN WOOL

ऊर्णायां स्यूतानि रहस्यानि

4:30 P.M.

Enclosed within the sanctuary of their guestroom at the Surya Chandra Inn, the family gathered in the intimate common area, a space that now doubled as an undercover meeting room. Ravi subconsciously locked the door, the definitive click of the bolt reverberating through the tension-laden air.

Cyrus looked up with concern, "Why didn't Raju and Siddharth come?"

Ravi answered, looking gently at his son, "We need a little family time. Okay?"

Cyrus nodded. "Okay."

A beat of silence followed. The room was thick with concerns left unspoken.

Amma's brow furrowed as she glanced between Ravi and

Sophie. "What is it?" she asked, her voice low. "Did something happen?"

Sophie hesitated, then shrugged off her coat and draped it over the back of the nearest chair. Before she could speak, Ravi said, "Just... some things that didn't sit right."

The ticking from the small clock above the fireplace pressed into the pause that followed.

Amma studied their faces, reading between the lines. She nodded once. "I see." She leaned back slightly, arms crossed. "But maybe we don't know them as well as we thought." Her eyes lingered on Ravi's. "Are we sure we should be this guarded?"

Sophie weighed in. "You have a point, Amma. Raju assisted Harrison in the bat cave, and they rescued us earlier at the bazaar. We've been too quick to judge."

"But, Amma," Harrison replied, "it was Siddharth who left me in the bat cave. That has to count against them."

Amma placed her purse on the table and left her hand resting there. She did not look up.

The silence stretched.

Ravi glanced at Harrison. He gave the slightest nod.

Harrison shifted in his chair before standing. "Amma," he finally said, "there is something I need to tell you and Pappa."

He waited until Amma lifted her eyes.

"While we were at the lake, the woman who sold us the tea and blankets warned me. She said not to trust anyone who is... well, she used the phrase 'bound by blood.' Then she handed me a paper with the Kumari Mandala on it."

He took out the crumpled paper and showed it to them.

Pappa looked at the paper and then at Harrison. "I had no knowledge of this."

"We wanted to be sure before sharing it with you," Sophie added.

"Bound by blood?" Pappa repeated, furrowing his brow. "I don't think she's suggesting *us*. No…it feels deeper. It's almost like she's implying—"

"That's what I thought," Harrison cut in.

"Well, Raju and Siddharth haven't done anything for us to alienate them," Amma remarked in their defense.

"They won't hurt us—they saved Sheepy!" Cyrus chimed in, clutching the toy close.

"Good thing we bought that bell," Pappa added. "Who knows if we'd have gotten him back without it?"

Cyrus checked the tiny knot to make sure the bell was secure. "Yeah…thanks, Amma and Pappa." He gave the toy a fierce hug. "I don't know what I'd do without you," he whispered to Sheepy.

Kiran nodded. "The truck almost hit me. Raju pulled me back." He paused, looking up, "And I like Siddharth's hair," he added quietly. "It's long and bouncy."

"He's been steady," Pappa's voice was sure. "Especially with the children."

Amma folded her hands. "They've helped us."

Sophie didn't answer. Her fingers traced the edge of her sleeve. She kept her gaze on the table.

Ravi did not look at her. "While that may be true, Harrison, Sophie, and I just feel that it's better to be safe than sorry. Let's maintain a low profile until we have more concrete information."

A murmur of reluctant agreement followed.

The room felt settled, almost ordinary again. Familiar roles quietly resumed, as if agreement itself could smooth what had been disturbed. Yet something in the air remained unaccounted for—not a fear, exactly, but a thin displacement, like time slipping a beat out of sequence. No one named it, and because it went unnamed, it stayed.

Harrison's unease gnawed at him. He needed a moment alone to collect his thoughts. "I'm going down to the vending machine. Anyone want something?"

"I'd like some chips," Cyrus called out, his attention fixed on his Nintendo Switch as his fingers moved expertly across the controls.

"Chips for me, too," Kiran added excitedly. He then turned to Cyrus, holding up the spinning tops they had received earlier. "Let's play with our new tops!"

"That's a great idea," Cyrus agreed, setting his game console aside.

"Could you grab me a coffee?" Pappa asked.

Sophie intervened. "Pappa, I'll brew a fresh pot for you right here in the room."

"That sounds perfect, Sophie. I'll have a cup, too," Ravi added, appreciating his wife's thoughtfulness.

Harrison disengaged the bolt, secured the door, and stepped out into the hallway. With a click, the door closed behind him.

Sophie busied herself with the in-room coffee machine.

"Do you need any help, Sophie?" Amma asked.

"No, I've got it covered. Why don't you check the drawer over there? I saw some takeout menus. Perhaps we should order something; I don't feel like going out tonight," Sophie replied with a note of fatigue.

"Yes, let's do that," Amma agreed as she picked up the menus and browsed through the options. One bore a faint emblem—two koi circling a lotus above the quiet words Sacred Balance. "How about some Indian-Chinese?"

The room collectively agreed. "Sounds good… Great idea."

Pappa wandered toward the corner cabinet—an old, low sideboard, carved from sal wood, its surface bowed from time.

One of the few pieces still original to the fort.

He opened the drawer. The metal pull stuck for a breath, then gave with a sigh. Inside: faded hotel stationery, a cracked fountain pen, a scattering of matchbooks. And something more. A groove. Subtle. Not drawn, not marked. Etched.

Pappa knelt, frowning, and angled the drawer toward the lamp. The grain caught the light just enough to show the stroke pattern.

He ran his thumb over it. Once. Then again.

"Strange," he muttered. "There's something carved here."

No one heard.

He leaned closer. Squinted.

The Devanagari script appeared as the light shifted: किरण- Below it, smaller, tighter—पञ्चमं सुरक्षितम्.

His breath caught. "Kiran," he said. "And something else…"

The room didn't answer. Then—

"What?" Kiran asked, still crouched beside the couch.

Pappa didn't reply. He touched the groove again, slower this time. "It's your name." He hesitated. "And a message."

Cyrus sat up. "What kind of message?"

Amma moved closer. "What does it say?"

Pappa traced the lower carving. "'The fifth is safe.'"

Sophie blinked. "What does that mean?"

Pappa shook his head. "No idea."

"I didn't do it!" Kiran's voice cracked. "I don't even know how to write like that!"

Amma set the menus down. "Ray?" Her voice was low, cautious.

Pappa stepped back, letting her kneel beside the open drawer.

She traced the name gently with her fingertip. "This script—it's old."

Pappa nodded. "The curves aren't modern. This...this was carved before the spelling reforms."

"How old?" Sophie asked, handing Pappa a mug of coffee.

"Eighteenth century, maybe earlier," he said. "Before the inn. Before it was called Surya Chandra."

Cyrus whispered, "Back when it was still a fort."

No one moved.

Kiran came forward, slowly, barefoot on the rug. He looked at the name, just barely visible in the light.

"That's not mine," he said, voice small.

"But it is," Pappa whispered. "It's spelled exactly the same."

He shook his head, backing away. "But I didn't write it."

"We know, baby," Sophie said softly.

"Then who did?"

No one answered.

The clock on the mantel broke the silence with a single, clear chime—three-quarters past four.

Pappa closed the drawer gently. "Maybe," he said, "it wasn't carved for someone."

He looked at Kiran, then at the drawer again. "Maybe it was carved for a time..."

Kiran's eyes stayed fixed on the wood. "What kind of time?"

The silence held. Tight. Watchful.

Cyrus whispered, "Maybe the kind that knows itself."

The silence lingered for a beat longer, then passed—like something brushing the edge of the room before leaving.

Cyrus and Kiran returned to their tops. No one mentioned it again.

Amma smoothed the menus with the flat of her hand. "I'll place the order," she said as she reached for the hotel's phone.

Just then, Harrison stepped back into the suite nudging

the door shut with his leg. The bolt clicked into place.

He crossed the sitting area, balancing an armful of snacks. As he passed the hearth, his gaze lifted.

The painting still hung above it—of the fort—cracked and heavy with twilight.

But something was missing.

He froze, staring. The slope that had once held a faint female figure near the edge of the ramparts now showed only stone and mist. The hillside was empty now.

He blinked. Looked again. The paint showed no trace of disturbance. As if she had never been there.

"What would you like from the Indian-Chinese menu?" Amma asked, her voice pulling him back.

"Chili chicken," he replied, sinking into a chair next to Cyrus.

The order completed, and the snacks disbursed, the family prepared to unravel the mystery before them.

Pappa pulled an old wooden upholstered chair to the coffee table.

"Here—let me take that," Sophie said, already reaching for her coat draped over it. She gathered it and hung it with the others by the door.

Pappa adjusted it.

But before he could sit, Kiran's voice cut through the room. "That chair's angry." He didn't say it loud, not quite looking at anyone, either—just at the scratch down one leg and the torn seam in the cushion.

Pappa paused, halfway to sitting. He glanced back at the chair, then at Kiran, then gave a short, almost amused breath. "All right," he murmured, pushing it back into the corner. "We'll choose another one."

The old chair dragged back, catching once in the red carpet. It stayed there—watching, in its way—while the family gathered around the table.

"Now that that's settled," Pappa declared. His gaze moved from one face to the next, lingering. "Let's set aside any issues we may have with Raju and Siddharth. We're facing a different mystery, demanding our full attention." Pappa paused, inhaling. "Let's lay out all our clues on this table. We must work together to unravel what's happening."

In that moment, Harrison experienced a longing for Raju's and Siddharth's insights. Their perspectives could shed light on his bewilderment. As his father had said, there was nothing certain to suggest Raju and Siddharth were a threat. However, his internal voice reminded him of the whisper from the woman at the lake—or the Spirit of Kumari, for all he knew—and cautioned him to be wary and stay alert to the undercurrents around him.

"You're right, Pappa. We need to focus." Harrison pushed aside his doubt and agreed. "Let's put all the cards on the table…so to speak." Harrison stepped over to the coffee table and emptied his backpack. He placed the small chest on the table and opened it, revealing the pot shards, the dark parchment, the arrowhead, the lump of beeswax resin, and a handful of small stones. He also added the piece of goatskin from the abandoned temple in Chitwan, inscribed with Sanskrit and the image of the Kumari Mandala.

Pappa followed his lead. He set his coffee cup aside, reached into his satchel, and pulled out an old, well-used bamboo flute, placing it gently on the table. As he rummaged further, something slipped from the bag and struck the floor with a metallic clang.

Harrison glanced down, eyebrows raised. "What's that?"

Pappa bent down and picked up the object, revealing an old, iron letter opener. "Oh, I forgot I put this in there," he said with a sheepish grin. "I found it in the library in Chitwan."

Amma picked up the letter opener, its sharp edge glinting. It looked more like a weapon than a tool. She turned to her husband. "Why did you think you needed this, Ray?"

Pappa hesitated, glancing at Sophie, who was with him when he took it. "I'm honestly not sure, Hema." He shifted, "I guess I was a little on edge back then," he admitted, rubbing the back of his neck. "We thought…maybe someone was watching us. But it turned out to be nothing—just our fear playing tricks on us."

Sophie nodded. "It was a strange place. We couldn't shake the feeling that we weren't alone, even though we were."

Pappa chuckled. "I'm a little embarrassed to admit it."

Harrison tilted his head. "Should we count it as a clue?"

"No," he finally said. "I don't think it's meant as a clue."

He set it aside and withdrew the brittle book from the Chitwan Jungle Lodge Camp library.

The spine cracked softly as he opened it to the torn page.

At the bottom, a caption read: Kumari Talisman—needed to find the Heart of Kumari. There was no image. No certainty. "This… I think this is a clue."

He didn't look up.

"Okay, my turn." Ravi approached the table and laid down his digital camera. The screen displayed the photo of peculiar wheels he had captured on one of the first days of their travels. "I have a feeling this image might be significant."

Sophie was next. With a calm reverence, she unclasped the beaded pendant hanging around her neck and placed it on the table. The blue, S-shaped stone at its center, surrounded on one side by the folded lotus petals, captured a universe within its crystalline structure, twinkling under the room's ambient light.

Amma caught her breath. "When were you planning

to tell us about this?" She lifted the necklace, her fingers recognizing something her mind had not yet named.

"I was waiting for the right moment," Sophie responded, "preferably when Raju and Siddharth weren't around. This is what we found last night. Just as Harrison's dreams had led us to Pokhara, they also led us to explore the tunnel. There, we found a magnificent chapel. And inside, on the altar, was this pendant."

"A chapel?" Pappa asked in disbelief.

"It's true, Pappa. We have pictures," Harrison confirmed.

Ravi nodded. "A chapel, hidden beneath our very feet."

Placing the necklace back on the table, Amma's breath shifted. She didn't smile. She didn't praise it. She only watched the blue stone catch the light.

Still processing the news of the previous night's adventure, Pappa eyed the eclectic pile. "Is this all we've got?"

Ravi looked around at the quiet faces. "Anyone find anything at the bazaar? Any clues?"

Silence.

Amma stared at Cyrus, pondering an unfathomable riddle. "Hold on," she finally said, her eyes narrowing on his stuffed lamb. "What if the lamb isn't as innocent as it seems?"

Confused glances darted around the table.

"You're saying Sheepy is somehow connected to our quest for of Kumari?" Ravi asked.

Amma shook her head. "I'm simply saying something doesn't feel right. I mean, who steals a child's toy?"

Cyrus hugged Sheepy closer.

No one answered right away.

The lamb's bell chimed softly as Cyrus shifted his grip.

Sophie seized the moment to address her son. "Cyrus, why would anyone want Sheepy? Is there something we're missing?"

Before his older brother could muster a reply, Kiran burst forth with eagerness. His eyes, wide and shining, turned to his mother's. He had been harboring this secret for days. "Oh! Oh! I know why they want the lamb! Cyrus hid the shiny thing in it—the one from the Monkey Temple." Kiran pointed toward the pendant on the table. "It looks just like that!"

Sophie gasped. "Could it be the missing half?"

The room fell silent.

"One way to find out," Ravi whispered. His hands trembled ever so slightly as they hovered above the toy lamb in Cyrus's grasp. "I need to see Sheepy for a moment. Trust me, I won't hurt him."

"Promise?" Cyrus asked.

"I promise. He won't feel a thing. And when I'm done, we'll fix him up as good as new."

Satisfied by his father's words, Cyrus relented.

Ravi plucked the toy from his grasp and looked at Sophie for final approval.

Sophie nodded, her face taut with anxiety.

The tension in the room bore down on them all. Every tick of the clock stretched time.

"Here goes nothing," Ravi whispered under his breath, finally breaking the silence. Carefully, almost reverently, he found the small hole Cyrus had used to conceal the pendant. Starting there, he pried apart the stitching of the stuffed animal. Finally, the last stitch gave way, and for a moment, nothing happened. Then, as if pushed by some invisible force, a beaded necklace tumbled onto the table.

The pendant—one half of a whole—held an S-shaped stone, shimmering with radiant blue. It lay there as though it had always belonged—and yet did not. A paradox. It caught everyone's breath.

Ravi looked up, locking eyes with his family. It was as

though time had frozen. The necklace and its S-shaped gem lay between them like an unanswered question, a clue to an enigma they were all desperate to solve.

Ravi handed Sophie the necklace, and she held her breath as she took the other chain from the table. Aligning the stone charms, they were drawn to each other like magnets. They fit together seamlessly, forming a perfect bond—the separate S-shaped stones now one, creating a perfect circle—completing a taijitu. The moment they touched, both gems emitted a glow that illuminated faces, bathing them in an otherworldly light.

Instinctively, Ravi lifted his hand—as if to steady it, or bless it, or pull it back. He stopped himself.

Silence enveloped them. The air seemed to thicken as something long still shifted—not awakened, but restored—settling into place without announcement. Somewhere nearby, the clock resumed its ticking, unchanged, yet no longer keeping quite the same company.

***

5:14 P.M.

The sun dipped below the horizon, casting a golden hue that reflected off the weathered façades of the buildings surrounding Mahendrapal Bazaar. Locals and tourists brought vibrant energy into the bustling marketplace, weaving through a maze of vendors. The air was thick with the fragrance of incense, spices, and tandoori, overwhelming the senses with rich aromas.

Even within the lively atmosphere of Mahendrapal Bazaar, Raju and Siddharth moved with a singular focus and intensity, their presence cutting through the throng. Both men were tall and imposing, their muscular frames suggesting strength and resilience. They wore stern, almost chiseled expressions and emanated an intense aura that accompanied a heightened awareness of every fleeting glance and subtle gesture in the surrounding crowd.

Raju turned to Siddharth as they walked with urgency toward their intended target. "We're losing them." His voice quivered as he spoke. A haunting nightmare surfaced—one he didn't want to believe. "I feel the Sharma family no longer trusts us."

Siddharth frowned. "How do you know that? We just put on a spectacular show by saving them from the thieves. I would think we have their trust."

Raju shook his head impatiently. "Siddharth, you can't be that naïve. Did you not see how they all rushed to their rooms the moment we returned? We should be planning to go into the hidden tunnel, but instead, they hid." He turned to his brother, frustration flaring in his eyes. "And do you know why?"

Siddharth's prayer beads clicked softly between his fingers. His voice was quiet, measured. "No. But I'm sure you'll tell me."

"Because they've lost trust in us." Raju quickened his pace as they walked. "Uncle Bhaskar is not going to be happy about this. Leaving Harrison alone in the cave was foolish. He probably would have found the clue with you there. Leaving him came at a cost. Your actions have riled the family's suspicions."

Siddharth pondered Raju's words. He was certain Harrison was the key to locating of Kumari—finding the chest in the cave had only reinforced this belief—but Raju did have a point. They needed to keep the boy close, and the family's distrust would present a challenge.

As the twins hurried through the alleyways, Laxman, tending one of the antique stalls, instantly identified the two men. He remembered them from the earlier chaos that had resulted in a frantic chase through the bazaar. A fleeting look of suspicion crossed his face as he watched them. However, he returned his focus to his wares when he saw their determined strides carrying them away from his stall. He stored this piece of information in the back of his mind to mull over later.

Raju leaned in, keeping his voice low as they navigated the crowds. "We need to make this fast, Siddharth. The last thing we need is for the Sharma family to suspect we've got our own agenda. And besides, we need to be at the inn in case they ask us for help."

Siddharth nodded, his gaze never lingering too long on any face or object. "Agreed."

Finally, they arrived at the edge of the market, where the sea of humanity dwindled into small clusters. Two local security guards were standing by a rickety wooden enclosure. The atmosphere here was less vibrant, filled with an air of authority and intimidation. Two teenage boys were crammed inside the makeshift cell. They were visibly battered, with fresh bruises discoloring their youthful faces and abrasions on their exposed arms. The elder between them, a youth with shoulder-length, tangled hair and eyes that had seen too much too soon, locked his defiant gaze on Raju and Siddharth as they approached.

Raju took a deep breath to steady himself before speaking. "Gentlemen, you have some young lads who were performing a minor task for us here. Consider it an internal security audit, of sorts."

Skeptical glances were exchanged between the two guards.

One—a stocky man with a handlebar mustache—retorted, "An internal audit? With children who were caught trying to snatch a toy?"

Taking the cue, Siddharth discreetly moved closer, ensuring his forearm brand—a daunting rook—was in plain sight as he extended his hand in a silent offer of understanding. "Perhaps this will settle any issues they've caused," he stated firmly.

The sight of the seared skin in the image of the rook was enough to unnerve the guard. He fidgeted nervously, a lump forming in his throat as his eyes lingered on the symbol—a mark of power and authority. With a reluctant nod, he acknowledged its significance. "All right, but keep them out of trouble from now on," he murmured, clearly intimidated by the rook tattoo.

With a flick of a rusty key, the enclosure was opened. As the boys stepped out, the elder winced from the pain of his injuries.

Raju discreetly slipped some bills into the teen's tattered pocket. "I regret the beating you had to take. But this should make it right," Raju murmured.

The youth clenched his teeth, glancing at the money before locking eyes with Raju. "It's part of the job." The beginnings of a sly grin formed on his battered face.

"Stay on standby," Raju added. "We may require your unique skill set sooner than you think."

The teens nodded almost imperceptibly, their eyes gleaming with anticipation as they heard the instruction. The pair turned and slipped back into the bustling maze of Mahendrapal Bazaar. A moment later, they melted into the crowd, disappearing among the throng of people.

Raju had a gut feeling he and his brother were skimming the surface of a much deeper, dangerous game. Involving these teens had just introduced a volatile element, forging a strange alliance in this already complex quest. It was a contest of tricky moves and countermoves, and the stakes grew with each decision.

Siddharth, too, considered the broader implications of what they had just set in motion. He knew that in this treacherous quest, sometimes the line between assets and liabilities was as thin as the edge of a blade.

* * *

5:30 P.M.

Priya sat in her office, the ceiling fan forming oscillating shadows on the papers strewn across her desk. The muted hum of the blades was the only sound until the door creaked open, sending a chill down her spine. She looked up, startled, as Uncle Bhaskar entered the room with an air of ruthless authority. Instinctively, she stood to show respect, her heart pounding in her chest.

"Bhaskar Mamaji," she greeted, her voice trembling slightly. She walked over to him and knelt, kissing her hands and then touching his feet in a gesture of submission. The floor was cold against her bare knees. "I wish I had known you were coming. I would have prepared tea for you," she said as she stood.

"That is not necessary, Priya," Bhaskar replied. He walked over to the bar and dropped two cubes of ice into a crystal glass. He opened a bottle of Scotch, the liquid glinting amber in the light, and poured a small measure. He took a slow, deliberate sip, savoring the taste before he spoke.

"Raju and Siddharth put on an amazing performance today at the bazaar. Operation Twin Rook was a success! I would have paid money to see it." A smug smile played on his lips, savoring his own words as if they were fine wine.

Uncle Bhaskar named it 'Operation Twin Rook'? When did this happen? Priya mused, trying to understand his proclamation that the day's misadventure had been a success. *I thought the plan was to get the toy lamb?*

"Oh," Priya replied. She kept her voice even, though her mind scrambled to follow his logic. "So…we're progressing in the right direction?"

"I am confident my plan to gain their trust is working. I need to think of more ways to entrap them and then save them. It's like a cat playing with a mouse." His voice took on a sinister lilt. "They will be eating out of our hands soon, willing to do anything for Raju and Siddharth."

"I am glad your plan is working, Mamaji," Priya remarked, her voice steady despite the turmoil churning inside her.

He picked an apple from the fruit bowl and tossed it upward. In a swift motion, he drew his knife from its sheath and sliced the apple mid-air. One half landed neatly in his hand, while the other fell to the ground, rolling to a stop at Priya's feet. He took a bite, the crunch signaling his satisfaction. He then walked over to her, looming like a dark cloud.

"Looks like we'll have in no time. I'm glad I put you cousins together. It's been a long time since you've worked like this. It's kind of nice," Bhaskar said.

A rare hint of sentimentality crept into his voice, though to Priya, it felt more like a veiled threat. "I guess, Mamaji," Priya responded cautiously.

Bhaskar's expression hardened as he shifted the topic. "Now, about the local businesses. I've heard rumors some of them are getting a bit too comfortable. We need to remind them who's in charge. I want you to oversee the racketeering operations. Make sure our cut from the money laundering is consistent."

Priya nodded, understanding her role. "I'll handle it, Mamaji," she replied, her voice firm despite the dread pooling in her stomach.

Before leaving, Bhaskar's demeanor turned menacing. "If anything changes with the Sharma family, you are to inform me immediately. Is that clear?" His voice was cold, commanding—a reminder of his ruthless nature.

Fear didn't just freeze her—it flared. Hot in her throat. Cold in her spine.

Bhaskar turned and fixed her with a piercing gaze. "Is everything okay with the Sharmas?" His voice dropped to a dangerous whisper, like the hiss of a snake.

Priya hesitated for a split second, her mind racing. Bhaskar's eyes narrowed, sensing her uncertainty. He grabbed her shoulder, his fingers digging into her flesh, pulling her close until his face was inches from hers. His grip was excruciating, causing her to squirm.

"Mamaji, you're hurting me," Priya whimpered, her voice cracking under the pressure.

"Don't lie to me, Priya. You know how I hate liars. I'm trusting you. Don't fail me," he growled, his breath reeking from his lunch.

"I won't, Mamaji. You have my word. I will let you know everything."

Bhaskar held her gaze for a moment longer, his eyes boring into hers like daggers, then let her go. "Good, because I have eyes everywhere, Priya."

"Yes, Mamaji. I won't fail you," Priya assured him, her voice trembling.

"Perfect," Bhaskar said, satisfied.

Priya knelt down once more, kissing his feet. Without another word, he turned and left the room, his presence lingering.

She exhaled shakily, the tension in the room dissipating with his departure. She sat back at her desk, the oscillating shadows continuing their dance over the scattered papers, as she tried to steady her breathing and gather her thoughts. The pain from Bhaskar's grip burned on her shoulder, a reminder of the darkness controlling her life.

-10-
THE MYSTERY DEEPENS

रहस्यं गाढतरं भवति

6:06 P.M.

Surrounded by the array of artifacts strewn across the antique coffee table, the atmosphere in the Sharma family suite was dense with apprehension, threaded through with a restless energy no one could quite name. It was reminiscent of the charged air that announced an impending thunderstorm, as the room vibrated with the residual energy of the recently united pendants. The sensation transcended any natural explanation.

The clock on the mantel chimed six times—a small sound. Ravi looked up. Then he checked his phone. He frowned, paused, but said nothing. No one else noticed.

Amma approached Sophie, her eyes alight with both curiosity and something deeper—almost awe. "Let me see the pendant," she said softly, her voice laced with quiet reverence.

Sophie, trying to grasp the importance of the artifact, nodded and handed it over. "Sure."

As Amma held the pendant, her fingers traced its design, her brow furrowing slightly in thought. She turned it over, her eyes narrowing as she examined the craftsmanship. After a long pause, she called out, "Ray, doesn't this look like something your mother gave you when we got married?"

Pappa stepped forward, his gaze fixed on the pendant. "Maybe," he murmured. "I vaguely remember something like this. Strange."

For a moment, the room fell into a heavy silence. The clock continued anyway.

Sophie's voice broke through the tension, though nothing about the room felt settled. "So, what now?" She placed the united pendant back around her neck, her gaze lingering on the other artifacts scattered across the table, as if she could unlock their secrets by sheer force of will.

The group stared the eclectic pile, each person lost in thought.

Sophie continued. "I suggest we go back to the hidden chapel. This time, we should all go together. Pappa, we'll need you to translate the inscriptions on the doors there. They might tell us how to open them."

"What doors in the chapel?" Pappa asked. "What else about this chapel haven't you told me yet?" He leaned forward, eager to hear the information.

Sophie pulled up a chair and sat down next to Pappa, keen to tell him what she knew. "Once we got past the first door, we entered a small tunnel leading to the chapel. Inside, there were ten doors. We could not figure out how to open them."

Pappa went still. He did not respond right away. His eyes flicked back to the photograph, then to Sophie.

"Ten," he repeated quietly. Not as a question. As if testing the word. "Harrison, you said you took pictures of the chapel. Did you happen to get pictures of the doors?"

"Mom took the pictures. They're on her cell," Harrison answered.

"I'll pull up the photos," Sophie said. She stood and walked toward her coat hanging with the others, her fingers searching the pockets for her phone as she picked it up. A moment of uncertainty passed before a wave of panic washed over her, unmistakable in her suddenly tense shoulders and the sharp intake of breath. "It's not here; my phone is gone."

Sophie checked the same pocket again.

"Are you sure?" Ravi asked, patting his own pockets.

"Yes, I had it in my jacket pocket. It's not here," Sophie confirmed.

"Maybe it fell out when we were chasing the boys who took Sheepy?" Kiran suggested.

Sophie stilled. For a fraction of a second, something unreadable crossed her face—then it was gone. She moved quickly, slipping her hand into her jacket pocket. "It was here," she said, almost lightly, as if reassuring herself. She checked again, slower this time, turning the lining outward. "I had it in the bat cave… I must have dropped it."

"We should inform the police and file a report," Ravi suggested.

Sophie frowned. "Do we really need to do that? I'm sure it will turn up."

"How about Priya's uncle, the chief of police? He could help," Amma offered.

"Didn't we meet him at the bazaar today?" Sophie interjected.

Pappa nodded. "That's right, we did. No need to rush. We'll let Priya know in the morning."

Sophie glanced at the clock on the mantel. Morning felt

farther away than it should have. Time didn't feel right.

Harrison leaned closer to his father, lowering his voice. "Dad, you said the inn might be involved in shady dealings after we heard the chief of police with Priya in the lobby. Are you sure we should trust him?"

Ravi paused, weighing his words. "It's just a missing phone," Ravi said. "And he is law enforcement." He did not sound convinced. "Filing a report won't hurt. Plus, he caught the thieves at the market today. He seems to be looking out for us—after all, we're just tourists, right?"

"If you say so, Dad." Harrison frowned.

"Priya gave me her cell number," Amma said, reaching into her purse and taking out her phone. "I can try texting her."

"I'm sorry, Pappa. This was really important, and I let everyone down." Sophie's words trembled on her lips, burdened with a disappointment she couldn't help but internalize.

"Don't worry, Mom. I took a picture of the first door; let me get it," Harrison said reassuringly. He retrieved his phone and displayed the image. "Here, Pappa," handing over the phone.

Pappa studied the photo with a puzzled expression. He rotated both his head and the screen, attempting to decipher the image. "Hmm. The Kumari Mandala is not right; it's off a little."

"Yes, we figured out we had to align the compass points on the mandala to open a small door leading to a secret passage. That's how we found the chapel," Harrison confirmed.

"Very clever," Pappa praised.

"Is this door the same as the others you mentioned?" Pappa continued.

"No, this door was different as far as I could tell. All the other doors had fixed mandalas that could not be moved," Ravi answered.

Pappa returned his gaze to the screen on Harrison's phone. He squinted and readjusted the image with his fingers to enlarge it. He read the message written over the threshold of the door.

यो ऽनाहूतः हृदयं स्पृशति,
दीर्घकालगुप्ताः छायाः आवहति
तस्यैव इच्छया नीयते,
अन्यथा मृतानां मध्ये भवति॥

He looked up. "These are not instructions on how to open the door."

Harrison's forehead creased in confusion. "They're not?" He leaned closer. "Then what does it say?"

Pappa drew a long breath, his gaze fixed on the screen. "It's a warning, a curse of sorts. I read about this in the book I borrowed from the library."

"A warning?" Amma exclaimed.

"What type of warning?" Harrison asked, eager for an answer.

Sophie's hand latched onto Pappa's arm, her fingers digging into his sleeve. "Read it, Pappa, read it!" Her words were a blend of fear and urgency.

With a nod, Pappa readjusted his glasses. A hush fell over the room. He waited longer than necessary before speaking.

"'*Whosoever reaches for the Heart unbidden, summons shadows, long been hidden. By its will alone be led, or find thyself among the dead.*'"

Sophie gasped as she clutched the necklace around her neck. Its energy intensified as the warning was being read.

Cyrus, who had been quiet until now, furrowed his brow. "What does that mean?"

Sophie's voice was a whisper, the reality of their quest settling like a heavy shroud upon her shoulders. "Oh my. You're right, Pappa. It's definitely a warning—not to seek the Heart without being called!"

Harrison, his back stiffening, recalled Raju's ominous words in the van on their way to Chitwan. "'Those who dare to seek the Heart without a calling have been met with fates darker than the deepest abyss,'" he repeated, the memory of Raju's grave tale adding depth to the ancient warning they now faced.

"But wait, there is more," Pappa said as he examined the photograph intently.

"What, Pappa?" Ravi leaned in.

Pappa squinted as he peered closely at the image on the screen. "I can't make it out. There is a glare from the flash." He sighed in frustration.

Ravi straightened from his position, leaning over Pappa's shoulder, and moved toward the coffee maker. He poured himself another cup, his movements deliberate. "So, let me think," he mused, considering Pappa's translation. He reflected aloud, "The warning was on the door we used to enter the chapel. Remarkably, we passed through unscathed," he recounted thoughtfully. "Yet inside, we found ten more doors, none of which we could open." He paused, lifting his hand to scratch his head. "And the diamond was nowhere to be found."

Sophie interjected eagerly, "And a pendant. Don't forget we found the pendant."

"Yes, the pendant," Ravi confirmed, nodding toward Sophie to acknowledge her contribution to his thought process. "So, the Heart is on the other side of one of those doors?" he mused. "Did everyone else come up with the same conclusion?"

"That sounds possible," Harrison affirmed.

"Well, considering we are still alive," Sophie said slowly, "the Heart hasn't turned us away."

"That's true," Harrison agreed.

Just then, Amma's phone buzzed with a text message from Priya. She read it aloud for everyone to hear. "'The inn didn't find your handy. I will contact my uncle Bhaskar to start a police report. We can finish up the paperwork in the morning.'"

"Uncle Bhaskar to the rescue again," Ravi joked.

Harrison grinned. "Nice having the chief of police in the family. Talk about a *handy* connection."

Pappa chuckled. "Ha! Handy. I see what you did there."

Ravi grinned. "I guess Priya picked up on the word 'handy,' too. Looks like it's catching on."

Sophie was not amused. "Well," she said, after a moment, "that's all we can do for now." She turned to Harrison. "Can you check 'Find My Phone'? Maybe it will show up on there?"

"Already did it, Mom. I got nothing, but I did change the settings so no one can access it."

"What about the cloud? Maybe my photos had already been uploaded?"

"Checked that, too," Harrison confirmed. "Nothing there either."

"Thanks, Harrison." Her expression was grim.

"Don't worry, Sophie; it's just a phone," Ravi reassured her.

She nodded, looking at her husband. "You're right."

Still scrutinizing Harrison's image, Pappa suddenly remembered something. "Hold on a minute. Ravi, you mentioned a photograph you took at the temple. Why wasn't it mentioned earlier?"

Ravi hesitated, his brow creased as though he were dredging up a distant memory. "Ah, yes," he finally said, "I nearly forgot. When Cyrus and Kiran spun the temple's prayer wheels, they inadvertently activated something astonishing. As the wheels spun, a fleeting pattern of Sanskrit numbers materialized, glowing faintly for only a second before disappearing. I can only explain it as the prayer wheels themselves being infused with some sort of ancient power. Fortunately, I snapped a picture just in time."

Ravi pulled up the photograph on his camera and presented it to Pappa, who studied it intently. The characters seemed almost alive, captured in a burst of unexplained light.

"You're right. They're random numbers, 'पञ्च, त्रि, सप्त, चत्वारि, द्व, एक, षट्.' Five, three, seven, four, one, six," Pappa murmured, awestruck yet bewildered.

No one knew what it could mean.

Amma looked over Pappa's shoulder and struggled to make heads or tails of the numbers. Suddenly, a spark of inspiration flickered across her face. "The book, Ray. Maybe there's something about this arrangement of numbers in there."

Pappa, ever the scholar, retrieved the book he had borrowed from the library in Chitwan. The pages seemed to whisper secrets as he skimmed through them. Flipping to the final page, his expression turned to disappointment. "I don't see this sequence."

Amma sighed, feeling the burden of the night's mysteries weighing down on everyone. "Perhaps all the answers won't come tonight. Let's rest and see what tomorrow holds."

Pappa stood and placed his journal on the side table. The book stayed open.

The group nodded in agreement, a collective resignation

that none of them welcomed. Still, no one moved right away.

In the contemplative stillness, a subtle but mesmerizing glow began to emanate from one of the objects on the table, drawing everyone's gaze. The *bansuri*, an ancient Tibetan flute, radiated with a mystical light. Everyone watched, transfixed, as tiny particles swirled and coalesced, forming a mesmerizing cloud around the flute. Slowly, the particles settled upon it, as if beckoning them to notice it.

Amma whispered, "It wants us to play it."

Pappa hesitated, his hands shaking from the sheer wonder of the moment. As he raised the bansuri to his lips, the room was held in a magical embrace. Each note he played was instilled with longing, as though it were weaving tales of old and summoning echoes of legends long forgotten.

The room trembled—not physically, but in some indescribable way each could perceive but not quantify. As the sound from the flute wove through the air, the artifacts on the table glowed brighter. They were not just illuminated—it was as though they were communicating. Each object appeared to be influenced by the ancient tune of the flute.

The mystery of the unfathomable enveloped them, as if the walls and furnishings pulsed in rhythm with the music. The air appeared to shimmer, a visual echo of the bansuri's melody, which seemed to exist simultaneously in multiple dimensions as though a veil between worlds had thinned.

As the final note dissolved into the silence, the shadows in the room seemed to shift. The old chair Kiran had called angry—still untouched in the corner—creaked once, though no one had moved. A seam in its cushion had split wider.

No one mentioned it.

But Cyrus pressed in tighter against Sophie's side, and Harrison's eyes flicked to the chair, then away. The room held its breath a little longer. It reverberates. Like the bansuri itself.

"What does all this mean?" Sophie finally asked. "What are we dealing with here?"

"It's like the story the man told us. The one about the bowls that sing," Kiran said, his mind processing the moment. He pondered the shopkeeper's words. *'Its rich, resonating sound had the power to heal the wounded hearts and troubled minds of those who heard it.'*

"You're right, Kiran! It's the same magical harmony," Sophie agreed.

Amma spoke with introspection. "I'm beginning to feel the world as we know it may hold more secrets than we ever imagined. There's a depth to our existence, layers we've yet to understand or uncover." She paused. "Perhaps this quest isn't about the pursuit of a diamond. Maybe, just maybe, it's a journey leading us closer to understanding something deeper within ourselves." Her words lingered with a gentle invitation to ponder the unseen and the unexplored.

In that quiet moment, a profound realization slowly began to bloom within them: perhaps the true essence of divinity was not found in external pursuits but deep within. The Sharma family started to see their quest in a new light, recognizing it was less about the quest for power or wealth in the form of this diamond. Instead, it was about being chosen by the Spirit of Kumari, a call to embark on a transformative journey of inner enlightenment. The Heart of Kumari, steeped in mystical significance, beckoned not to those driven by material desires but to those seeking a deeper understanding of their true selves. They were starting to realize this journey was about confronting personal fears, peeling back the layers of their existence, and unveiling the essence of who they truly are. It was a path not just to a fabled artifact but to the core of their own being, where the most profound discoveries awaited.

Among the sea of reflective faces, Kiran broke the mystified silence. Drawing upon memories of the concealed charm given to Cyrus, he posed a question that resonated with innocence and profound insight. "How did somebody else know the necklace was hidden inside Sheepy?"

Cyrus stiffened at Kiran's question, his heart racing. He knew the answer, but a deep-rooted fear kept his lips sealed. He remembered it vividly—the stranger who had taken him aside, a cold hand gripping his shoulder a little too tightly, the voice a low, menacing whisper. *'If you say a word about the necklace, something very bad will happen. You don't want that, do you?'*

His mind flashed back to the moment the man tried to take Sheepy from him, his fingers brushing against the hidden necklace, eyes gleaming with a sinister knowledge. *The bad man saw it; he knew I put it in there.* Cyrus had been terrified, too scared to stop him, too scared to tell anyone. *What if something bad really did happen?*

He couldn't bear the thought. It's why he had begged for the little brass bell earlier—it was for Sheepy's protection. If someone tried to take him again, Cyrus wanted to hear it. He wanted Sheepy to make noise.

His stomach churned with guilt and fear. He wanted to speak up, to tell the truth. *But what if he's still watching? What if he's listening right now?* Cyrus cast a quick glance around the room, feeling eyes on him even when there were none.

The room's contemplative atmosphere dissolved, pierced by an incisive question that cut through the air as tangibly as the wind rustling the leaves outside the open window. This query exposed a vulnerability, a flaw in the armor they had thought to be impenetrable. It let in a chilling draft of uncertainty, forming a shadow of doubt that hovered over the group. The moment marked a shift, a subtle crack in the façade of certainty they had built and believed in, leaving them adrift in the complexities of their quest.

Ravi promptly got up and closed the window, the lock clicking into place with finality. "We need to be more cautious. Someone must have seen Cyrus put the pendant in the lamb. The temple square was a sea of people." He paced back and forth, as though the act could help untangle his thoughts. "Literally anyone could have been watching him. We're not as inconspicuous as we'd like to think."

Cyrus shifted uncomfortably, pulling himself closer to his mother. His small body pressed tightly against her side as he nestled his head into her shoulder, seeking comfort to shield against the rising worry he couldn't escape.

Sophie sat on the couch, diligently stitching Sheepy's torn fabric with a hotel mending kit. She couldn't help but express her anxiety. "It's unsettling to think we might be under surveillance." She then looked up and added, "Perhaps it's those men we encountered at the lake. You know, the ones in the boat with the suits."

Harrison contemplated the situation. "You mean the men staying in this inn," he clarified.

"What?" Amma turned to him.

Pappa's voice came slower this time, measured. "What do you mean, 'staying in this inn'?"

Harrison shifted. "Before the bat cave…when I went back for my phone. I saw them. Same suits. Same faces. Just a few doors down."

Pappa didn't speak at first. His gaze lingered on Harrison. Then, he looked past him, toward the drawn curtain. "Could be nothing," he said at last. "Coincidence, maybe. Or not."

Kiran's voice broke the hush. "Mama…is someone watching us?"

Sophie stopped stitching and pressed a hand to his cheek. "I don't know, baby." Her eyes flicked to the door, then she turned to Ravi. "Shouldn't we say something about them?"

"No…" His voice caught, then steadied. "Pappa's right. Their presence may not be related to our quest, or they could be a ruse to distract us. Besides, their suits give them away; they look too much like some sort of officials."

Harrison stroked his chin. "Had we met Raju before we went to the Monkey Temple?"

"What does that matter?" Pappa grumbled.

"I'm trying to piece together the timeline."

Amma looked up, her gaze unfocused as she searched her memory. "Yes, we had already been introduced to him. He had saved Kiran from the truck the morning before. But he is so nice and helpful. I can't imagine Raju has anything to do with this."

Sophie pulled Kiran close.

Harrison sat there, Amma's words circling back through him. He couldn't shake the unease settling low in his stomach. "Yeah…maybe."

"There's no reason to believe it's Raju," Sophie said, biting the thread clean with her teeth. "Like Pappa said, there were hundreds of people at the temple that day. It could have been anyone."

Pappa nodded slowly. "We may be looking in the wrong direction entirely." He rested his hands on the table, fingers steepled—not thoughtful. Calculating. "Or," he added quietly, "we're looking too narrowly."

No one spoke.

Ravi stopped pacing The silence shifted when he did. "Whether it's Raju or not…" he said at last. He didn't finish the sentence right away.

The room seemed to wait for him. "What matters," he continued, voice lower now, "is that this didn't begin at the temple."

Harrison felt it land.

"It didn't begin at the lake," Ravi went on. "And it didn't begin in the cave."

Sophie's stitching slowed.

Cyrus's bell gave a soft, accidental chime. Ravi didn't look at it. "It means," he said evenly, "we weren't stumbled upon."

The words settled like weight.

Kiran swallowed. "So…someone is watching us?"

Ravi met his eyes. "Yes." No elaboration. No softening. "From now on," he said, "we assume that's true." He paused. "And we assume it's not random." The words did not rise. They settled.

No one argued. No one reassured.

Sophie's fingers tightened in Sheepy's wool.

And for the first time, the room didn't feel like theirs.

***

6:55 P.M.

As darkness fell upon the Surya Chandra Inn, Priya and Anil were immersed in their tasks at the front desk. The bulb of a lamp cast an eerie light on their work, highlighting the ancient stone masonry of the lobby. Their responsibilities were varied—organizing the next day's bookings, updating guest records, and meticulously planning the breakfast service for the morning. The lobby, usually a hub of activity, had quieted down, a stillness after the bustle of the day. The faint scent of burning wood and the gentle rustle of leaves in the evening breeze filtered through the open window, bringing with it a sense of quiet serenity.

The quiet atmosphere was abruptly disturbed as Siddharth and Raju ran through the front door, nearly toppling a takeaway delivery man in their haste.

Siddharth rushed to Priya, his breath uneven, his words tumbling out. As he moved, the binding at the back of his head slipped loose. His long hair fell forward, half-shadowing his face. "Priya, we need to talk. Right now." His eyes were too bright. "It's…it's important. You need to contact Sunjata—the curator…at the museum—"

"I know who Sunjata is," Priya interrupted.

Siddharth blinked, momentarily thrown off, before quickly continuing. "Right, right. Sorry. I've got Sophie's handy, and…and there's information on it. Photos—there are photos. Of the discovery Harrison made…in the bat cave today." He reached back to secure his hair, but the knot wouldn't hold. "These could be…I mean, they might be…really important clues."

Raju, sensing the need to clarify, interjected. "Let me explain." His face showed a complex blend of irritation and earnestness. "It's becoming clear the Sharma family's trust in us is declining," he admitted, his cadence carrying an undertone of frustration.

Priya was quick to respond, and she didn't mince words. Her voice was sharp, cutting through Raju's façade. "You mean *your* actions have led them to distrust *you*, not *me*." She challenged him with a piercing gaze.

In an attempt to maintain his composure, Raju brushed off her pointed correction, a spark of annoyance etched across his face. "That's just a minor detail," he responded, attempting to downplay her accusation. "What matters now is we need Sunjata to mislead them. She must make them believe the gold box they found is meaningless. Perhaps a prop from the movie they are filming." His voice grew more calculating, deceit creeping into his words. "She should be able to spin a tale that will throw them completely off track." His proposal revealed the depth of his scheming.

Anil, silently observing the exchange, chose that moment

to express his concern. Stepping forward, his brow creased in puzzlement, he looked questioningly at Raju and Siddharth. "Why are we trying to mislead the Sharma family? Don't we need them to find the Heart of Kumari?"

His question remained, highlighting the potential conflict in their plans and casting doubt on the path they were choosing to take.

Realizing he had acted impulsively—spurred on by Siddharth's excitement—Raju took a deep breath, striving to approach the situation with composure and thoughtfulness. "We can't discuss this here. Let's find a quiet place to sit down and have a calm conversation."

"Why don't you all come to my office?" Priya suggested. "It's a quiet and comfortable space, perfect for discussing this matter in more depth. I have some refreshments there, and we can have a productive conversation."

***

6:58 P.M.

The glow from the bansuri had long since faded, but the room did not feel entirely returned to itself. The air held a thin aftercurrent, as though something had passed through and left the door slightly ajar.

Harrison sank onto the couch and drew the brittle library book back into his lap. The spine gave a soft crack as he turned the torn page again, though he already knew what it said.

His eyes lingered on the caption written on the torn page. Kumari Talisman—needed to find the Heart of Kumari.

He looked up—just briefly—toward the pendant resting at his mother's throat. Then back to the page.

Amma was the first to move. "I'll set the table," she said

gently, as if restoring balance required something practical.

She crossed to the old sideboard and opened its lower cabinet. The hinges gave a soft protest. Inside, a stack of porcelain plates sat wrapped in thin paper. She unwrapped them one by one and set them on the dining table near the window. The sound of ceramic touching wood felt louder than it should have.

Pappa joined her, drawing out cutlery from a felt-lined drawer—forks, knives, a few mismatched spoons. He aligned them carefully beside each plate, the metal catching the lamplight.

Cyrus rang Sheepy's bell once, absentmindedly. The chime carried.

Sophie glanced at the clock above the mantel. "It's getting late," she said, almost to herself.

Ravi checked his phone. "Seven," he replied. "It'll come."

She nodded, but her fingers went to the pendant at her throat. The stone felt warmer than the room.

Kiran peered toward the door. "Do you think they're lost?"

"No," Amma said lightly. "Food always finds its way."

Another minute passed. Then another.

Sophie stood and moved toward the door, as if listening for something beyond it. "It's been a while," she murmured. "Maybe we should call."

Ravi looked up. "Let's give it a few more minutes."

The clock ticked. Steady. Unbothered.

Sophie exhaled slowly and returned to the table, smoothing a napkin that didn't need smoothing. The pendant rested against her collarbone, still, as though it were waiting too.

She turned toward the sideboard.

"I think I'm going to have a little wine," she said, almost lightly.

Ravi looked up. "Long day."

Amma gave a small nod. "Pour me some as well."

Sophie opened the cabinet beneath the carved wood. A bottle stood beside two unused glasses, faint dust along the rim. She wiped them with the edge of a towel and poured carefully, the soft glug of liquid briefly louder than the ticking clock.

She handed one to Amma.

"Thank you," Amma said.

They took a sip. The warmth spread—but it did not quiet the room.

A knock came at last.

Not loud. Not urgent. Just three firm raps against the wood.

Ravi stood, paused, and looked through the peephole before sliding the bolt back.

Steam drifted in with the delivery man—cardboard containers stacked in his arms, the scent of garlic and soy and chili cutting through whatever lingered from the flute.

Ravi stepped aside to let him in just enough to set the bags on the entry console. He counted out the cash from his wallet, added a few extra notes, and accepted the change without checking it. The delivery man gave a quick nod and left as quietly as he had arrived.

The bolt slid back into place.

Ordinary. And yet, as the door shut and the bolt clicked again, the family did not quite relax.

Harrison rose from the couch and carried the brittle library book to the coffee table. He left it open to the torn page before joining the others at the table.

***

7:15 P.M.

Priya's office exuded sophistication, with dark wooden furnishings and subdued ambient lighting. A well-crafted bar stood in one corner, its polished wood boasting a mirror-like gleam. The couch, a plush leather masterpiece, sat invitingly in the center, its deep burgundy hue beautifully complementing the room's earthy tones.

Along the far wall, the bookcase rose toward the ceiling, its dark wood set deep into the old stone, as if the room had been built around it. Above the top shelf, a smooth plaster band ran the width of the wall. Near the ceiling, a narrow iron ventilation slit cut through it, dust clinging faintly to its ribs. Just below the vent, a hairline seam traced the plaster—straight, deliberate, easily mistaken for a settling crack.

With a calm demeanor, Priya poured herself a generous measure of whisky, the rich amber liquid nearly filling her glass. She then turned her attention to Raju and Siddharth. "Would any of you like something to drink?"

"I'll have what you're having," Raju replied.

Siddharth echoed his sentiment.

Anil strolled over to the opulent couch and settled into its embrace. The couch featured decorative leather stitching, and it cradled him in comfort. His drink from earlier in the evening had already been placed neatly on a coaster sitting on the side table.

Raju accepted his glass from Priya and seated himself beside Anil. He leaned in and said, "Do you want to know why we don't need the Sharma family to lead us to the Heart of Kumari?" His words held a menacing subtlety.

Intrigued, Anil responded, "Yes. I thought they were the chosen ones."

Raju leaned back, taking a sip of his drink. A calculating

look played in his eyes. "Yes, they are. But their trust in us is waning. We know where the key is, and we now possess the last clue to the diamond's location. Our success depends on Sunjata at the museum. We are more than capable of finding the Heart without the Sharma family."

Priya mulled over his cunning strategy; the allure of securing the diamond without involving the Sharma family gnawed at her thoughts. She recognized the merit in Raju's assertion—they could acquire the Heart of Kumari independently. In her view, the Sharma family was becoming more of an impediment than an asset. Yet, a hint of doubt crept in.

"How can we be certain Sophie's photographs will uncover the diamond's whereabouts?" she queried.

"That's where Sunjata comes in," Siddharth assured her. "She'll analyze the photos of the box and extract the needed information. I'm confident it will show the way to the diamond's location."

Anil hesitated before addressing the question that had been weighing on him. "What about the part of the legend that says only the chosen one can seek the diamond?"

Raju's eyes blazed with determination. "The legend says *our* family is destined to find the Heart. This quest is *ours*, and I won't let the Sharma family steal our legacy. The Kumari stared into my eyes as well—I'm certain I'm the one who is destined to find the diamond." His gaze swept across the room, locking eyes with each family member. "We are the chosen ones. *Our* bloodline! Not that boy!"

Siddharth pondered his brother's words. "When I looked at the goatskin, I felt a deep calling. It changed something inside me, leading us to the clue. I'm convinced you're right, brother. We've been chosen for this mission."

A hush fell over the room as Raju and Siddharth's words sank in. The weight of the moment was undeniable. Their family legacy was written into the ancient books and legends, stretching back generations. Raju, Siddharth, Priya, and Anil had always believed they were destined for this quest—a belief that had only grown stronger after discovering their family names inscribed in the very book found in the inn where they now gathered.

This conviction wasn't theirs alone; the Shatranj Ke Sipahi, too, supported them, holding their breath in anticipation for their success.

Priya had once felt the same fire in her veins, a passion that had slowly dulled over the years as doubt crept in. Yet with Raju and Siddharth's return, something had stirred within her. Their resolve had rekindled a spark she thought long extinguished, pulling her back into the fold of destiny. She met Raju's eyes, a flicker of her old conviction reigniting. *Could they truly be the ones? Was this my moment?*

With the weight of generations resting on their shoulders, Priya knew there was no turning back. "We should inform Uncle Bhaskar of the change of plans," Priya suggested hesitantly. The very mention of his name sent a shiver down her spine.

Raju almost choked on his drink, his eyes wide with panic. "No," he said, quickly regaining his composure but not his color. "I mean, not just yet. Let's not make him aware the family has lost trust in us. He's counting on that trust. We don't need to worry him unnecessarily."

"But if he finds out without us telling him," Priya countered, her voice trembling, "his anger might be even worse. You know how he gets when he's deceived."

Siddharth frowned, his expression darkening as he considered the consequences. The room seemed to grow colder, shadows creeping along the walls, as if drawn by their fear.

They all knew too well how Bhaskar could react—his temper was a living thing, unpredictable and deadly.

"Raju's right," Siddharth said, his voice steady but low, almost a growl. "We need to have all the pieces in place first. Then, we can confront him with the evidence—we can find the Heart without the Sharmas."

Raju nodded, swallowing hard. "Exactly. If we go to him now, without any proof, he'll see it as a sign of our failure and lack of confidence. It's better to handle this on our own and present him with the results later."

Priya sighed. "I just hope we're making the right decision."

Anil stood up and paced the room. "What about the pendant hidden inside the toy lamb the boy, Cyrus, possesses? We need that to present to Uncle Bhaskar." He ran a hand through his hair, exasperated. "Our last attempt ended in failure."

Priya's voice hitched. "Ha! Not according to Uncle Bhaskar." She turned toward Raju and Siddharth, addressing them directly. "He came in here touting your praises. Even had a name for it: 'Operation Twin Rook.'" She took a sip of the liquid swirling in the glass. "Apparently, he does not understand the importance of the Talisman."

"Uncle Bhaskar is all about strategy," Siddharth commented, leaning back against the plush cushions. "Operation Twin Rook was not about getting the necklace; it was about gaining their trust. We knew exactly how the scene was going to play out, and it did, perfectly."

He retied the leather cord at the back of his head, tighter this time. He met Raju's eyes. "Well done, brother."

His twin let the compliment settle before lifting his glass. "Thank you, Siddharth."

"Too bad it didn't achieve our goal," Anil smirked. "I thought we already had their trust."

"Yeah, well…" Raju faltered. "Apparently, Uncle Bhaskar wasn't as convinced."

Priya's eyes narrowed as the realization hit. "So, it was

never about getting the lamb?" The sharp sting of betrayal spread through her thoughts. *It was my idea, and he changed it. Uncle Bhaskar had assured me the street boys would retrieve it, but now it all makes sense—his strange demeanor in my office earlier, the fact that he said it was a success, the shift in plans.* "I get the feeling he wants to draw this out, like he enjoys watching the Sharma family squirm."

"Well, he's putting us through anguish, too," Anil added, slumping into a chair and rubbing his temples as if trying to ward off a headache.

Priya sighed, her fingers caressing the glass containing her drink. "You're right. I think he likes to make us suffer as well." She continued, her tone bitter. "He gets a thrill out of it." She lifted the glass, her eyes narrowing as she studied the way the ice glimmered through the crystal, and a memory suddenly resurfaced with brilliant clarity—a brutal memory that she had been trying to bury.

She saw Khan's lifeless body dragged before her, the scene seared into her mind like a scar. His dead eyes, hollow and vacant, stared back at her through the bruises and burns that marred his tortured frame.

She blinked, trying to shake the memory. "We need to be careful. We're caught in his dangerous game."

Anil pressed on, trying to wrap his mind around the situation. "Raju, why did you and Uncle Bhaskar give the lamb back? We were so close."

Raju crossed his legs and leaned back. His response was deliberate. "As I said, our intention was to preserve their trust," he explained. "Unfortunately, it seems to have yielded the opposite result. Now, I think they're starting to get suspicious of us."

Anil's jaw tightened, but he gave a curt nod. "I see," he said, his pride preventing any further questions. Clearly, he had been left out of the plan.

Priya spoke. "Another reason why we can't tell Uncle Bhaskar. If he realizes Operation Twin Rook has failed, he will blame it on us, and it will be our necks."

They all contemplated this unsettling truth in silence.

Priya turned to Raju, "And Sujan? Sunjata's twin. Did he report anything after taking the Sharmas out on the lake?"

Siddharth's words slipped out through his teeth. "Bhaskar won't risk his son. Sujan is only another pair of eyes."

Anil shook his head. "He must have seen or heard something."

Raju answered. "Nothing. Only that others may be watching."

"Others?" Priya questioned.

"Then we move quickly," Anil said.

Something tightened behind Priya's ribs—an instinct, sharp and unwelcome. The room seemed to narrow around her. She caught Raju's glance, seized the thread he had offered. "I'll suggest they go to the museum in the morning. Sunjata can get the box, and while they're out, I'll have the street kids search their room. We'll see what clues they might have hidden."

Raju leaned in. "We've just returned from the Mahendrapal Bazaar," he explained. "We bailed out those street kids; they're eager and fully prepared for their next assignment."

"Fantastic. At least we have them on our side," Anil remarked.

Priya rose from her seat. "Then all we need now is the pendant." She moved like a shadow toward the window, her thoughts as dark as the night outside. She stared into the abyss, the curtains rippling around her like the whispers of specters conspiring with her silent musings.

The faint stir of air was like a breath, wrapping her in

its subtle veil, as the wheels of treachery turned in her mind.

"I'll take care of that myself," Raju declared assertively. "I'll patiently await the perfect moment to secure it. Once we possess the necklace and the precise location of the diamond, we will inform Uncle Bhaskar—and we will execute the retrieval ourselves."

Anil glanced at him, hesitant. "What about the Sharmas? Won't they be in the way?"

Raju's smile was cold, calculated. "If they become an issue, we'll deal with them. One way or another, they won't stand in our way."

"Then it's settled," Priya proclaimed, a devious smirk on her lips. The weight of blame in the case of failure had shifted from her shoulders to Raju's. She pivoted away from the window, the curtains swirling in her wake like dark waters. Raising her glass with the poise of a chess master moving into checkmate, she toasted with steely assurance. "To the Heart of Kumari!"

Raju, Siddharth, and Anil followed suit, holding their glasses aloft as symbols of their unified front.

With a collective tilt of their heads, they downed their drinks.

Out side, the wind shifted.

Inside, the glasses touched the table one by one.

-11-
A DAY AT THE MUSEUM

संग्रहालयदिवसः

NOVEMBER 13TH
7:00 A.M.

A gentle breeze stirred the lace curtains as the family gathered for breakfast in the dining hall. It was a grand affair, an expansive spread of culinary offerings that paid homage to Nepali traditions and Western comforts. Fruits, cereals, bread, pastries, local cheeses, and various popular dishes filled the table.

The aroma of freshly baked naan mingled with the pungent scent of yak cheese, while plates of glistening *gundruk*, fermented leafy greens, sat next to bowls of *chatamari*, a kind of Nepali rice crepe. Traditional masala tea perfumed the air, its spiciness contrasting with the sweetness of mango lassi. Everyone had a glass in front of them except for Sophie, who had opted for freshly squeezed orange juice.

"Everyone, dig in. The food is getting cold," Amma said, breaking the silent appreciation for the meal.

Sophie picked up a slice of naan, its warm fluffiness absorbing the seasoned ghee she spread. She savored the first bite, letting the harmony of flavors and textures settle on her palate before speaking. "So, we have a mystery box from a bat cave, and we have no idea how it fits into the puzzle for the Heart of Kumari. What's the plan?"

Already halfway through his serving of spiced *daal* and rice, Ravi swallowed before responding. "It is an anomaly, yes. Perhaps a detour is warranted. We could visit the Pokhara Museum. Their collections include artifacts dating back centuries. There's a good chance they'll have something similar, or at least, information leading us to understand its significance."

Amma, who had been placing pieces of fried okra onto her plate, looked up. "I agree. Besides, the museum also has several displays on local folklore and mythology. There might be background information we've overlooked. Not to mention, we can inquire about the Kali Raatri and our ancestor Gopal."

Harrison, enjoying a cheese-filled pastry, weighed in. "I guess it can't hurt to look into it. But I doubt we'll ever find his last name." He paused and looked contemplative. "On the other hand, it's weird, though, isn't it? We find this box, and it doesn't have the Kumari Mandala on it. It doesn't seem to fit in. Like it's a red herring or something."

Pappa chuckled, lifting his cup of masala tea for a sip. The warm, spiced liquid awakened something in him. "Ah, but life is full of red herrings, Harrison. Do they distract us, or do they lead us to something more extraordinary?"

Kiran, who had been quietly enjoying his mango lassi, finally spoke. "I want to go to the museum."

Amma nodded. "Perfect! I felt this might be important, so I did some groundwork for Sophie, and I filled out the police report for her lost phone this morning. Priya says the museum is a short drive from the inn." She looked down at her watch. "It opens in an hour. That gives us plenty of time to wrap up breakfast and get ready." She paused and mentioned, "Priya also suggested it's a worthwhile visit."

No one questioned it. Priya and Anil ran the inn. Whatever history they carried, the Sharmas hadn't glimpsed it—at least not clearly. Ravi might've caught a flicker. A name offered too smoothly. A pause too rehearsed. But he said nothing.

Not yet.

His hand rested on the table, steady but tense. Then Ravi interjected with a note of caution. "Let's be clear, we don't say a word about the Heart of Kumari. Our official reason for the visit is to learn more about Harrison's treasure box from the bat cave and anything they might know about Gopal. Understood?" His gaze circled the table, making sure everyone was in agreement.

A chorus of nods and murmurs met his statement. As each family member turned his or her attention back to the diminishing breakfast spread, there was an unspoken understanding that their trip to the museum would be anything but ordinary. What they would find at the Pokhara Museum was anyone's guess, but as forks were set down and the last sips of tea and lassi were taken, each knew this detour could offer answers as vital as those sought in the original quest for the Heart of Kumari. After all, in the complex game of destiny and choice, unplanned detours often lead to the most astonishing revelations.

09:11 A.M.

In the glow of the Surya Chandra Inn's lobby, where the hum of gentle conversations mingled with the cascade of piano melodies trickling down from hidden speakers, Kiran and Cyrus trailed behind their mother, followed by Harrison. Their expressions were illuminated by the light of the sconces as they walked across a marble floor resembling a giant chessboard. They marveled at the details of the room.

In the corner was a table crowned with a chess set. It was an unassuming piece of the lobby's charm, its figures polished by the hands of countless guests seeking a quiet respite. The game stood ready, the bronze and pewter pieces arranged in their starting positions, inviting a moment of thoughtful battle.

Sophie navigated through the lobby's gentle murmur. She found Raju and Siddharth seated discreetly in a corner by the grand bookcase dominating the back wall, their heads close together in earnest discussion. As Sophie approached, she gave a warm smile. "Well, don't you look nice today, Raju."

Raju, dressed sharply in a suit and tie, returned her smile with a slight nod. "Thank you, madam. I do try to look my best."

"Well, it's working," she said with a playful lilt.

Siddharth, observing the exchange, raised an eyebrow at his cousin before turning to Sophie with a small grin. "Anything we can do for you, Sophie? Any plans for the day?"

"Actually, yes," Sophie replied, her voice bright with curiosity. "We were hoping you might take us to the museum. We think there could be some significance to Harrison's box he found yesterday, and we'd love to know more about it."

Raju and Siddharth exchanged a quick, meaningful glance, understanding the significance of her request—*Priya was able to convince the Sharma family to go to the museum.*

Meanwhile, Cyrus, whose curiosity was as boundless as his energy, was the first to spot the chess table. The table stood as an island of quiet retreat amidst the sea of soft laughter and clinking cups.

"Look over there, Kiran. Do you want to play?"

"Oh. That looks like fun!"

Seeing his brothers' interest, Harrison caught up and offered his knowledge. "You want me to teach you? Come on." They moved toward the chess sanctuary they had discovered.

Raju watched the Sharma boys walk over and sit down. He contemplated for a moment. His gaze settled on the rook before he focused his attention back on Sophie. "Of course, madam," Raju said smoothly. "We'd be more than happy to take you there."

He folded the map he had been studying and placed it back in his pouch. His attentive demeanor displayed optimism.

Siddharth, too, perked up at Sophie's suggestion, offering a grin. "The museum it is, then. The exhibits might speak to us in more ways than one."

Harrison slid into the chair like a seasoned player, his movements slow and deliberate. With the impulsive joy of youth, Kiran bounded onto his lap, his eager expression fixed on the gleaming pieces. More reserved but no less intrigued, Cyrus pulled out his chair and sat opposite, his gaze tracing the patterns of the chessboard's squares, which copied the design of the lobby's marble floor. He looked up to the staircase and was struck by the sight of the pillars anchoring the railing, their forms mirroring the pawns arranged before him.

Sophie called over to her children. "Don't be too long. We're leaving soon."

"This is the king," Harrison began, his finger resting on the tallest piece, its crown commanding respect even in miniature. "The object of the game is to capture the king." His hand shifted to the queen—her form elegant yet fierce. "The queen, however, is the most powerful piece on the board."

Kiran's hand hovered over the smallest of the warriors. "And what is this one called?"

"That," Harrison replied with a gentle tilt of his head, "is the pawn."

Kiran furrowed his brow. "And what does the pawn do?"

Harrison's face softened as he regarded the pawn, thinking it was, perhaps, a reflection of his youngest brother's innocence. "The pawn is like the little hero—until it isn't. It's small, but it's very brave, and sometimes it goes on a big adventure to protect everyone else, especially the king. It's all about being courageous, even when you're not the biggest or the strongest." His words were gentle, a bittersweet lesson on the harsh realities of sacrifice and duty.

"Do you think I'm a pawn?" Kiran questioned. "I'm small and brave."

Harrison didn't answer right away. "Maybe," he said finally. "But don't worry." His eyes stayed on the board. "The pawn is the one that goes first."

From the other side of the room, Siddharth's attention lingered on Harrison, who was guiding Cyrus and Kiran through the game. Then, feeling the press of time, he interjected. "As always, time is of the essence." He took one last sip of his jasmine tea before the china cup met the saucer with a soft clink.

"We'll get the van ready," Raju said with a smile.

Raju and Siddharth got up from their armchairs, their movements synchronized.

As they walked past the front desk, Priya flashed a smile. "Enjoy your day."

Harrison, Cyrus, and Kiran became further engrossed in the complexities of the chess game, Sophie's voice reached across the room to them. "Boys, it's time to go to the museum."

"We can continue this later," Harrison suggested, lifting Kiran from his lap and standing up.

Cyrus grabbed his lamb and rose to follow.

The game paused; the lessons of chess would have to wait. With one last look at the pieces—each carrying a story yet to unfold—the brothers returned to the world, their minds a little wiser, their bond a little stronger.

As the Sharma family exited the lobby, the light shifted causing a glint to run across the chessboard's edge. Beneath the queen's square, three letters caught the sun for the briefest instant—B L O—then vanished.

***

10:17 A.M.

With a gentle push on the gas pedal, Raju pulled away from the curb, his eyes caught by the sight of Cyrus clutching his lamb in the back seat. With its hidden secret, the lamb seemed to sense Raju's intentions, and its glass eyes held a glint of misgiving. Raju's mind churned, not with the guilt of the impending theft but with its mechanics. *How do I navigate the delicate dance of deception to relieve Cyrus of his cherished toy without arousing suspicion?*

As they left behind the sanctuary of the inn's lobby, the car hummed toward the museum. Raju's grip on the steering wheel tightened, the thrill of the hunt sparking in his veins. Meanwhile, oblivious to Raju's inner dialogue, Cyrus gazed out the window, lost in thoughts of the chess game—its kings and queens, the strategic battles on the board, and the pearls and perils of each calculated move.

With a blend of trepidation and excitement, the Sharma family ventured toward the museum, absorbed in their individual thoughts but united by a singular mission. Unbeknownst to them, a shadowy, hooded figure had been observing their movements, waiting patiently for the Sharma family to leave. A cryptic smile formed on his lips as he watched them disappear into the cacophony of Pokhara's streets.

***

11:00 A.M.

The museum rose in pale stone and dark beams, its eaves strung with prayer flags that snapped in the cool wind. Two lions flanked the entrance, their jaws frozen in eternal warning.

Inside, the air pressed heavy and still. Heat radiated from the stone walls, pulling the chill from their skin. The Sharmas unzipped their jackets, exchanging murmurs about the warmth.

The grand lobby spread wide, the floor a grid of polished stone. At its center stood a great prayer wheel, bronze and shoulder-high, its surface carved with mantras worn smooth by touch. Bands of vermilion and turquoise paint clung to its fluted sides, the pigments faded but still vivid in the half-light. Gold leaf lingered in the deeper grooves, catching glints of the sun that fell through the high windows. It seemed to wait, steady and silent, for the next pilgrim to set it turning. No one did.

To the right, a bank of lockers lined the wall, each marked with a shiny brass number. Raju lifted his chin toward them. "It's warm in here," he said. "You may prefer to leave the jackets here. Easier than holding them all afternoon."

Ravi glanced at Sophie. "We'll keep them."

"As you wish." Raju's smile held.

As they walked deeper into the structure, Raju slowed

beside Cyrus. "You know," he said, "six is a fine age. Young men seldom carry toys. People may stare."

Kiran stepped between them. "He's not too old. I have my superheroes, and we're almost the same age."

Amma heard the exchange and turned. "He will grow out of it in time. For now, he is a boy." She paused. "Does it trouble you if he carries a toy?"

Raju straightened his tie. "Only a thought for appearances, madam." He smoothed his jacket. "I mention it only for his comfort, nothing more."

Siddharth lifted a hand. "Wait here. I'll see if we can speak with the curator." He moved off toward the desk, his steps measured.

Raju followed.

The Sharma family drifted along the displays that lined the main corridor.

Annapurna rose in a wall-sized relief—ridges and passes named in tiny brass plaques. Harrison's eyes traced the high line toward Thorong La, and a shiver passed through him.

Beneath the ridge, one plaque bore letters nearly lost to age—O O D L—their edges softened by tarnish, the meaning forgotten. The metal flared, then dulled, and no one saw.

Sophie was caught by a case of Gurung ornaments: silver crescents, coral beads, a comb of hammered gold that seemed cut from sunlight.

Kiran pressed his face close to a diorama of Phewa Lake, complete with miniature boats. The temple glimmered like a jewel in the water. "We were just there," he whispered, his breath clouding the glass.

Cyrus stood before a map of caves and karst, rings inked around dark mouths in the stone—Mahendra, Chamero. Sheepy's bell gave a faint chime.

"Chamero Gufa," Harrison said. "The Bat Cave. That's

where we were—I found the box there." His voice thinned as he looked again at the map. "I didn't know it had a name."

Ravi stopped before a panel titled FOOTSTEPS OF BUDDHA. The display showed a narrow path cut through stone, pilgrims bent against wind and snow. Beneath it, the inscription read:

SIDDHARTHA OF LUMBINI, BORN IN NEPAL, LEFT BEHIND HIS PALACE AND CROWN TO WALK THE ROADS OF MEN AS A SEEKER. ON THESE PATHS HE TURNED FROM THE WORLD OF KINGS TOWARD THE TRUTH OF SUFFERING, BECOMING THE BUDDHA.

Ravi whispered, almost to himself. "I didn't know Siddhartha, the Buddha, was born in Nepal."

They turned a corner. The Seti River cut the earth in a deep, white gorge on the wall photograph. Pappa stood a moment longer than the rest, listening to the roar the picture could not carry.

As he stepped away, something caught his eye—a stone rook half-hidden in a shadowed display. Beneath it, a weathered plaque described the late Kali Raatri period, the fracture within the Order, and a term recovered from damaged manuscripts: Kaali Shakti.

He paused, drawn to the carved edges of the rook and the unfamiliar phrase below it. He slipped his notebook from his coat and scratched a few quick lines, determined to hold the memory before it slipped into the noise of the day.

Amma lingered nearby, her attention fixed on a faded thangka that hung high on the wall. The deity's face was nearly erased by time, yet the eyes remained—dark, steady, watching. A chill rose on her arms as she studied them, a feeling she could not name settling at the base of her spine. She pulled her jacket close.

From behind them, Siddharth's voice called out. "Sunjata will see us now. This way." He gestured back toward the lobby.

Kiran broke from the group and ran toward him.

"Kiran—don't run," Amma called.

But Siddharth was already stepping forward. He caught the boy easily and lifted him, settling him against his hip as though it were the most natural thing in the world.

Kiran reached out and touched the loose curl that had fallen near Siddharth's cheek. "Your hair's longer than Mama's," he observed seriously. "Why don't you cut it?"

Cyrus hovered close, studying the dark waves. "It looks happy," he added.

A faint laugh moved through Siddharth's chest. He adjusted his grip on Kiran, then brushed the curl back from his face.

"Happy is good," he said.

Kiran leaned closer, still curious. "But why don't you cut it?"

Siddharth's fingers found the leather cord tied at the back of his head. "Because I promised not to." He set Kiran down gently. "Come," he said, turning toward the waiting wheel, heavy with mantras no one had yet dared to turn.

***

11:20 A.M.

As Raju, Siddharth, and the Sharma family wandered through the brightly lit corridors of the Pokhara Museum, the displays from various civilizations held their fascination. Sunjata, the museum's curator, guided their journey through the vast archives and exhibits, drawing her energy from their mysteries. Her smile wasn't merely warm; it expressed a thousand tales waiting to be told. Her countenance ignited, not with a spark of mere interest, but with the blaze of a storyteller deeply connected to the past. Her presence radiated history, much like the artifacts surrounding them, infusing the air with an aura of mystery.

"Harrison, you exude the spirit of an explorer. It's electrifying, like the air before a storm." Sunjata's voice personified a genuine excitement that elevated her words into something almost powerful. "I've heard our staff murmuring about a family—the Sharma family." She pivoted to make eye contact with each of them. She extended her arms outwards as if to present them to royalty. "Your family," she proclaimed with dramatic effect before wheeling around. She then resumed her stride across the room, her stilettos challenging the marble floor.

The family fell into a meditative silence, lulled by the clicks of Sunjata's heels as they echoed through the corridor. Riveted by her commanding presence, everyone's attention was fixed on her.

Breaking their trance, she continued, "Bringing your own artifacts into the museum is not an everyday occurrence. We welcome such remarkable discoveries with open arms."

Harrison, touched by the compliment, felt the flush of excitement rise in his cheeks. "It's been a family effort. We've all been bitten by the bug of curiosity. We want to learn the history behind this box we found."

Sunjata leaned in conspiratorially, her voice a blend of revelation and intrigue. "Your discoveries have resonated beyond these walls. Your family's adventures are arousing interest in certain circles and being whispered about in the hushed tones of folklore enthusiasts. You're rattling cages and tantalizing minds in realms you may not be aware of."

A shiver trickled down Harrison's spine, mingling with a surge of exhilaration and foreboding. It was becoming more apparent that their simple family vacation was transcending into something far more complicated, perhaps even dangerous.

Amma pulled him back to the present. "It feels like the universe helped us find these pieces. Their stories may be just as interesting as the circumstances that led us to them."

Sunjata's merry laugh filled the air. "Oh, artifacts are the world's best storytellers. Each object, each chiseled detail, waits for the perfect moment to become a chapter in the grand epic of history."

Their imaginations ignited, and the Sharma family followed Sunjata to a secluded nook far away from the general bustle of the museum. It was a refuge for objects that defied conventional categorization, items hinting at alternate histories, worlds colliding, and timelines merging.

"May I?" Sunjata's gaze was fixed on the ornate box Harrison carried, a gleam of uncontainable interest lighting up her features.

"Certainly," Harrison replied, cautiously handing over the box he had discovered in a hidden chamber within the bat caves. The moment it left his hands, an inexplicable sense of vulnerability washed over him. "We came upon this during our cave exploration. It's been a riddle ever since. At first, I thought it was a prop for the movie they are filming in the cave, but there's something about it that makes me believe that's not the case."

Sunjata didn't look up as she turned the box in her hands. "You're right to doubt first impressions," she said quietly.

She delicately opened the box to peer at its ancient contents. A look of fascination swept over her. "Do you mind if my colleague documents these discoveries?"

Before Harrison could respond, she handed the box to a distinguished Nepali man working at the museum. He was of medium height, with weathered hands that spoke of years spent handling ancient artifacts. His salt-and-pepper hair framed a face marked by wisdom and experience, and his warm, crinkled expression exuded a deep knowledge of history and archaeology. With a respectful nod, he accepted the box and walked away, his every movement reflecting a deep reverence for the treasures of the past.

Then, without a word, Sunjata led the family through a maze of exhibits to a glass display case mirroring Harrison's discovery down to the finest detail. The caption read UNEARTHED: FABLED TREASURES FROM THE BAT CAVES OF ANNAPURNA.

"These artifacts were from a specific group of indigenous people who had occupied the caves about five hundred years ago—the Chorangi people," Sunjata explained. She hesitated, treading delicately as she confessed, "Sadly, these items, though intriguing, are not of any significance. They are remnants of a bygone era and hold little historical value."

Sensing something amiss, Harrison pressed further. "But why aren't they important? What's the true story behind these treasures?"

Sunjata hesitated, a secret lurking behind her somewhat forced explanation, as she concealed the truth from the Sharma family. "The Chorangi people were known for their superstitions and legends. Many of these artifacts are believed to be associated with mythical tales, which, while fascinating, aren't always grounded in historical fact. That's why they may not be as important as other historical finds."

Sunjata continued to craft her narrative. "As you can see, your box isn't an isolated find. But that doesn't diminish its uniqueness! You've stumbled upon a sibling to a relic that we've admired for years. Who's to say how many more remain hidden, waiting to be discovered?"

Harrison's brow furrowed in dissatisfaction, sensing the curator might be withholding something. "Thank you, Sunjata, but…"

Just then, Sunjata's phone buzzed. She glanced at the screen. "Excuse me." With a graceful nod, she stepped aside, her voice softening as she moved out of sight. "I must take this."

For a moment, the Sharmas stood alone with Raju and Siddharth. The quiet of the museum pressed in.

The boys lingered nearby, absorbed in their own quiet game.

"I think she's lying," Harrison said suddenly, his jaw set. He fixed on Siddharth. "You told us the clue would be in the cave. This has to be it."

Siddharth met his gaze without blinking. "I thought the cave would yield more," he said carefully. "Perhaps we missed it. The box may not be what the goatskin meant."

Raju leaned in. "The curator has no reason to deceive us. Still, Siddharth is right—we did not search thoroughly."

"Then we should return," Harrison insisted.

Siddharth tilted his head. "Agreed. It seems we are back at the beginning."

Amma frowned. "That's unfortunate."

A moment passed.

"What about the tunnel?" Siddharth asked, breaking the silence. "We have yet to explore it."

Pappa's brow creased. "Oh, we didn't—"

Harrison cut him off "You're right. We still have to explore the tunnel."

"Yes. The tunnel. Will you take us, Raju?" Pappa asked.

Kiran traced a square on the floor with his shoe. "Is it my turn now?"

Raju exchanged a glance with Siddharth. "I think we can arrange that."

Sophie caught Siddharth's gaze. "Tonight?" she inquired.

Siddharth's tone softened. "Yes."

"Good," Sophie answered, adjusting her silk scarf. The hidden pendant felt warm against her chest. "Then it's settled. We'll go back to the tunnel tonight." She did not look at the boys.

Ravi nodded once. "We should be quick."

Near the patterned floor, the boys slowed, their game coming to an end. "Seven," Kiran said, stopping short.

They cheered, "We get to see the monster!" They were already turning their attention elsewhere.

Sophie smiled despite herself.

A moment later, the sound caught up with her.

Just then, Sunjata returned, sliding her phone into her bag. Her smile was bright, practiced, as though no time had passed. "I hope I did not keep you waiting. Don't mistake me—what you hold is curious, even precious in its own way."

Just then, the Nepali man working in the museum returned. "The chest and its contents have been photographed and recorded. Thank you." With that, he whispered something into Sunjata's ear before handing the box back to Harrison.

As he reclaimed the items, Harrison felt a flicker of confusion. He quietly stowed the parchment, lump of beeswax, flint arrowhead, small stones, and pottery shards inside an interior zippered pocket of his jacket before securely placing the decorated box back into his backpack.

"You are right to think that it looks like a movie prop," Sunjata said.

Harrison's fingers tightened briefly on the strap of his backpack.

"Don't be disheartened." Her smile attempted to convey to the family that the artifact still held meaning. "While this box may not fit the mold of conventional historical value, it does appear to be old—and there are those who will cherish its significance."

"So, we're just free to keep it?" Ravi asked.

"The laws of Nepal are very strict as to what qualifies as 'treasure.' Given the items' lack of declared historical value, you are indeed free to do with them as you wish," Sunjata lied.

Cyrus hurried over and stopped, looking up at Sunjata. "It is important," he said quickly. "People keep looking at us. Yesterday, too. They don't stop."

Sunjata's cheerful visage faded, replaced by a solemn, burdened expression. "Artifacts like these," she began, her words carrying an air of importance, "often serve as keys to both metaphorical and literal doors. Doors that may unveil histories better left buried, shadows better left unexplored. These 'treasure hunts' don't align with the history we aim to convey at the Pokhara Museum. They are folklore, legends that don't quite fit our intended portrayal. However, it's crucial to acknowledge there are individuals who genuinely believe in these tales, and they're willing to go to great lengths for them. These artifacts can be the source of fervent devotion and even danger."

"Danger? Should we be worried?" Sophie looked visibly concerned.

Sunjata exhaled a heavy sigh, her gaze meeting Sophie's. "Caution can never hurt. Your simple adventure may have crossed into the territory of those who have spent a lifetime believing in things they cannot solve. Tread carefully, for not all who walk these paths are mere scholars."

"We'll be careful," Ravi said, pivoting to turn. He met Sophie's expectant gaze. "Oh, right." He turned back to Sunjata. "We have another question not related to the box we found."

"Yes?" Sunjata said, curious.

"We recently found out my six-times-removed grandfather was from Nepal."

"That's fascinating," Sunjata said, not impressed.

Ravi leaned forward. "We're trying to uncover his last name. From what we've learned, he changed it when he fled Nepal during the later years of the Kali Raatri—near the end of the eighteenth century. He was supposedly a member of the royal court. Any information you can provide would be incredibly helpful."

Sunjata composed herself, but a trace of tension crept into her voice. "The Kali Raatri—or 'Dark Night'—was indeed a dark era in Nepal's history, a period of unrest and suffering that cast a shadow for decades." She paused, her gaze slipping past them, as if measuring what to say next. "It followed the weakening of the old courts, when the Malla line became ceremonial and power began to move behind curtains—quiet at first. Administrative. Hidden."

She let a beat pass.

"One of the key figures attached to that era was Chancellor Jayendra of the Shatranj Ke Sipahi," she continued carefully. "Historians often conflate him with his grandson," Sunjata added. "They shared the same name—Jayendra—but not the same moment. The earlier one turned influence into leverage. Leverage into rule. And when historians speak of the moment the darkness arrived, they often point to 1769—because that is when the rupture became public. The year the people finally felt what had already been forming in the dark."

Ravi's posture sharpened. Sophie stilled.

"But that," Sunjata added, her voice lowering, "is not the true beginning."

Her smile did not reach her eyes.

"The Kali Raatri did not arrive in one clean strike," she said. "It began earlier—quietly—through purges, sealed orders, disappearances. The first coup was not staged in daylight. It was staged in corridors. In 1695, Jayendra consolidated power through force and fear, removing rivals, sealing records, turning the old order into a shell. By the time 1769 came, what remained was only ceremony—and the illusion of rule."

She looked at them with intensity, letting the weight of it settle. "So yes—many loyalists fled after 1769, because the last veil tore. But others fled long before that. Some hid. Some changed names. Some waited for decades before crossing into India."

Ravi furrowed his brow, glancing at Sophie before turning back to Sunjata. "Our genealogy records state that our ancestor entered India in the late 1800s. That doesn't seem to line up."

Sunjata didn't flinch. But something tightened at the corner of her mouth, as though the question had struck closer than Ravi knew.

"Not all crossings are recorded when they happen," she said. "Not all names remain intact when a family is trying to survive. It is possible your ancestor fled during the worst years—then lived under another name, in the hills or along the border, for generations. And it is also possible the record you have marks the first documented entry, not the first escape."

Her gaze sharpened—warm on the surface, unreadable beneath.

"In times like that," she murmured, "people vanish for decades…and reappear as if they were born new."

Sophie sighed, her voice tinged with frustration. "That's too bad."

Sunjata wasn't done. Her smile remained, but something colder moved behind it. "Most people don't know that," she said softly. "Because the ones who did…didn't survive to write it down."

A brief silence settled over them—thick as dust in a sealed room.

Pappa then spoke, his brow furrowed. "There's something I still don't understand. If the Shatranj caused such a dark period in Nepal's history, and they are now active today, why are they allowed to operate?"

Raju and Siddharth exchanged a nervous glance with Sunjata.

Sunjata hesitated, her smile faltering for a brief moment.

She glanced down, fingers lightly tapping on her thigh before she spoke. "There's more to the story. You see…that was over two hundred years ago." Her voice softened. "The Kali Raatri ended when a group of reformists, led by the Jyoti Sangha—a brotherhood of monks and scholars. With the help of the local people—farmers, craftsmen, temple guards, and those who remembered the old ways—they overthrew Jayendra's regime. The Shatranj Ke Sipahi were driven into hiding. For nearly a century, the Order vanished from public life."

She paused, her eyes flicking toward the window as if weighing her words. "But when they reemerged, they had rebranded themselves. The Shatranj Ke Sipahi kept their original name but aimed to return to their original purpose—protecting the people of Nepal. They helped stabilize the country when new external threats arose in the late nineteenth century. Since then, they've worked tirelessly to rebuild their reputation. Today, they're involved in charity work, running hospitals, supporting local law enforcement. You'll see their name on hospitals, police stations, and various charitable organizations. The community trusts them, sees them as protectors—a modern order of guardians."

She paused again, letting her explanation sink in. "But it wasn't easy for them to shed the shadows of their past."

Sophie nodded slowly. "So, it's true then—the Order is intact, living among the people of Nepal…serving them?"

Sunjata's expression darkened slightly, her voice dropping. "That's part of the reason you won't find much about the history of the Shatranj. Their darker past has been deliberately erased. They prefer to be remembered as protectors."

"That's what the historian in Kathmandu said," Sophie responded.

"That's because it's the literal truth. The Shatranj Ke Sipahi have done much for the country. Their contributions are woven into the very fabric of Nepal's progress. It's no wonder they're held in such high regard."

Ravi stepped forward. "What about finding out our ancestor's last name?"

"That would be nearly impossible," Sunjata said, shaking her head. "Like I said, many records were lost or destroyed. You might want to try the Shatranj headquarters in Kathmandu. They might have some records, but it's doubtful."

Sophie edged closer to Ravi and whispered, "Should we ask if the Shatranj was in possession of the Heart of Kumari during the Kali Raatri?"

Ravi's expression tightened, and he quickly shook his head. "No. We can't let on that we know anything about the diamond."

Turning back to Sunjata, Ravi offered a polite smile. "Thank you, Sunjata. You've given us much to think about."

Sunjata nodded. "Stay safe on your journey," she said, her eyes lingering on them as if she, too, were considering the gravity of what they might uncover.

Raju straightened his cuffs. "I'll bring the van around. Come, Siddharth."

Siddharth gave a short nod.

The two stepped away together, their movements measured, their presence leaving behind a faint ripple of unease.

3:00 P.M.

As they emerged from the sanctuary of history into the outside world, the Sharma family fell into silence, each turning over what they had learned. None of them trusted Sunjata. It was clear she knew more about the box—and more about them—than she was willing to reveal. *But why?*

What had begun as a simple family vacation had spiraled into something far stranger. The museum had left them with more questions than answers.

They were no longer mere tourists.

Part II

The Loom of Fate
विधेः तन्त्रम्

"...When the Time... Bloodlines..."
— Doctrine of Balance, Fragment 9

"Oh, what a tangled web we weave, when first we practice to deceive."

— Sir Walter Scott

-12-
WOVEN LIES

विन्यस्ताः असत्याः

3:56 P.M.

No one could ignore the unsettling atmosphere as they stepped into their rooms at the inn. The once familiar space lay disturbed, foreign. Someone had been here. For a moment, no one spoke. Ravi drew a slow breath through his nose as his eyes moved across the room without settling. Amma remained still, listening.

The stacks of neatly arranged papers were scattered like leaves after a storm, and personal belongings had shifted just enough to signal an invasion of their private space. Everyone was immediately on high alert, though no one moved to break the stillness.

Sophie didn't move at first. She tilted her head in concern. Her lips parted slightly, her breath hitching, as she observed the violated sanctity of their space. "This is extremely unsettling." She reached down, picked up a throw pillow, and set it back on the sofa, smoothing the fabric as if it might answer her. She caught her reflection faintly in the glass—eyes older than this morning.

Pappa's focus narrowed. His gaze scanned every inch of the room, searching for an invisible intruder. "Who would do this? And what were they looking for?"

Pappa crouched to retrieve a drawer that had been pulled from the desk and left askew on the floor. As he lifted it, his eyes caught on the grain—the old grooves, the shape of the letters. किरण पञ्चमं सुरक्षितम्. The same as before—THE FIFTH IS SAFE. He didn't say it aloud. He just put the drawer back.

Harrison's hand instinctively sought the hidden pocket in his jacket where the relics were hidden. "Could they have been looking for the artifacts?"

"Thank heavens we took them with us to the museum," Amma replied. "Otherwise, we might have lost them."

"Not like they mean anything anyway," Harrison huffed.

Cyrus clutched his stuffed lamb to his chest, the little brass bell at its neck giving a nervous chime. "Is someone after Sheepy again? I don't like this."

Pappa's words, usually so reassuring, carried a new level of gravity that made everyone listen intently. "They weren't looking for money."

"Maybe it's the men in suits," Harrison suggested.

"Possibly, but I think they're here to throw us off," Ravi added. "It's like a distraction. You worry about them, but the real danger is under your nose."

Harrison frowned. "How so?"

Ravi's gaze drifted, the lines at his brow tightening. His thoughts slipped back to his days with the U.S. military. "Once, on patrol in Iraq, we spotted a group of fighters on a ridge—loud, careless, easy to see. Everyone thought they were the threat. But while we watched them, the real team slipped in through the gullies below, close enough to strike. If one of our scouts hadn't caught the glint of metal, we'd never have known."

"Or, they could be trying to scare us off, so we'll abandon our quest," Amma mused, her voice filled with thoughtful consideration. She puzzled over the fact that nothing had been stolen.

"Hey, like in Scooby-Doo?" Kiran asked.

"Yeah!" Cyrus cut in quickly. "They always pretend to be ghosts so everyone gets scared."

Pappa looked toward his wife as he walked to the door. "You may be right, Amma. Whoever or whatever their motive is, it's clear they want us to know they are closer than we think." He crouched, found the seam where the door met the jamb, and traced it. There was no splintered wood, no new gouge. He examined the keyhole, finding only the faint oil of an old key, with no fresh scratches that would indicate the lock had been picked. "They didn't get in through the door," he finally said, straightening.

Ravi exhaled slowly. "If they wanted us scared, they would've taken something."

Sophie walked over to the window and tested the latch. It held. She peered cautiously through the glass, then she looked down. Three stories of emptiness stared back. "They didn't come in through here," she said, drawing the curtains closed.

In the corner, the old wooden chair lay on its side, the cushion slightly askew and one leg twisted against the floor.

Kiran moved in closer to his mother, his voice a murmur. "I don't like it."

The room fell silent. No one corrected him. Yet, Amma bent, righted it, and nudged it back into place with her foot.

"We need to be careful with what we say and do from now

on. For all we know, there could be hidden microphones or cameras here," Pappa cautioned.

"Mama, are we playing a game? Is this fake, like in the television?" Kiran reached up his arms.

"No, love. It's not a game, but I promise we'll be okay." She picked him up and held him close, infusing her voice with a bravery she hoped was more than pretend. "Just like in the stories, remember? The heroes are always quiet when the dragons are near."

"Will the dragons hear us?" he asked, pressing against her shoulder, his fingers clutching her shirt.

"Not if we're smart and brave," Sophie whispered back. She kissed the top of his head. "And we are both, aren't we?"

Kiran nodded, his trust in her absolute. "We're super brave, Mama. Not like Shaggy and Scooby!"

Sophie's heart tightened. "Yes, we are." She drew the curtains tighter, the world outside vanishing like a bad dream. "And that's why we'll always stay safe."

Harrison began checking the seams of the cushions and the edges of the furniture as a precaution. "I think it's time to switch rooms…or hotels."

"Let's not jump the gun," Pappa interjected. "We may have an advantage. If the intruder is after the pendant, he must believe it's still in the lamb. We could use that misinformation to protect ourselves."

Harrison frowned. "How?"

"Well, if they're watching the lamb, they're not watching us, right?"

"Yeah," Harrison acknowledged.

"It's like your father said. It becomes the distraction. They keep their focus on the lamb, and we use that space to move, to plan, to stay a step ahead."

Cyrus held Sheepy tighter. "Please don't let them hurt

him."

"No one will hurt Sheepy," Pappa assured, his tone firm. Then, softer, "But we must be clever. Let them chase what they think is the prize. All the while, we decide how the game is played."

"In the meantime, should we call the police?" Amma asked.

Pappa shook his head. "No. We don't want whoever did this to think we're rattled. That would play into their hand. If they believe we're afraid, they've already won."

"Pappa's right," Sophie asserted. "Let's keep our heads down and continue what we started. It appears nothing was actually stolen, so I doubt the authorities would be interested anyway."

She tugged at her scarf as if to settle it, her eyes lowering to the floor.

"Let's at least inform the inn's management," Ravi chimed in. "If they have security footage, or if any of the staff saw anything, it could give us a clue."

Harrison nodded, but the unease in his chest wouldn't quiet. *This wasn't an advantage—it was a mark.*

The impact of the situation settled on them all. Sophie shifted Kiran on her hip, grabbed her bag, and headed for the door.

* * *

4:20 P.M.

Their tension permeated the lobby as the family descended the staircase, their footsteps a series of muted thuds echoing in the cavernous hallway. As they reached the front desk, a slight shiver ran down their spines; they were stepping back into a world they no longer fully trusted, one that had demonstrated its capability for betrayal.

Raju and Siddharth were seated in a shadowed corner of the lobby. Engrossed in a private conversation, they looked up as Ravi and his family approached. Their expressions changed subtly from relaxed camaraderie to urgency, mirroring the family's faces.

Ravi's voice broke the uneasy angst. "Raju, our room was broken into. Nothing seems missing, but you can imagine how troubling this is."

Raju stood so fast his chair nearly tipped. "Are you sure?"

"Pretty sure," Ravi answered. "Not sure how they did it, but they were looking for something."

Siddharth rose from his seat. "We should call the police. Perhaps Priya's uncle can help."

"No police," Pappa said firmly. His statement carried weight, leaving no room for debate. "We don't want whoever did this to think we're rattled. That would play into their hands."

For a lingering moment, the air thickened.

Raju adjusted his cuff. "Of course," he said quickly. "Best not to show fear." His eyes flicked to Cyrus clutching the lamb, then back to Ravi. "Still… Perhaps we need to let the hotel know."

"That's why we came down," Amma said.

Raju nodded. "Good. Let's see what they have to say."

Just then, Priya entered the lobby. Her gaze took in the grim scene before her, widening with mock concern. "What's happened?"

Ravi and Amma exchanged a glance, debating how much to reveal.

Finally, Ravi spoke. "We thought it prudent to inform you our room appears to have been searched. Nothing is missing, but the intrusion is unnerving."

Siddharth looked at Ravi, then turned to Priya. "There's no need to trouble your uncle. Let's keep this quiet."

Priya nodded.

Siddharth faced the family. "Your discovery has attracted more attention than we anticipated." He paused, letting his words sink in before continuing with rehearsed caution. "The museum curator warned us. Treasures like what we found in the bat cave can draw dangers we might not be prepared for." Siddharth softened his tone, "this is no coincidence," he asserted. "One of us will stand guard at your door tonight for your safety."

Ravi's jaw tightened. He did not meet Siddharth's eyes. "Very well, Siddharth," he said.

As Sophie passed, she touched his sleeve. "Thank you," she whispered. "For protecting us."

For a fraction of a second, Siddharth forgot the script. His throat worked. "Always," he replied, though the word came rougher than he intended.

Just behind them, Priya's features tightened—just enough to register a flicker of strain. She stepped forward with the poised assurance of an innkeeper doing her duty. "This is quite concerning," she stated with a practiced seriousness. "I'll immediately look into the security footage and implement extra measures for everyone's safety."

Yet beneath this concern, there was a fleeting hint of detachment, suggesting her words might not be as genuine as they appeared.

Ravi didn't say a word. Instead, he crouched and gently lifted Cyrus into his arms. The boy clung to him, still clutching Sheepy.

Amma stepped forward and scooped up Kiran, who was beginning to rub his eyes, wearied by the weight of the day. Without fanfare, the family turned toward the staircase. Their steps were steady, measured—but there was no mistaking the tension drawn tight between their shoulders. Whatever trust had once existed in that room had begun to dissolve.

As they climbed the first few steps, Ravi leaned toward Sophie and whispered, just for her: "I don't think we can trust Raju and Siddharth anymore."

Ravi hadn't meant for anyone else to hear his worry, but Cyrus had. The boy shifted slightly in Ravi's arms, pressing his face into his father's shoulder. He didn't speak, but the way he held Sheepy tighter said everything.

Behind them, Raju and Siddharth stood motionless in the dim lobby, their faces unreadable. Though the air remained still, something had shifted—subtly but irreversibly. They did not look back.

***

After the Sharma family departed, Siddharth, Raju, and Priya stood in the empty lobby. The low hum of a ceiling fan failed to stir the heat pressing in from the walls.

"That did not go very well," Priya said, turning to Raju. "Looks like the Sharmas are onto you."

Raju's jaw tightened. "Maybe."

Siddharth's voice carried its usual steel. "We still hold their trust enough to guide them. If we point them back to the cave, they will follow."

Priya's laugh was dry, without mirth. "You still believe that? Did you not see Sophie's eyes? Or hear Ravi hesitate? They have already stopped trusting you—both of you. They nod. They smile. But beneath it, they are pulling away."

Raju looked at her sharply, but her words left no room for denial.

"They will not follow blindly again," she said. "If we mean

to control this, it must be now. Before they close the door on us entirely."

"I'll figure something out," Raju said through clenched teeth, though he knew in his marrow his cousin was right.

For a moment no one spoke.

Then, Siddharth's voice cut the air, smooth and cool. "What about the box?"

Raju turned to Priya. "Yes, the treasure box. Any word from Sunjata?"

Priya nodded. "Her team ran the parchment and the box through everything—spectral scans, infrared, x-rays, UV light, microscopic imaging, even bacterial swabs. They tried humidity chambers, high-resolution models, laser mapping. Nothing. Not a trace of ink or any sign that the clue was ever in the box." She paused. "They want the parchment back to run more tests. They think that may be the key."

Siddharth frowned. "Why the hell don't they still have it?"

"She returned it to Harrison with the box," Priya admitted.

"If it was so important, why didn't they swap it out?"

"We thought of that, but she said switching it was too risky. And I agreed with her. If the Sharmas were to discover she'd deceived them, they'd be on to us."

"Of course," Siddharth muttered.

Priya continued, lowering her voice. "Sunjata thinks the writing could be in a special ink—something ancient, only visible under very specific conditions. She wants to have another look." She gave a small shrug. "She might have enough information, but she wants the original to be sure. You know how thorough these museum types are."

Raju gave a short laugh. "Perfect. So now, I'm supposed to borrow it back. Fine. I'll just add it to my growing list of items I need to take from the Sharmas."

Priya's brow lifted. "And the Talisman? Any plan yet?"

The twins exchanged a look.

"Well." Raju paused for a moment, shifting uneasily. "We don't have a plan yet," he confessed, running his fingers through his hair. "We're playing this by ear." His voice wavered, revealing a note of hesitancy and reflecting the unpredictability of the evolving situation they found themselves in.

Priya frowned. "That's not very reassuring. Let me know if you need anything." With a final click of her stilettos, she turned and walked out.

"You haven't done any better," Raju called after her.

But the door to her office had already closed behind her.

***

In the quiet of the inn's lobby, Raju and Siddharth were left to themselves. The anxiety was palpable. The silence was broken only by the tics of the grandfather clock.

Raju finally spoke. "We need to figure out how to get that pendant."

"And gain their trust back." Siddharth added.

"Forget about that. We've already played that line."

The ticks of the clock grew louder in the stillness, mirroring Raju's sense of unease. It was as though the passage of time was underscoring the critical nature of their mission—a reminder they were in a race against the clock.

At that moment, the bond between Siddharth and Raju was clearer than ever.

"Whatever you decide, I'm right there with you, brother."

"Thank you," Raju replied, leaning in as he placed a firm hand on Siddharth's shoulder. His voice softened. "I know the toll this is taking on you."

Siddharth gave a wry smile. "It's a hard road for both of us. But we each have our roles to play."

Raju clapped Siddharth on the back. "Now, let's head to the Sharmas' door. We've got our part to play there, too."

Together, they turned toward the marble staircase.

They climbed.

Slow.

Measured.

Deliberate.

-13-
THE HEART OF DECEPTION

प्रपञ्चस्य हृदयं

5:44 P.M.

Determined to stay one step ahead, Ravi pressed his ear against the wooden door, listening intently for any trace of Siddharth and Raju's conversation outside. Assured they were on guard, he gestured for the family to gather in a remote corner of the suite.

Cyrus and Kiran had dozed off on the weathered couch, its faded floral pattern worn from years of use. The cushions had settled into familiar grooves, perfectly contoured from generations of guests relaxing into their cozy warmth.

"Let's go into my room and close the door," Amma suggested. "I don't want to wake them. It's been a long day."

"That's a good idea," Pappa agreed. "We need to make sure our conversation remains private. After all, the walls may have ears."

Sophie hesitated, her gaze flicking toward the sleeping boys. "Our room was just broken into. You think it's wise to leave them alone?"

Ravi lowered his voice. "We're still in the suite, Sophie. It's not like we're leaving them. We'll hear if anything happens."

They tiptoed past the slumbering duo and into Amma's room, shutting the door behind them. Ravi, Sophie, Harrison, Amma, and Pappa huddled around the antique desk serving as a makeshift investigation hub. Papers were strewn about, the desk lamp forming long shadows on the wall.

Outside, the wind dragged its fingers down the windows, slow and searching, as if seeking a way in. Behind them, the unmistakable tinkling of Sheepy's bell broke through the quiet.

Sophie peeked into the adjoining room. The children were asleep. Cyrus had curled up into a tight ball, his arms wrapped around Sheepy. The lamb's brass bell dangled from its neck like a tired ornament. A draft pushed through the space, and the bell gave a tiny chime, high and metallic, like a laugh swallowed in the dark.

"Must've left the window open in our room," Sophie murmured, almost to herself.

"I'll get it," Harrison said. He stood and walked off quietly.

"Thanks," Sophie replied, but he was already gone.

Pappa sat at the desk, sifting through the mess the intruder had left behind. Crumpled takeout receipts, stained with sauces and greasy fingerprints. A menu from the inn's restaurant, creased down the center. One of Kiran's picture books—closed, but placed upside down.

"Anything missing?" Sophie asked. She stood in the doorway with her arms crossed, waiting for Harrison to return.

"Nothing important," Pappa murmured. "Just clutter. Receipts. Ticket stubs. That sort of thing."

"You sure?" Sophie pressed. "You didn't leave anything

out? Notes? The books from the library?"

Pappa hesitated. "No. Everything's in the safe. Books, passports, the translation pages from the temple."

"Still. Maybe check again," Sophie said.

"I already did," Pappa said reassuringly.

Amma looked up from folding laundry. "Do it again," she said flatly.

Pappa stood without another word. He walked across the room to the closet. The door groaned open.

Inside, the safe sat like a forgotten tombstone—squat, gray, and half-buried under folded towels and old throw pillows. Pappa knelt and turned the dial.

Click. Click. Clunk.

The door swung open. Pappa stared at the contents for longer than was necessary. Passports. Notebook. Bansuri. The felt pouch with the temple coins. Even the letter opener was present. He closed the door with a dull thud.

"Everything is here," Pappa called back.

Sophie dropped onto the bed, the mattress springs squealing. The pendant throbbed faintly beneath her sweater. "This would be a great time for a television. Some terrible soap opera. A cooking show. Anything."

"The hotel doesn't have one," Pappa said. "Guess that's the charm of coming to a country that doesn't believe in distractions."

"You mean charm like spiders in the shower?" Sophie replied. "That kind of charm?"

No one laughed.

Harrison walked in and sat cross-legged on the floor near the wall. "Window's closed," he announced. He took out his phone and began to scroll through the photos. His thumb stopped. He zoomed in, focusing on the writing over the ancient door. "Do you think the markings above the tunnel door are a curse?" he asked the room, not looking up.

Pappa reached for his phone. He studied the screen like it was a mirror that might reflect some hidden truth they had yet to notice. "It says, 'Only the chosen may seek the Heart.'"

"Why me?" Harrison asked, looking up. "Why was I chosen? Why not someone else?"

Pappa handed the phone back with a smile. "It must see the same special soul we all see."

Harrison leaned his head against the wall. "What if we just left? What if we got on a plane and went home? Forget about the Heart, the curse, and everything else."

"You think the Heart would let us?" Sophie asked, too quietly.

Harrison didn't answer right away. "Siddharth said it would find someone else. But I don't believe that."

Ravi stepped away from the window, where he'd been staring through the curtains as if something might be staring back. He looked at his son, the shadows upon the young man's features revealing the weight of his struggle. "Harrison, I know this feels like you're walking through a pitch-black house. No lights. No map. Just darkness. And you're reaching for a switch that's not there."

Harrison nodded slowly. "That sounds about right."

"Maybe there's no switch," Ravi said. "Maybe you have to learn to see in the dark."

Everyone fell silent. Even the wind outside seemed to hold its breath.

***

6:05 P.M.

The doorknob to the Sharma family's suite gave a delicate click, and a thin blade of light crept with intent across the carpet. The glow stretched against the faded red pile before climbing the edge of the couch where Cyrus lay.

Raju entered first. His polished shoes sank into the fibers, leaving no sound, no trace. Behind him came Siddharth, his shadow looming long, his steps just as muffled. For a moment, both men stood motionless at the threshold, listening. From the next room came the hum of voices—the family speaking.

Raju moved closer to the boy. His body leaned into the light, his eyes fixed on the lamb nestled in the crook of Cyrus's arm. The child stirred faintly in his sleep, rolling his cheek deeper into the toy. His lips parted, whispering some half-formed dream.

Raju crouched. His hand hovered above Sheepy, then lowered. The wool felt warm beneath his fingertips. Carefully, he tugged.

The boy shifted. His arm tightened instinctively, clutching the toy closer.

Raju's pulse hammered in his temples.

He tried again, inch by inch. The lamb slid half out of the child's grasp. *It's almost free.* Raju's hand trembled as he pulled.

Then Cyrus rolled, and Sheepy slipped loose.

The lamb struck the carpet. The sound should have died there, smothered by the fibers, but the brass bell betrayed them. It gave a sharp, bright chime that cut through the room.

Both men froze. Their eyes shot to the door separating them from the family. The voices beyond carried on.

Raju bent quickly, snatching up the toy. But as he straightened, Cyrus shifted again. His eyelids fluttered.

A groggy voice broke the hush. "Raju? Why are you here?"

Raju stiffened, caught.

Siddharth crouched quickly, his face calm, composed. "We just needed to make sure that you were safe."

In an unexpected flash, Cyrus reached out and tore Sheepy from Raju's grasp. He buried his face in the toy's wool, the familiar scent comforting him. Suspicion stirred in his eyes. "My mom and dad don't trust you anymore."

The words fell like a stone in water. The silence rippled within them. *Priya was right*, the twins realized. *Cyrus just confirmed it.*

Siddharth's gaze flickered, but his voice was steady. "Cyrus, listen. We are not bad. Do you remember who saved Sheepy in the bazaar? That was me. I would never let anything happen to him. You can still trust me."

Cyrus's arms locked tighter. The brass bell dug into his chest. "You need to go away."

Siddharth lowered his head, pleading. "Can we borrow Sheepy for a while? Nothing more. You will have him back after your nap, promise."

The boy shook his head fiercely, his curly hair sticking to his damp temples. "No. I'm not leaving him. Not ever."

The pause that followed was brittle, suffocating. The painting over the fireplace hung unchanged.

Then, they sensed movement from behind the door. Desperation set in. It was now or never.

Raju's expression hardened. His whisper came sharp. "We'll take them both." He stepped forward and scooped up the boy from the couch.

Cyrus struggled, but sleep dulled his strength. His small fists flailed weakly, his grip still locked on Sheepy.

Raju pushed through the doorway. "Quiet," he hissed.

Cyrus writhed against him, the lamb clutched tight.

Siddharth followed, his thoughts spiraling at the sudden change in course. *Stealing the toy was one thing; kidnapping a child was something else entirely.*

As he reached back to close the door, a sudden rush of air met his retreat. The chill was ominous, as if summoned by some unforeseen force. Before he could react, the door slammed behind them.

The sound cracked through the corridor like a gunshot.

***

Back in the sanctuary the Sharmas had made, the silence broke with a slam—sharp, jarring.

Every head turned.

Sophie was already halfway out of her chair. The sound had come from the direction of the sitting room. From the boys. "Harrison, I thought you closed the window?" Sophie asked.

"I did," he replied quickly, his eyes darting toward the closed door.

"Maybe it was in the hallway," Ravi offered. "These walls are thin."

Sophie hesitated. Just a beat. Her hand hovered near the doorknob—then fell back to her side.

Just then, they were startled by a buzz as Amma's phone lit up on the side table.

Amma snatched it up. "It's from Priya," she said, her voice wavering. "She says: 'Checked the security cams. Nothing unusual captured.'"

Sophie stayed where she was. "How is that possible?" she asked, incredulous.

"Are we looking at a professional job here?" Ravi mused, rubbing his temples.

Visibly troubled, Amma pondered, "Or perhaps someone tampered with the footage? It would have to be someone with connections to this hotel, but who?"

Pappa, wearing an expression of deep concentration, ventured, "Could it be Priya herself? Or maybe Anil? They both know the inn intimately. It would be easy for them to avoid detection. In fact, maybe there's no footage at all." He looked around the room, hoping the walls could whisper back the answer.

A hush settled over the room. The thought that someone that close might be involved was chilling. The air grew oppressive with the weight of their suspicion.

"She didn't seem as concerned about our safety as I expected," Harrison said, frowning. "Yeah, she said they would implement more security measures, but…"

"What else could she have done?" Sophie asked. "We told her nothing was actually stolen and not to call the police."

"True," Harrison said slowly, "but Pappa makes a good point."

"For now," Amma said, "let's keep our theory to ourselves. If it is Priya or Anil, confronting them could put us in more danger."

"They're bound by blood!" Harrison nearly shouted. He composed himself slightly before continuing, his hushed voice awash with both excitement and concern. "Remember the women at the lake? She said to be cautious of those who are bound by blood!"

Sophie blinked. "Anil and Priya—they're related! Why didn't we see it?"

Pappa spoke. "Sometimes the people closest to the fire cast the darkest shadows."

The room seemed to shudder in stunned silence.

"We should leave this hotel," Pappa added softly.

"I'll start looking," Ravi said, already pulling out his phone. "We leave tomorrow. First light."

The room filled with reluctant nods. Though their thoughts raced with questions and suspicions, they knew caution was their best ally. They were grateful that the two sleeping boys in the other room were blissfully unaware of the web of deception tightening around them.

Then, the desk phone rang—sudden, slicing through the tension. They exchanged startled looks.

"Who could that be?" Sophie wondered aloud.

Ravi reached for the receiver—paused—then lifted it. Priya's voice came through on the other end. His complexion turned pallid as he listened.

Suddenly, Ravi dropped the phone and ran toward the door. "Two men have taken Cyrus and left the inn! Priya said they were running as they went through the exit!"

Sophie's heart began to pound as if trying to escape her chest, and a pit formed in her gut. "What?" she wailed as she sprinted toward the sitting room. Her mind raced. *This has to be some cruel joke, some inexplicable prank.*

But as she and Ravi burst into the room, her worst fears were confirmed. The place where Cyrus had rested beside Kiran on the couch now sat vacant, with Kiran peacefully lost in his dream world, unaware his brother was missing.

Sophie spun in all directions, frantically searching for her child. But Cyrus was nowhere to be found. Only the unlocked door remained, mocking their earlier sense of security.

"I forgot to lock the door!" Ravi shouted, his words filled with regret.

For a moment, time froze, unwilling to move forward with the realization of their horror.

Panic, raw and unfiltered, filled the room.

6:25 P.M.

The air grew suffocating as Ravi, Harrison, and Pappa rushed down the grand staircase of the Surya Chandra Inn. Each step struck the marble floor like a drumbeat of panic. Their chests heaved with adrenaline. Urgency propelled them forward.

As they neared the point of breaking into an all-out sprint, Priya's voice pierced the lobby like a shard of ice. "It was your guides, Raju and Siddharth! They took Cyrus!"

Her words were a dagger to their hearts.

The realization hit Ravi like a ton of bricks, confirming his darkest fears. *So, it's true*, Ravi thought bitterly. *I never should have trusted them!* And now, Cyrus's life hung in the balance.

The intensity of the moment was palpable. The betrayal was shattering.

Ravi turned toward Pappa and Harrison. Without speaking a word, they knew what they had to do. Time was running out, and they had to act fast.

They burst through the inn's front doors, the chill of the evening cutting against their faces as they hit the street.

For a split second, Ravi froze—rage and fear warring inside him. Then, Harrison's shout cut through the haze.

"Dad—there!" He pointed down the road. "It's Raju and Siddharth! They're getting away!"

As they exited the inn, Ravi's eyes were ablaze, like two embers in the dark of night. He gestured to an auto-rickshaw idling nearby. "Pappa, Harrison, get in! Now!" he bellowed.

Pappa jumped into the single driver's seat as Ravi and Harrison slid into the vehicle's rear bench. The three-wheeled auto-rickshaw burst to life with a roar, its four-stroke engine awakening like a feral beast unchained.

As they pulled away from the inn, they were thrust into a frantic journey through the maze-like streets of Pokhara. The strong odors of exhaust fumes and sizzling street food swirled through the air, overpowering Ravi's already-heightened senses. With each jarring jolt of the rickshaw, a nerve-jangling vibration surged up Pappa's arms. His knuckles turned ghostly white from the strain of his grip.

As they rounded a winding corner, Raju emerged from the shadows, also driving an auto-rickshaw. The distinct silhouette of his face caught in the glow of passing streetlights created a haunting image that sent a jolt of shock through Ravi.

Pappa's breathing became rapid and shallow, and the scent of his perspiration grew intense, filling the space around them. Beside Ravi, Harrison's eyes were wide with horror, as he grappled with the magnitude of the situation.

Summoning a voice filled with ferocious determination, Ravi hollered, "Faster! We can't let them escape!"

Pappa twisted the throttle, and the auto-rickshaw responded with a sudden burst of speed, its tires screeching as it devoured the distance between them and Raju. Each heartbeat amplified the adrenaline coursing through their veins. The distant city lights became a surreal blur, their colors merging and warping like a nightmarish dream in the wake of their relentless chase.

As they closed the gap, Ravi peered through the rear window, locking with Cyrus' terror-stricken eyes. His son's face was a portrait of fear and uncertainty, a mirror image of the turmoil raging within Ravi.

Over the roar of the engines, Ravi called out, "Pappa, pull up closer. I can reach him!"

Pappa shifted gears and accelerated. The vehicle surged forward, drawing level with Raju's auto-rickshaw. For an instant, their eyes met. Ravi's glare burned with a vow of retribution.

Driven by pure instinct, Ravi leaned himself out of his

vehicle, his upper body hanging precariously as he strained toward Raju's auto-rickshaw. His arm flailed wildly in a desperate attempt to rescue his son. Cyrus stood on the seat and tried to climb over Siddharth, his small hands reaching out toward his father.

Pappa emitted a guttural cry of anguish, echoing the raw torment of a father in distress. Among the cacophony of blaring horns and screeching tires, his focus was split between keeping the two speeding vehicles aligned while navigating the perilous road. Forced to drive on the wrong side, Pappa swerved around oncoming cars, their horns deafening in a chorus of alarmed warnings. The auto-rickshaw's engine roared in protest as he darted his gaze between the road ahead and the vehicle beside them, struggling to maintain a straight course. Glancing to his side, Pappa saw the chaotic scene of Ravi and Siddharth locked in a desperate struggle over Cyrus.

Suddenly, a looming threat materialized as a truck turned directly into their lane, its massive form barreling toward them with a thunderous growl. In a split second of terror, Cyrus, suspended between the two rickshaws, released his grasp on his father and retreated to safety beside Siddharth, fear coursing through him.

Amid the blinding glare of the truck's headlights and the relentless blare of its horn, Pappa executed a swift and desperate maneuver. He veered their auto-rickshaw sharply out of the truck's path. The tires screeched against the asphalt, piercing the chaos with their shrill cry. The vehicle swayed precariously, teetering on the edge of control as they narrowly avoided a catastrophic collision. The bright lights disoriented them, and the tires' screech reverberated through their bones, heightening the adrenaline-fueled moment of near disaster.

As the auto-rickshaw's engine whined, it slowed, losing pace with Raju's. Through the rear window, Cyrus's face, pressed against the plexiglass, grew smaller in the distance. Harrison's cry cut through the tension. "Pappa, we're losing them!"

In response, Pappa changed course, steering the auto-rickshaw down a cramped alley. The narrow space amplified the roar of the engine, its echoes bouncing off the walls with deafening intensity. The vehicle hurtled dangerously close to the alley's shopfronts, weathered doors, faded signboards, and shuttered windows. Street vendors' goods, precariously perched outside, rattled as the auto-rickshaw sped past. Garbage cans toppled with a clatter and the debris, disturbed by the vehicle's passage, spiraled into the air, creating a whirlwind in the auto-rickshaw's turbulent wake.

As they burst from the alley, they found themselves unexpectedly ahead of Raju's auto-rickshaw. Pappa expertly maneuvered the handle, his hands working in tandem with the clutch, slowing just enough for Ravi's bold move.

Ravi, sensing his moment, climbed to the rear. His feet teetered on the fender of the back wheel, a precarious balancing act as the auto-rickshaw swayed. With a firm grip on the sidebars, he steadied himself. In a fluid motion driven by rage and desperation, he launched himself forward.

He landed with agile precision on the decorative mudguard of Raju's front wheel, the ornate patterns blurring beneath his foot. For an instant, the street flared around him—neon bleeding through smoke and dust.

A sign above a shuttered storefront flickered, most of its tubing dead, only four letters alive in trembling red glass: I N E S. The glow stuttered once and died, swallowed by the dark.

Ravi's hand shot out, grasping Raju's windshield, obscuring his view for a split second as he pulled himself into the back seat, sliding in next to a startled Siddharth. Ravi's grip was unyielding; his resolve mirrored in the iron-tight hold on the sidebars. He whipped around to face Siddharth and drove his fist into his shoulder. Ravi's knuckles connected with a resounding thud, the force of the blow freeing Cyrus.

Meanwhile, Raju pushed the vehicle faster, pulling up alongside Pappa's rickshaw. Now Raju was in the opposing lane.

Ravi, his movements swift and desperate, reached over Siddharth to grab Cyrus, his son's small hands flailing toward him. But as Raju swerved sharply to avoid an oncoming car, Ravi was thrown off balance, tumbling back into the seat next to Siddharth. Ravi swung his arm again, his fist connecting with Siddharth's nose in a splatter of blood. From there, the two men engaged in a ferocious brawl, throwing punches with raw, unbridled force.

Raju, his attention torn between the road and the violent struggle in the back, lost control. The auto-rickshaw swerved erratically, veering dangerously close to Pappa's vehicle. The sudden motion nearly sent Ravi tumbling out. Clinging on with sheer determination, he fought against Siddharth's hands clawing at his grip, prying his fingers loose.

In the chaos, Cyrus caught a familiar glimpse in Siddharth's eyes, and a spark of recognition flared. *Those were the eyes from the fire festival.* "You're the one who took me!" Cyrus screamed. "You wanted to take Sheepy from me!"

Fueled by a burst of unexpected courage, Cyrus struck out at Siddharth. Each hit became a desperate attempt to break free from his iron grasp and save his father.

The auto-rickshaw rocked and swayed with the ferocity of their movements, teetering on the brink of disaster as the battle for control intensified. In a critical moment, with Ravi dangerously dangling over the road, gripping the metal bar for dear life, Harrison made a daring move. He leaned out, extending his arm across the treacherous gap between the speeding vehicles, reaching desperately for his father.

Spotting Harrison, Ravi released the bar with one hand, stretching toward his oldest son. Their hands met, and Harrison pulled his father back toward safety with a firm, determined grasp. Ravi tumbled into the back of Pappa's auto-rickshaw—the wind knocked out of him.

Driven by a surge of adrenaline and paternal instinct, Ravi quickly recovered. He lunged forward with every ounce of strength, extending his arm across the perilous gap between vehicles. His fingertips barely brushed the fabric of Cyrus's pajama sleeve.

"Pappa, closer!" Ravi's yell sliced through the mayhem with piercing intensity.

Pappa edged the auto-rickshaw forward in response. Seizing the moment, Ravi latched onto Cyrus's arm. But Siddharth's grip tightened around Cyrus's leg, locking them in a heart-stopping standoff.

Once again suspended in a perilous balance over the gap between the two rickshaws, Cyrus became the focal point of a terrifying tug-of-war.

Ravi's heart pounded relentlessly. He pulled with every fiber of his being, trying to seize Cyrus from Siddharth's hold. For a few endless seconds, Cyrus hung dangerously, a young face taut with fear, caught in the middle of this high-speed battle.

In that tense moment, time appeared to freeze, and the world around them held its breath. The familiar night sounds faded, leaving behind an eerie stillness that clashed with the escalating chaos. As the blurring pavement below Cyrus seemed to fade into the background, Ravi's attention was drawn to Siddharth's forearm. Amidst the turmoil, a seared mark resembling a rook from a chess set came into view, burned on Siddharth's skin. This unexpected sight brought the surroundings back into focus and intensified the significance of the life-and-death struggle unfolding with the rushing wind and the roar of engines.

Harrison, his face twisted with a mix of fear and determination, clung to the seat, his fingers white from the intensity of his grip. He watched with horror as his father valiantly fought to rescue his brother, his own breathing in sync with the desperate rhythm of the struggle.

Then, with a yank that strained every muscle in his body, Ravi pulled Cyrus into his rickshaw. He stumbled back, his chest heaving, as Siddharth's desperate grip finally gave way.

In the frenzy, the toy lamb tumbled from Cyrus's grasp. The bell chimed once. Then it was gone.

With the backdrop of screeching tires and the distant wail of approaching sirens, Ravi held Cyrus close, his arms wrapped protectively around his son. Tremors of adrenaline coursed through him, and his breaths came in ragged gasps.

Harrison and Pappa let out a collective sigh of relief, their faces drained of color but etched with profound gratitude. As they clung to one another, Ravi's senses filled with the comforting scent of Cyrus's shampoo, a soothing counterpoint to the whirlwind surrounding them.

"You're safe now, little buddy," Ravi whispered, his words hoarse but steady.

Cyrus's lip quivered with both relief and longing as he called out, "My lamb!" His small hand instinctively reached behind him, fingers outstretched, ready to grasp the cherished toy, but it was already lost to the receding darkness, swallowed by the vanishing auto-rickshaw. His wide eyes tracked the vehicle's disappearance with a blend of sadness and yearning.

Harrison, still breathless, placed a reassuring hand on Cyrus's shoulder. He leaned in close, his words a soothing balm. "It's okay, Cyrus," he said tenderly. "We don't need the lamb. We have something far more important."

Pappa's eyes, still reflecting the worry he had carried through those heart-stopping moments, met Cyrus's gaze through the rearview mirror. "That's right. We have you, safe and sound. The lamb is just a toy, but we could never replace you."

"Dad, I just realized it was Siddharth who took me at the fire festival. He told me not to tell anyone or Sheepy would be stolen." Tears welled up in Cyrus's eyes as he continued, "I promise, I never told anyone, Dad. Now my lamb is gone."

"It's okay, Cyrus. You did nothing wrong," Ravi said. He did not finish the thought.

Pappa slowed the auto-rickshaw, and for the first time that night, he felt his heart cease its frantic pounding. Turning to Ravi, he saw a reflection of his relief, triumph, and hard-won wisdom. Some things—like trust—could shatter in a blink.

***

7:22 P.M.

Exhausted and on edge, Ravi, Pappa, Harrison, and young Cyrus returned to the sanctuary of the inn. A haze of adrenaline clouded their senses. After lifting his son out of the auto-rickshaw, Ravi's arms wrapped around Cyrus with a fierce protectiveness, as though he could shield the boy from the world's darker truths. He was a cauldron of roiling emotions—rage at betrayal, confusion at inexplicable motives, and dread for what might lie ahead. He wondered what could make a diamond worth the life of his child.

Pappa's voice snapped Ravi out of his contemplative abyss.

"My son, this is far worse than I could have imagined. I thought we were stepping into a child's adventure, a harmless puzzle to add a layer of wonder to our family holiday. But we've stumbled upon something much darker, more treacherous."

Ravi's glare met his father's as he clutched Cyrus close to his chest. "This is insanity, Pappa. Nothing, not even the so-called Heart of Kumari, is worth endangering my son's life."

Ravi looked down at Cyrus, whose expression was filled with the innocence only a child could possess. His resolve hardened. "I couldn't care less if a mystical rock calls out to us. My family—their safety—that's my calling. That's my purpose." He walked back into the inn's lobby.

Sophie ran toward them. The moment she saw Cyrus, her face crumpled with relief. "My baby!" she cried, rushing forward and pulling him from her husband's grip. Holding him tightly, she murmured, "You're safe now. You're safe." She hoped that by saying it, she could make it eternally true.

Sophie turned to Ravi. "I want us out of here. Now!" Her voice was like steel wrapped in velvet. "This place—this adventure—this is no place for children or adults who value their lives. We need to protect what's most important to us." With a final, lingering look, she turned and took Cyrus to their room.

Priya watched Cyrus disappear into Sophie's arms, her eyes unreadable. Too unreadable. Then she emerged from behind the front desk, scanning the lobby before settling on Ravi and his family. "Anil will oversee the guarding of your room tonight. We will notify you when Raju and Siddharth are apprehended. Furthermore, we've arranged for local law enforcement to stand guard outside the inn. They'll be available if needed."

Just then, Police Chief Bhaskar entered the lobby. Concern arranged neatly across his face. "My men have captured Raju and Siddharth—they are in our custody as we speak. I assume you'll be pressing charges."

Ravi listened, nodding.

"We'll handle everything from here," Bhaskar said. "There's no need to come to the station tonight."

"Tonight?"

Bhaskar adjusted his cuffs. "I will need your passports for the report. Standard procedure in cases involving foreign nationals."

Ravi's gaze lingered a fraction too long. "They're in the safe upstairs."

"That's fine." Bhaskar lifted a hand as if to reassure him, then let it fall against Ravi's shoulder, "I'll collect them shortly."

His eyes flicked once toward Priya. Then he stepped back, already turning away.

"Trust us," he added, before leaving.

Ravi watched him go.

Then he turned to his father. "Raju and Siddharth… They were supposed to be trusted allies, and they betrayed us. Pappa, who can we trust now?"

Pappa exhaled slowly. "Trust is not a single stone you set in place, Ravi. It shifts. It tests the hand that holds it. Sometimes…"

While listening to his father's reply, Ravi's attention slipped. His gaze fell upon the chess table in the back corner. The room's noise and Pappa's words seemed to melt into the background as he was drawn to the mesmerizing scene. Two men sat across from each other, deep in thought, their brows furrowed as they contemplated their next moves.

The board between them was old, its surface worn smooth. Along one edge, faint letters had been carved and nearly sanded away with time—SACRED BALANCE—so shallow they looked more like a flaw in the wood than words at all.

Ravi's gaze lingered a second too long. Something about the scene unsettled him. Not the game. Not the players. The shape.

The rook stood near the center of the board, squat and unyielding.

"Are you okay?"

Ravi blinked and shook himself from his trance. "Yeah, why?"

"You looked like you were in another world," Pappa observed. "As I was saying, trust is a complicated matter, my son…"

"You're right, Pappa," Ravi interrupted. "Now, come on," he continued, yanking his father's arm and pulling him along the checkerboard tile. They took the stairs two at a time.

The Board had tilted beneath them.

-14-
THE UNSEEN TIES

अदृश्यानि बन्धनानि

8:00 P.M.

Bathed in the soft glow of the sconces, Sophie sat in her suite, tense and anxious. Cyrus, unaware of the mounting uneasiness yet exhausted from the harrowing event that had just taken place, lay sleeping on the couch next to his younger brother, Kiran.

Her gaze fixed on her peacefully sleeping children, Sophie clutched a cup of tea that had long gone cold. The necklace that had once hung at her throat lay discarded on the table.

The ordeal of Cyrus's kidnapping cast a heavy shadow over her spirit. She replayed those harrowing moments in her mind—the fear that had clenched her chest, the gut-wrenching panic of not knowing if she'd ever hold her son again.

Her countenance, usually so full of life, was now weary with the burden they had borne.

In that moment, a flash of anger stirred beneath her fatigue. *How could I have been so naive?* She had trusted Raju and Siddharth with everything—her family, their safety. But they had been careless, and it was Cyrus who had paid the price. A bitter taste rose in her mouth as she thought about how easily she'd let them into her life. She hated herself for it—hated that she had placed so much trust in them.

Yet as she watched Cyrus sleep, his small chest rising and falling, something in her eased. They were still here. That would have to be enough.

In the stillness, her heart skipped a beat as the door creaked open. She exhaled a sigh of relief seeing Pappa, Amma, Ravi, and Harrison step in. Anil remained in the hallway. His shadow crossed the threshold. He did not.

Harrison closed the door. The latch clicked. The lock slid home. The sound settled in the room and did not leave.

Ravi moved across the room, drawn to Sophie by an invisible thread. As she stood up, his eyes met hers, and without a word, she folded into him, seeking solace in his familiar presence.

"Thank God you are okay," she whispered.

Ravi held her close, his embrace a familiar shelter. His gaze drifted to Cyrus, in quiet slumber, his arms curled as though still clutching the stuffed lamb. It was a serene, innocent scene amidst the chaos. With a tender smile, Ravi reached out, his fingers lightly brushing Sophie's cheek.

This simple touch drew her gaze back to his. "I'm so sorry," she said, trembling. "This is all my fault."

"No," he said softly. "I was the one who left the door unlocked." He looked at Cyrus. "He's here."

The intensity in his expression was a powerful demonstration of their family's unbreakable resilience.

"I love you so much." Sophie's touch was gentle as she

traced the contours of Ravi's bruised jawline. Her attention lingering on the dried blood from his cracked lip.

A knock came at the door. Not loud. Not urgent. Measured. Three deliberate strikes.

Ravi looked up before anyone spoke. "It's him," he said quietly.

Another knock.

"Mr. Sharma?" came the voice from the hallway. Smooth. Public. "Police Chief Bhaskar."

Ravi stepped away from Sophie. He glanced once at Cyrus and Kiran, then toward the room with the safe.

"I'll handle it," he said.

He slid the chain into place before unlocking the latch and opening the door just wide enough to see through.

Bhaskar stood framed by the corridor light, uniform immaculate, expression arranged into concern.

Behind him, the hallway stretched empty. But not entirely. Anil's shadow lingered further down, half-swallowed by the light.

Ravi kept his hand on the door.

"I won't take much of your time," he said quietly. "I need your passports for the paperwork."

Ravi hesitated. "Is that necessary?"

Bhaskar inclined his head slightly. "You're welcome to accompany me to the station instead. It would expedite the formalities."

Sophie moved closer to Ravi at once. "No." Her hand caught his sleeve. "Stay. Please. Just give them what he needs."

Her voice trembled despite her effort to steady it.

Bhaskar waited. Patient. Certain.

Ravi looked back at his family. At Cyrus, sleeping. At Kiran's small hand curled into the couch cushion.

"It's just paperwork," Sophie whispered.

Ravi turned to his father, "Dad, would you get them?"

Pappa held Ravi's gaze for a moment, then nodded once. He moved toward the closet without comment.

The safe door groaned open. *Click. Click. Clunk.* The sound felt louder than the last time.

One by one, the passports were lifted from the dark interior. The small navy covers looked thinner in Pappa's hands.

He returned and passed them to Ravi.

Ravi hesitated, the passports still in his hand. "Should we contact the embassy?"

Bhaskar regarded him calmly. "You may. However, the embassy is closed at this hour."

A measured breath.

"I will file the necessary report tonight. In the morning, once your passports are returned, you are welcome to visit them yourself, if you wish."

Behind Ravi, Sophie's voice was low. "Stay. Please."

Ravi looked down at the small navy booklets in his hand. The gold crests caught the light. He felt their weight—paper, ink, stamps, entry marks. Identity. Exit.

Paperwork, he told himself.

His eyes lingered on Bhaskar a beat longer than courtesy required. Then he passed the passports through the narrow gap.

Bhaskar accepted them calmly, stacking them with precise care. "They'll be returned first thing in the morning," he said.

Then he stepped back. The corridor swallowed him.

Ravi shut the door. The lock slid into place with a final, metallic click.

For a moment, no one spoke.

Sophie pressed her palm to her chest as if steadying something beneath it. "We go to the embassy first thing," she said softly.

Amma's gaze lifted to the clock on the mantel.

Outside, a faint draft brushed the door and moved on. At the far end of the corridor, a shadow did not.

Pappa lit a fire in the fireplace to dispel the evening's tension. As the kindling blazed to life, he added logs to the growing flames. "Looks like we missed our window to go to another hotel," he said quietly.

The fire popped.

"Maybe," Ravi replied, pulling the old chair from the corner. He sank down beside the fire. He opened his mouth to speak—but paused. His brow furrowed, eyes narrowing slightly, as though the thought he'd meant to say had just slipped through his fingers. "Hmm," he said, placing his hands on the arms. "I had a point…"

"Ravi?" Sophie prompted gently.

He blinked, as if surfacing from water. "Never mind. Must've lost it." He stood abruptly, as though embarrassed by the silence, and pushed the chair back into the corner.

Harrison's eyes flicked to the chair. He didn't say anything—but he didn't look away either.

The fire cracked. The pendant pulsed. The silence resumed.

Amma pulled her shawl tighter around her shoulders. "Perhaps this is all too much. Maybe Harrison was right. Maybe we should think about going back home."

Sophie looked at her son with a torrent of emotions. Seeking comfort in Ravi's presence, she nodded in agreement with Amma, her eyes shimmering with unshed tears. "I'm scared. I want to go home. Let's do as Amma says."

Pappa, his face a mix of empathy and determination, stepped toward them. He placed a firm hand on Ravi's shoulder and touched Sophie's arm comfortingly. His gestures acknowledged the heavy burdens they had all shouldered. With a slight nod, he seemed to say it was time to leave behind the strife of their quest and seek the safety and peace of home.

Harrison was drawn to the table where the pendant lay, its subtle glow casting a mesmerizing aura. It drew their attention, refusing to be ignored. "We can't abandon our quest now. We're so close." He looked at his mother with urgency. "Mom, I didn't want to go on this vacation. I wanted to stay with my friends. But look at us now. We've grown so much, come so far." His words were filled with sincerity. "When we were in the jungle, and you were so gung-ho, I thought you were being reckless. But you were right, Mom. There's something about Nepal that's calling us." Harrison pointed to the pendant with profound emphasis. "This is bigger than us. I think we need to be here. We need to finish this."

Sophie's gaze softened, but her heart ached with the fear of what they'd endured. "But what if we lose more? What if we're risking too much?"

Pappa considered this before speaking up. "Sometimes, the greatest risks hold the most important rewards, Sophie. We didn't come all this way by accident. The Heart of Kumari isn't just a legend—it's part of us. Turning back now wouldn't undo what's already happened."

Harrison nodded. "That's right, Pappa. We can't. It's a part of us!" He then turned to his father. "Dad, you've always said it's darkest just before dawn."

The pendant pulsed once. Not brighter. Just steady. "That's right," Sophie said.

Harrison frowned. "What do you mean, Mom?"

She didn't look at him, her eyes still focused on the glow. "It's overwhelming... Like when you step out of a cave and into the sun after too long in the dark."

Harrison blinked. "Which cave?"

Pappa's gaze flickered toward the pendant, its glow pulsing like a heartbeat. "She's speaking of the cave in Plato's allegory. Remember, I read it on the drive to Chitwan? At first, the light wounds. It strips away the comfort of shadow. But only then can you see the world as it truly is."

The room stilled.

Sophie's fear, sharp as glass, cracked under the weight of understanding. The kidnapping, the betrayal, the ache of mistrust—they weren't signs to turn back. They were the sting of eyes opening.

Her gaze fell to the pendant. Its glow grew bolder, as if answering. In that moment, her apprehension reshaped into resolve. The resolve came without clarity, and she did not wait for it.

Harrison stepped closer, the light mirrored in his eyes. "It hurts because we've left the shadows," he said softly. "And we're not going back."

As the words left his mouth, a fleeting thought from his dream in Chitwan resurfaced. *Seek the Heart. Only you can restore balance.* His gaze shifted to the softly glowing necklace, its light holding his attention. Determination surged within him. This wasn't just about the legend—it was about them, their family, and the bond they shared.

An inexplicable stillness settled over the room. The pendant's glow was a beacon, reigniting their resolve. The magnitude of their ordeal transformed into a challenge they were forced to carry, knowing that the Heart of Kumari wasn't just waiting—it was *calling* them.

Harrison's face grew serious. "The Heart is guiding us. If we stop now, we'll leave something unfinished—something that could change everything. This isn't just about us. There's more at stake, and we can't turn away."

The room fell silent as the weight of Harrison's words settled over them. No one said whether they understood them the same way.

Ravi nodded slowly. "If we leave now, we might be abandoning more than we realize. This is no longer just about treasure or a vacation. The Heart of Kumari holds a power we don't fully understand yet, and it's calling to us for a reason—calling us into the light."

Sophie bit her lip, torn, but as she looked at her son, standing tall with the pendant's glow reflecting in his eyes, she realized the truth. They had come too far to walk away now. This was no longer just a quest; it was a responsibility—one they couldn't abandon without consequence.

"Okay," Sophie said quietly. "We'll finish this. We'll step out into the light—even if it still hurts. But under one condition."

"What's that?" Amma asked.

"We need to leave this hotel."

"Of course, Sophie," Pappa said. "First thing in the morning."

Amma's gaze settled on the necklace, transfixed by how its glow grew more intense. It was as though the light reached out—an invisible thread tethering her to the ancient artifact. A gentle smile formed on her face. "I do believe you're right; it's beckoning to us." She then turned to her husband. "Ray, could you please play the flute?"

"That's a wonderful idea," Pappa praised as he stepped away to retrieve the bansuri from inside the safe. Its bamboo surface captured the orange light from the fire as he raised it to his lips. The first notes were haunting, filled with a sense of longing that seemed to transcend time and space.

As the melody filled the room, the pendant stirred in response to the flute's notes. Each radiant pulse moved in harmony with the music, forming an aura of hope and enchantment around them.

Amid the flute's serenade, the charm gleamed brilliantly. The music seemed to gather them in, leaving little room to remain where they were. This journey, imbued with wonder and mysteries yet to be unveiled, pressed itself forward.

Surrounded by the ancient music, they resolved to support Harrison in his pursuit of the Heart of Kumari, a choice now as inevitable as the harmonious notes floating around them.

A whisper stirred within Harrison, urging him toward the glowing necklace. He lifted it carefully, warmth seeping through his fingertips. When he placed the gem around his neck, it settled snug against his chest. At that moment, something stirred, and a deep current surged within him, old and unfamiliar.

***

8:10 P.M.

Priya sat on the leather couch in her office, staring at the open window. The curtains churned from the evening breeze, mirroring the storm brewing inside her. She contemplated what she would say to Uncle Bhaskar. A heavy sense of foreboding pressed down on her. He would come, and she would be blamed for Raju and Siddharth's actions. They weren't here—but she was.

The door burst open with a thunderous crash, startling Priya. Uncle Bhaskar stormed in, clad in his police uniform, flanked by his two thugs pretending to be officers. His presence was overwhelming, his eyes burning with a controlled fury.

"Why did Raju and Siddharth kidnap the boy? I was not informed of this action!"

"I don't know, Mamaji," Priya stammered, fear flashing in her eyes as she looked away. "I had no idea either. It caught me off guard, as it did you. I promise."

Bhaskar glared, his face twisted. "Hmm," he muttered. "Now, the family doesn't trust them anymore. How are we going to get the diamond?"

"Maybe if Sunjata can get the last clue from the box, we won't need the Sharma family anymore," Priya said. The words came out too fast. Her stomach dropped. "If Raju and Siddharth secured the pendant from the boy, then we can find the diamond without them." She stopped, bracing for his reaction.

"The lamb! This is about that toy?" Bhaskar growled.

"I think so." She hesitated. "We need the necklace inside the lamb to find the diamond chamber."

Bhaskar walked over and slapped her, the sound sharp.

She winced, her face turning away. When she brought it back to meet Bhaskar's eyes, tears were streaming down her cheeks. "I'm sorry, Mamaji."

"Always sorry," Bhaskar sneered. He placed his hand on her chin and lifted it to look into her eyes. "You're lucky you look like your grandmother."

"Nani? You never told me that." She sniffled, seizing the moment to try and reason with him. "Look, if Raju and Siddharth have the Talisman, then send us to get the diamond. I know we can do it."

Bhaskar pondered this, his eyes narrowing to slits. "You know what happened to the last Seeker who failed me."

"Yes, Mamaji, I remember." She grimaced.

Bhaskar's expression darkened further. "Don't let the Sharma family leave the inn. At least they trust you and Anil."

Priya nodded, swallowing.

Bhaskar reached inside his coat and pulled out a stack of navy booklets.

"Their passports," he said.

Priya stared at them. "But how?"

Bhaskar walked over to the desk and placed them next to the lamp. "Paperwork," he said. "Fear makes people compliant. Confusion makes them obedient. Even mistakes can be positioned."

A breeze slipped through the open window and flipped the top booklet open. Ravi's photograph caught the lamplight.

Bhaskar watched it for a moment.

Then he unholstered his service weapon. Checked the safety with calm precision. The click was soft. Final.

He wrapped the gun in a dark cloth and set it beside the passports. "They will not leave this inn. Do you understand?"

Her jaw tightened once. That was all. "Yes."

He stepped closer. "Do not fail me, Priya," he said. "You better pray Raju and Siddharth got the lamb, or you will suffer the same fate as Arshad Khan." To emphasize his point, Bhaskar motioned to his officers.

One of them grabbed a vase from a nearby table and smashed it against the wall, sending shards flying. The other thug approached Priya, grabbing her arm with a painful grip, his knuckles white with tension.

Priya recoiled.

"Do you understand how important it is that the Shatranj find the diamond?" Bhaskar hissed with deadly intent.

"Yes, Mamaji," Priya gasped, the pain in her arm radiating through her body.

Bhaskar watched her for a moment, his eyes cold and calculating. Satisfied, he turned sharply, the buttons of his uniform gleaming in the light. He walked over to the bar and poured himself a generous measure of scotch, the amber liquid glinting as he raised the glass. He took a slow, deliberate sip, savoring the taste before slamming the glass down on the bar with a loud crack. "Release her," he ordered, gesturing to his men.

His point made, Bhaskar and his thugs turned and left the room, the door slamming shut behind them. Priya exhaled shakily, rubbing her bruised arm. She knew she had to tread with caution. Bhaskar was ruthless, and any misstep could be her last.

As the silence settled in her office, Priya's mind raced. The passports. The weapon. The hope that the twins had found the Talisman flickered, but it was drowned by a deeper fear—the dangerous game Bhaskar was playing with their lives. She pressed her back against the door, hands covering her face, trying to steady her breath. Shattered glass lay scattered around her.

She would wait a few more minutes, ensuring her uncle had left the inn before heading up to the Sharma family's room to meet Anil, who was keeping watch in the hallway.

* * *

8:40 P.M.

Ravi reached for his phone. He scrolled to his music app and tapped play on his '80s playlist. "Careless Whisper" by George Michael began to play. The saxophone drifted through the room, soft and familiar, loosening the tightness in the air.
"Now, we can get to work," Ravi said. "We have a mystery to solve."

"Mom, did something happen?" Cyrus asked, rubbing his eyes. The saxophone had woken him up.

"No, baby," Sophie said. "We just needed some music."

"Okay," Cyrus murmured, his eyes falling. He missed his lamb.

Ravi sang a line under his breath, slightly off-key, letting the sound carry. He crossed the room with exaggerated ease, then lowered himself beside Cyrus, offering him a cheeky grin.

Cyrus smiled, then drifted back asleep.

The saxophone wailed.

Outside the door, heels clicked on marble.

Inside, conversation resumed, lighter now.

***

8:43 P.M.

In the shadowy hallway of the Surya Chandra Inn, outside the family's suite, siblings Priya and Anil leaned against the rich mahogany paneling. The golden glow from an antique chandelier scattered light across the corridor.

Next to them, an elaborate oil painting of the Annapurna Mountain range drew the eye, its snow-capped peaks and lush valleys glowing under the soft light. The peaceful, untouched landscape provided a stark contrast to the clandestine exchange unfolding beneath it.

The strains of a classic 1980s track began to seep through the door. "Careless Whisper" by George Michael drifted down the hallway.

"I don't think the boy came back with the lamb," Anil remarked, a note of satisfaction in his voice. "It's likely Raju and Siddharth have it."

Tall and slender, Priya exuded elegance in her fitted pencil skirt. Her sharp eyes narrowed. "So, they've secured the lamb? Then do we have the necklace?"

Together, they pondered the implications. Finding the Kumari Talisman would mean Uncle Bhaskar's approval and a step closer to locating the diamond.

"Most likely," Anil said confidently.

"Then Raju did it!" Priya mused, surprise mingling with

newfound respect. She had harbored doubts about him, but now, those were swept away by their plan unfolding successfully. The thought of finally laying their hands on the Heart of Kumari drew a malevolent smile across her lips.

-15-
THE DRAGONS ARE NEAR

नागाः समीपे सन्ति

8:45 P.M.

Each passing minute in Raju's auto-rickshaw was suffocating as both men drowned in pools of thought and regret. For more than an hour, they had been circling the outskirts of the city, dodging familiar streets, their eyes scanning for any sign of danger. The weight of Bhaskar's looming wrath pressed down on them, tightening with each passing mile. Every corner they turned delayed the inevitable, the fear of retribution gnawing at their nerves. Yet, beneath it, something colder coiled—an unseen pressure urging him forward, not back.

Siddharth sat in the back seat, his left eye swollen and a bloody handkerchief pressed to his nose. His hair had come undone. It fell forward, half-veiling his face. He finally broke the oppressive silence, his voice filled with anguish. "Raju, this wasn't supposed to go this far. We only needed the lamb, not the boy." He searched Raju's face, looking for some clue of remorse or reconsideration—he found none.

Raju exhaled slowly from the driver's seat. Each breath was a battle. "The boy clutched that lamb like it was his lifeline. What choice did we have? We had to act fast. Time is running out," he continued, trying to justify his actions. "They'd stopped trusting in us. We needed the Kumari Talisman—had to act."

Realizing they were spiraling into a dark pit of complications, Raju veered the auto-rickshaw off the road. He parked alongside Mahendrapal Bazaar, the ancient marketplace still pulsating with life. Known for its rich, diverse array of vendors, the bazaar also served as a hidden ground for discreet exchanges and covert tasks.

As Siddharth exited, his eyes widened at the sight of a plush leg sticking out from under the seat. His mouth fell open in shock. "Raju, look here!" he exclaimed, pointing with a trembling hand. "The lamb! Cyrus must've dropped it during the struggle!"

A rush of adrenaline coursed through them. Grasping the stuffed lamb, Raju eagerly tore open the stitching. His face fell almost immediately.

The toy was empty.

"The pendant is gone. The family must've discovered it…They moved it." Every word carried the weight of disillusionment, suffused with an escalating sense of dread. A pit formed in Siddharth's stomach. "We've messed up, Raju. Not only did we not get what we came for, but we've also revealed our true intentions. Uncle Bhaskar is not going to be happy. What do we do now?"

Raju looked out into the busy atmosphere of the Mahendrapal Bazaar. His gaze hardened. Something in him shut. "We adapt, just like we've always done. We need to find those boys—you know the ones, street-savvy and cunning. Maybe they can get into the family's room unnoticed and retrieve the pendant."

In the dimly lit streets of Mahendrapal Bazaar, Raju and Siddharth stood, and the weight of their choices pressed upon them. The faint, cheerful hum of the marketplace surrounded them, a stark contrast to the turmoil churning within. With a shared glance, they acknowledged the gravity of their situation and the uncertain path ahead.

As they prepared to navigate the intricate web of secrets and consequences, neither spoke of what this would cost. They steeled themselves, and the city swallowed them whole.

* * *

8:50 P.M.

Compelled by a sudden, inexplicable instinct, Harrison rose from his chair, his senses acutely sharpened. "Tainted Love" by Soft Cell, pulsed through the room. The beat was thin and metallic against the walls.

He crossed to the window and pulled the curtain tighter. Checked the lock. Then the next. Then the door.

"What are you doing?" Amma asked.

He didn't answer at first. He listened. "I don't feel safe."

"Anil is outside," Amma said gently.

"Chief Bhaskar said the police are staged outside the hotel," Pappa cut in.

Harrison's jaw tightened. He turned the deadbolt anyway.

Sophie was already watching him. The shift in him unsettled her more than his words. She reached for Ravi's phone and turned the volume up.

The beat intensified. Mechanical. Hollow.

A shadow passed beneath the threshold.

For an instant, the sliver of hallway light bent around the doorframe and broke against the floorboards—E T R—before the angle shifted and the line went clean again.

Kiran, now roused from slumber, blinked against the firelight. He turned toward Cyrus first, who had fallen back asleep.

Kiran's gaze dropped to the space where Sheepy should have been. He frowned.

"Siddharth?" he asked quietly. The name was soft. Uncertain.

No one answered.

Sophie looked up from across the room. "No, sweetheart," she said gently. "Siddharth isn't here."

Kiran searched her face. "Did he take it?" he asked. The question barely rose above the crackle of the fire.

Sophie held his gaze. "We're going to get it back," she said.

Kiran nodded once. He didn't ask again. His eyes tracked Harrison moving through the room, checking locks. With each turn of a latch, a thread of worry wound tighter around Kiran's chest.

He slid off the cushions and padded toward his mother—but veered wide around the old chair on the way, giving it a nervous glance without slowing. Then he scurried into her lap, seeking refuge in the safety of her arms. He looked up and asked, "Mama, are the dragons near?"

Sophie held her son close, her heart aching at the innocence in his question. She brushed his hair away from his eyes. "Yes, my love, the dragons are close, but remember what we've talked about?" She held his gaze. "We are brave and clever, and dragons can't hurt us if we stand strong." She held his gaze a second too long. "We'll outsmart them."

Kiran nodded, but he did not smile. He studied her face. "Is Siddharth a dragon?"

Sophie did not hesitate. "Yes," she said. She drew him closer. "He chose to be."

Kiran pressed his face into her shoulder.

The room had settled into a fragile calm, the kind of quiet that felt borrowed. For a moment, the music paused between songs. The silence stretched, drawn out just long enough to be noticed. Then, the mellow chords of "Drive" by The Cars curled softly around them, and for a flicker of time, the room was almost normal again.

Amma rose and moved to the sideboard, the electric kettle hissing softly. "Tea, anyone?" she asked.

Sophie nodded. "Yes, please." She lifted Kiran from her lap and settled him beside her on the couch. He leaned against her arm, watching his grandmother pour the liquid.

Amma crossed the room and handed her a cup. "Here, dear. This will help."

"Thank you, Amma." Sophie accepted it with both hands, the warmth seeping into her palms, anchoring her.

Amma set her purse on the table, tightening the clasp.

"We need to talk," Ravi said, his voice grave.

The room's atmosphere shifted, the fragile peace shattered by the weight of his words. Sophie looked up, sensing the change. "What's wrong?" she asked, her hold on her cup tightening slightly.

Ravi took a deep breath, pacing slowly across the room. "There's something I need to tell you all…"

"What?" Sophie asked.

"Chief Bhaskar told me they apprehended Raju and Siddharth."

Sophie let out a breath. "Oh, that's wonderful."

Ravi's expression darkened. "But wait," he added, "Something didn't sit right."

Amma leaned forward. "Oh, why is that?"

Ravi took a moment to choose his words, "He was very quick to tell us not to come to the station," he explained.

"Maybe he was trying to spare us," Amma offered.

"Maybe," Ravi said. But he didn't sound convinced.

His mind moved backward. Raju driving. Siddharth watching the rearview mirror. Routes chosen for them. Stops arranged. Yet, they had never once set the course themselves.

Ravi's jaw tightened. "In the rickshaw…his sleeve rode up. I saw a mark on Siddharth's arm. It was of a rook—you know, like in chess."

"What's so strange about that?" Pappa asked, walking over to the tea pot and helping himself to a cup.

Sophie shifted, her gaze briefly flicking away. Her attention was drawn to a distant thought.

Harrison nodded, taking a quick breath. "Was it burned into the inside of his wrist?"

"Yes! How did you know?" Ravi asked.

"Raju had the same mark—I saw it yesterday at the bazaar when he handed me my bag."

The room lapsed into an oppressive quiet, each person contemplating the association of the burn marks.

"A rook?" Ravi pondered. "And Raju has a rook, too?" The information tracked with the revelation he had downstairs.

"Wait, there's more," Harrison said, as a memory surfaced in his mind. "I saw a king burned onto Arjun's arm back in Chitwan. He showed it to me—mentioned something about how it's guiding his path." He leaned in, his voice low and conspiratorial. "Police Chief Bhaskar also has a mark on his wrist—it's not a chess piece, but it looks like a crown entwined with a serpent. That's how I knew it was him at the bazaar;

I saw the same burn mark on his arm when we were in the stairwell leading to the basement."

A pit formed in Ravi's stomach.

"Priya has a queen on her neck," Sophie said, adding to the growing list of odd connections. "I saw it when she walked away the other day at breakfast. I thought it was odd at the time, but I figured she liked to play chess." She whispered so as not to be heard through the door.

"A queen!" Ravi exclaimed in a low hush. He turned to the group, his expression tense. "Has anyone seen any more markings like this?"

Kiran spoke up, uncertain. "I saw a burn mark on the lady who worked in the jungle. I can't remember her name."

"Ms. Reena? Raju's mom?" Sophie asked.

"Yes, that's her name. She had a queen, too. I saw it on her neck," Kiran confirmed, his memory becoming clearer.

"Just like Priya," Sophie said, a shiver running down her spine.

Pappa's voice hitched in shock. "By the stars! Meera had a queen on her neck as well. I asked her about it."

"What did she say?" Sophie pressed.

"Something about being in a sorority in college."

Amma chimed in, "Yes, and when we were on the tour of the fort, I saw a knight burned onto Anil's arm."

"Oh my God!" Sophie exclaimed.

"Shh," Ravi hushed her. "Keep your voice down."

"I'm sorry—it's just that I remembered something." Sophie turned to Pappa. "Do you remember the book we found in the Chitwan library? The one with the diamond on it?"

Pappa's brow tightened. "Of course. The one about the Shatranj—the chess order."

"The same order Sunjata mentioned today," Sophie pressed. "The one that 'rebranded.'"

"The same order that used to occupy this inn when it was a fort," Harrison said.

Ravi went still.

"That wasn't just history," Pappa murmured.

"Mom, what did it say?"

"It said something about being bound... by blood and oath." The words tasted different now. "Do you think..."

"Sophie," Pappa's voice slowed. "You might be onto something."

Harrison frowned. "Onto what?"

Pappa didn't answer immediately. His eyes moved from one face to another. "We've seen the brands," he said. "The rook. The queen. The knight. They aren't random."

"Chess soldiers," Kiran said.

"They're ranked," Ravi said quietly.

"Yes." Pappa nodded once. "And if it's ranked... then it's organized."

Silence.

Sophie's voice dropped. "And if it's organized..."

Kiran looked up at Harrison. "Like a real game?"

Harrison met his brother's eyes. For a second, he saw it—not the board in the lobby, not the polished bronze figures—but something older. Something moving. His gaze dropped briefly to Kiran's hands. Small. Unbranded. Unmarked. He looked back up slowly. "Yes," he said.

No one corrected him.

"Then they are not just guides," Harrison finished.

Ravi exhaled slowly. "No."

Amma looked between them. "What are you saying?"

Pappa met her eyes. "I'm saying some legacies aren't chosen." He reached for his teacup. Beneath it lay a folded newspaper, a headline half-blurred by spilled tea appeared—THE WORLD ENDS NOW. SHATRANJ HAILED AS SAVIORS—bold letters from an old article about a temple collapse in eastern Nepal.

No one noticed. The stain bled into the words, darkening them as Pappa finished. "They're inherited."

The words settled.

Sophie swallowed. "You mean—"

"Yes," Ravi said. "Raju and Siddharth aren't just guides."

Harrison's voice barely carried. "They are Shatranj."

A window rattled.

"What's wrong with that?" Amma asked, her brow furrowed in confusion. "Sunjata said the Shatranj changed their image—doing good for Nepal."

"Good people don't hide what they are," Ravi said quietly. "Not when they're guiding your children through caves."

No one spoke.

Ravi continued, "They drove us. Fed us. Moved us from city to city." His jaw tightened slightly.

"And they never once said they belonged to the Shatranj."

The door stood between them and the hallway.

Amma's fingers stilled around her teacup.

Sophie's eyes drifted to the small gold chain latched above the handle. It hung there, delicate.

Harrison swallowed.

The room fell into a heavy silence, each family member processing the revelations that had come crashing down around them.

Harrison's voice pierced the stillness. "We have a crown with a serpent, a pair of queens, a knight, a king, and two rooks." He looked at each of them. "We have every piece accounted for." He swallowed.

"Except the one that gets sacrificed first."

The room did not feel safer. It felt smaller.

-16-
BLOODLINES AND BETRAYALS

रक्तवंशाः च विश्वासघाताः

9:00 P.M.

The bustling streets of the Mahendrapal Bazaar teemed with life as Raju and Siddharth hurried through the crowd. The mix of faces mirrored their turmoil—fear, hope, desperation, resolve—as people wove through the stalls.

Through the press of bodies and bright lights, a glint of copper rose above the haze—the temple dome, gleaming like a promise. The sight drew Siddharth's gaze, and a quiet insistence stirred within him.

A faint chime drifted from the courtyard, the fragrance of sandalwood threading through the evening air.

Siddharth felt a compelling pull to step inside.

"Go on without me," he urged. "I want to offer a prayer."

"Fine," Raju retorted sharply. "I'll go search for the street boys myself. Send a message to Anil to keep him informed."

"Without a doubt, my brother," Siddharth assured him. And with that, he walked toward the temple.

* * *

Inside the temple, Siddharth lit an incense stick, its fragrant smoke curling upward as he lowered his head and spoke. His cadence was a tender whisper amidst the sacred silence. "Divine guidance, grant me the wisdom to discern the path ahead," he implored, each word saturated with his inner turmoil. His voice grew more fervent as he continued. "Bestow upon me the courage to honor my devotion to my brother while not forsaking the burning desire in my heart to walk the path of righteousness and seek redemption for my Order."

Images of the recent events flickered through his mind like shards of a once beautiful mosaic, now fractured and scattered. The faces of those they had crossed, their choices, and the consequences they had set in motion all presented themselves before him. But in Siddharth's heart, a faint glimmer of hope persisted. It was a belief that maybe, just maybe, they could find redemption, that the narrative of their lives remained open, not yet written in unyielding stone. He harbored a conviction—that finding the Heart could restore honor to the brotherhood of the Shatranj Ke Sipahi. His soul ached for a sign, a divine spark to illuminate their path of righteousness and cleanse the sins of past misdeeds. And so, he pressed forward, teetering on the precipice of an existential cliff, his faith unwavering.

* * *

When Siddharth emerged from the temple steps, a gust of wind funneled through a narrow alley. It struck him sideways, catching the hem of his jacket. He looked up, and his gaze settled on a young family—a mother and father walking together with their child, who he thought to be around the same age as Cyrus. The child clutched a stuffed toy to his chest. His countenance sparked with simple joy.

The sight pierced Siddharth's conscience. His chest tightened as if an invisible hand had grasped his heart.

How can I be a part of something that would shatter a family and harm a child? he questioned, a tremor of moral doubt coursing through his veins. He was visibly shaken, his hands trembling, his conviction cracking under the weight of his conscience.

Drawing a deep breath, Siddharth steadied his hands and summoned the will to update Anil. The message was simple, the truth heavier than words: The necklace was not in the lamb.

* * *

9:05 P.M.

Back at the Surya Chandra Inn, Anil's phone vibrated in his pocket, breaking his train of thought. He glanced at the screen; Siddharth's name flashed. Unlocking the device, he read the message, and his expression sharpened into surprise. "It's from Siddharth. They've got the lamb, but the pendant is missing."

At first, disappointment overcame Priya, but then her mouth curved into a sly smile. "So, the Sharma family found the Kumari Talisman. It's in their room."

"It must be," Anil agreed.

Priya turned to Anil. "Or around someone's throat," she

said with a venomous grin. "Now, we will play this my way. We'll use the hotel's hidden passages to access their suite. Let's enlist the street boys again. I'm confident they'll succeed this time."

The light flickered, then steadied.

"We must get the pendant, whatever the cost. Once we have it, the Sharma family will be obsolete."

Anil nodded.

"Send Siddharth our plan," Priya commanded.

Hesitantly, Anil's fingers moved over the phone's screen, typing out the message. The thought of enlisting the street kids again weighed heavily on him; their involvement seemed fraught with potential complications. He wrestled with the idea, seeking an alternative route to secure the necklace that didn't include them or harming the family, but Priya's plan, risky as it was, emerged as the only feasible option. The thought of confronting the family directly didn't bear consideration. He had never done anything like that; he avoided anything that would put his carefully crafted reputation in jeopardy.

Anil's heart was heavy, yet driven by the urgency of their quest. Reluctantly, he pressed 'send.'

9:06 P.M.

Ravi reached for the room key on the side table. When he lifted it, the metal pawn charm swung in the lamplight.

No one spoke.

Pappa stared at it for a long moment. "We're on the Board," he said quietly.

Kiran leaned forward, squinting at the charm. "But we're

not even playing," he said. "Are we?" He nudged Harrison's arm. "You know how to play, right?"

Harrison glanced at him. "I've played." He shifted his eyes to Pappa. "He's the expert." The charm in his father's hand mocking them. "What does it mean?"

Cyrus slept on the couch, arms folded tight against his chest, fingers closed inward.

Pappa did not smile. "Pawns move forward," he said. "Only forward. They never go back."

He looked at the charm.

"They're placed first," he continued. "And they're often the first to fall."

Ravi swallowed. "So what do we do?"

Pappa's gaze remained on the small metal charm. "We stop playing the way they expect."

Ravi looked up. "Then we need to understand who they are."

The fire popped.

Harrison turned to his mother. "Mom, what else did that book say about the Shatranj?" he pressed.

Sophie hesitated, frowning as she tried to recall. "I... I don't remember exactly. I wish we'd taken the book. I didn't realize it would be so important."

Harrison gently encouraged her. "It's okay, Mom. Just think."

Sophie took a sip of her tea before speaking. "It said something about them being guardians of a secret legacy."

Pappa jumped in. "Chosen to protect the Heart of Kumari from those who would misuse it."

"That's right!" Sophie said, relieved that Pappa had jogged her memory. "Thanks."

"Guard it from those who would misuse it," she repeated. She looked up. "But the legend says the Heart keeps equilibrium. If it holds balance… then why does it need guardians?"

"You're right to question it," Pappa said. "Balance doesn't collapse on its own."

Harrison nodded slowly. "So… the Shatranj were guardians." He hesitated. "What if it wasn't outsiders who misused the Heart?"

The room stilled. "What if it was them?" he finished quietly.

Sophie's expression changed. "Back in Chitwan, Raju said they were searching for the Heart because they believed it would give them unlimited power." Her fingers tightened around the cup. "If they were already its guardians…" she said, almost to herself, "then why would they be searching?"

"It doesn't fit," Harrison said.

A log collapsed into the embers.

Pappa reached for the poker and pressed the burning wood deeper into the coals. "If guardians begin to believe the power belongs to them," he said, "protection becomes possession."

Harrison stared into the hearth, watching the flames bend and recover. "So the change… wasn't in the Heart," he said slowly. "It was in them."

Sophie swallowed. "And possession becomes conquest."

"And that," Pappa said quietly, "is how a dark age begins."

"The Kali Raatri," Sophie breathed.

"Wait. I thought the diamond was good?" Amma questioned, her tea cup paused mid air. "How could it cause the dark age?"

Harrison turned to his grandmother. "Maybe it depends on who is controlling it. Maybe, it's like it takes on their intentions."

Amma placed her cup on the side table. "Oh," she said, "like how a knife can be used to cut food or to harm someone. It's not the knife itself that's good or bad—it's the one holding it."

"Yeah," Harrison said. And for the first time, the diamond did not feel like something to find. It felt like something to survive.

The fire flared.

Pappa turned toward Harrison, the glow of the flames caught his eyes. "And when possession replaces protection," he said, "they stop guarding."

Harrison frowned. "And if they stopped guarding... then at some point they lost it."

Sophie's fingers tightened. "In Chitwan, Raju said they were searching for it." She looked up slowly. "If they were once its guardians... and they're searching now..."

"Then they don't have it." Harrison finished.

Sophie set her teacup down too carefully, aligning it with the grain of the table as if precision could steady her. "And now..." Her voice faltered. "Raju and Siddharth might be trying to reclaim the Heart of Kumari." Her mouth went dry. "To take back what they lost." The words hollowed her out.

The room felt suddenly too warm. She pressed her palms into her knees to keep them from shaking. She swallowed. A small, sickness coiled low in her stomach. She did not look at Ravi. No one noticed.

"So we're not just looking for an artifact," Harrison said. He rose and crossed to the hearth, nudging a log with the metal poker. Sparks lifted and died. "We're in the middle of it."

He stared into the flames. Light flared, then folded back into ash. "To keep the Kaali Shakti from coming back."

Ravi's eyes narrowed. "What did you just say?"

Harrison blinked, as if waking. "I—I don't know." The poker slipped slightly in his hand. He set it back against the stone. "It just came to me."

Sophie looked up.

He took a deep breath, steadying himself. "In my dream in Chitwan…an angelic figure—the Spirit of Kumari, I think—she showed me a world where the Kaali Shakti had taken over. It just hit me now! Cities destroyed…people suffering…everything swallowed by darkness." His voice cracked slightly, the images flooding back. "It was terrifying."

Pappa's expression hardened. "The Spirit of Kumari showed you this? In a dream? That's not something we ignore."

The air shifted—not louder, not sharper—just thinner.

"What is the Kaali Shakti?" Amma asked. "How does that fit in?"

Pappa didn't answer immediately. He crossed to the side table and opened his notebook. The pages were creased, graphite smudged at the edges from travel and handling.

He flipped once. Twice. Then stopped. "There," he murmured.

Beneath a rough sketch of the museum panel, a word circled in the margin. Kaali Shakti.

"I didn't translate it fully at the time," he said quietly. "It appeared in an older reference tied to the Shatranj records." He looked up. "It means… 'the dark force.' But not merely evil." He hesitated. "More like… power unrestrained."

Amma inhaled too quickly. Tea caught in her throat. She coughed, pressing her napkin to her lips. "Power unrestrained," she managed.

"It's not a demon," Pappa said softly. "It's what happens when guardians forget what they were guarding."

Ravi leaned back, arms crossed, his face shadowed by the firelight. "So the Shatranj Ke Sipahi aren't just looking for the diamond," he said slowly. "They're trying to take it back," he paused, "and whatever happened during the Kali Raatri… they want it again." The words lingered.

Sophie glanced between them. "That would explain their

obsession." Her voice was thinner now. "The Heart isn't just an artifact. It's a hinge." She swallowed. "If it turns… something ancient turns with it."

Silence stretched. Pappa spoke at last. "If they're tied to the Kaali Shakti," he said, "then this isn't ambition."

He looked toward the darkened window.

"It's resurrection."

The word settled. No one spoke.

Kiran looked from face to face. "What's a resurrection?"

Pappa studied him for a long moment before answering. "It means something that was gone… comes back," he said. "Sometimes it's a person. Sometimes it's a belief. Sometimes it's power." He glanced toward the fire. "It doesn't always come back the same."

"Like when my fish died and we got a new one?" Kiran asked.

"No," Harrison said quietly. He was still staring into the flames. "Not new."

Silence followed. The fire shifted and bent.

Kiran frowned, trying to understand.

His stomach growled. "I'm hungry," he announced, almost apologetically.

Sophie exhaled, as if grateful for something she could solve. "Let's eat."

"We could order something," Amma suggested, pulling open the side-table drawer where the takeout menus were tucked.

Ravi shook his head before she finished. "Let's not."

That was all he said. No one asked why.

Sophie crossed to the mini-fridge. Cold light spilled across the firelit room as she pulled out the leftover takeaway containers.

The microwave hummed. Too loud.

Ravi glanced toward the door.

Kiran watched the door while the dishes turned.

Amma tore the bread into smaller pieces than necessary, her fingers working steadily.

The fire burned low

"They were supposed to be good," Amma said, a crease forming between her brows. "That's what the curator said."

Pappa nodded once. "They probably were."

Amma looked at him.

Ravi didn't look up. "That's the story they want told." He leaned forward, elbows on his knees. "Benevolence is the mask. Underneath, it's control." A pause. "They've just learned to hide it better." He exhaled sharply. "They already proved that." He pressed his palms to his forehead, steadying himself. "The other night in the basement stairwell—Harrison, Sophie, and I—we overheard Priya and Chief Bhaskar. It wasn't a casual conversation." His jaw tightened. "Priya handed him a folder. Evidence. Bhaskar said he'd 'take care of it.'"

The microwave beeped.

Sophie crossed to the sideboard and pulled out seven chipped plates. The ceramic clicked softly against the wood.

"Take care of it how?" Amma asked, gathering her purse and shawl from the table and setting them on the old chair beside her to make room.

Ravi didn't hesitate. "Destroy it."

Sophie spooned rice onto the plates.

"For who?" Pappa asked quietly.

"For himself," Ravi said. "Or for them." He looked up then. "Remember those suited men we saw in the boat? I don't think they were watching us. He leaned back, jaw tight. "I think they were watching the inn."

The words landed heavier than he intended.

Amma's fingers stilled. "Then maybe we approach them,"

she said carefully. "Ask for help."

"Not so fast." He leaned forward again. "They've already seen us with Raju and Siddharth. If they're investigating something illegal, we walk up to them now—" He shook his head. "We look involved."

Silence.

"We don't know who's watching who," he added. "We don't know who answers to who."

"We need distance," Pappa said. "From this inn. From Raju. From Siddharth."

Pappa didn't raise his voice when he spoke. That made it worse.

Ravi didn't answer. Distance required documents. Documents sat in Police Chief Bhaskar's desk drawer.

Amma nodded slowly. "If that's true," she said, "then the Heart matters even more."

"Yes," Ravi said. Then, softer, "That's what we're saying."

Amma didn't answer.

He exhaled, shoulders lowering. "I'm sorry. That came out wrong."

She gave a small nod. "We're all trying to understand."

Sophie set a plate of rice and daal in front of Kiran. "I wouldn't be surprised if Priya and Anil are related to Raju and Siddharth," she said, almost to herself. "After all… doesn't 'bloodline' mean family?"

Kiran chewed slowly, looking around the table.

Harrison, intrigued, asked, "Why do you say that, Mom?"

Sophie paused, considering her words. "I can't quite put my finger on it… It's more than how they look," she remarked, a spark of certainty igniting within her. "It's the way they interact with each other," she continued, her ideas gaining clarity. "It's like they have a shared past," she submitted, remembering the knowing smiles and exchanged glances among the four, hinting at a hidden secret.

"I noticed that with Police Chief Bhaskar," Harrison said. "The way he interacted with Raju and Siddharth at the bazaar made it seem like they knew each other well, almost like the whole scenario had been rehearsed."

Ravi's eyes glazed over as he stared into the fire, contemplating this new development. "It would make sense if they were family," he muttered, half to himself.

"How do you mean?" Amma asked.

Ravi's focus sharpened. "We already know they're Shatranj," he said. "The marks prove that." He leaned forward. "But what if this wasn't coincidence?" He looked at each of them in turn.

"What if we were guided exactly where they wanted us?"

Harrison remembered the odd feeling he had while at dinner in Kathmandu—the uncomfortable sensation. "Remember when we were at Hareti's Kitchen on our first night, and I told you I felt like someone was watching us?"

"You're right," Pappa chimed in. "Raju approached us, led us to the Himalayan Guest House, and later introduced us to Siddharth in Chitwan... I bet they were watching us at dinner."

"And Cyrus said he recognized Siddharth from the Pashupatinath Temple back in Kathmandu. He said Siddharth tried to take him—wanted to steal Sheepy back then," Ravi added.

Sophie's eyes widened as her stomach twisted into knots. "Siddharth! I had no idea!"

"Cyrus figured it out only tonight when he was kidnapped," Ravi explained.

"Why didn't he tell us before?" Sophie gasped.

Kiran froze.

"Wait." He looked from face to face. "Cyrus was kidnapped?"

No one answered fast enough.

He swallowed. "Is that why Sheepy's gone?"

Cyrus, overhearing their conversation, stirred from his sleep on the couch. He sat up slowly, his voice trembling. "I was too scared. He said he would hurt Sheepy if I told anyone."

Sophie dropped her fork and moved quickly to her son. She pulled him onto her lap. "I'm so sorry you had to go through that," she said, kissing his forehead. "Is that why you wanted Sheepy to have a bell?"

"Yes," Cyrus murmured softly, burrowing deeper into his mother's arms.

"I'm so sorry, baby," Sophie said again.

Pappa's face darkened. "It seems they knew Harrison was the chosen Seeker before we did. They've been targeting us since we landed in Kathmandu, using us for their own gain."

"It all makes sense now. I should not have doubted myself—they deliberately led us to this hotel! I knew something was off!" Sophie said, clenching her fists, her eyes burned with resolve.

"Mom, it's okay," Harrison said softly. "We all wanted to believe they were good. After all, they put on a convincing show."

Sophie's heart clenched at her son's words, a bitter mix of shame and regret. She forced a nod, trying to swallow the heaviness in her throat. "I just…" Her voice wavered. "I should have seen it sooner."

Feeling a sudden chill, Amma reached for her shawl where it rested atop her purse. It slipped. Fell.

The purse hit the ground with a thud, spilling half its contents across the tile.

Amma blinked. "Oh—" She reached down, flustered, gathering scattered coins, folded papers and a lipstick tube.

"This chair never seems to cooperate. I thought… wasn't it back in the corner?"

Sophie looked up. "It was."

Harrison turned toward the chair.

No one said anything else.

Ravi stepped forward, quietly picked up the chair, and carried it back to the far wall. He placed it there without comment. Straightened it. Brushed his hands on his pants, then turned back toward the group.

The fire crackled.

Just then, Amma's mouth dropped open, her eyes wide as she stared at a business card that had fallen out of her purse. "Meera and Neeraj Chandra. Himalayan Guest House Kathmandu," she read.

"They're cousins." Sophie breathed.

"They have been manipulating us since day one," Pappa said.

For a fleeting second, something in Harrison recoiled.

Amma nodded, her face reflecting a mixture of disbelief and realization. "Meera and Neeraj—the couple who ran the guesthouse in Kathmandu—they're Priya and Anil's parents." She looked around the room, her voice tightening with urgency. "And Arjun—the man who ran the jungle camp in Chitwan—he's Raju and Siddharth's father. He's Meera's brother. That means Meera and Arjun are siblings. They're all connected." Sophie's eyes widened. "Raju didn't just work in Kathmandu for anyone…he was helping his aunt run the guesthouse."

"And they're the ones who sent us to Pokhara," Ravi muttered, the weight of it settling over him like dust.

"Bound by blood," Sophie whispered. "That's what the woman at the lake meant, Harrison."

"And Bhaskar must be their brother," Pappa finally said.

"The bloodline of the Shatranj Ke Sipahi," Harrison whispered.

A beat of silence followed. The air in the room felt heavier, as if the words had tilted something off balance.

Harrison stepped back, needing air. He turned toward the hearth—and froze. The painting loomed above the mantel, its twilight scene unchanged. But the hillside was no longer empty.

She was there again. A faint silhouette on the rampart. A woman, barely distinguishable, caught mid-turn, as if she'd been walking away and just now looked back. Not at the fort. Not at the sky. At him.

He blinked hard. Still there.

The sound of Ravi's footsteps behind him broke the moment. Harrison turned, heart thudding. He didn't speak.

And above the hearth, the fort watched on.

Sophie's face paled as the connections sank in. "We've been staying in the heart of their operations this whole time."

"It was their plan all along, and we fell for it, hook, line, and sinker," Ravi said.

Pappa looked around at his family, his expression one of fierce determination. "This isn't about finding the Heart anymore."

Amma's hands trembled as she spoke. "We have to be very careful... They may know we're onto them."

Ravi went still. "They may not know we're onto them.," he said quietly. "But we just gave them control." His eyes shifted to the room were the safe was.

Harrison's jaw set. "Then we give them nothing."

His eyes flicked upward—just for a second—to the painting above the hearth. She was still there. Watching. As if she already knew what came next.

He opened his mouth to speak—then closed it. What would he even say?

Pappa's hand settled on Harrison's shoulder. "They've made their move," he said quietly. "Now we make ours."

***

9:20 P.M.

In the winding alleys of the Mahendrapal Bazaar, Raju made eye contact with the street-smart youngsters. It was an exchange that acknowledged the high-stakes gambit they were entering. As they met in a dark corner of the bazaar, Raju leaned close.

"I have a critical task," he whispered. "You must infiltrate the Surya Chandra Inn discreetly, just as you did last time, and make your way to the Sharma family's suite. The objective is to locate a necklace with a pendant. It's a simple piece with beads and a blue stone at its center. However, it's not just any necklace—it holds immeasurable importance." Raju reached into his pocket and retrieved a neatly folded slip of paper, handing it to the older boy. "This is what you're looking for."

The boy unfolded the paper to reveal an image of the Kumari Talisman.

"Do whatever it takes to retrieve it," Raju continued. His demeanor was chillingly calm as he drew his index finger across his throat in a haunting gesture, leaving no room for misunderstanding. He paused, making eye contact with each of them to ensure his message was sinking in. "Failure is not an option."

The boys exchanged a glance. Their young expressions were a complex web of emotions—fear, curiosity, and even a glint of excitement.

The younger of the two shook his head. His expression

changed as the impact of what was being asked dawned on him. "I'm out," he mumbled. A wave of relief washed over him as turned and walked away, blending back into the maze of the market.

The older boy, his face hardened by the harsh life he'd led, wasn't so easily deterred. "How much?"

Raju leaned even closer, his demeanor sharpening with calculated intensity. "I'll make it worth your while for a job well done... Very worth your while."

The boy's eyes shone with both skepticism and interest.

Raju sensed the wavering in the boy's gaze and pressed. "Once you retrieve it, you'll give the necklace to the lady behind the reception desk. Her name is Priya. She will have an envelope for you with one hundred twenty thousand rupees."

"I know Priya," he hissed. His eyes fixed on Raju. "Fine. It's a deal." He almost spat the words, torn between the magnitude of what he agreed to and the reward's enticement. "I'll be in that room at one in the morning. You'll have your necklace shortly after. But let's get one thing straight: I'm not cleaning up my mess. Got it?"

As the words left his mouth, a noticeable tension fell upon the scene—a strain that hinted at the moral consequences and the undeniable risks of their illicit endeavor. At that moment, they both realized the lines they were crossing.

With a lingering sense of foreboding, Raju turned and walked into the throng. The pact he had just struck bore down on his conscience. This new move in their precarious game was a gamble, one that had the potential to bring either salvation or ruin in its wake.

As the bustling activity of Mahendrapal Bazaar engulfed him, its heady scents mingling with the sea of people, Raju felt disoriented, almost unmoored. The lines that once demarcated loyalty from betrayal, ethical from corrupt, had dissolved into a murky fog of moral ambiguity. In that dizzying moment, one haunting question refused to leave him. *What will be the ultimate cost of this next fateful step we are about to take?*

A complex mix of emotions churned within him. They had crossed another boundary and added a layer of risk to their already fraught endeavor. Raju felt like he was teetering on the edge of a cliff, uncertain whether the next gust of wind would push him to safety or send him plummeting into an abyss. As he stood there, grappling with these unsettling thoughts, he knew they had reached a point of no return. He had made his move. The Board would answer.

* * *

9:30 P.M.

With quiet caution, Harrison walked over to the door and leaned in to listen. He strained to hear if Anil was still outside. The ticks emanating from the clock on the mantel were intensified by the prevailing quiet that shrouded the room. Amidst this hush, he could discern the distinct clicks of heels on the marble floor.

"They're out there; I can hear Priya's shoes," Harrison whispered. He scribbled a note on a piece of paper and handed it to Amma, knowing silence was now their safest ally.

As she unfolded the note, her expression reflected the shock of the scratched words staring back at her.

OUR ENEMY IS RIGHT OUTSIDE THE DOOR.

An icy shiver rippled through her body. In a solemn silence that spoke volumes, Amma turned over the slip of paper, her hand shaking as she inscribed another damning revelation.

WE ARE TRAPPED. WE NEED TO FIND A WAY OUT.

Holding it aloft, she presented her words to the assembled family members, who exchanged concerned glances. The once-trusted innkeepers now cast long shadows of doubt; those who were supposed to protect them were their greatest threat. The irony was suffocating—their guardians were their jailers. It was a realization that highlighted the significance of the choices they would make henceforth.

Amma's fingers, trembling, scribbled another note.

WHAT DO WE DO? THE POLICE ARE IN ON IT!

Pappa leaned in, his gaze meeting those of his family. He took another piece of paper from the desk, wrote a reply, and held it up for all to see.

WE NEED A PLAN. FAST.

Ravi moved to the closet without a word. He opened the safe. The hollow space stared back at him. He closed it again. Slowly.

Sophie watched him. "Ravi?"

He didn't answer immediately.

Then, low enough that only those nearest could hear, he said, "Even if we leave… we don't have our passports."

The words did not need to be written down. They settled heavier than the notes.

The once safe confines of the Sharma family suite no longer felt like a sanctuary—a dramatic shift from its former sense of security. The family nodded, eyes meeting in a silent agreement. Whatever their next steps were, they would have to tread with caution on this dangerous ground. The enemy was closer than they had ever imagined, and the room, once a place of comfort, had become a theater of invisible warfare. Their trust had been shattered, but their resolve had not.

* * *

9:45 P.M.

Siddharth continued to scan the throng at the Mahendrapal Bazaar, searching for Raju. His gaze fell upon something familiar amidst a discarded heap of trash. It was Cyrus's toy lamb, its once-vibrant wool now tainted with dirt and neglect. Clearly, Raju had thrown it away, deeming it insignificant after discovering the pendant was missing.

In a heartbeat, Siddharth's feet carried him toward the toy lamb. He picked it up, akin to cradling a fragile piece of someone's soul. With tender care, he brushed off the grime and dirt that had marred its wool.

This... I can make this right, he thought, his eyes misty with relief and newfound determination. He placed the lamb in his backpack, securing the zipper reminiscent of locking away a promise. I will get you back to Cyrus, Siddharth silently vowed. It wasn't just a promise to return a lost object; it was a commitment to trust in the greater plan, a belief that the divine would guide him through the darkness.

His phone buzzed, and a new message from Anil lit up the screen. Siddharth's thumb hovered, lingering in a moment of hesitation. Anil's words flickered on the display. Priya wants you to find the street boys and hire them to go back to the family's room. She wants the Talisman whatever the cost.

Raju was already on the lookout for the street boys, so the cousins were aligned in their thinking. Maybe this wasn't just a coincidence; it was confirmation they were making the right choice. Yet, a fierce battle raged within him, a clash between his conscience and his duty. As the conflict wore on, a sharp clarity cut suddenly through the tumult of his thoughts.

It's too late to turn back.

The gears of their intricate plan were already in motion, and his role was not just necessary—it was pivotal. He was a steadfast member of the Shatranj Ke Sipahi, and though the path ahead was shrouded in darkness, he couldn't waver. With his ancestral duty driving him forward, Siddharth understood that to reach the Heart of Kumari, he would need to embrace the very path that troubled his soul.

Now, there is no room for doubt—only faith.

ON IT, he typed. He sent the reply with newfound resolve. With that action, Siddharth committed himself to the journey, to the promise seared into his very essence. There would be no turning back—not now, not ever.

***

9:46 P.M.

The hallway of the Surya Chandra Inn seemed to shrink around them, its confines becoming oppressively narrow. Priya paced back and forth, a restless energy about her. "Did Siddharth reply yet?"

"No," Anil responded, trying to inject a note of calm into the tense atmosphere. "Give him some time."

Just then, Anil's phone vibrated. He glanced at the screen, anticipation and anxiety mingling in the pit of his stomach. "He says they will take care of it."

Priya's demeanor radiated a blend of thrilled excitement and danger, a relieved smile touching her lips as she contemplated their next move. "Perfect. Those street kids are like shadows, slipping through every hidden corner of this city. They'll secure the necklace without any suspicion. Soon, the Heart of Kumari will be in our grasp."

Anil shared a glance with Priya that reflected a tacit understanding interlaced with an undeniable excitement. Together, they were balancing on the precipice of a treacherous game, each maneuver fraught with peril yet exhilarating. Every action they took was a gamble, where a single misstep promised not just danger but catastrophe, ready to engulf them. But this dance with ruin, this flirtation with disaster, wasn't just a necessity—it was a thrill Priya relished.

"Stay alert. We need to make sure they don't leave," Priya warned, her heels clicking rhythmically against the marble floor as she walked away.

* * *

9:47 P.M.

Raju maneuvered through the crowd at the Mahendrapal Bazaar until he finally spotted Siddharth.

"Did you manage to do everything you needed to do at the temple?"

"Yes, brother." Siddharth paused, changing the subject to a more pressing matter. "Were you able to enlist the street kids? It seems Priya had the same idea."

A smile spread across Raju's face, satisfied they were finally in agreement. "Yes, the older of the boys will sneak into the room at one and retrieve the pendant."

Across the alley, a boy waited in the shadow of a shuttered shop. Too thin. Too eager. Raju gave a nod and he ran off.

"Good. I'll keep Anil in the loop."

With a few swift taps, Siddharth composed the message. THE STREET BOY WILL ENTER THE ROOM AT ONE O'CLOCK. RAJU IS GETTING RESTLESS. WE'LL WRAP UP SOON.

As he sent the update, a heavy sense of resignation settled over him, sealing his commitment to a plan that twisted his soul. Pocketing the phone, Siddharth felt a surge of dread wash over him.

Raju was already walking. The plan was in motion now. Siddharth followed. Behind them, the temple lights flickered in the wind. Siddharth sensed he was now walking a razor's edge, teetering between redemption and damnation, unsure whether this moment was the last chance for a moral reckoning or the path of no return.

* * *

9:48 P.M.

As Priya reached the end of the hallway, Anil's phone buzzed again.

"It's Siddharth," Anil called out as he caught up to her. "Raju is getting restless. The street boy will be here at one."

Priya whirled around, a sharp intensity flashing in her eyes. "Then tonight, we strike."

When she disappeared around the corner, the hallway felt longer than it had before.

Anil remained where he was for a moment, staring at the marble tile beneath his shoes. The scent of smoke drifted faintly through the vents. He adjusted the cuff at his wrist, smoothing the fabric carefully over the old scar there.

His phone buzzed. One last message from Siddharth.

WE ARE HEADED BACK TO THE INN TO GET SOME SLEEP BEFORE THE EXCITEMENT BEGINS.

Returning to his post outside the Sharma family's suite, he leaned back against the door. The wood was warm from the fire inside. Through it, music pulsed faintly—too loud, too careless. A burst of laughter followed.

He closed his eyes. Not to sleep. Just to steady himself. Bhaskar's warning echoed in the back of his mind. He did not knock. He did not move. He stayed where he was.

Part III

Hidden Passages
गुह्यमार्गः

"...When the Time...Bloodlines and Betrayals..."
— Doctrine of Balance, Fragment 9

"Not all those who wander are lost."

– J.R.R. Tolkien

-17-
UNVEILING THE CLUE

सूत्रस्य उद्घाटनम्

9:50 P.M.

Ravi had resumed his pacing around the room in the Sharma family suite, his eyes flicking over the table where each family member had carefully placed their discoveries. They were determined to solve the mystery hidden within the riddle inscribed on the goatskin they had discovered in the abandoned temple in Chitwan. Only by solving this riddle could they hope to move forward and discern their next step in locating the Heart of Kumari.

With his head cocked, Harrison looked at the mysterious box from the cave. He felt an impulse. Picking it up, he ran his fingers over its detailed markings. "There must be more to this," he guessed. "Do these symbols mean anything to you, Pappa?"

Pappa squinted through his reading glasses. With precision, he cross-referenced the markings on the box with the ancient book he'd borrowed from the library in Chitwan.

Every eye was fixed on Pappa and the ancient book set before him. Just when the tension seemed too much to bear, Cyrus, sitting on the couch, glanced at the sea of adult faces. He couldn't help but laugh at his father, who was singing along to the song playing from his phone.

"I bet Sheepy could've solved this mystery ages ago!" Cyrus announced.

Ravi looked at Cyrus. He stopped singing and placed him on his lap. "I miss Sheepy, too. I promise we'll get him back."

Pappa set the book down, his wrinkles deepening in frustration. "No, these markings are so different from anything in the book."

Beside him, Harrison's face mirrored Pappa's disappointment, his own brow creasing as he took another glance at the cryptic items on the table. He reached out and picked up the goatskin, wondering if they had overlooked something. A shiver ran down his spine as his fingers traced the ancient markings that had been beautifully transcribed onto its underbelly. The ink was faded, but the Sanskrit letters were apparent in the flickering firelight.

The windowpanes gave a faint rattle in their frames. No one looked up.

"Hmm. Maybe we need to take a step back," Harrison suggested.

At that moment, the song changed to "Believe It or Not," the theme song from the sitcom "The Greatest American Hero," sung by Joey Scarbury.

"Okay," Pappa agreed. "Let's try that." He then reached for his worn-out journal and flipped to the page where he had transcribed the meaning of the Sanskrit riddle.

Just then, the song changed. "'…on a wing and a prayer…'"

Ravi called out. He couldn't resist reciting the lyrics, jumping to his feet with a grin. He swooped toward Sophie and tugged her into a sudden twirl.

Sophie barely had time to react, stumbling before catching herself. She sat back down with a small gasp and shot him a look. "We need to focus," she said, concealing a giggle.

"You're right," he replied, settling back into his seat.

Harrison leaned over Pappa's shoulder to get a closer look. Everyone gathered around as he read the riddle. "'In the land where scales touch the sky…'"

"That's Pokhara," Pappa chimed in.

No one disagreed.

Harrison continued. "'Seek the dark where winged creatures fly.'"

Kiran spoke up. "That's easy. It's the bat caves."

"Not the dragons?" Sophie said playfully, tickling Kiran's belly.

"No, Mama. The only dragons are outside the door."

The room fell silent. Even the music seemed to pause. The innocence of his comment cast a chilling shadow over them.

Harrison's heart skipped a beat, his eyes darting to the door. He swallowed hard, forcing himself to focus. With a determined nod, he steadied his voice and read on. "'Mark the stream that follows a tale…'"

With a perplexed look, Sophie asked, "Could that be Phewa Lake? I don't remember any streams."

"We might have missed something," Harrison added.

Sophie observed the map that lay open on the table and sifted through her memory. "Remember when we were downstairs the other day? Raju pointed to a river on the map." She looked up, searching for the right words. "He said it flowed beside the concealed tunnel leading from the old fort."

With a sudden look of revelation, Pappa added, "He mentioned it could lead to the mountains. Yes, here it is—the Seti River." Pappa pointed to the map.

Ravi's expression turned reflective. "Yes, I remember."

Pappa returned his attention to the goatskin clue. "Sophie may be right. The river mentioned here may follow the tunnel."

A spark of realization glimmered across Sophie's face. She leaned forward eagerly. "Of course! I think I'm right, Pappa. It must add up. The river *is* the one running alongside the tunnel!" She gestured with her hands, a motion akin to piecing together a puzzle. "The riddle says the stream 'follows a tale.' The 'tale' is the tunnel itself—the tunnel whose lore is colored by ancient stories and myths. That's the 'tale' the riddle refers to!"

Harrison rubbed his chin in contemplation. "I guess that makes sense. Maybe? I'm not so sure, Mom. That might be a stretch. But if it isn't, then we've identified the river."

Kiran, rubbing his eyes, chimed in, swaying along with Tears for Fears' "Everybody Wants to Rule the World." "What's next in the clue?"

Harrison continued reading, "'…and find the cave hidden beyond the veil.'" He furrowed his brow in contemplation. "Wait. We've already identified the cave, haven't we? The bat cave, 'where winged creatures fly.' Why is it mentioned twice?"

Sophie considered the possibility and suggested, "Maybe there is another cave with a waterfall? The riddle mentions two caves. Right?"

Amma sought clarification, feeling a bit mixed up. "So, is this the bat cave we explored?"

Harrison tried to explain his theory. "Maybe the first cave is something different. Maybe the chapel under the tunnel is the first cave. We did go there first, and there were bats there, too, remember?"

Sophie stood and began pacing. "Which cave is the one where winged creatures fly? The chapel? Or the bat cave Siddharth took us to? I'm so confused! We need to figure that out." She plopped back down onto the sofa. The cushion compressed under her, emitting a sigh that seemed to echo her exasperation.

The group grappled with the possibility of two caves and the mystery of which one the clue referred to as the place where winged creatures fly. They realized their journey was fraught with questions and uncertainties, and they needed to find clarity to move forward in their quest for the Heart of Kumari.

As the group debated the cryptic riddle, Ravi sank into the armchair, his gaze distant, lost in thought. Then, a spark of realization brightened his face. "Hold on, you both are onto something. The first part of the clue is about the location. 'Seek the *dark* where winged creatures fly.' It doesn't specifically mention a cave. At least, not yet. The subsequent lines provide the directions to that place, clarifying that we're looking for a hidden cave. Siddharth must have understood this."

"There's only one cave that fits this description?" Sophie questioned.

Ravi nodded thoughtfully. "It seems that way. The riddle first hints at a general location—near Machapuchare where the bats can be found. Then, it tells us how to get there and what we're looking for—follow the river, and you will find the cave hidden by a waterfall. The 'dark where winged creatures fly' and 'the cave hidden beyond the veil' are referring to the same place."

Pappa added, "According to the clue, we should have located the stream that represents the Seti River and followed that to the cave." His finger tapped the spot on the map he was referring to. "But we don't have to do that because we already did it. Siddharth read the goatskin while we were sitting in the lobby, remember? He figured it out and took us there."

"But we didn't find the clue in the bat cave," Kiran spoke up.

"You're right, Kiran," Pappa said. "We need to take another look at the bat cave. Something's missing."

Just then, Sophie had a revelation about Raju and his intentions. "Hold on! We should have seen through their deception sooner. I distinctly remember Raju claiming he couldn't read Sanskrit. It was back in the abandoned temple." Turning to Ravi, she continued, "Remember? You asked him about deciphering the Sanskrit on the goatskin. He flat-out denied knowing how to read it. Doesn't it stand to reason that if Siddharth could translate the goatskin, so could Raju?"

"I could argue that just because one twin learns something, the other is not imbued with that ability. That's not how it works," Ravi teased. "But given what we now know about their family, I'd say you're right. All things considered, Raju claiming that he couldn't translate the Sanskrit was just another lie—one that solidifies my point. They've been deceiving us right from the beginning." Ravi seethed, his anger simmering beneath the surface.

"Let's refocus," Pappa announced before their frustrations could get the better of them. He turned to Harrison, urging him to continue reading.

"It says, 'Not all darkness is empty, or so they say, for in the cave, the next clue lay.'"

"That sounds like another cave," Sophie commented, counting on her fingers. "One. Two... Three?" Her face scrunched in confusion.

Pappa shook his head gently. "No, it's the same cave. Read it again." He pointed to the journal. "See, '*the* cave'—it's singular."

Sophie's shoulders dropped. "So, it's just one cave. But how does the river fit in? I thought it led from this inn to the cave."

"Mom, forget about the river," Harrison urged.

Pappa reassured her, "We don't have to worry about the river anymore because Siddharth knew how to get to the right cave, and he took us there directly."

Sophie's face brightened. "I'm starting to understand. I think the chapel and the secret tunnel are throwing me off. It's not in the clue at all?"

Pappa shook his head. "No, it's not."

Just then, the song on Ravi's playlist switched again—"Every Breath You Take" by The Police.

Ravi sank back into the armchair. His mind was a whirl, turning over each detail. "We are definitely missing a piece of the puzzle. I feel like the bat cave hasn't revealed all its secrets to us." His words haunted him, a reminder their quest was far from straightforward, and more answers might be hidden in the shadows of the cave they had already explored.

"Dad and Pappa are right," Cyrus urged. "We're supposed to find something with the bats. Something's wrong."

"Does that mean we have to go back? Do we know the way?" Sophie asked.

"No, Mom, I don't think we have to go back." Harrison's face lit up with understanding as he finished reading the clue aloud. "Listen to this. 'For in this cave, the next clue lay. Unveil the secret, bathe in its glow, and the path to the Heart of Kumari will show.'" Harrison looked up. "When I found the box, it was *bathed in a glow*. A light came from nowhere, and it directed its beam to the box on a pedestal. I'm certain the treasure box is the clue. It just has to be!"

There was an air of expectancy in the room. All eyes were drawn to the enigmatic box that now sat at the center of the table. They were trying to understand how it fit into the puzzle.

As the tension in the room escalated, Ravi stood up and drifted toward the in-room bar. His movements reflected his inner turmoil, yet he could not help but sing along to the '80s hit playing on his phone. Pausing with a thoughtful expression triggered by the lyrics, he mused aloud, "Could Sunjata from the museum have intentionally misled us?" He poured a small measure of whiskey from a miniature bottle, holding the glass contemplatively, hoping it might reveal some hidden truth.

Harrison responded with suspicion. "You might be onto something, Dad. Remember how she had that display set up? It was like a scene straight out of a movie." He paused, his mind retracing their steps. "The caption in the display case read, 'Fabled Treasures from the Bat Caves of Annapurna.' Now that I think about it—"

Pappa chimed in, his face creased with a frown. "Yes, something about that whole museum visit felt off to me, as well."

Ravi took a sip, then set the glass down. "You're right, Dad."

As he spoke, a thin smear of condensation marked the polished counter. In the blur of moisture, four faint letters—A N D B—took shape before the warmth of the room dissolved them. No one noticed.

Amma gazed curiously at the box, hoping the mystery might reveal itself more clearly. "May I have a look?"

"Of course," Harrison replied.

As she took the box from the table, her fingers slipped, and the box tumbled onto the floor. Colliding with the marble, the upper surface of the metallic chest gave way, revealing a hidden compartment within.

They gasped.

Harrison stepped forward and collected the box, its hidden base now lying open on the marble floor. An image of the Kumari Mandala caught his eyes as he inspected its interior. "Everyone, this *is* a clue! Look, it's the Kumari Mandala!"

Ravi rushed over to examine the revelation. "You're right, Harrison. How did we miss this?"

Harrison furrowed his brow, perplexed. "But there's nothing inside! It's like something has been deliberately removed."

"Remember the man at the museum? He took the box. It was out of our sight for a while. Could they have taken the clue?" Amma questioned.

Ravi nodded gravely, taking a sip of his drink. "If that is the case, they probably know the location of the Heart of Kumari by now."

Harrison's expression turned to one of understanding. "It all makes sense. That's why Raju and Siddharth kidnapped Cyrus. They don't need us to find the diamond anymore. They must already know where it is! But maybe they need the necklace."

"And they knew that Cyrus hid the pendant in the lamb, as Siddharth was the one who took Cyrus at the Pashupatinath Temple," Ravi said.

Pappa was struck by the magnitude of the situation. "They were so desperate for the necklace, they risked everything." His words underscored the depth of their adversaries' determination and the lengths they were willing to go to achieve their goal.

"What they did not anticipate is that we had already found it," Ravi said.

Sophie's expression unexpectedly radiated excitement as she added, "That definitely means the necklace must be the key; it's the Kumari Talisman needed to access the diamond! I was right!"

"It would appear so," Pappa said.

Harrison looked around at the group. His hand gripped the pendent around his neck, and there was a sense of urgency in his words. "What do we do now? Without the next clue, we can't find the Heart of Kumari."

The clock ticked past ten, unnoticed.

"I vaguely recall Sunjata at the museum mentioning a parchment among the relics in the box," Pappa commented. "Maybe the clue is on that parchment?"

"It was just a blank piece of paper." Harrison fumbled with his jacket, opening a zippered pocket. With a trembling hand, he extracted the parchment. "But, here it is, Pappa. I didn't want to lose it, so I kept it safe."

"Good thinking," he said as he took the parchment from Harrison.

At that moment, the familiar tune of "Don't Stop Believin'" by Journey spilled from Ravi's phone.

Pappa leaned forward, the sheet gripped between his fingers as he brought it nearer to the fire. The glow of the flames brushed across the parchment. He turned it over once, then again, searching each side. The surface held nothing—no ink, no hidden lines, only the rough weave of the fibers.

The museum staff had already tested it with every tool at their disposal and had found nothing.

Pappa's careful inspection only confirmed what they already feared—the parchment was blank.

Harrison's shoulders sank. He had wanted it to reveal something, anything.

With a quiet sigh, Pappa handed the paper back. "Perhaps it will respond to you, like the goatskin we found in the jungle. Do you see anything, Harrison?"

Harrison turned the parchment over in his hand, studying both sides, but it remained stubbornly barren. "No...nothing."

"Wasn't there something else in the box?" Kiran asked.

"You're right." Harrison set the paper aside on the table and reached for his jacket. His fingers brushed the contents in his inside pocket. "There was a lump of wax, a few small rocks, and an arrowhead." He held each up briefly before slipping them back into their hiding place. "Oh, and some pottery shards. They were wrapped inside the paper."

Pappa's head lifted. "Pottery shards? Where are they now?"

"In my backpack," Harrison said, already moving. "But they're just plain—nothing on them." He dug into a side pocket and pulled out a cloudy zip-top bag. The fragments clinked faintly as he set the bag on the table.

They leaned in closer. Firelight slid across the broken pieces, highlighting faint painted lines.

Pappa murmured, "We should have looked at these a long time ago."

Harrison tipped the bag, and the shards spilled across the table like a scatter of teeth, pale and jagged.

Sophie picked one up, turning it between her fingers. A dull curve of vermilion shimmered faintly—then brightened as it neared the flame. She set it down, then lifted another. Her eyes lit. "It's a puzzle," she breathed. "These pieces... they're meant to go back together."

"A puzzle?" Cyrus leapt from the couch, a smile spread across his face. "I'm good at those—let me try!" He snatched up a piece and turned it, grinning as it slid neatly against Sophie's selection.

The cracks aligned almost perfectly.

"See? I told you!"

"Keep them close to the fire." Sophie said. "The heat brings out the design."

Kiran crowded beside him, already reaching. "Wait—this one goes next. Look, the edge is jagged the same way." He pressed his shard against Cyrus's, and the two pieces kissed together.

"Careful," Amma said gently, steadying their hands. "Don't force it. Let the pieces show you where they belong."

Cyrus laughed. "This is just like that dinosaur puzzle we did. But way cooler!"

"It's older than dinosaurs," Kiran declared with mock seriousness. "Lots older."

"Maybe millions of years older," Harrison added with a faint smile, handing Kiran another piece. "Try this one. I think it goes with the one you are holding."

Kiran grinned. "Perfect!" But as he let go, the pieces wobbled and fell apart.

"It's not staying," Harrison said, frowning. "We're missing something. We need something sticky."

Kiran looked up. "Mama, do we have any glue?"

Sophie shook her head, then paused. "No glue…but I *might* have some chewing gum in my backpack." She unzipped the side pocket and pulled out a stick. "It's mint. That okay?"

"Awesome!" Cyrus said, grabbing it. "Gum to the rescue!"

He and Kiran started chewing, giggling as they pinched off sticky bits and pressed them between the shards. This time, the pieces held…but not well. They shifted. They slid. The fit wasn't precise.

"It's better," Sophie admitted, adjusting one shard, "but

not ideal."

Pappa narrowed his eyes, watching the gum stretch between the cracks. Then he turned to Harrison. "Wait. Harrison—you said there was some wax in the box?"

"Yeah." Harrison nodded, reaching for his jacket. "Right here."

Pappa took the lump from him, turning it in his fingers. "Yes…this is brilliant! It must've been included so someone could rebuild the bowl."

They passed the beeswax from hand to hand, softening it with their palms and breath. When it was pliable, they used small pinches between the shards. The wax took the exact form of each edge. This time, the fit was perfect.

"Wow!" Kiran cheered, fitting another piece.

The children's chatter filled the room as they considered their next moves.

Sophie hushed them.

Ravi, who had been watching quietly, leaned over the box. His eyes narrowed. "Hold on," he said, tapping the box's inner lining. "Do you see this? A circle—pressed into the base. It's like something round was meant to rest here."

Sophie's breath caught. "The bowl. It belongs inside the box."

"Exactly," Pappa said, his voice firm. "Build it here. The circle will guide the pieces."

"Quick, let's try it!" Cyrus urged. "I'll put the big one in!"

"No, me first!" Kiran protested, picking up the largest shard.

Pappa chuckled, reaching to settle the quarrel. "Together," he said firmly, guiding both boys' hands as they lowered the piece into the circle.

It fit perfectly.

"Ha! I knew it," Kiran whispered in triumph.

"Here, here—this one!" Cyrus hurried to add another piece.

Sophie steadied the next addition into place. "I think this one goes here."

Harrison leaned forward, pinched off a bit of the warm beeswax, and handed it to his mother. She pressed it between two edges before sliding in the next fragment. The resin held fast as the vessel took shape.

Amma shifted behind them, scanning the room for a place to sit closer.

"Amma, take this," Sophie said, reaching behind the table. She dragged the wooden chair from the corner without thinking, placing it beside the hearth.

She glanced at it. The torn cushion. The scratch down one leg.

"No, no," she murmured. "I'll sit here." She lowered herself beside Kiran instead, folding her shawl beneath her.

The chair stayed where Sophie had left it. Out of the corner. Closer to the firelight. No one moved it back.

Piece by piece, the artifact rose from its long silence. As the cracks closed, black strokes of Sanskrit stretched along the inner rim.

"Look!" Cyrus gasped. "The funny letters!"

"Yeah," Kiran whispered. His voice was lower, reverent. "It says something. We made it come back."

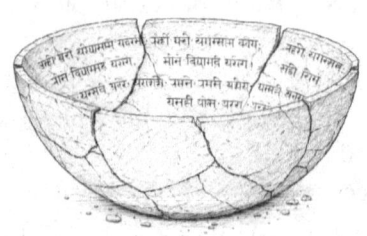

Pappa adjusted his glasses, bending low. His voice softened, carrying the weight of awe. "Yes. I think this is the clue."

The script emerged faintly, each letter a ghostly whisper of history, resplendent and almost magical across the rejoined shards. Under their hands, the broken bowl remembered itself. In its wholeness, the wisdom of ages past stirred again.

Pappa's glasses slid down his nose as the script came into focus.

भूमेः अधः गूढचैत्येषु, यत्र भिक्षवः जपं वहन्ति।
आशीर्वादचुम्बितेन कुञ्जिकया मार्गं पश्य।
अग्निसंयोगेन जलप्रवाहेण च,
शुध्यते तव आत्मा, वर्धते तव चेतना।
शिखरे जगतः, यत्र दिवं पृथिवीं स्पृशति,
तत्र ते पन्थाः विश्रामं लभते, भाग्यं च प्रतिगृह्णाति।

He nodded in awe. "It's the clue! It was hidden in the pottery shards all along." He traced the restored lines with his fingertip and read aloud. "'Beneath the earth in chapels deep, where chanting monks their vigils keep. Find the key by blessings kissed, to ascend the mountain's peak and mist. Through fire's embrace and water's flow, purified, your spirit will grow. Atop the world, where heavens meet, your journey ends, and destiny greets.'"

Cyrus crinkled his face. "But what does that mean?" he asked with frustration. "There are so many mountains nearby. How can we ever know which one is the right one?"

A silent glance passed among them, heavy with unspoken questions. The fire dimmed, mirroring the mood.

From his perch near the window, Ravi studied the transcription he had hastily jotted on the back of a receipt from the bazaar. "Let's take it from the top," he insisted. "Slower this time. We can't afford to miss anything."

Pappa nodded. He adjusted his glasses and reread the first line, his words cutting through the tension. Steady and reassuring, like an anchor in their emotional storm. "'Beneath the earth in chapels deep, where chanting monks their vigils keep.'" He lifted his attention from the page. "Sophie, here's your chapel."

"Finally," Sophie mused.

Pappa unraveled the next part of the riddle. "'Find the key by blessings kissed, to ascend the sacred mountain's mist.'" He paused, gathering his thoughts. "If you are right, Sophie, this must be referring to the pendant you found in the chapel—the necklace Raju and Siddharth are so desperately after. That's 'the key by blessings kissed.'"

Harrison instinctively placed his hand over the pendant around his neck. A subtle but unmistakable sensation confirmed Pappa's words as he touched it. The necklace resonated with a quiet acknowledgment, signaling to Harrison they were indeed on the right path. "And the key will lead us to the mountain?"

Pappa looked up. He found every eye in the room fixed on him, the surrounding expressions a blend of anticipation and amazement. "I can't say for certain, but yes, I think that it will." Readjusting his glasses, he continued. "'Through fire's embrace and water's flow, purified, your spirit will grow.'"

Sophie leaned forward. "What does that mean, Pappa? How can we be purified by fire and water?"

Pappa gave a half-smile. "I'm not sure. I guess we will find out soon enough."

In the warm, unsteady light of the fire, determination shone on Ravi's features. "We have a key," he said with conviction. "And we know where the chapel is. The Kumari Talisman should open one of the doors in the chapel. After all, we have ten doors to choose from. From there, we see if things lead to the right mountain."

Pappa interjected, "Wait, son. The photo also revealed something else is needed to open the door, but I couldn't make it out due to the flash."

Ravi paused, considering their options. "You're right, Pappa, but I believe our next step is to return to the tunnel. We'll use the key and see what unfolds. It seems fairly straightforward. It would be foolish to hesitate any longer." He scanned the room, waiting for any objections or concerns.

No one spoke.

No one moved.

A low rush of wind moved down the chimney. The flame bent, then steadied. Something shifted in the hallway—a whisper of fabric, a muted footstep. The air felt thinner.

For the first time that night, leaving did not feel like a plan.

It felt like a point of no return.

Then Ravi looked at Pappa, who motioned in approval.

Ravi took a slow breath. "Are we ready for this?"

With purpose, Sophie walked over to Harrison. Her hand hovered for a moment before she reached out and touched the pendant around his neck.

It flared.

The room went still. Harrison felt the heat through the fabric of his shirt. No one spoke. Even Ravi stopped pacing.

On the mantel, the clock ticked—10:56.

They had done it. Solved two clues—without Raju. Without Siddharth. The realization settled slowly, almost carefully. They were not being led anymore.

The clock ticked again.

Relief tried to rise. It didn't make it far. If the necklace was the key, then it was not simply important. It was wanted. Wanted badly enough to steal a child. Wanted badly enough to stand guard outside their door.

Harrison closed his hand around the stone at his throat. The glow did not warm him. It felt like recognition.

Across the room, the fire shifted. Shadows lengthened along the walls. The second hand moved again.

They had solved the puzzle. The next move was theirs. Only two obstacles stood between them and the door. Priya and Anil.

-18-
THE GRAND ILLUSION

महो माया

11:00 P.M.

Anil lay curled outside the Sharma family's suite, his shoulder pressed against the carved teak door as though proximity alone could guarantee obedience. The marble beneath him held the night's chill, seeping slowly through cloth and bone. He had meant only to rest his eyes. Only for a moment.

The grandfather clock in the lobby began to toll. The sound did not simply rise through the stairwell; it entered him. Each strike settling into the hollow behind his ribs.

Tow hours until one. And with it, the return of memory. He was seven again. The courtyard had smelled of damp stone and smoldering resin. Smoke gathered low along the earth like something living. At the center, the flame burned—not wild, not flickering—but steady. Controlled.

The Rite of Ahora. The fire that did not consume. His name had already been taken from him for three days. No one had spoken it. No one had answered when he whispered it into his own hands at night. The elders called it the Stillness of the Sigil—silence so the Pattern could listen.

He remembered the loneliness of that silence more than the fear. He walked the Circle of Eight barefoot at dawn, one measured step for each piece upon the Board. The stones were cold. The sky barely lightening. He had tried not to look toward the ring of witnesses. But he had.

And he had found Raju. Older. Already marked. The Rook lay dark against his wrist. A tower, bold and unshifting.

Anil remembered thinking the mark looked permanent in a way he was not ready for.

When he completed the eighth step, the elder lifted the brand from the flame. It was smooth. Unformed. He had hoped, foolishly, that perhaps it would not change. That perhaps it would stay blank.

The metal touched his inner wrist. The pain came, sharp and white. But what truly undid him was the movement. The brand shifted beneath his skin. Lines bending. Curves rising. As though the metal recognized him before he recognized himself.

He gasped.

When the brand lifted, the shape stood revealed— Knight. The curved horse's head. Sudden change.

A single bell rang. The sound did not celebrate him. It confirmed him.

Anil's gaze had drifted instinctively to Raju. And he would never forget what he saw there. Not anger. Something deeper; a quiet recalculation. As though a piece had been placed on the Board, and Raju was already imagining how it might move.

The eleventh chime from the grandfather clock brought Anil back to the present. His eyes blinked open slowly. For a moment, he did not know which sound had woken him—the bell from years ago, or the clock in the lobby below. Footsteps approached. Measured. Unhurried.

Raju stepped from the bend in the hallway, lamplight catching the faint sheen along his brow. His presence altered the air before he spoke. "Why are you sleeping?" The words were not shouted. They did not need to be.

Anil pushed himself upright at once. "I'm sorry. I didn't mean to."

Raju studied him for a moment, then turned his gaze toward the suite door. Music hummed faintly beneath it.

"They're still awake," Anil offered, eager to steady the moment.

"Yes," Raju replied. His voice carried something heavier than irritation. It carried displacement.

Raju had undergone his own Rite years before. He had stood barefoot before the flame and endured the shaping of metal against flesh without flinching. The Rook had revealed itself then.

A foundation piece. Steady. Necessary. Unmoving. He had accepted it. Or told himself he had.

Raju listened to the muted sounds within the suite. A laugh. A chair scraping. The soft murmur of Sophie's voice. He imagined Harrison. He remembered the way the Kumari had looked at him. *Seeker.*

The word did not rise; it spread. Raju had felt the Pattern shift that day. He simply had not felt it claim him. Instead, it had bent toward a foreign boy with unmarked skin and questions in his eyes.

Raju's jaw tightened. It wasn't that Harrison had done anything wrong. That was the part that burned. The boy had simply stepped into something that should have been his.

Raju flexed his wrist. The Rook does not chase. It guards.

It holds the line while others are permitted to move. "You know what unsettles me?" Raju said quietly, still facing the door.

Anil did not answer.

"They did nothing to earn it." The words were not loud. They were heavy. "They walked into this country by accident… and the Pattern opened." His gaze drifted downward, toward the seam of light beneath the door. "My whole life I was told it would return to us."

Silence settled between them

Raju drew a slow breath and straightened. "He'll be here soon," he said, his voice steady now. There was no excitement in it, no hunger—only resolve.

He stepped forward and took Anil's place directly in front of the door, close enough that the light brushed the edge of his shoe. The gesture was not aggressive. It was positional. The Rook returning to its square.

In the hallway, stillness, the grandfather clock shifted into its next minute. One was coming.

***

11:30 P.M.

Perched on the mantel, the clock chimed the half-hour. The sound spread, then fell away. Unnoticed. The air was already filled with the opening notes of "Should I Stay or Should I Go" by The Clash. The upbeat rhythm clashed with the somber scene. Sophie paced with the rhythm, her movements an expression of defiance and determination.

"Can't we just leave? They don't have to know what we're up to," she protested, her words floating over the steady cadence of the melody.

Ravi shook his head. "It's not that simple. They're not just guards; they think we're on the same side. Sneaking past them would alert them we don't trust them anymore."

Sophie shot back, "I don't care if they know we don't trust them. It's obvious we don't."

Cyrus spoke into the room, cutting the air. "Why not go out the window?" He got up, walked to the sill, and pulled back the curtain.

They were three stories up, and the landscape below was a bed of jagged rocks and manicured shrubbery—moonlit and menacing.

Ravi stepped toward the window. Cold air pressed faintly through the frame. Below, the courtyard dropped away into shadow. A loose shutter somewhere along the exterior wall knocked once, then went still.

Sophie frowned. "The wind's picking up."

Pappa set his journal aside and walked to the window, peering down at the treacherous drop. "It's risky, but it's not impossible," he announced, already formulating a plan. "Hang on."

The family watched with intrigue as Pappa darted into the nearest bedroom.

When he reappeared, he carried the sheets he had yanked off the bed. "Look, if we tie these together, we can make a makeshift rope to climb down. It will be challenging for Amma, but we'll help her."

Amma stood behind her husband like a rooted tree, her stance full of unwavering courage. "All right. Let's find more sheets," she declared, rallying the troops. She walked toward her bedroom, her strides purposeful and confident.

Sophie exchanged a look of disbelief with Ravi. "Are they seriously thinking we're going to 'Mission Impossible' our way down three stories with no one noticing?"

While searching for more sheets in the closet, Amma discovered a rickety shelf cluttered with forgotten trinkets. Amid the disorder, barely visible, sat a small golden statue of an elephant—symbolic of Lord Ganesha. Overcome by a surge of devotion, she tenderly kissed her hand and reverently placed it upon the figure as a prayer for their safety.

The instant she touched the statue, an almost inaudible rumble filled the small space. Dust particles floated and coalesced as though disturbed by some ancient magic. Slowly, the outline of a door within the closet became distinct. With a muted click, the hidden passage revealed itself, its entrance swinging open to expose a mysterious tunnel extending into the darkness.

Amma stepped back into the living room, breath uneven. "I found something."

"What?" Sophie responded.

"In the closet. There's a door. I don't think it's meant to be found."

The Sharma family followed Amma into her bedroom and crowded around the closet, filling the space with bodies. One by one, smiles crept across their faces. This enigmatic passageway offered them the promise of escape. The clock kept ticking anyway.

***

11:40 P.M.

Following a brief stop in his office to send word that Raju had taken the watch, Anil turned down the narrow corridor that led to the room Siddharth was staying in room 266. The inn had settled into its midnight quiet. Only the low hum of the heater and the distant tick of the lobby clock marked the hour.

He did not knock. He took out the master key and inserted it into the lock. The door swung in.

Inside, Siddharth was not asleep. He lay on his back, staring at the ceiling, fully clothed. His eyes shifted toward Anil without surprise. "Priya asked for you," Anil said.

"Then it's time." Siddharth rose at once. No questions. No hesitation.

The hallway swallowed their footsteps as they moved toward the front of the inn. Light pooled faintly beneath Priya's office door.

Inside, Priya stood behind the desk, her sleeves were rolled up. The passports lay stacked beside the brass bell. Navy covers. Gold crests catching the lamplight.

She did not look up when they entered

"Raju?" Siddharth asked.

"Still at the door," Anil replied.

Priya closed a ledger and aligned it with the edge of the desk. "I'm going up to see him. Wait here."

With that she turned and left.

The grandfather clock shifted toward the hour.

Siddharth moved to the window that overlooked the courtyard. Anil remained near the doorway. The desk lamp cast long shadows across the marble floor. The passports did not move.

Outside, somewhere beyond the inn's gates, footsteps approached.

* * *

11:45 P.M.

At the edge of the Mahendrapal Bazaar, the noise thinned into pockets of shadow.

The street boy fastened the clasp of the black cape around his shoulders. The fabric was too large for him. It swallowed his frame and brushed his calves when he walked.

His younger brother watched from a few steps away.

"You look silly in that thing," the younger boy muttered.

The older one didn't smile. "It keeps me hidden."

"It makes you look like you're pretending."

Silence.

"You don't have to go," the younger boy said. "Baba said we could manage this month."

The street boy shook his head. "Manage how?"

His brother hesitated. "Are you really going to kill them?"

The older boy looked toward the road that led to the inn.

"If I do it, we get paid."

The words sat between them.

"And if you don't?"

"Then someone else will." He adjusted the cape again, more tightly this time. "Go home," he said.

The younger boy didn't move at first.

"I said go."

The street boy stepped into the dark.

A gust swept through the thinning stalls, lifting loose paper and carrying the scent of wood smoke. His black cape snapped once behind him, ballooning wide before collapsing back against his legs. He caught it at the collar and pulled it tighter.

The cloth folded around him until he was part of the shadow.

November 14ᵀᴴ
12:00 A.M.

Raju pressed himself against the grainy texture of the Sharma family's door, his ear angled toward the seam, straining for anything beyond the music that might betray them.

Music spilled into the hallway—steady, unhidden, almost careless. It should have reassured him. It didn't. Beneath the rhythm, there were no voices. No movement. No shift in tone. The hallway felt suspended, as though waiting for something it had not yet heard.

Time seemed to freeze. The grandfather clock in the lobby had just gonged twelve times, sending deep vibrations up the three flights of stairs. Each second thereafter echoed Raju's heightened heartbeat. He counted without meaning to, then stopped when he realized he was counting. Glancing at his phone, the glowing digits of 12:02 A.M. intensified the unease coiling in his stomach.

"The boy will be here soon," Raju mused.

He pressed his ear against the door once more, straining to catch any movement—a footstep, a door closing, anything to indicate the family was awake.

Raju's thoughts swung like a pendulum in the oppressive silence, oscillating between hope and apprehension. The stillness was punctuated only by the occasional creak of the old building, doing nothing to ease his tension.

Just then, the clacking of shoes broke the silence. The sound came closer, then stopped.

Raju stood. He waited, unsure why he didn't move right away.

The hallway narrowed as she stepped into the light. It was Priya.

She handed him a mug of coffee. "Here. I thought you

could use this."

"Thanks," he said, taking a sip. "Why the nice gesture? Trying to poison me?"

She gave a quiet laugh. "I just thought you might be lonely up here."

Priya pressed her ear against the door. Raju didn't follow—he listened instead.

For a moment, neither of them spoke. The silence between them held.

Then Priya said, "We can't let them leave," though her eyes stayed on the floor.

"I know. I'm hoping the street boy will take care of that."

"Uncle Bhaskar took their passports," she added. "He said it was for paperwork."

"And they believed him?" Raju asked.

"Ravi handed them over."

Raju exhaled slowly. "They won't leave without them."

Priya stirred at the floor a moment longer. "I hope you're right."

Raju watched her fumble with her mug. "You all right, Priya?"

"I'm fine. It's just Uncle Bhaskar paid me a visit. He's not happy about our change of plans."

"I was wondering when he was going to let me have it."

Priya's mouth opened as if to speak. Instead, a tear slid down her cheek, and she turned away.

"I'm sorry, Priya," Raju said.

Her shoulders rose once, then settled. She didn't face him when she spoke. "We can't fail. I never told you this, but it was Bhaskar who ordered Khan's death. He wanted him to suffer for trying to flee the Order."

"What? He tried to break away?"

She turned now to look at him. She could see the confusion in his eyes.

"Bhaskar was furious when he found out Khan had tried to leave. Khan denied it when confronted. I thought Bhaskar was going to kill him on the spot. Instead… he let him go." She hesitated. "Only to have him hunted down later."

Raju swallowed. "I knew he was ruthless, but…" He didn't finish. Couldn't. And for a moment, he looked like the boy Priya used to know—the one who used to dream.

Priya waited. When he didn't continue, she nodded once. "Now you know," she said. "Don't fall asleep. If anything changes, let me know."

"Will do. And thanks for the coffee."

With that, Priya turned and walked away, the sound of her steps trailing behind her.

Raju stayed by the door, listening to the quiet return.

* * *

12:20 A.M.

Back in Priya's office, the Sharma family's passports lay stacked beneath the desk lamp. Navy covers. Gold crests catching the light.

Siddharth stood near the window, watching the courtyard. Anil lingered by the doorway, arms folded, listening to the hum of the heater and the distant tick of the lobby clock. The office felt smaller at night.

Just then, the door opened. Priya stepped inside and closed it softly behind her.

"Well?" Siddharth asked.

"No word."

Siddharth turned back toward the window. "He should be there by now."

"He will be," Priya said, though her voice lacked conviction.

Anil shifted his weight. "And if he isn't?"

Priya's gaze hardened. "Then we do it ourselves." She crossed to the cabinet against the wall and opened it. Then, she removed something wrapped in dark cloth and set it on the desk without unwrapping it.

Anil stiffened.

Siddharth's gaze dropped to the bundle. A thin glint of metal showed through the fold before the cloth settled again. "We let the street boy do his job," Siddharth said evenly. "First."

"And if he doesn't?" Priya pressed.

"Then we handle it. But we let the street boy do his job first." He paused, "If he fails we'll finish it."

"What if they leave?" Anil asked quietly.

Siddharth glanced toward the desk—toward the stack of blue passports beside the cloth. "They won't," he said. "Bhaskar made sure of that."

Priya held his gaze a moment longer. "Then we wait"

12:45 A.M.

Sophie stared at the newly revealed tunnel entrance, her flashlight illuminating its cobweb-strewn darkness.

"Remember what Priya said about this inn? It used to be an ancient fort with countless secrets. Looks like we've stumbled upon another one."

Peering into the dark maw, Ravi pondered, "I wonder if this leads to the basement. We need to find the passage that takes us to the chapel."

Pappa came up beside him. "Do we go now?"

Ravi checked his watch. "It's almost one."

Amma hesitated. "What if we wait until morning?"

No one answered at first.

Ravi glanced toward the hallway door. The seam of light beneath it hadn't moved. A shadow was still there. "Morning won't change anything," he said quietly. "They'll still be watching. The police will still be theirs. And the passports will still be gone."

Sophie's voice was tight. "So we just leave them?"

Ravi didn't look away from the tunnel. "We won't get them by staying in this room."

The song playing from his phone drifted to its end. The room did not rush to fill the silence.

Sophie exhaled. Then she turned toward the others gathered in the doorway. "All right, everyone, take only what's essential. Keep in mind you'll have to carry it on your back. You'll appreciate the lighter load later."

The group stepped outside the bedroom and began the painstaking process of sorting through their belongings, handpicking only the necessities.

"Water," Pappa said suddenly. "We need water."

Ravi crossed to the in-room fridge and pulled it open. The light flickered on. Two small bottles. Half a carton of juice. Leftover naan wrapped in foil. A bruised apple.

"Take it," Sophie said.

Harrison stuffed the bottles into his pack. Cyrus grabbed the apple. Kiran hesitated over a chocolate bar, then slipped it into his pocket without comment. No one mentioned breakfast. The fridge door swung closed with a soft suctioned thud.

The room dimmed again.

A thud came from the hallway. No one looked up.

While digging through his bag, Harrison pulled out the flashlights they had bought at the Mahendrapal Bazaar and handed them to his father and Pappa.

"Why don't you use your phone, Harrison?" Kiran asked. "Wouldn't that be easier?"

"Just wait a little, buddy. The tunnel we have to go through is really dark," Harrison replied. "The flashlight on the phone isn't strong enough. These will be much better." He held up one of the flashlights to demonstrate how bright it was. Its beam sliced through the room.

Just then, Pappa interrupted the preparations. "Wait. We must leave the phones behind."

Ravi nodded, his expression firm. "Pappa's right. They have connections within the police department, which means they could easily track us. We need to go off the grid. Remember, no slip-ups."

The digital clock on the dresser changed to 12:52.

Sophie gathered the phones one by one, a touch of reluctance in her movements. "Where should we put them?" she asked, glancing around the room, secretly hoping her husband and Pappa would change their minds about leaving the phones behind.

"Put them in this," Ravi instructed. He retrieved an old satchel from inside the closet, its worn leather suggesting it had seen better days. "When we get through this adventure, I'll buy everyone new phones if these disappear."

Sophie considered his words. "Wait. Can't we just take the SIM cards out? That way, we won't be tracked."

Ravi scanned the room, his gaze settling on a bag of potato chips they had bought from the inn's vending machine. He emptied the chips into the trash.

"What are you doing with my chips?" Cyrus protested.

Everyone looked perplexed.

Ravi explained, "I'm making a makeshift Faraday bag. The aluminum in the bag should block any cell signals."

Sophie pleaded with him one more time, "But Ravi..."

Her husband stood firm. "Your phone is already gone. Who knows if they have it? We can't be certain what they might have extracted from it if they do have it, nor can we guess the extent of their technology," he emphasized.

Sophie nodded in understanding.

Methodically, Ravi powered down each device and set them on the table. "Sophie," he said, holding out his hand. "I need one of your earrings."

She blinked. "My earring? What for?"

Ravi glanced at the phones lined up before him.

"Oh, I get it," Sophie said, realizing his intentions. She removed a small stud and handed it over.

Ravi used the earring's post to pop out the SIM card tray from each phone. He removed the SIM cards and slipped them into his pocket, separating them from the devices. Next, he took the empty potato chip bag and carefully placed the powered-down phones inside. "Just to be safe," he muttered, mostly to himself. He sealed the bag, placed it inside a worn leather sack, and tucked it into an aged wooden box, shutting the lid tight. "Just in case someone tries to find us," he said. "Now, they're deaf and blind."

Sophie, still apprehensive, expressed her concerns. "But what if we need to communicate? Maybe we should take one of them with us just in case."

Ravi faced her directly, placing his hands on her shoulders, his message clear and firm. "Look, we are dealing with the Shatranj Ke Sipahi—an order that constitutes an evil, powerful bloodline. We don't know how dangerous Raju, Siddharth, Priya, and Anil are. We don't have the police on our side. And we don't know who else is after us. We can't risk anyone following us." With a deliberate calmness, he secured the chest's latch, each click punctuating their perilous reality. He then turned back to face her, meeting her gaze with an intensity that bridged their unvoiced fears. "And as for the last clue…" Ravi's words hung for a moment, a prelude to the enormity of their next step. "It beckons us to the Himalayan mountains. Into a landscape beyond the reach of any call for help. No cell service, no lifelines. Okay?"

"No slip-ups," Sophie reiterated.

Ravi nodded, letting the truth of their situation settle around them. The air charged with the magnitude of their journey ahead. "We'll need to rely on something stronger than signals and satellites," he concluded. His words were filled with conviction.

"What is stronger than cell phones, Dad?" Kiran asked.

"Faith," Ravi declared. "We'll have faith in each other."

Kiran's expression held childlike inquisitiveness and concern. He searched his father's face, seeking an anchor in the uncertainty before them. The boy found a promise in his father's steady gaze that their bonds would prove stronger than anything man-made. It was in that moment, with his father's conviction wrapped around him like a warm cloak, that Kiran understood—faith wasn't just an empty word; it was their unyielding trust, their shared strength.

Sophie absorbed her husband's words, recognizing their irrevocable truth. Her reply was simple, but her voice carried a steely assurance. "Together, we'll get through this."

Just then, Amma's keen eye caught the camera slung over Ravi's shoulder, and she raised a cautious eyebrow. "Is that a good idea?" she said with a nod.

Ravi reconsidered, realizing the potential complications the camera might pose. With deliberate and careful hands, he stowed the camera inside a suitcase, hiding it within their clothing.

"Last call," Ravi said, his gaze sweeping across each family member. "Does anyone else need to put something in this suitcase before I close it?"

Harrison spoke up. "Wait, Dad." He walked up to the suitcase, his cherished Nintendo Switch in hand. He reached in and placed the console inside. "Come on, Cyrus and Kiran," he urged, "it's time to let go of our electronic devices."

Reluctantly, both Kiran and Cyrus walked up and placed their game consoles next to Harrison's Switch, following his lead.

Harrison patted his brothers on the back. "Don't worry, guys," he said with a comforting conviction, "we won't need those games. We have each other. It's a sacrifice, but it's for a greater purpose." He looked at them with a loving and approving grin.

Ravi closed the suitcase as Sophie ensured their bags were neatly packed before they embarked on their journey, leaving behind any non-essential items that would hinder them.

Pappa crossed to the dresser and pulled open the top drawer. "I left my reading glasses in here," he muttered. The drawer slid halfway before catching. He tugged it free. As he reached inside, his fingers brushed the faint Devanagari letters carved along the inner wood—THE FIFTH IS SAFE.

He froze. The inscription was nearly worn smooth. He had dismissed it before. Now, with the tunnel open behind them, it felt less like graffiti. More like a warning.

He removed his glasses. Closed the drawer carefully. "Ready," he said.

Harrison checked all the rooms making sure nothing was left behind. A scrap of paper lay half-hidden, tangled in the knot of bedsheets. He bent to pick it up.

"We don't want to leave this," he said, holding up the receipt with Ravi's transcription of the clue.

Ravi's eyes flicked to it, then he gave a quick nod. "Good

catch." He took it and shoved it into his pocket without another thought.

Harrison gave a small nod, satisfied. "Now, we're ready."

Somewhere in the inn, a door shut.

Ravi reached for the switch. The lamp clicked off. The room fell into shadow.

With finality, they all looked at each other, holding their flashlights.

Just then, Kiran's shoelace came loose. He crouched, fingers fumbling in the beam of his flashlight. The knot would not catch.

Sophie knelt without thinking. "Hold still," she whispered, looping it tight. It took longer than it should have.

The room held its breath.

No one noticed, but in the painting above the hearth, the woman had turned. Just slightly. Not toward them, but toward the open doorway.

As they made their way into the bedroom, their flashlights caught across each face. Determined. Quiet. Not afraid, but not unshaken.

The opening waited. Black. Unlit. Narrower than it had seemed before. The room was silent, filled with a collective anticipation that was almost tactile.

Pappa, his features stern and full of resolve, stepped forward to lead the way. "No turning back," he declared.

For a moment, they remained where they were. Then Ravi nodded. Amma reached for Cyrus. Harrison angled his light forward.

As the others stepped through the hidden doorway, Sophie paused at the edge of the room, her flashlight sweeping across the space one last time.

Her light passed the painting. Something in it felt altered. She did not look long enough to name it. The air behind her cooled. Not enough to notice. Enough to register.

Just then, the beam caught on the old chair in the sitting room. Still near the hearth. Still out of the corner. Still not where it belonged. No one had moved it. A torn seam curled like a smile. A shadow fell across the cushion. She didn't speak. Just watched. Then she turned—and followed her family into the dark.

-19-
INTO THE ABYSS

अवसादे प्रवेशः

1:01 A.M.

Yielding to the pull of the unknown, the Sharma family pressed deeper into the faintly-lit tunnel within the inn's interior. The stone walls seemed to close in around them, and the light from their flashlights cast unnatural apparitions that lingered and flickered like ghosts on a moonless night. The tunnel twisted and turned, leading them down a series of uneven stone steps that descended further into the bowels of the ancient building. The tunnel bent again.

They arrived at an old, weathered door over which the word ATTIC was carved into a tattered wooden lintel. The door was not locked.

"Should we open it?" Sophie questioned. "We know the way to the basement from the attic."

Ravi did not answer at once. His hand hovered over the handle.

A breath.

"We can't risk it," Ravi finally said, lowering the light.

They continued along the passage, their footsteps muffled on the damp earth.

Amma, squinting to make out the details in the half-light, noticed fresh footsteps in the years of accumulated dust. "It seems like this tunnel is still in use."

"Probably staff," Ravi said.

"I wonder if this is how someone entered our room undetected. Each room may have its own hidden access point," Pappa pointed out.

"I'm almost certain that's how they did it," Ravi replied.

They pressed onward, the tunnel growing darker and narrower, until they came upon another staircase descending deeper. The air felt heavier here.

"This should lead to the basement," Ravi said, taking the first step cautiously.

Pappa opened his mouth to speak. Then stopped.

Sophie lifted her hand, then let it fall.

The quiet around them intensified, and they could almost hear their heartbeats.

And in that silence, they descended.

***

1:07 A.M.

The marble floor in Priya's office held the cold. It climbed through the soles of Anil's shoes as he stood at the desk. The lamp cast a hard circle of light over the stacked passports. Beyond it, the corners of the room receded into shadow.

A pipe ticked somewhere behind the plaster. Then silence.

A small monitor glowed on the corner of the desk, its light colder than the lamp. The lobby camera showed an empty front desk. The staircase feed flickered faintly. The hallway outside the Sharma suite held steady—Raju's shoulder visible at the edge of the frame, unmoving.

Anil drew the top passport toward him. The navy cover was smooth beneath his thumb. The gold crest caught the lamplight and flared, then dulled as he flipped it open. The pages whispered when he turned them.

Across the room, Siddharth stood near the window. The courtyard beyond the glass was empty. No movement. No dark figure cutting across the stone.

Siddharth checked his phone. 1:07. Nothing.

The hallway feed did not change.

Priya did not sit. She remained beside the cabinet, one hand resting lightly on the sofa.

"He would have gone in by now," Anil said quietly, still looking at the passport in his hands.

No one answered.

The clock in the lobby ticked. The sound carried through the air and into the room, thin but insistent.

Siddharth turned. "You left the panel unlatched."

Anil's jaw tightened. "Of course I did." He turned away flipping through another passport.

"Enough," Priya said. "Listen."

Anil closed the passport and aligned it back into the stack. His fingers adjusted the edges until the corners met perfectly.

From somewhere above them, faintly, a board creaked. All three heads turned toward the vent near the ceiling.

The monitor continued its silent loop. No shadow crossed the lens. No door opened.

The pipe ticked again. The second hand moved.

***

1:08 A.M.

As the Sharma family ventured through the secret passage leading from their suite, the groan of wood echoed through the small space, followed by the sudden thud. Spinning on their heels, they snapped off their flashlights. A wedge of light spilled from the level above, cutting across the stone. A silhouette crossed it. Then vanished..

Sophie leaned in, whispering, "A person just walked through the door above us."

They froze.

"Headed to our room," Amma breathed.

The tunnel felt smaller now, the stone pressing closer to their shoulders. Cyrus's fingers tightened in Pappa's sleeve. "Sheepy," he whispered.

"We'll find him," Pappa murmured, though his eyes remained fixed on the seam of light above.

Silence stretched.

The building creaked.

Dust loosened from the ceiling and drifted down in the dark.

Kiran shifted his footing.

His flashlight, still dim in his hand, tilted.

A faint glint caught the edge of the wall.

He frowned.

"I see something," he whispered.

***

1:09 A.M.

Navigating the dark, narrow tunnel that led to the Sharma family's room, the street boy's heart pounded in rhythm with his quickened footsteps.

His black cape billowed slightly in the narrow draft of the passage. The plan was supposed to be simple: a quick in-and-out job—one rewarded by a big payout—but the felt wrong. The tunnel felt tighter than it had before.

At the secret door to the Sharma family's suite, he hesitated. He wiped his palm against his thighs before pressing his hand to the panel.

1:10 A.M.

The Sharma family did not move. Above them, wood creaked. A door eased shut. Stone pressed cold against their backs.

Kiran shifted his footing. His flashlight, still dim in his hand, tilted toward the wall. A faint glint caught. He frowned. "There," he whispered.

Ravi turned. "What?"

Kiran crouched. The beam of light slid across a narrow iron ventilation slit set at knee height in the tunnel wall, half-veiled in dust. Faint light pulsed through its ribs. Not bright, but steady. Beside it, a hairline seam traced the plaster—too straight to be stone.

Harrison lowered himself beside his brother. He brushed dirt away with his sleeve and pressed upward along the seam. The plaster shifted. Loose. With careful precision, he slid the concealed hatch up into the wall cavity.

Through the opening, a room came into view. A desk. A

lamp. The blue light from a monitor. Then a figure crossed the floor.

Harrison's breath stopped. "Mom… look."

Sophie leaned down beside him. "That's impossible," Sophie whispered.

Below them, Siddharth stepped into the light. Not in a cell. Not restrained. Standing. Alive and free.

"Ravi," Sophie said quietly. "You need to see this."

Ravi lowered himself, steadying one hand against the stone.

For a moment, he watched Siddharth move. Then his gaze shifted. Near the edge of the desk lay seven navy booklets stacked neatly beside the lamp. The gold crest caught the light. Ravi's jaw tightened. "They never booked him," he said under his breath.

No one spoke.

The air above them shifted again.

* * *

1:11 A.M.

A shiver crept down the street boy's spine as he paused at the bedroom doorway, his breath caught. He hesitated, thoughts spinning as he crafted his next move, each heartbeat thudding more heavily. He carefully turned the knob. He allowed the door to open enough to slip in. Stepping quietly inside, he was struck by the emptiness of the room—a bed, hastily abandoned, and the faint scent of fear-laced sweat lingering like an unseen guest. His eyes fell to the bedpost, where a rope-like structure caught his attention. Bed sheets, knotted and tied together, dangled from the window, fluttering slightly. *A makeshift ladder.* He traced it with his flashlight, watching as it slipped out into the night, like a secret escape route.

The boy's pulse quickened as he crossed the threshold into the living room, where the shadows shifted with an almost sentient malice, dancing in the flickering glow of the dying fire. Moonbeams streamed through half-drawn curtains, casting a pale, ghostly light that mingled with the warmth of the embers. The room seemed to hold its breath, as if aware of his presence. Every step sank into the plush carpet, muffling his movement; yet, even the silence seemed louder—a haunting reminder that he was unwelcome.

His breathing shallow, he pulled out his dagger from its leather sheath and tiptoed toward the first bedroom, his vision sharpening in the darkness. Opening the door, he expected to see the sleeping form of a child, the coveted necklace lying somewhere close to or perhaps around his neck. But the bed was mockingly empty.

Realizing the suite was abandoned, he moved quickly to the second room, then the third. Each was a replica of emptiness and eerie solitude.

What in the world…?

* * *

1:12 A.M.

Ravi did not look up from the narrow opening. The office below lay in half-shadow.

Siddharth moved to the desk. He picked up one of the navy books and opened it slowly. His finger traced the edge of the photo. He flipped a page. Another. He tilted it toward the light, studying the visa stamp. "Bahrain," he murmured. He reached for the next one.

"They're right there," Sophie whispered.

"Oh my god." Amma breathed. "They were never going

to give them back."

Priya crossed the room. "Stop looking at them. Give me that." She took the passport from Siddharth's hand and gathered the rest. She moved to the sideboard, knelt, and opened the cabinet beneath it. A metal door swung outward. She placed the passports inside. For a moment, her hand hovered. Then she reached deeper into the compartment and withdrew something wrapped in cloth. She rose, glanced at the security monitor mounted beside the shelves, and set the bundle on the table. The safe door closed with a muted click. The dial did not turn.

"Now what?" Sophie whispered.

"We leave them," Ravi said immediately. "We already made that decision."

"That was before we knew where they were," Pappa replied.

Ravi looked at him. "We thought they were at the police station. Gone. Out of reach." Pappa nodded toward the room below. "They're right there."

"It's too dangerous."

"And walking into a checkpoint without identification isn't?" Pappa asked quietly.

Ravi's jaw tightened. "The nearest embassy is in Kathmandu," he said at last. "We won't make it."

"And we don't have our phones." Sophie reminded them.

Silence pressed in.

Through the slats, Siddharth stepped toward the table. He unwrapped the cloth.

Steel caught the light.

"They don't need to be everywhere," Ravi said under his breath. "Just ahead of us." His eyes shifted to the sideboard. The safe. The dial. Unturned.

"Right now," Pappa said softly, "they think we're upstairs."

The words settled.

The concealed hatch sat high in the plaster band above the shelves. Dust rimmed its thin frame. Harrison touched it lightly. It shifted. Just enough.

Ravi looked at the narrow opening. Just beyond, shelves descended directly beneath it, built into the old stone wall. Then he looked at his three sons. His gaze landed on Kiran.

The realization settled.

"No," Sophie said immediately, reading his face.

Kiran swallowed. "What?"

Ravi crouched fully now, lowering his voice to almost nothing. "You're the only one who can fit."

Kiran stared at the vent. Then at the shelves below it. Then back at his father. "I don't want to," he whispered.

Above them, something scraped across the floorboards.

No one breathed.

Harrison leaned close to his brother. His voice was steady, but not loud.

"Remember when you asked if you were the pawn?"

Kiran blinked. "You said the pawn was small,"

Harrison continued. "And brave."

Kiran shook his head slightly. "Pawns die first."

Harrison held his gaze. "Only if they stay where they're put."

Ravi's hand rested lightly on Kiran's shoulder. Not forcing. Not pushing. "We're right here," he said.

Another sound above.

Kiran looked at the grate again. Then he nodded. Barely.

* * *

1:13 A.M.

The street boy stepped back into the center of the suite. His mind raced faster than his heartbeat. *The necklace is gone— the boy and family with it. But where could they be?* He supposed it didn't matter.

He dashed to the open window for one last futile attempt to spot them. He half-expected to catch a trace of their presence, but he did not. *They're not here.*

A decision loomed before him: should he disappear as quietly as they had, or should he report this unexpected turn of events to Priya? The instructions had been explicit: return with the necklace, no exceptions. A cold shiver of dread ran through him as he considered the consequences of coming back empty-handed.

His eyes darted frantically around the room, landing on the digital clock's relentless march. Time was a river swiftly escaping his grasp. A tumultuous battle waged within, pitting cowardice against conscience. *This is stupid. I'm leaving.*

As he turned on his heel, the air in the room shifted, plummeting into an icy chill. The curtains took on an eerie life of their own, rustling and swirling. An unseen force had filled the space with an unusual surge of energy, snuffing out the last ember in the fireplace.

Fear, cold and sharp, pierced his heart. He couldn't shake the burgeoning sense of danger clawing at him. The temperature dropped further, preying on his surging panic.

The wind intensified, sending the twisted bed sheets soaring upward from the ground. They started to twirl and whirl around him in a mesmerizing dance, wrapping around his limbs as he attempted to break free. Hopelessly ensnared in the sheets, he ceased struggling.

***

1:14 A.M.

Through the narrow ribs of iron, the office below unfolded in fragments of light. The shelves rose directly below them, dark wood pressed tight against old stone. From this height, the top row of books was nearly level with Ravi's eyes. Beyond the shelves, the rest of the room stretched outward—the angled desk, the leather armchair, the oriental rug pooled in shadow.

Priya stood near the desk, her eyes glued on the security monitor, her expression drawn tight with impatience. Anil hovered near the doorway, glancing toward the corridor as though expecting movement at any second.

"Let me check the lobby again," Priya said quietly, "he should have come."

Anil did not answer. He opened the door and stepped into the hall.

Priya lingered a moment longer, scanning the room once more—the desk, the lamp, the safe—then followed.

The door clicked shut behind her.

Only Siddharth remained.

From above, they saw only his upper body when he moved closer to the shelves, and the top of his head when he crossed toward the sideboard. He poured himself a drink. The liquid slipped into the glass in a slow amber ribbon. He did not hurry.

Above, the family remained motionless.

"The gun," Sophie whispered.

Ravi's eyes tracked it where it lay on the table near the lamp.

"Where is Raju?" Amma breathed.

Ravi searched the visible edges of the room again—the door, the desk corner, the chair legs visible beyond the shelf line. "Not here."

Below, Siddharth lifted the glass to his lips. From the office floor, the hatch was flush and narrow, blending seamlessly into the plaster band.

Ravi tested its edge gently. The hatch shifted a fraction, then settled back into place with the faintest scrape.

Sophie slid her jacket between the metal frame and plaster, pressing fabric into the seam.

Ravi pressed upward. The concealed panel slid slowly into the cavity above, revealing a dark opening. He held it there with one hand.

Below them, the shelves offered a vertical path down.

Ravi studied the spacing between ledges. Solid. Built into stone. "That's your way," he murmured to Kiran.

From the hallway came Priya's voice, sharp and sudden. "Siddharth." He turned at once. "What?"

"Come here."

He set the glass down. For a suspended second, he looked back toward the desk—then stepped into the corridor. The door remained ajar.

The office breathed open and empty. No one moved above for three long heartbeats.

Ravi lowered his gaze to Kiran. "This is not about being brave," he said softly. "It's about being precise."

Kiran nodded, his face pale in the dim light. "You drop onto the top shelf," Ravi continued. "Stay close to the wall. Don't rush."

Kiran swallowed.

"You go down the shelves. Stay on the rug. Not the floor. Go to the sideboard. The cabinet underneath. The metal door will be inside. Open it slow."

"How does it open?" Kiran whispered.

"Don't turn it," Ravi said. "Just pull. It wasn't locked."

He leaned closer.

"Take all seven. Close it the way you found it. No noise. If anyone steps in, you freeze. Not for anything."

Sophie pressed the jacket tighter along the metal lip. "Slow," she whispered.

Kiran eased forward. The stone grazed his elbows as he slid through the opening. For a moment he hung suspended between levels, small hands gripping the top shelf. Then his feet found wood. He crouched there, pressed against the old fort wall.

Above him, six faces hovered in shadow.

Below, the lamplight pooled across the desk. The shelves descended like steps into the room.

The safe waited.

***

1:15 A.M.

Back in the Sharma family's suite, a faint light caught the street boys attention. At first, an apparition shimmered into existence, a mere wisp of otherworldly mist. The air stirred; dust lifted from the floorboards, drawn into its orbit. For a breath, the motes aligned—E T R—before scattering like ash in wind.

The ghost hovered, quivering in the moonlit gloom, then swelled into a more definitive shape.

It was no longer an ethereal whisper but a terrifying specter who unfurled his future before him—a grim picture if he continued down this path of malevolence. The room conspired to confront him with his darkest potential: a life deprived of light, devoid of redemption.

In this eerie reflection, the boy beheld a distorted image of himself, marred by vice, with his soul reduced to a hollowed husk. Each wrongful act carved deeper scars into his very essence, an unrelenting torment that refused to release its grip. It was an instinctive jolt, a sudden and harrowing moment of clarity amidst the growing turmoil. He came to realize the ominous path he was heading down, fraught with peril at every turn. This encounter served as the pivotal moment that would determine the course of his destiny.

True and profound terror tore at his chest, a beast with talons of ice. It was a fear not of the apparition but of the life it promised—a life he was on the cusp of claiming.

He knew then, with a certainty that eclipsed all else, that this was the crossroads of his existence. His choice was to continue the descent or ascend from the darkness.

"Help me," he uttered, not to the ghost, but to the remnants of goodness buried within him. "Guide me away from this darkness."

Hearing the sincerity in his plea, the apparition began to morph once more, its frightful visage softening. The bed sheets fell to the ground in a twisted heap. The ghost extended a hand, not in menace, but in salvation, beckoning him toward a new dawn.

Something in him irrevocably altered. He turned and retraced his steps, exiting the room with adrenaline coursing through his body. He rushed through the secret door and ran down the tunnel without looking back. The image stayed with him, impossible to unsee.

***

1:22 A.M.

Kiran landed softly on the rug. The fibers cushioned his palms. He stayed still. From the floor, the room felt enormous. And close.

The bottom half of the office door glowed faintly. Hallway light cut a thin blade across the wood just beyond the rug's edge. Voices drifted—Priya's sharper tone, Siddharth's lower reply.

The desk blocked most of the room from the doorway. He stayed behind it. To his right, the sideboard stood against the wall, polished and tall.

He moved.

He kept to the rug as long as he could, sliding along the shadowed edge of the desk. The wood floor beyond gleamed too bright. Too loud.

He reached the sideboard and lifted the cabinet door carefully.

The hinge gave the faintest click.

He froze.

The hallway voices continued.

Inside, the metal safe waited.

The dial sat exactly where Ravi had seen it. Untouched.

Kiran reached up and pulled. The door opened. A thin breath of air escaped.

Inside, the passports lay stacked.

Seven. He gathered them carefully, counting by feel. One. Two. Three. Four. Five. Six. Seven. He closed the metal door without turning the dial, then he closed the cabinet with a soft click.

Now the climb. He turned toward the shelves. They rose like a wall. The lowest ledge reached just above his chest. He placed both hands on the wood. It was cool. Solid. Built into stone. He pulled himself up, sneaker scraping lightly. A book shifted beneath his knee. He steadied it.

Nothing moved at the door.

He climbed higher.

The second shelf bit into his toes. He pressed his shoulder into the stone backing for balance. The room widened beneath him—the desk lamp a small island of amber, the rug dark and still.

Above him, the hatch waited in shadow.

Close now. He rose onto the narrow lip of the top shelf, balancing carefully, passports clutched tight against his ribs.

He reached for the hatch. He pushed. The plaster gave slightly beneath his thumb. A faint spill of dust loosened. It settled in a pale line across the top edges of the books. The panel shifted. A dark opening appeared. Six faces hovered beyond.

Ravi's hand reached out. "Slow," he breathed.

Kiran lifted the stack toward him.

One slipped.

It fell.

The passport struck the wood floor with a flat, unforgiving sound.

Kiran's hands tightened around the remaining passports.

The office door moved. Not wide. Just enough. The thin blade of hallway light widened across the rug.

From the corridor, Siddharth's voice cut in. "What was that?"

Kiran dropped down a level and pressed himself flat against the shelf, hidden in shadow between spines and stone.

The fallen passport lay near the desk leg, half in lamplight, shielded from the doorway by the bulk of the desk.

In the same breath, something tore through the tunnel behind them.

A body. Fast. Unsteady.

Harrison barely had time to turn before a shoulder

slammed into him. The impact drove him against the stone. Dust burst loose from the ceiling. A hand scraped across his jacket, searching for balance.

The street boy did not look at them. His eyes were wide. Wild. Not with pursuit—something else. He tore past them from the Sharma's suite, breath ragged, cloak snapping against the walls. The sound of him echoed forward and vanished into the dark.

For one suspended beat, the tunnel held the shape of his passing.

Just then, the heavy thud cracked somewhere beyond the inn—sharp enough to fracture the quiet.

Above the opening, six bodies went rigid.

From the corridor, Anil's voice answered, faint. "Outside."

Ravi released the panel. It dropped softly into its seam. The wall became whole again.

A pause. Then footsteps approached.

The door opened fully and Priya stepped into the office. Near the desk leg, the fallen passport lay where it had struck, its navy cover turned slightly toward the light.

She took a step toward the desk—then halted. A flicker of hesitation. Instead, she pivoted toward the table. She lifted the cloth. Steel caught the light as she unwrapped it and raised the gun.

Only then did she still.

The room held its breath. Something in the air shifted.

Her gaze lifted. Not to the floor. Up. Toward the shelves. Toward the plaster band near the ceiling.

The upper wall sat in shadow. Books lined tight against wood. The hatch above them looked like nothing more than another seam in the plaster band.

Priya held her breath one moment longer. Then—

"Anil," she called.

"A shutter fell from a third floor window." He called back.

"Impossible." She turned toward the door, gun in hand. Footsteps receded.

Silence returned.

On the shelf, Kiran did not move.

Above him, the panel shifted again.

Ravi's hand reappeared. "Kiran," he breathed.

Kiran waited one heartbeat longer. Then he climbed down, dropping the last foot to the rug. He snatched the fallen passport and pressed it back into the stack. Seven.

He climbed up again. Shelf. Stone. Top ledge. He finally reached the access point. Just then, strong hands caught his wrists and pulled him through. The panel slid down, back into place.

The tunnel swallowed them whole.

**

The office stood empty. The door was closed. The lamp burned in its hard circle of light. A black cloth lay open on the desk, its corners no longer squared. The shelves stood pressed tight against the old fort wall, rows of dark spines aligned in practiced order. Almost.

Near the top shelf, one book leaned a fraction forward from the rest. Not fallen. Not misplaced. Just shy of perfect. Above it, the plaster band lay pale and smooth. The cabinet beneath the sideboard sat flush.

Closed.

The safe behind it remained unseen.

The pipe ticked once inside the wall.

Then silence.

***

1:25 A.M.

Harrison slid the metal plate back into place. It settled with a faint scrape against stone. The tunnel darkened. The meager light from the flashlights struggled against the pressing darkness. For a moment, no one spoke.

Amma exhaled. "That was a close call."

No one disagreed.

Sophie pulled Kiran against her, one hand firm at the back of his head.

"You were super brave," she whispered. "Just like Superman."

He pulled back, eyes still wide. "Like Spider-Man," he corrected softly. "When he climbs the buildings… and fights the dragon."

A flicker passed through her face. "Just like spider-Man," she said.

Kiran nodded once. Then he slipped from her arms.

Ravi pulled the passports free just enough to thumb the edges. Seven. He tucked them back inside his jacket.

Pappa glanced over his shoulder into the dark. "Let's go. Before they realize they're gone."

That did it. They moved. Faster now.

The tunnel narrowed as it bent. Their shoulders brushed stone. Every scrape of fabric sounded too loud. Behind them, the darkness felt awake.

No one said it. But they all thought the same thing. Someone might have seen.

The tunnel dipped sharply, then split. Three mouths opened in the stone ahead of them.

Ravi slowed only long enough to sweep his light across

the walls. "Which way?"

"Left," Harrison said, too fast.

"How do you know?" Ravi asked, his flashlight beam jittering over the stone.

Harrison pointed to a faded plaque, its letters almost gone. The sign read CELLAR, with an arrow pointing left.

Ravi did not argue. He turned. The wooden door at the end of the passage groaned when he pushed it open. He scanned once. "Clear."

They moved.

The basement felt wrong.

Sophie slowed, her light catching the far wall. "Wait."

"The kukri swords and shields are gone," Ravi noted.

Amma frowned. "That's unsettling."

Ravi turned back toward the tunnel. "Block it."

He and Harrison shoved a supply shelf across the entrance. Cans clattered, then steadied.

"If someone comes through," Ravi said, breath short, "we'll hear it."

"We need to hurry," Sophie said turning toward him. "Do you remember where the entrance to the secret tunnel was?"

Ravi nodded, panning his flashlight across the room. Its beam sliced through the darkness like a knife. "It should be right around…"

"There!" Harrison suddenly exclaimed. "Behind that pile of old crates!"

Ravi's light confirmed it: the hidden door was there. It loomed like a dark mouth, offering escape…or something worse.

-20-
Passage to Dread

अगम्यभीतेः पन्थाः

1:20 A.M.

As the Sharma family stood before the door, Cyrus clutched Pappa's hand, his eyes wide with fear. "We have to go in there?" he whispered, pointing toward the sinister-looking door Anil had warned them about.

Harrison curled his fingers around the pendant on his beaded necklace. Its protective powers were both a comfort and a mystery. "We have no choice," he said, determined. "We've come too far to turn back now."

With a blend of anxiety and resolve, Ravi unlatched the door. As it creaked open, a cold gust of wind whooshed out, as if the tunnel beyond was exhaling, disturbed by their presence. The light from their flashlight pierced the darkness, but the void seemed to swallow it whole. The tunnel stretched ahead, an endless maw waiting to consume them.

The group hesitated, every instinct screaming to turn back. But they couldn't…wouldn't. They stepped into the abyss.

As the door closed behind them with an ominous thud, a low growl rumbled from deep within the tunnel, shaking the ground. A shadow, darker than the surrounding gloom, encompassed them.

Fear gripped them like a vice, but it was too late for second thoughts. With hearts pounding, they plunged deeper into the labyrinthine dark, each step taking them further from the world they knew and closer to the terrors that awaited them.

The stone in the necklace began to glow.

And somewhere, deep in the earth's bowels, something ancient and malevolent stirred.

***

1:55 A.M.

Harrison's firm grip on the flashlight led the way through the ancient tunnel. The need to escape pressed against the Sharma family from all sides. Harrison remembered it was a forty-minute walk to the tunnel's next crossroads, though it felt endless. Their steps were hurried, each footfall resounding through the cold emptiness, trying to outrun the darkness that engulfed them.

Above, the tunnel's ceiling was an uneven canopy of rock and earth, its surface jagged with grotesque stalactite formations that looked like the fangs of some primordial beast. Sconces lined the walls at irregular intervals, their hollow brackets long empty, untouched for centuries.

Sophie's flashlight flickered for a moment before steadying. She shuddered. "Let's hurry to the chapel and get out of here before—"

Her words were cut off by a sudden screech reverberating through the tunnels, drowning out all the other sounds—an animalistic wail, unlike anything they had ever heard before.

Everyone froze in their tracks, paralyzed with a fear that clenched at their stomachs and crawled up their spines.

"What was that? We didn't hear that before!" Harrison insisted, though he wasn't sure he wanted to know the answer.

Kiran clung to Pappa's leg, his grip firm, holding on for dear life. His face drained of color, and fear coursed through him, making it hard to breathe. With a trembling lip, he uttered, "Pappa?"

As Pappa looked down at him, his flashlight briefly illuminated the whites of his eyes, revealing the palpable terror within.

"Whatever it was, we don't want to stick around to find out," Ravi replied, gripping his flashlight and wielding it like a weapon. "We need to keep moving."

Increasing their pace, they reached the crossroads, their breaths short and heavy.

"Harrison, can you recall which way we went?" Ravi inquired.

"Of course," Harrison replied, masking his trepidation with a show of confidence. He led them down the path he recalled from their prior journey.

As they moved deeper down the new tunnel branch, unsettling noises grew around them—water dripping in an unseen reservoir, rustling and scuttling from hidden corners. But most concerning was the persistent, low, haunting roar echoing through the tunnels.

Harrison's light skimmed the wall as they turned a bend. For a breath, the beam caught on a smooth patch of stone where no tool had touched. Letters shimmered out of the damp surface—faint, breathing, alive. ...*THE WORLD ENDS NOW. (DOCTRINE OF BALANCE, FRAGMENT IX)*

The words glowed once, as if remembering themselves, then vanished when the beam shifted. No one noticed. Only the earth seemed to exhale, the sound folding into the roar ahead.

For a moment, no one moved. The tunnel seemed to listen—to wait. Water dripped once, twice, and was swallowed by the dark.

Pappa whispered, "Whatever that is, it doesn't sound human."

"Let's pray it stays away, wherever it is," Sophie said, her face ashen. She clutched Kiran's hand, her knuckles white with the force of her grip, as if holding on to him could anchor them both in safety.

"Let's not find out," Cyrus advised, his arms wrapped around Amma as they quickened their pace.

Finally, they reached the ancient door that blocked their path. Harrison looked at each face, their expressions a tableau of dread and determination. "This is it. The next steps we take could change everything."

"Can we go back?" Kiran asked.

"No," Ravi said, "we can't. We must go forward."

Sophie caught her breath in astonishment as she beheld the ancient structure. "Look, Pappa," she uttered with reverence. "This is the Kumari Mandala Harrison manipulated."

The portal before them was a breathtaking piece of history, expertly carved from the rich sal wood native to Nepal. The elaborate details evoked a sense of awe, each geometrical shape a narrative of ancient craftsmanship. A legacy of excellence now forgotten in the rush of modern times. The slight skew of the Kumari Mandala hinted at a secret—a hidden entrance that beckoned to be revealed.

Pappa's eyes, filled with the wisdom of age, scrutinized the door's ancient façade. His brow furrowed in confusion. "The inscriptions say that the chosen may pass, but that others will need a key to unlock this barrier." He paused, considering the message. "Others? What others?" he murmured, the wrinkles on his forehead deepening with concentration. Turning to Harrison, he asked, "How can those who are chosen pass without a key?"

"We rotated the ring around the lotus petals at the center and aligned them with this word." Harrison pointed to the term 'कुमारी' written on the outer ring of the dial, his finger hovering over the characters that had once shimmered with an otherworldly light. "It was aglow then. The Spirit of Kumari…she guided me, showed me how to open it." Then he leaned in, his voice lowered. "When I touched it, the carvings stirred to life. The ring shifted under my hand, and the door opened. But when Dad tried…nothing."

Harrison placed his hand on the door, and for a moment, it glowed to life. When he pulled his hand away, the light faded. "Like that."

Pappa watched Harrison with grave interest, the silence filled with unspoken thoughts as he contemplated the revelation. "Then it responds to *you*. Not to strength. Not to chance. To resonance. To *your* resonance. The door knows your frequency, Harrison—it knows you are the Seeker."

A brief glimmer of shock flashed across Harrison's face. "You mean I'm the only one who can…?" He stared at the door in disbelief as his words trailed off.

Pappa nodded as a satisfied grin spread across his face. "Without the key, yes. You are the only one who can open it. As the chosen Seeker, you have that honor."

Harrison slowly extended his hand again, but Pappa's words drew his arm back.

"However," Pappa continued, "if I understand things correctly, there is another option." Pappa's gaze lingered on his grandson before he finally turned back to the mandala. "Let's see if the Kumari Talisman can open the door, too," Pappa finally suggested.

Harrison lifted the necklace from around his neck and handed it to his grandfather.

"Well, here goes nothing," Pappa declared, his hands pressing against the gem at the center of the locus petals. Its energy pulsed through him. "Now, where might this fit?" Pappa mused, his palm skimming the door's surface, feeling for any clues.

"Pappa, quickly!" Sophie urged.

Just then a thought popped into Harrison's head. "The Mallas used patterns to hide latches."

"Let's just open it the way we know how," Sophie insisted.

"What did you say, Harrison?" Pappa asked, ignoring her.

Harrison, a bit flustered, replied, "Um… When we were in the bat cave, Siddharth said that during the Malla reign, they used carvings on the doors to hide things."

Pappa paused, engrossed in the puzzle before him. "I remember a paper that said the Mallas built with misdirection. Every pattern meant to confuse—except one. The true line always breaks the symmetry."

"Let's just open it the way we know how," Sophie repeated sharply. "We don't have time for a history." She turned, glancing behind her into the tunnel's dark.

The sound rose again.

"Here!" Harrison directed, indicating a subtle indentation artfully concealed in the door's design.

"Aha! Well spotted, Harrison. I think you found it," Pappa praised. He slotted the pendant into place with a satisfying click.

The images on the threshold began to glow faintly with an emerald light, and a soft, musical hum vibrated through the air. The mandala shivered, then turned of its own accord—rings aligning with symbols as though an unseen hand guided them. The smaller door, once indistinguishable from the intricate carvings, creaked open.

"Wow!" Kiran exclaimed, his expression lit with surprise as the panel swung open as if touched by magic.

"I can see how people might believe this was sealed by enchantment," Pappa mused, his face lit up with wonder.

"Before we proceed," he said, turning his attention to the obscured section of the door, "I want to translate the writing the flash of your camera concealed."

The family was visibly tense, wanting Pappa to be as quick as possible so they could get out of the tunnel and away from that horrifying roar.

"Yes, this is the warning," Pappa murmured.

"Can't we hurry, Pappa?" Sophie interjected, panic setting in.

"A warning…plus, something more," Pappa replied. "I can't quite figure it out." He paused. A look of bewilderment crept onto his face. "Pasang?" he questioned. "Who is Pasang?"

Anxious to move forward, Harrison interrupted his grandfather. "Pappa, the chapel is just ahead." He pointed to the small opening that beckoned them. "We found the second half of the pendant there."

A shiver of uncertainty passed among them as they shared silent glances. The roar of the unknown creature reverberated again in the distance, a haunting reminder they were not alone.

Sophie spoke up. "We need to move into the chapel. Pappa, there are ten doors in there." She paused before continuing. "We are going to need to figure out which one to take and how to open them, too. We're at a dead end here. We must move forward now."

"But we have Harrison. He is the key," Pappa argued.

Sophie called his name again. "Pappa!"

Then, as though on cue, the roar rose again—closer.

Cyrus clutched Amma tighter, his expression filled with both curiosity and apprehension. "Are we going to meet that noise?" he whispered, afraid of the answer.

Amma held Cyrus closer. "We'll face whatever comes, but we'll do it together." Her gaze met Pappa's.

Pappa motioned in approval, taking a steadying breath. "All right, let's see what's in the chapel. We stick together, no matter what."

With a determination that overshadowed their trepidation, most of the group lowered themselves to their hands and knees and entered the smaller passageway, the cold earth pressing against their palms and the narrow walls brushing their shoulders.

Just behind them, Harrison lingered at the threshold. His hand darted to the slot, fingers deftly reclaiming the pendant. As he pulled it free, the door began its slow, inevitable swing toward closure. With the artifact now secure in his grasp, Harrison dove forward, propelling himself into the cramped passageway mere moments before the stone sealed them in.

Ahead of them lay the secret chapel, its mysteries veiled by darkness and uncertainty. They crawled forward, the space around them tight. All the while, a chant—ancient and resonant—grew steadily louder: a single low tone holding the dark, then a quiet swell of voices, then a fine lattice of sound unfurling through the stone as their slow, deliberate advance through the tunnel carried them onward.

* * *

2:22 A.M.

In the quietude of night, the fate of Raju's mission hung in the balance, shrouded in the stillness that enveloped the hallway in the Surya Chandra Inn. There, in the faint light that struggled against the encroaching shadows, Raju sat motionless, his every breath a silent question. *Has the boy managed to accomplish the task? Or has the plan unraveled in the dark, unseen corners of the room?*

Raju's mind, caught in a tumult of scenarios, left him paralyzed in anticipation, a statue awaiting the verdict the silence refused to reveal.

As the clock's hands inched their way through the night, its ticks became a relentless companion. Wearied by the weight of anticipation, Raju found his eyelids growing heavy. His back melted into the cold, unyielding door. He slipped into a fitful slumber.

In this dreamscape, Raju found himself at a crossroads. Two distinct paths unfurled before him. One path shimmered with the noble intention of aiding the Sharma family in their quest for the Heart of Kumari, a journey marked by honor and the potential for redemption. The other path was more tantalizing and alluring, conforming to his own dark aspirations to claim the diamond for himself—to possess its rumored, boundless power.

Consciously, Raju had never contemplated the righteous path; it was a façade. Yet, there were moments that broke through, revealing the underlying goodness deep within him. His inclinations often lay with the latter, a path that resonated with his self-serving desires. As he turned down this shadowy path, his vision became increasingly clouded by the lure of power. Unseen by him, this road held the peril of a descent into an abyss—one that threatened to engulf his very essence. And still, he pressed on.

Amidst the torment, a vivid flashback surged through his thoughts, like an accusatory specter from his past. He saw himself orchestrating Cyrus's kidnapping, the darkness in his heart consuming him as he plotted the sinister deed. The memory of stealing the innocent child's lamb, an act of callousness driven by his own ambitions, also haunted him.

As these scenes unfolded, Raju's mind began constructing a narrative to rationalize his behavior. The dreamscape twisted his willingness to manipulate and use the Sharmas into mere brushstrokes on a canvas of inevitability, portraying his ruthless and malevolent choices as mere misdeeds, absolutely necessary in order to achieve his dark ambitions. After all, in his quest to obtain the Heart of Kumari, the ends justified the means. With each justification, the last remnants of his humanity dissolved, sealing his intentions and hardening his resolve toward a path of increasing wickedness. In this twilight of understanding, Raju's subconscious became a crucible, forging a new, unyielding purpose from the depths of his growing darkness.

As his journey down this dark road continued, the jewel now consumed his thoughts, its siren calls echoing through the vastness of his ambition. This coveted jewel was not just a treasure but a beacon of untapped power, a promise of a future drenched in authority and control. Raju envisioned himself wielding its influence, a future where he rose from being a mere rook to becoming a master of his destiny.

As the darkness of his intentions increased, the dream warped around him, painting a vivid masterpiece of his innermost desires. There he was, a silent marauder lurking in the shadows, patiently waiting as the Sharma family, oblivious, inched ever closer to their own ruin. Raju imagined himself deftly outmaneuvering them, the Kumari Talisman slipping from their grasp and into his own. Each step the Sharmas took toward finding the Heart of Kumari would bring Raju closer to his moment of triumph.

The dream intensified, projecting Raju into a space devoid of morality, where the diamond represented the ultimate prize in his game of deceit. Raju remained in the clutches of this revelation as the night waned, his subconscious mind crafting a justifiable narrative for the betrayal and ruthless cunning that would eventually manifest itself in the real world.

* * *

2:23 A.M.

A collective gasp escaped their lips as the Sharma family emerged from the tunnel into the vast expanse of the ancient chapel. Though Ravi, Sophie, and Harrison had been here before, the scene was now transformed. Once barely lit by the feeble glow of their cell phones, the chamber now shone with an ethereal radiance. The architecture was otherworldly, beyond any of their wildest imaginations. Stone pillars reached up like the fingers of ancient gods, beautifully carved with symmetrical patterns that were highlighted by the brilliant light. The pews rose around them, hewn from the bedrock, each a masterful blend of artistry and *Vastu Shastra*—an ancient form of Indian architecture highlighting natural forces and elements. Ten imposing doors, perfectly spaced apart, encircled the chapel. A grand podium stood as a focal point, sculpted to imitate the rising sun, a fusion of spirituality and geometry that left them in awe.

The Sharma family hesitated near the entrance, noticing they were not alone.

A hundred monks sat in pews, lost in a ceremony. Clothed in vibrant maroon and saffron robes, the monks began chanting in harmonic unison, a blend of baritone and tenor voices that echoed off the stone walls in a haunting rhythm. They sang the age-old hymns of a Buddhist Puja ceremony, offerings to the divine that resonated in the cave's recesses.

The Sharma family huddled behind a formation of jagged rocks, unseen. Pappa's breath hitched, while Ravi's fingers tightened around Sophie's hand. Even in silence, their widened eyes and brief glances betrayed how the ceremony unsettled something deep within them.

"The monks from the clue," Harrison whispered, his voice barely rising above the rhythmic cadence of the chanting.

Pappa did not look away. "'Beneath the earth, in chapels deep, where chanting monks their vigils keep.'" His voice was low. "It fits."

The gathering concluded. The monks rose and exited through separate doorways. All except for one, who remained.

The lone monk approached the podium and stopped. He did not search the shadows." Harrison," he said. "Come forward."

The name carried through the chamber without force.

Shock rippled through the family. Pappa's jaw clenched. Beside him, Sophie's heart skipped a beat. Ravi gripped his flashlight tighter. Kiran covered his mouth in disbelief. Cyrus and Amma held on to one another.

Harrison felt like he was in a dream, surreal and distorted. Summoning every ounce of courage, he approached the monk.

"I am called Pasang," the monk offered, reaching out his hand in acknowledgment. He paused, then continued, "Harrison, we have been waiting for you."

The word settled differently than Harrison expected.

"We know the Heart of Kumari calls to you. But first, you must prove you are the destined Seeker."

"What? How?" Harrison's voice hitched, unsure of where

he found the courage to speak.

"These trials will test your mind, heart, and spirit. Only those who are purified by fire and water can proceed on the path to the Heart of Kumari."

A rush of fear overwhelmed him.

As Harrison stepped closer, Pasang looked down at the pendant. Harrison, sensing the monk's request, lifted the necklace over his head and handed it to him.

"I thought the Kumari Talisman would lead us to the diamond," Harrison said as the pendant left his grasp.

"If you are not the chosen Seeker," Pasang said, turning the pendant in his hand, "the Kumari Talisman becomes the key. It unlocks the ancient doors that guard this chamber. But there is more than one path to the diamond. The Heart chooses the way. And it has led you to me."

The Kumari Talisman radiated a more brilliant light than it ever had before. "This way, please." Pasang crossed to one of the ten doors. The metal found its hidden slot with a quiet click.

Kiran, almost absently, began to count under his breath. "One... two... three..." The third door responded. A thin line of emerald light traced its frame before the hinges released.

The door opened.

It did not welcome them.

Part IV

The Chamber of Trials
संघर्षमराडपः

"...When the Time...Bloodlines and Betrayals...Sacred Balance...The World Ends Now."
— Doctrine of Balance, Fragment 9

"The only journey is the one within."

— Rainer Maria Rilke

-21-
A Secret Heritage

गुप्तपरम्परा

Looming before them, the door moaned on its hinges, reluctant. Beyond it lay a library, with stacks of ancient texts and manuscripts piled high. Pasang ushered the Sharma family through the opening to what waited.

Twelve towering stone shelves encircled the room in the shape of a dodecagon. The higher levels loomed far above, reachable only by a rickety wooden ladder. At eye level, some of the most precious books were encased in glass cabinets, showcasing their worn bindings and ancient pages. These displays also housed an array of ancient items—delicate scrolls with faded ink, carved stone artifacts, and gleaming jeweled relics—all exhibited on velvet-lined surfaces.

Beneath it all, the floor stretched out like a great chessboard, carved from alternating squares of obsidian and gold-veined quartz. It did not seem ornamental. It felt ceremonial.

Framing the entrance were two stone horse heads, weathered but regal. Their hollow eyes faced inward. They bore no reins, no riders. Only silence. And carved into their foreheads, just above the brow, was the sigil of the Knight—the broken L—the path that bends.

Set into the twelve walls, almost hidden among the alcoves, were narrow towers of black basalt—rooks, not built, but born of the stone. Each faced outward, as if anchoring unseen lines across the room, stabilizing something far older than the structure itself.

In the center was a large copper fire bowl, crackling with a smokeless intensity. The fire moved as if it were aware—alive. Above, the ceiling arched into a stone vault, shaped like a celestial dome, giving the impression of a vast and sacred space. This dome seemed to shelter the ageless wisdom within, emphasizing the room's importance as a sanctuary of knowledge. Set into this firmament, stars gleamed—each one a raw, uncut diamond. From within this sky, the bishops emerged. Not as living figures, but etched in eternal profile along the curve of the dome. Hooded. Faceless. Their robes traced in gold leaf so fine it caught the subtlest flicker of firelight. None faced inward. Each turned toward a cardinal point—east, south, north, west. They bore no staffs, no scrolls. Only their hands, lifted mid-gesture. Neither blessing nor curse. Something older. Something watching.

Off to the side, on a tall pedestal, lay an open book. It was immense in size, seemingly fashioned for the hands of a giant. Its thick pages, wrought from ancient parchment, promised secrets of old. A frayed ribbon marked the heart of the tome, drawing the eye to its mysterious contents. There, on the exposed page, the Kumari Mandala was visible, its delicate design glowing faintly, as if infused with the breath of ancient magic.

This was no ordinary room. This was a reflection of the Board.

Pasang stood at the entrance of the space, letting the family walk through in single file. Once they were all inside, he began to speak. "The Pattern has fractured. It is wisdom that will be the light that guides us through the darkness. This room, filled with the relics and knowledge of ages past, holds the key to understanding your place on the Board."

"The Board?" they questioned in unison.

"Ah, yes. The Board," Pasang answered. "It is the grand field of life—where fate is played out. Every move shapes the world. Kings, Pawns, Guardians, Seekers…we all have our place."

"What is the Pattern?" Pappa asked.

Pasang tapped his chest. "The Pattern is what lies beneath it all. It is the current behind the river—the aspirations, the doubts, the truth that drives each move. To understand your place on the Board is only the beginning. To sense the Pattern…that is enlightenment."

He paused, his gaze sweeping over the ancient texts and artifacts. "The Heart of Kumari is not merely a physical relic. It is a spiritual journey. To comprehend its power and know the way forward, you must seek answers within this sacred space."

He stepped back, gauging their reactions. "This book," he gestured toward the immense tome on the pedestal, "holds a test left by the ancients. Unravel its riddle, and it will not only reveal the Heart's location, it will prove your right to stand upon the Board. To solve this puzzle is to show you can walk the Pattern with clarity. The Heart, they say, is not lost. Only hidden. And it will reveal itself only when the Pattern calls the one it has always known. Do not be afraid. The Heart's favor is with you. Be wise, and you will touch the stars in the heavens. Fools, however, will be removed from the Board."

Pasang moved toward the door. "May you prove worthy." With a solemn bow, he exited the room, the heavy door creaking shut behind him—sealing them inside.

The Sharma family was alone in the silence of the ancient library, the only sounds being the beating of their hearts and the soft crackling of the fire.

After a long pause, Kiran turned to his older brother. "I thought the diamond would be here."

Harrison stooped to his level. "I know. Me too. But I think the Heart of Kumari is testing us, making sure we're worthy of its power."

"Kiran," Pappa instructed, "we must first understand it."

"But how?" Kiran asked.

Pappa looked at the massive tome lying open on the pedestal. He took a deep breath. "Pasang said this book is more than text. It's a puzzle, a test. The Heart of Kumari isn't just an object; it's a journey."

"I don't get it. I want to go back to my room, to my bed. I'm so tired," Kiran said.

"Kiran, we can do it," Cyrus said, placing a hand on his brother's shoulder. "I'm tired, too, but I'll help you."

"We need to keep moving forward. Going back to the inn is not safe. The dragons are there," Sophie said, scooping Kiran up into her arms.

Kiran shuddered. "Are we safe here? I don't feel safe."

Sophie looked into his eyes, her voice soft yet firm. "Remember, if we are wise, we will be safe. And we are wise, right?"

"Yes, Mama, we are wise," Kiran whispered, his small arms wrapping around her with a grip that felt desperate, like he was afraid to let go.

His heartbeat thudded against her chest.

Pappa walked over to the book and traced the glowing Kumari Mandala on the page. "We need to decipher its secrets. Each symbol, each word, holds a truth. Solve this, and the diamond's location will be revealed."

Kiran leaped out of his mother's arms and approached the pedestal. "I can read," he said, standing on tiptoes to reach the pages. He looked up with wide, curious eyes. "So… this book knows?" he asked, placing his hand over the mandala.

"Exactly," Pappa nodded. "The ancients ensured only the worthy can find the Heart. We must use our knowledge and intuition. Only then can we move forward."

Harrison joined Pappa at the book, its letters glowing faintly. At first, the writing appeared in Sanskrit, but then, as if by magic, the words transformed into English. "Look, I can read it," he exclaimed.

"Me too," Sophie said.

"It's like it wants us all to understand, not just Pappa," Harrison said. The words no longer resisted them.

Harrison began to read, his voice carrying through the space. "'Long ago, in an era when gods and mortals walked the earth together, there existed a powerful gem known as the Heart of Kumari. Within the gem, a radiant emerald fire blazed, a beacon of wisdom piercing through the darkness—this was Parā, the living flame. This diamond, a gift from the goddess Kumari herself, embodied purity, wisdom, and immense power. As humanity evolved and reached a new level of development, the gods saw that their direct involvement was no longer necessary. They did not vanish—but withdrew, as if stepping back to let the Pattern unfold. Their breath remained in the flame, but their voices grew still. In their final act upon the Earth, they entrusted the Heart—and the flame within—to the Shatranj Ke Sipahi, guardians of the Pattern, sworn to preserve harmony across the Earth. But in time, as the Order grew divided and the Pattern began to dim, the balance fractured. The flame within the Heart no longer recognized all who sought it. Some say it withdrew. Others say it waits. But all agree: the one who would find it again must be aligned—not by name, not by claim, but by truth.

"'The Shatranj Ke Sipahi was not an army, but an order ordained by the Pattern—a living mirror of balance. Each member was aligned not merely by blood, but by resonance—a frequency deep within their souls that drew them to one of the Four Paths, North, South, East, and West, and to the balance they were born to embody. Direction and role were not chosen separately; they emerged together—threads of a single fate revealed in harmony. And thus, each warrior moved not by will alone, but as part of the greater design upon the Board.

"'At the age of seven, each child was brought before the Path Lords to undergo the Rite of Ahora—a sacred trial meant to reveal their alignment within the Pattern. Through fasting, meditation, and guided visions, the child's inner essence was unveiled. Some heard the wind in the stones and were named rooks. Others felt the pull of sacred geometry and were marked bishops. The remainder stood still in the silence of paradox, and these blessed few were chosen as Kings.

"'At the Rite's conclusion, the child received their mark—a sigil burned into their skin, its shape determined by the role the Pattern had revealed. It was not merely symbolic. The mark pulsed when the Pattern shifted, a living reminder of duty, destiny, and the price of imbalance.

"'The Rite was not a choice; it was a revelation. Those who passed became Sipahi. Those who failed...they were never spoken of again.'"

"We were right about the tattoos!" Harrison gasped. "That's why everyone in Raju and Siddharth's family is marked."

Ravi nodded. "According to this legend, they're all Shatranj Ke Sipahi. Keep reading, son."

Harrison found his place and continued. "'For centuries, the Shatranj Ke Sipahi protected the diamond with devotion. But over time, their hearts grew corrupt, twisted by the gem's allure. They sought to wield its power to rule the world. From this desire emerged a malevolent force, a darkness that seemed to seep from the Heart of Kumari itself. As the balance of good and evil was disrupted, the scales of destiny tipped precariously toward chaos. The ancient laws had warned of this. Obedience preserves balance. Ambition fractures it. And so, when the Pieces tried to rule the Pattern, the harmony of existence was shattered. Thus, the Kali Raatri began.

"'A great battle ensued between the corrupted guardians and the forces of light and wisdom—the latter led by a group of ancient monks. These holy men, dedicated to reestablishing and upholding the sacred balance, understood the Heart of Kumari was not just a source of power but a focal point of destiny, capable of tremendous good or unimaginable evil.

"'The monks, skilled in both combat and spiritual arts, wielded their knowledge and strength against the dark forces. Their chants and rituals resonating with the ancient energies of the land, empowering them in battle. Their movements were a seamless blend of martial prowess and mystical invocations, a formidable combination.

"'In the chaos, the monks, guided by righteousness, managed to seize the diamond. They vowed to protect it from those susceptible to its temptation. They hid the Heart of Kumari in a sanctuary deep within the Himalayas, creating intricate puzzles and trials to test the purity and wisdom of anyone who sought it. They ensured that to reach it, one must not merely be brave or strong, they must…'"

He paused, his eyes scanning the ancient script again.

"'They must recognize the Pattern. For the Codex warns: the Heart is not a prize. It is not a weapon.'" Harrison looked up. "'It is a mirror.'"

"A mirror?" Sophie questioned. "Reflecting what?"

His throat tightened. "I… I think we're about to find out."

"Is there more?" Pappa asked.

Harrison gave a solemn nod.

Though the setting frightened him, his brother's calm storytelling had eased Kiran's tension, and he implored him to continue. "Keep reading, Harrison."

Harrison smiled at his brother's innocence. "All right," he said, looking back to the gospel. "'The monks foresaw that only those with true understanding and pure intent could find the diamond. Their prophecy declared when the balance of good and evil tipped once more, the Spirit of Kumari would choose a Seeker to restore harmony. They foretold that under the shadow of the blood moon, a Seeker shall rise from the ancient bloodline. This chosen one, driven by wisdom and not power, shall embark on a journey both spiritual and physical to find the Heart of Kumari. This path will test the soul and spirit of the Seeker, leading through trials that will reveal the Seeker's true nature. Only through purity of intent and depth of understanding shall the Seeker unlock the gem's secrets and restore balance.

"'Centuries passed, and the tale of the Heart of Kumari became a myth, a whisper in the winds of time. Yet, the gem remained, waiting for the worthy to uncover it.'"

Harrison paused, looking up from the book.

"The books says that 'a Seeker shall rise from the ancient bloodline,'" Sophie recounted, "but that doesn't make sense. We are not in the bloodline, yet here we are."

The family considered this quandary.

"Unless…" Sophie whispered, the explanation sinking in.

Pappa took a deep breath and looked at his family. "You're right, Sophie. It appears there's a truth about our family that has remained hidden until now." His heart grew heavy with the realization laid bare before him. "To seek the diamond, we must acknowledge a connection we never fully understood. Pasang's cryptic words were pointing us to this revelation. We must be bound to the ancient order, a lineage steeped in mystery and power."

"Pappa," Harrison replied, "do you mean…?"

Pappa nodded. "Yes, Harrison. If you are the Seeker, we must be in the bloodline of the Shatranj Ke Sipahi."

"No!" Harrison exclaimed. "I'm not one of them! I'm not evil!"

Pappa placed a reassuring hand on Harrison's shoulder. "No, you're not evil, Harrison, none of us are. But it appears that you have been chosen, and it's up to us to discover how that was possible and to determine the purpose of your selection." He then glanced at the giant tome before them. "Let's see what else this book can tell us."

Pappa flipped to the next page, revealing intricate, handwritten notes and sketches that seemed to bring history to life. As Pappa summarized what he read, his voice carried a mix of reverence and urgency.

"This section describes a man called 'one of the last pure rooks of the Shatranj Ke Sipahi,'" he murmured. "A scholar-strategist. Devoted to the Heart. Keeper of the Pattern. He was known for his foresight and unwavering principles."

He paused, his eyes scanning the ornate script. "It says he was once a loyalist who was trained in the old codes, obedient to the Order. But over time, he began to see a change. The rituals had grown hollow. The bishops had ceased listening. Power had replaced purpose."

Pappa's voice deepened. "It was not betrayal that moved him—but revelation. He came to understand a simple truth: the Heart cannot be mastered. It responds only to balance. To resonance. When the Council ignored his warnings, he acted. He stole sacred scrolls—fragments of the Lost Laws—and disappeared into the eastern Himalayas. Not to destroy the Order, but to redeem its truth."

Pappa paused. His finger stopped moving.

His eyes narrowed—as if the page had shifted beneath him.

"What, Pappa?" Cyrus asked, too quickly. "What is it?"

"There's a break in the script," Pappa murmured. "A single entry—half-burned, like someone tried to erase it." He swallowed. Looked up at them.

"In the year seventeen seventy-seven…"

A pause. Small, involuntary.

"The Spiral Temple was lit with blood."

No one spoke.

Harrison felt the word spiral catch somewhere deep in his chest. As if this moment had happened before.

Sophie's voice came quieter now. "Pappa… is he mentioned by name?"

Pappa looked up at her flatly. Without a word, he looked back at the page and adjusted his glasses. He traced a line with his finger, silently confirming the note scrawled in the margin.

"His name…"

Pappa's voice faltered as the color drained from his face. He breathed deep, almost shuddering.

"His name was Gopal Bhattarai…"

A stillness fell over the room—thick, reverent.

The fire cracked once.

No one spoke.

The past had found them.

The family gasped. For a moment, the room lost its air.

Pappa took an unsteady step backward, his wide eyes fixed on the page, unable to tear himself away from what he had just read.

Harrison's breath caught.

Ravi's mouth dropped open.

Sophie's hand flew to her mouth.

Amma's body stiffened.

"Yes. Gopal Bhattarai," Pappa repeated. His face softened with the realization. "My hunch was correct. We are of the bloodline," he murmured, almost to himself.

The family silently contemplated this revelation, each considering the ramifications of this discovery. Their involvement in this quest had suddenly become clearer. And yet, this clarity had also clouded their insight into their lineage.

For a fleeting second, Harrison remembered the stillness of the lake. The warning that had followed him since.

Bound by blood.

The words did not feel like an accusation anymore. They felt closer.

Pappa took a deep breath and straightened. "All right, let's regain our composure and start reading again. We are meant to understand this."

"Agreed," Ravi stated confidently, determined to inspire hope among the others. "Please, keep reading."

Pappa cleared his throat. "Gopal Bhattarai was a man of unparalleled foresight and wisdom. Born into the prestigious Bhattarai family, a Brahmin caste deeply respected for their priestly and advisory roles in royal courts, Gopal Bhattarai was not only well-versed in spiritual matters but also trained in the arts of governance and strategy. He quickly discerned the growing corruption and dark influence within the ranks of the Order of the Shatranj Ke Sipahi.

"The Kali Raatri marked a period of great turmoil in Nepal, as the Order sought to dominate the land through the power of the Heart of Kumari." Pappa paused, allowing everyone to ponder the ancient text.

The family had been listening intently, their expressions a blend of curiosity, amazement, and concern.

Amma spoke up. "So, Bhattarai is a Brahmin name. He never had to change it. He just…switched to a new one."

Pappa nodded, continuing the story. "Exactly. Gopal didn't change his caste; he just changed his identity to protect his family. When he fled to India, adopting the name 'Sharma' wasn't about abandoning who he was; it symbolized a new beginning rooted in purity and strength. His mission was clear: to preserve his lineage so that one day a descendant with a pure soul could rise to seek the Heart of Kumari and restore balance."

Harrison's eyes widened as he listened, feeling the profound connection to his ancestor. "So, Gopal's foresight and wisdom were meant to save the world from the dark forces of the corrupt bloodline. And now, I'm chosen to find the Heart because I am of his family line."

Pappa nodded. "Yes, Harrison. You are chosen because you embody the purity and strength Gopal wanted to preserve. You are not like the others in the Shatranj Ke Sipahi. You are meant to counter their darkness and protect the Heart from falling into the wrong hands."

For a moment, the word bloodline did not feel triumphant. It felt old. Heavy. As if something had survived not only through them—but beneath them.

Ravi, moved by the revelation, added, "Gopal knew this day would come. His actions were driven by a deep sense of duty and love for his descendants. He wanted to ensure that when the time came, his family would have the strength and wisdom to face the challenge."

Amma's eyes glistened with pride. "This is a great responsibility, but you're not alone, Harrison. We are all in this together, and we will support you every step of the way."

Sophie placed a comforting hand on Harrison's cheek. "You have a good heart, Harrison. That's why you've been chosen. We believe in you."

"Thanks, Mom."

Pappa turned back to the ancient tome laid out before them. With a flick of the page, his eyes scanned the new script that appeared. "It's another riddle!"

"Read it, Pappa!" Cyrus said.

"Solve this riddle, and only then will you be purified to seek the heart," Pappa read. He paused, hesitant to continue. "Purified?" he whispered. He then readjusted his glasses, taking a deep breath. "In the vault where wisdom breathes, the Pattern veils what none perceives. Above the board, where Watchers peer, mark the word to shift the sphere."

Pappa lifted his eyes from the aged parchment, his thoughts turning inward. As he did, the ink caught the fire's pulse. Between the curling vines, faint letters shimmered—A Y A L—before the page settled back into stillness. He was too engrossed with the riddle to notice.

"The vault. It's this room," Amma said, looking upward.

They all followed her gaze, their eyes drawn to the arched expanse. A vast dome hewn from dark stone towered above them, inlaid with gemstones so precisely set that it mimicked a living sky. Sapphires and onyx formed a field of deep night, while flecks of diamond and amber flickered like stars. At its center, a crescent of blood-red ruby curved, pulsating from the fire burning beneath, casting a shimmering glow that made the celestial sky above seem alive with dancing light.

Pappa nodded. "We need to use the knowledge in this room to find the answer."

Just then, the room began to shake. The atmosphere suddenly became stifling, making it difficult to breathe. Panic began to creep in, tightening its grip with every second.

"What's happening?" Harrison asked.

"I don't know," Ravi answered, trying to keep his composure. "But we need to stay calm."

Kiran wrapped his arms around Amma's leg, his body quivering with fear. "I don't like this!"

Cyrus dashed to the door, past the twin knights, wanting to escape, only to realize there was no handle. "It won't open! There's nothing to grab!"

"What are we supposed to do now?" Harrison asked.

As if in response, the shaking suddenly ceased.

Pappa turned toward the door to examine it. Its surface was smooth and featureless, seamlessly integrated into the wall with no visible seams or hinges, as if it were part of the room itself. "The only way out is to solve the puzzle," Pappa said.

"But, how?" Amma insisted.

They looked around, the weight of their situation becoming clear. As their confusion grew, a fog seemed to rise, mirroring their uncertainty and blurring the room's boundaries. The shelves holding ancient texts and manuscripts appeared distorted in the mist's ascent. The fire in the center of the room began to crackle, creating spectral fingers that oscillated across the stacks of books.

Harrison wheeled around, looking at Pappa. "What did Pasang say? Wisdom is the light that guides us through the darkness?"

Pappa returned to the giant book, his fingers traced the ancient tome, sensing the pulsating energy within its pages. He paused at a phrase that caught his attention. "In the diamond's heart, wisdom's flame; where fire burns, there is no night." His eyes lit up in understanding. "Fire. Of course! Fire symbolizes wisdom, illuminating the darkness."

Suddenly, a forceful gust of wind swept through the room, sending the pages of the giant book fluttering wildly, as if an unseen force were hastily searching for something hidden within its ancient text.

Ravi ran over and read from the page where it settled. "To find the next clue hidden in plain sight, seek the scroll that burns with light. Within this room where secrets lie, beware the face where truth abides."

"A clue," Amma exclaimed. "The book! It's pointing us in the right direction."

"Look for a scroll that looks like a flame," Ravi said.

With determination, the Sharma family dispersed, each member searching intently for the scroll that would reveal their next clue.

Harrison squinted and looked up. High on one of the shelves, a faint glimmer caught his eye. *Was that always there? Or is it just the play of the firelight?* "I think I see something. It looks like a scroll."

Amma followed his gaze. "You're right!" she agreed. "It looks important, almost as if it's glowing like fire. Just like the book described."

"I see it, too!" Kiran shouted, breaking away from Amma. He darted to the stone wall where the shelf was but realized it was out of reach. He stood there, staring up. The rook loomed above him, as if mocking him. Heart pounding, he turned to his father. "It's too high. Dad, can you help me get it?"

Ravi looked around and spotted a ladder. "Sure thing, Kiran. Pappa, can you give me a hand with this?"

Pappa nodded, moving toward the ladder. "Of course, son. Let's get this in place."

The ladder was old and worn, and its rungs looked splintered. Ravi and Pappa each took an end, lifting it off the ground.

"I don't think this will hold our weight," Pappa said.

Ravi tested a rung, which wobbled under his touch. "You're right, Pappa." He scanned the room for another option but found none. "Kiran is the smallest and lightest. It'll have to be him."

As Ravi and Pappa positioned the ladder, Harrison stepped in to help steady it. "I've got this side."

"Thanks, Harrison," Ravi replied, appreciating the extra support.

"Kiran, you're going to have to go up and get the scroll," Ravi said, turning to his son.

"Okay, Dad. I can do this," Kiran said, trying to sound confident despite the nervous flutter in his stomach.

"Kiran, start climbing slowly," Ravi instructed, his eyes never leaving the boy. "We'll keep the ladder steady for you."

Kiran took a deep breath and placed his foot on the first rung. The ladder creaked under his weight. He hesitated, but it held firm. He began to climb. Each step grew more precarious. His heart pounded.

"You're doing great, Kiran," Pappa encouraged from below. "Just a few more steps."

Kiran's hands quivered. He climbed past the carved face of the rook, trying to ignore its gaze.

He had climbed in worse places. In darker ones. But this room did not feel dark. It felt as if it were measuring him.

Kiran reached the top. The scroll rested in a narrow cradle of stone. He stretched out his hand, feeling the grit beneath his fingers as he dislodged it. Dust filled the air, making him cough, but he grasped the scroll with a tight grip and began his careful descent. When he finally reached the ground, he let out a breath he didn't realize he was holding.

The group sighed in relief.

"Well done, Kiran," Ravi said, ruffling his son's hair. "You did great."

Kiran smiled, holding the scroll. "Thanks, Dad." He passed it to Harrison. "Here you go."

Harrison held it up to the flames. The parchment gleamed, its wax seal bearing the imprint, 'कुमारी'.

"It says 'Kumari' on the seal," Pappa read, squinting at the intricate letters.

"Open it, Harrison," Sophie urged.

Harrison broke the seal and unrolled it, revealing a cryptic riddle penned in English.

I AM NOT ALIVE, BUT I GROW. I DO NOT HAVE LUNGS, BUT I NEED AIR. I DO NOT HAVE A MOUTH, AND I CAN DROWN. WHAT AM I?

"That doesn't make sense," Cyrus said, frowning.

"Let's think about this," Pappa mused.

Amma nodded. "The riddle speaks of something that grows and needs air but can drown. Let's split up and search for anything that might relate to these clues."

They spread out, each member of the family examining different parts of the library. Sophie explored a section of old manuscripts, her finger tracing the spines as she searched intently. Amma and Pappa studied the various artifacts displayed in glass cases, their eyes searching curiously. Meanwhile, Cyrus focused on the inscriptions carved into the stone bookshelves, his brow wrinkled in concentration.

As Harrison stared into the flames, his mind churning with the riddle's cryptic lines, a sudden hissing noise drew his attention. He turned to see the mist in the room rising again and creeping along the floor. *Is it leading me?* Then, he noticed the familiar symbol of the mandala that had been guiding them, not set in obsidian, but in a tile of gold-veined quartz. It began to glow faintly, hidden within the shifting fog. "I think there's another clue here. I see the Kumari Mandala!" Harrison called out.

They all ran over and examined the engraving with its concentric circles. Above the mandala, attached to the wall, a torch burned, illuminating the inscription.

Pappa squinted at the designs. "You're right, Harrison." As he spoke, his breath made the flame in the torch grow.

Harrison's eyes widened as he connected the clues. "Flames…growing…needing air…" He stared at the flame, watching as it flickered and grew, rising and shrinking with each of Pappa's breaths. He stepped closer and blew just enough to fuel the flame, and it rose in intensity. *The riddle says, 'I am not alive, but I grow.' Fire grows but isn't alive.* "Pappa, do you think the answer is fire?"

Pappa raised an eyebrow, intrigued. "Why do you say that?"

Before Harrison could respond, Kiran's excited voice cut through. "Look! The mandala isn't lined up!" Kiran knelt down, recalling the ancient door they had encountered earlier in the tunnel. The stone rings, slightly raised from the floor—they were just like the rings on that door. He reached out and tried to move the outermost ring, grunting in frustration as it refused to budge. "The rings move," he said with urgency, his hands straining against the cold quartz, "but I can't do it. I need help."

Harrison and Pappa exchanged a look.

"Come on, Pappa."

Harrison crouched beside Kiran, placing his hands next to his brother's, while Pappa knelt on the opposite side. Together, they pushed with all their strength, but the heavy stone barely shifted.

"We need more leverage," Harrison said, sitting back on his knees.

"You're right," Pappa said, wiping sweat from his brow. "But how?"

As they paused to catch their breath, Harrison noticed something—the flame from the torch illuminated a small hole carved into the surface of each ring, as if waiting for something to be inserted. "Look, Pappa. Holes."

Pappa leaned closer, studying the rings. "We need to slot something into these holes to create a handle. Something strong enough to give us more leverage to turn the rings."

Sophie scanned the room. "What about that?" she said, pointing to a copper fire poker resting against a bookshelf.

Harrison wasted no time. He scrambled to his feet, ran over to the poker, and grabbed it. Returning in a flash, he slipped the poker into one of the carved holes. It was a perfect fit.

With everyone gathered around, they pulled together.

Slowly, a deep, rumbling noise filled the chamber. The rings began to shift, turning as the gears hidden beneath the floor ground against one another. The intricate mechanism beneath the floor creaked to life.

As they rotated the ring into place, the gears clicked into alignment, settling with a loud thud. Then, with a resounding groan, a hidden compartment above the torch opened, releasing a stream of water that cascaded down, extinguishing the flame with a sharp hiss. Steam billowed around them, swirling in the cool air.

Ravi, Kiran, and Pappa exchanged triumphant glances. Amma and Sophie smiled.

Harrison's mind raced as he observed the extinguished flame. *'I do not have a mouth, and I can drown.' Fire doesn't have a mouth, and it can be drowned by water.* "The answer *is* fire," he called out.

The family turned to him, surprise and understanding dawning on their faces.

Pappa nodded, impressed. "Of course, it makes sense. Fire isn't alive, but it grows. It doesn't have lungs, but it needs air. And it can be 'drowned,' or extinguished, by water."

"We have a bigger problem—the water is coming!" Cyrus exclaimed.

Sophie dashed toward the bookshelf. "There must be something here to stop it!" she called out, frantically searching through the ancient texts and artifacts.

Ravi reinserted the copper poker into the mandala, desperately trying to reset it. "The rings are locked; they won't move."

"Let me help," Pappa said, gripping the copper poker as he joined his son in pushing against the stubborn ring.

They strained with all their strength, but the ring wouldn't budge. Sweat beaded on their brows as they tried again, to no avail.

"It's stuck!"

Pappa stepped back, eyeing the mandala with concern. "If we can't align this, I fear the compartment above will remain open and the water will continue to flow." He glanced around the room, his worry deepening. "We need to find another way."

Ravi glanced over and saw Sophie, panic written across her face. He rushed to her side, gripping her shoulders gently but firmly. "Sophie, stop!" he said, locking eyes with her, trying to steady her with his voice. "We're not going to stop the water like this. We need to think."

"Ravi's right. We need to focus," Pappa urged, trying to bring calm to the chaos.

"The answer to the last riddle! We need fire to move forward," Amma realized, her eyes widening with understanding. "But how?"

The water gushed out with greater force, pooling rapidly around their feet. It cascaded from the wall, spreading across the floor in waves. The air thickened with moisture, and the room filled with the echo of surging water, a sound that grew more ominous by the second.

Water lapped at the base of the copper bowl at the room's center, but the fire within still burned. Harrison grabbed a torch from the wall and ignited it. The flame flared up with a whoosh, projecting twisted shadows that pulsed across the bookshelves. As it did, a low groan rose from the floor, as if the library itself were resisting the answer. The water churned violently, waves crashing against the walls and sending ripples in all directions. Books tumbled from the shelves, splashing into the rising water. The family crouched low, trying to stabilize themselves on the trembling floor.

When the shaking subsided, Harrison rose and stepped forward, his boots sloshing through the growing mire. The cold, murky water lapped at his ankles. He held the torch high, its light gliding over the rippling surface, and approached the Kumari Mandala, which was now fully submerged.

The mandala appeared distorted. The once-distinct symbols now twisted, shifting under the flickering torchlight. Tiny bubbles clung to the edges, rising to the surface and causing undulations that added to the mesmerizing effect.

Harrison looked up and focused on the source of the water, searching for a way to stop the relentless flow. His eyes locked on the compartment from which the water gushed, cascading down and striking the base of an iron torch holder. The water splashed outward before pooling at his feet, a steady stream that showed no signs of slowing.

Determined to find a solution, Harrison studied the torch

more closely. Its flame had been extinguished earlier, leaving only damp wood and metal, but something about the way the water was splashing against the holder caught his attention.

He brought his lit torch closer, the flickering light revealing the soaked wood beneath the water. He didn't know why—but he had to pull it.

He reached out and yanked the torch free.

A series of low, mechanical clicks reverberated through the chamber.

High above, one of the etched bishops seemed to catch the firelight differently—its lifted hand now casting a longer shadow across the dome.

Across the room, one of the massive stone bookcases began to tremble. The water collected around its base, swirling and lapping against the stone.

The ground began to vibrate.

With a loud creak, the bookcase began to pivot, scraping against the wet floor. As it moved, water cascaded into the dark beyond.

Harrison froze, clutching both torches, watching the water spill through the opening. The water did not retreat. It only redirected. "I was trying to stop the water," he said, breathless. "But I think…"

Pappa finished his thought. "I think you just found our escape."

For a fleeting second, Harrison felt no triumph—only recognition. As if he had stepped into something already waiting for him.

-22-
BORN OF WATER AND FIRE

आपो ऽग्निसंभूतः

Slowly, the bookcase continued to turn until it opened, exposing a dark chamber beyond. Water flowed steadily into the room, forming a narrow stream that snaked across the floor, glinting in the torchlight.

"You did it!" Kiran shouted. "We found the way out!"

"The water's filling the room!" Amma screamed.

"This way!" Pappa urged, taking the lead. They followed closely behind him. The water churned at their feet.

"Agh!" Harrison jumped in terror as he entered. A towering mirror caught his reflection—and the torch's. The appearance of the flame wavered, as if reflecting his fear. The image looked like him, but something was off. Staring back at him was a more sinister version of himself—one he couldn't quite place, filled with foreboding. The air inside felt cool, carrying a sense of dread that wrapped around him like a cold shroud.

Once inside, the Sharma family noticed the room was

small, almost claustrophobic. The light from the torch birthed long fingers on the walls that twisted and danced like specters. There was no way out; every direction felt like a dead end. The darkness pressed in from all sides, giving the unsettling impression the space was shrinking—closing in on them. The only sound was that of water flowing into the room, heightening their sense of dread.

Harrison's heart pounded, as though the room itself were alive, waiting.

As they moved deeper into the room, their sense of anxiety grew, and the mist thickened. Their skin prickled with unease. In the center of the room, twelve candlesticks stood in a perfect circle. On the floor, within the circle of candles, the Kumari Mandala was carved into the stone.

"I don't think this is the way out," Pappa admitted.

"What is this, Mama?" Kiran looked up at his mother.

"I don't know, baby," Sophie replied, gripping his hand tighter. "It looks like a ritual," she whispered.

The mist began to shift—thinning, retreating, as though exhaled by the chamber itself. Within moments, it vanished entirely, leaving an eerie stillness in its wake.

"Look! There's something written on the mirror," Harrison said, wiping away the fog.

The letters remained, as if by some strange magic.

As water rises and shadows play, reveal the path without delay. Light the candles from dawn 'til night, leave the heart out of your sight. In the flicker, a false flame lies. Solve each riddle, do not deny. Complete the puzzles, one by one, Before the drowning has begun.

"We need to light the candles to stop the water!" Sophie said.

"No, read it again! It's worse," Ravi shouted. "We need to complete all the puzzles correctly to get out alive!"

"What? How many puzzles are there?" Sophie exclaimed, turning frantically as the water climbed, now lapping at her knees.

"I don't know," Ravi admitted.

"Let's light the candles. Hurry, Mama!" Kiran screamed.

"Not so fast, Kiran," Sophie cautioned, putting a hand on his arm. "We need to be very careful." She paused. "How do we know which ones to light? Which one is the false flame?"

"There must be another puzzle to figure it out!" Cyrus hollered.

Sophie looked around in panic. "We must hurry. The water is rising!"

Dread coursed through them as they struggled to stop the encroaching water. The oppressive, damp atmosphere pressed in around them, heightening their sense of urgency and terror.

Amma scanned the room. "We need to find a way out of here. Fast!"

Their hands trembled as they examined the twelve candlesticks closely. All were made of pure gold. And each one bore a unique symbol—a sun, moon, star, tree, river, mountain, flame, book, heart, sword, crown, and a key.

"We need to decipher these symbols," Pappa said, his voice steady despite the water rising up to his knees.

Harrison's heart pounded. "They must have something to do with the order to light them."

"Mom!" Cyrus cried, the water rising around them.

A look of puzzlement spread across the group's faces.

Harrison ran back into the library, trudging through the rising floodwaters, his mind racing. He scanned the shelves, desperate for an answer to reveal itself. "Dawn to night…" he muttered, his eyes darting around. Then, he noticed the same symbols from the candlesticks engraved at the tops of the bookshelves. "Hey, I found something!" he shouted.

"What did you find, Harrison?" Sophie asked, trailing behind him, her clothes weighed down by the water.

The group followed.

"'Light the candles from dawn 'til night,'" he repeated. "We have to light the candles in a specific sequence!"

"But what sequence?" Sophie inquired.

"Look!" Harrison said, peering up. "The same symbols on the candlesticks are carved above each of these bookshelves."

Pappa nodded decisively. "He's right. The order on these shelves starts with the sun." He gestured around the room, pointing at each in turn, starting with the one closest to the first doorway. "See, the moon is next to the sun, so the sun—dawn—must be the first candle to light, then we proceed around the room this way…" He circled the shelves with his finger. "Ending with the moon—night—as the twelfth candle to light. Twelve shelves, twelve candles."

"That's the order! But which one is false?" Ravi asked.

The water continued to rush around them.

"The heart," Sophie supposed.

"Why the heart?" Pappa turned to Sophie to understand her logic.

"Because the riddle says, 'leave the heart out of your sight.'"

"Good point, Mom," Harrison praised.

"Let's try it," Amma announced.

Harrison continued to carry the lit torch, its blazing fingers licking the air, creating long shadows that shimmered across the water's surface. With the torch held high, they waded back into the smaller chamber—all except for Pappa, who continued to study the shelves.

"Okay, here goes nothing." Harrison inhaled, taking a deep breath to steady his nerves. He approached the candles. "I'm lighting the sun first," he said, more as a statement than a question.

"Correct. The sun should start the sequence," Pappa called out from the library.

Harrison lit the candle. "Okay, it's done!"

"Next is tree, then river, book, and key," Pappa said.

Harrison lit the candles in turn. "Okay, what's next, Pappa?"

Pappa looked at the images and continued. "Mountain, book, flame… The next is heart—don't light that one!"

Harrison lit the candles as instructed. "Got it. What are the rest?"

"Crown, sword, star, and the last is moon." Pappa trudged back into the room with the mirror to join the group.

As Harrison lit the last wick, the room began to quake, the stone walls shuddering as if coming alive. The family huddled together, clinging to each other in fear.

Suddenly, an ominous face materialized in the mirror. Staring back at them, its eyes glowed with malevolent intent. The surface of the mirror rippled like disturbed water, distorting the features into a grotesque mask that seemed to mock their very presence. "Wrong!" the face sneered, its voice dripping with malice and foreboding.

Chilling, hollow laughter echoed through the chamber, sending shivers down their spines. Suddenly, a cold wind surged from nowhere, sweeping through the room and extinguishing the candles and the torch in an instant. Fear enveloped them as the room plunged into darkness. Then, a distant rumble rose, and the sound of falling water thundered louder.

Ravi dug into his pocket and retrieved his flashlight. Turning it on, the beam shuddered and waned, as if some unforeseen force had drained the charge from the batteries. The dim, diffuse light illuminated the scene in a haunting glow.

"I messed up! The heart is not the false flame!" Sophie

cried. "I'm sorry!"

"The water is coming out faster!" Amma cried.

"It's not your fault, Mom. We all agreed," Harrison reassured her.

"We need to figure this out!" Amma roared as the water reached her waist.

"*Flame*!" Harrison shouted. "The false flame is the flame!"

"No, it can't be that simple… Can it?" Ravi supposed.

"But it is," Harrison argued, his voice growing stronger. "Think about it—this whole place is designed to deceive us. The last riddle was about fire, and fire was the solution. But this time, it's a warning. The riddle says, 'In the flicker, a false flame lies.' What if the flame isn't real at all?"

Sophie looked puzzled. "But we've lit the candles. Those flames are real, aren't they?"

"The candles are real," Harrison replied, wading through the water swirled around him. "But the flame we're focusing on—that's the decoy. Like what Dad said about the men on the boat: they weren't a threat. They were only a distraction. The false flame doesn't burn because it's never meant to. It's a lure, a trick, a *lie*."

"Still…" Sophie challenged. "What if the men on the boat weren't just a distraction? What if they were part of something bigger?"

"That doesn't matter right now," Harrison said, shaking his head. "The point is, they pulled our attention away from what was really happening."

Pappa's eyes widened, suddenly understanding. "Of course! The flame isn't just false because it doesn't burn—it's false because it's meaningless. This whole place is filled with illusions, testing us to see what we'll fall for."

Sophie caught on. "Exactly! The riddle says, 'leave the heart out of your sight.' The heart was the obvious choice because it draws our attention, but that was the deception. It was never about lighting the heart."

"So," Harrison nodded, his thoughts racing. "We need to ignore the candle with the image of the flame and light all the other candles."

"Well, we'd better hurry," Amma yelled.

"I need to relight the torch," Harrison shouted. "I'll be right back."

Harrison waded into the ancient library, the water now lapping at his waist. The gust of wind from earlier had extinguished the fire in the copper bowl, but he held onto a flicker of hope—perhaps some embers remained. Blindly, he felt his way through the room until his hand brushed the edge of the bowl. His heart sank as he realized it was submerged beneath the waterline. The fire was completely smothered, leaving nothing behind. Dread tightened in his chest. *What am I supposed to do now?*

"The fire is out!" Harrison called back to the others.

"Oh no!" Kiran cried, pressing into his mother.

"You have to find something to light the torch!" Pappa yelled.

Harrison twisted around and rummaged through his backpack. He found his flashlight and jammed down the button.

Nothing.

He shook it, smacked it, and tried again.

Still dead.

"Seriously?" he muttered. "I should've known not to trust a five-rupee flashlight from a street bazaar."

He shook it one last time. When it didn't respond, he sighed and flung it into the water. "Rest in peace, Discount Beam Deluxe. At least you got us through the scary tunnel."

The splash echoed faintly before being swallowed by the silence.

Harrison tried to look around the room, the damp air chilling his skin. He squinted into the darkness, his heart thumping. *This is impossible. I can't see anything. Think, Harrison, think. How do I light a torch without fire?* Panic surged through him, but he pushed it down, forcing himself to focus. His eyes darted reflexively, his mind searching anxiously for a solution.

Suddenly, he remembered the flint arrowhead from the box they found in the bat cave. He reached into his pocket, rifling around for its sharp edges. Finally, he pulled it out. *Now what?*

Desperation surged as he waded through the rising water, blind in the inky darkness. He couldn't see a thing, but he remembered the glass cabinet on the far side—where artifacts had been displayed. *That cabinet could hold something useful, something that might help me light the torch.*

He forced himself forward, each step heavier as the floodwaters dragged at him. Finally, his hands collided with smooth glass. Relief was fleeting. He fumbled for the handle and pulled, but the doors held firm. Panic set in again. He yanked, harder this time, but the cabinet stayed sealed, trapped beneath the crushing weight of the flood.

Panic rising, he frantically felt along the wall until his fingers brushed something cold—the copper poker. Gripping it tightly, he swung it with all his strength. The glass shattered, water rushing in as shards splintered and floated around him. He plunged his hands into the cabinet, feeling blindly through the water-soaked shelves. His fingers grazed over various objects, desperate to find something—anything—that could strike the flint and spark the fire he so urgently needed.

Inside, he touched a variety of ancient artifacts: worn leather books, delicate glass vials, and intricately carved wooden figurines. His fingers brushed against something cold—an iron statue. He felt along its surface, tracing the sharp edges of wings frozen mid-flap and the snarling features of a dragon caught in mid-roar.

Relief washed over him as he grabbed the statue, feeling its cold, solid weight in his hands. *This could work.*

Harrison made his way back into the smaller chamber. "I found something—but I need help!"

Ravi waded through the water, his forehead creased with worry. "What is it, son? What did you find?"

"Here, take this," Harrison said, handing the unlit torch to his father. "I'm going to use the flint arrowhead from the box we found in the bat cave and this statue to light the torch."

"Good thinking."

"But I need a dry piece of cloth."

Without hesitation, Ravi shrugged off his backpack, pulled out a cotton shirt, and wrapped it around the torch. "Let's make this work," he said, holding the torch out to be lit.

Harrison gripped the flint in one hand and the statue in the other, striking the flint against the iron dragon with growing desperation. Sparks flew, briefly illuminating the darkness and casting flickering reflections on the rising water. After several attempts, a spark finally landed on the cloth wrapped around the torch. It smoldered, then caught fire.

Ravi cupped his hands around the small flame, shielding it from the drafts. His heart pounded as he waited anxiously, watching until the flame burned steadily.

"Hurry, light the candles before the wicks are under the water!" Sophie urged.

Harrison began lighting the twelve candles in the precise order: sun, tree, river, book, key, mountain, heart, crown, sword, star, and finally, moon. He left the flame candle unlit.

The room held its breath as the candle wicks burned.

Slowly, the mirror's surface began to clear, and letters started to shimmer, revealing another riddle glowing in the firelight.

"It worked!" Harrison exclaimed, relief washing over him.

For a moment, it seemed as though the room might yield.

The water kept rising.

No one spoke.

"We solved it—why are we still drowning?" Cyrus screamed.

The water said nothing.

It kept rising.

"Help, Mama! The water's getting too high!" Kiran cried, reaching out with trembling arms.

Sophie scooped up her son. "We have to reach higher ground!"

Ravi snapped out of it. "We're not going to drown," he said sharply. "We just need to solve the next puzzle—now."

Pappa waded forward through the rising water and began to read from the mirror. "Find the object that breathes life into words, but beware, for it hides in the shadows." He whipped around to address the others. "Books breathe life into words! We need to go back!"

"Hurry, Pappa!" Sophie implored. "The water is rising fast!"

As they reentered the library, they were met with a haunting scene. The once-grand room was now partially submerged. Books floated tauntingly on the water's surface, their pages and covers bobbing and churning with the current.

Pappa waded through the now chest-deep flood, his arms pushing through the liquid and creating a wake that fanned out behind him. The cold water swirled around him as he scanned the titles. "Books…words…but which one?" he muttered, as he searched for clues.

The family glanced back at the room with the mirror. They watched the lights from the candles flicker and dim, each flame succumbing to the rising water. One by one, the flames sputtered and hissed, the water licking at the wicks until the last candle was extinguished, plunging the room back into darkness.

"Mama!" Kiran exclaimed.

Harrison held the torch high above the water, his hands shaking as he struggled to keep the flame alive.

"Climb up on the shelves, boys. We need to get higher," Sophie urged.

"I can't, Mama. They are too narrow!" Cyrus screamed.

"We are wise. We are wise," Kiran repeated as he scampered up a bookcase.

Harrison's eyes widened in horror as he watched the smaller chamber vanish beneath the rising water. *How are we going to get out of this?*

"Come. Let's solve the next puzzle," Amma urged. "What book breathes life into words?"

"They all do!" Sophie replied hopelessly. Her eyes darted over the old tomes as she pulled them off the shelves, sending them splashing into the rising water. "We need to get higher!" she shouted.

Kiran's heart raced as he continued to scamper up the towering shelves, his movements cautious yet urgent. Amid the chaos, he spotted a dark leather-bound book that seemed to glow in the flickering torchlight. He leaned closer. On its spine, large, faded letters shimmered back at him in gold. "Buh...ruh...ee...th," he whispered, sounding out the word. "Breath," he said excitedly. "Breath of..." He paused, tracing the last word with his finger. "Luh...eye...fuh..." He squinted in determination. "Life. Breath of Life!" he said confidently.

He reached up with a trembling hand, feeling the rough texture of the spine beneath his fingertips. He pulled the book from its resting place, revealing a hidden compartment behind it marked with a Kumari Mandala. "I found something!" Kiran shouted.

"What?" came a chorus of shouts. The water was now over their heads, and the group struggled to stay afloat.

"It's the Kumari Mandala!" Kiran shouted, the water splashing against the ledge he was on.

"Can you move it?" Ravi called out.

"I don't know!" Kiran pushed on the mandala, and a small door creaked open. Beyond lay an ancient quill, its tip glistening softly, as if infused with a mysterious light. Kiran reached inside and retrieved the quill. "Look what I found!" he exclaimed, holding the quill up high. "A feather!"

"A feather?" Amma gasped, struggling for air.

"Hold on to the shelf, Amma," Sophie called out, treading water as she swam over to safely guide her mother-in-law.

"Let me see that," Pappa demanded. Now swimming, he took the plume in one hand while grasping the shelf with the other, his weathered hands trembling. "This, Kiran, is more than just a feather. It's a pen! And a pen breathes life into words!"

"I get it!" Harrison exclaimed.

"But what words, Pappa?" Kiran asked, climbing higher to the next shelf.

"I think we need to write down our answer," Harrison explained. "Remember, one of the riddles said to 'mark the word to shift the sphere.'"

"But mark it where?" Sophie asked. "And how?"

"Look around for some ink," Pappa instructed. "It should be in a little jar."

"Maybe we write it in the giant book," Cyrus suggested.

"But the book is underwater! How do we do that?" Kiran exclaimed.

"I don't know," Harrison yelled back. "Let's find the ink first, then we'll figure it out."

"We are running out of time!" Amma screamed.

The group frantically scanned the room, desperately examining the artifacts on the shelves. The water continued to rise rapidly, forcing them to tread water. They glanced upward in terror, realizing the ceiling was closing in on them, their air supply dwindling with each passing second.

Pappa's gaze swept across the room until it settled on the highest shelf among the stacks. On it sat an inkpot and a pristine piece of parchment sat waiting. "There! Over there! I see the ink!" Pappa struggled to keep his head up. With purposeful strokes, he cleaved through the rising water to reach the ledge.

"But what word?" Harrison interjected.

Pappa paused, his eyes scanning the ancient symbols etched into the chamber's walls. The "false" flame from the previous riddle, once high at the top of the chamber, now stared at him at eye level through the lapping water, drawing his attention. *Fire symbolizes wisdom, illuminating the darkness.*

"Hurry!" Sophie shrieked.

"Mama!" Cyrus cried.

"Let's try 'fire,'" Pappa suggested. He reached out with one hand and grabbed the shelf where the inkpot was, his legs kicking to stay afloat. He dipped the tip of the pen into the ink and grabbed the paper with his other hand. A sudden wave of water splashed over him, soaking the paper and causing Pappa to drop it. "The paper is gone!" he bellowed.

The water was now almost to the ceiling, forcing them to tilt their heads back and press their faces against the cold stone. Panic set in as the water continued to rise, leaving them with only a sliver of space to breathe, their fingers scrabbling desperately at the unyielding rock where the red crescent moon was placed.

Amma spat water, struggling for breath.

Pappa swam over to help her, handing the quill to Harrison along the way. "Take the pen, Harrison!" Pappa yelled, his voice muffled as the water covered his face. "You need to keep it dry! Write the word on the ceiling!"

As Harrison took the pen, he shouted, "That's it! The ceiling is above the board where Watchers peer! We never needed the paper!"

"You're right!"

"Okay. Here it goes! Hold your breath and pray!" Harrison kicked desperately, trying to stay afloat, the cold water closing in around him.

"Stay up! Stay up!" Sophie screamed, trying to keep Kiran and Cyrus' heads above water.

Just then, the pen slipped out of Harrison's hand, spiraling down into the darkness. "I dropped the pen!"

"Dad, help me!" Cyrus choked between gulps of air.

Ravi, supporting his son, screamed out, "Harrison, use the flint arrowhead in your pocket and carve the word into the ceiling!" His voice trembled with desperation as the water rose at a faster pace.

"I need to use the quill!" Harrison's mouth dipped below the surface as he gasped for breath, the water lapping over his face.

"Maybe you don't need the quill! Just use *anything*!" Ravi shouted, his voice breaking with panic.

Harrison reached into his jacket and gasped. "It's not here!" Desperation sank in. "I'll be right back," Harrison said, taking a deep breath before diving down. His pulse raced. *I need to find something! Anything!*

The icy water stung his skin as darkness enveloped him. He groped blindly along the floor, his fingers scraped rough stone and loose debris. Panic surged as his lungs ached for oxygen. As he thought he'd have to resurface, his hand closed around something sharp and metallic at the base of a bookshelf. An old, iron letter opener. *Pappa's letter opener from Chitwan! He must have dropped it!*

Harrison kicked off the floor and surged upward. The water had reached the ceiling—there was no more air. His lungs screamed. His vision blurred.

He pressed the letter opener to the stone, fingers shaking. With one last, desperate effort, he scrawled the word 'fire.'

As the blade lifted from the final letter, the chamber shook. Waves slammed the walls.

Light cracked across the surface.

A flash—

A pulse—

And then—

Silence.

Grip loosened.

Vision dimmed.

He let go.

And the darkness received him.

-23-
THE UNSETTLING QUIET

अशान्तशान्तिः

6:58 A.M.

Siddharth jerked awake on the leather couch, the stiffness in his neck reminding him he hadn't meant to sleep. The office was dimly lit. Disorientating. For a moment he didn't remember where he was. Then he did.

From across the room, his eyes met Priya's. She sat behind her desk, upright, fully dressed. She hadn't slept.

Anil stood near the window, the curtains barely parted, watching the sky pale over the courtyard.

"Did the street boy deliver the pendant?" Siddharth asked, his gaze unwavering.

A flash of worry clouded Priya's face. "No," she said. "The boy never showed up. I assumed something must have gone wrong, and I've been waiting for either you or Raju to come with me to check the room."

Siddharth felt a sickening band of dread tighten around his chest as she spoke. Priya's words confirmed the nagging fear that had settled in him, an inkling that something had indeed gone terribly awry. "Let's go. The family trusts you. I can't afford to be seen."

Priya rose. She reached for the gun.

"No," Siddharth said sharply.

She paused, fingers brushing the grip. "If he didn't show," Siddharth continued, voice controlled, "that means the family still believes in you. In Anil. We don't escalate until we have to."

Anil didn't move, but his eyes shifted between them.

Priya considered this. Her thoughts drifting back to the unsettling events of the previous night. Sophie's face rose in her mind—the shock, the betrayal, the moment Cyrus was taken. For a fleeting moment, it tugged at her heart—then she pushed it down, hard. The Sharma's still trusted her. That was all that mattered. For now.

She exhaled, "You may be right."

She crossed to the sideboard with the gun still in her hand. "We don't leave it unattended," she said, crouching before the safe. The dial turned beneath her fingers—familiar, mechanical clicks in the quiet office.

Behind her, Siddharth's voice remained steady. "Besides, everything we need is in that room.

The safe door released with a muted sound.

Priya opened it. She didn't look inside. She was still looking at Siddharth. "But what if they captured him?" she asked. "What if he failed because they fought back?"

"If they had," Siddharth said, "we would have heard or seen something."

"Unless it was quick," Anil added

Priya's hand hovered. The dark interior of the safe sat

open beside her knee. For a fraction of a second, she could have glanced down, but she did not.

Siddharth stepped closer. "Put it away."

She straightened instead. "No. I think I'll keep it." The words were quiet.

She swung the safe door closed. Turned the dial. Locked it.

The gun remained in her hand. "If I'm wrong," she said, meeting Siddharth's eyes, "we adapt."

Fine lets go

They rushed up the three flights, each step echoing in tandem with Siddharth's accelerating heartbeat. The golden sunbeams sliced through the darkness, heralding a moment of reckoning. In the hallway outside the Sharma family's suite, they found Raju asleep against the door, his body twisted into an uncomfortable position.

"Raju, wake up!" Siddharth nudged him urgently with his foot.

Raju's eyes flickered open, filling with confusion before snapping into clarity. "What? What's happened?"

"The pendant. There's been no word from the street boy. Priya never received it. Have you heard anything from the room?" Siddharth's composure began to crack under the strain.

Raju sat up and rubbed his temples. His face flushed. "No, absolutely nothing," he admitted. "I heard no movement from inside the room." Siddharth studied him for a beat.

Too quiet.

Raju looked at the door.

"Should we knock?"

No one answered immediately.

The hallway felt narrower than it had a moment ago. Morning light spilled across the tile in pale bands. The inn below was beginning to stir—distant clatter, a chair scraping.

Priya stepped forward. "You shouldn't," she said softly — not to Raju, but to the moment itself.

Her hand hovered over the wood. For a second, she didn't touch it.

Siddharth felt it then—the shift. The sense that whatever waited beyond the door would not be simple.

Priya drew a breath and rapped lightly. "Mr. Sharma?" Her tone was polite. Measured. "It's breakfast time, sir. Madam Sophie?"

Silence answered. Not the silence of sleep.

The silence of absence.

With a bolder movement, Priya knocked again.

Still, nothing but the haunting emptiness responded.

Raju turned to Siddharth. "What if something's gone horribly wrong?" His voice trembled. "What if the street boy killed the family and stole the pendant?"

The possibility settled between them.

If the street boy had done what they asked—and then decided the necklace was worth more than the payout—the Heart was already out of their reach.

Siddharth's jaw tightened. His fingers brushed the leather cord at the back of his head, grounding himself. "We would have heard something," he said. "A scream. A struggle."

The hallway seemed to absorb the words. "The night was silent." He held to that. It was all he had.

"But what if…" Priya started, her voice tinged with the dread that fills in the blanks of unfinished sentences.

"We'll cross that bridge when we get to it," Raju concluded. "

The stood there—the moment stretched.

"Well? Are you going to open the door?" Raju urged.

Her hand trembled as she reached into her pocket to pull out the master key. A metal charm in the shape of a chess queen dangled from it. Grimly, she inserted the key into the lock and turned it. With a mournful creak, the door opened.

Slowly, cautiously, she peeked inside.

It was a disturbing sight. The room was a picture of disarray. Sheets had been yanked off the beds, their chaotic folds suggesting a hurried, frantic act. In glaring contrast, the family's luggage sat undisturbed, silently awaiting their return. The paradox was jarring, a room both violently disrupted and hauntingly still.

Priya felt a surge of fear intensify within her, a visceral reaction to the scene's unsettling inconsistencies. She looked over at Raju. "See for yourselves."

Raju's expression sharpened in scrutiny as he stepped into the room. The bed sheets were not merely disheveled or strewn about; they were interwoven and deliberately knotted together, fashioning a makeshift rope that snaked out of the window. The frayed end was anchored to the leg of a heavy couch at the center of the room.

Siddharth's heart drummed a frantic rhythm against his ribcage. Each beat stressed the gravity of the mystery in which they found themselves. The eerie quiet they had felt earlier metamorphosed for them into a stifling haze, somehow solidifying the air and consuming every morsel of certainty. The shift left a dark cloud of perplexing doubt in its wake.

"Do you think they tried to escape through the window?" Priya asked.

Raju and Siddharth exchanged a glance, disbelief mounting.

"They wouldn't take such a risk," Raju murmured. Yet, the makeshift rope told a different story. He approached the window with urgency, peering down. The sheer drop spanned a menacing three stories, with jagged rocks waiting ominously below, a treacherous cushion for any fall.

Siddharth, joining him at the window, took a deep breath. "I can't imagine they'd be desperate enough to try this, but perhaps it was their backup plan. Maybe just having an escape route gave them some solace."

Raju walked over to the side table where a solitary business card lay. Driven by curiosity, he snatched it up and ran his eyes over the details. "They know," he blurted out, disbelief twisting in his gut.

"Know what?" Priya inquired.

"They know we are related," Raju responded.

"How?" Siddharth chimed in.

"Look at this," Raju said, gesturing with the card toward his cousins. "It's the business card from the Himalayan Guest House. They've made the connection."

"I wonder what else they know?" Siddharth queried.

"Let's see what they left behind," Anil remarked, gesturing toward a waste bin placed next to the desk. As he sifted through the garbage, his fingers brushed against a pile of chips. Amidst the crumbs lay a crumpled slip of paper. With his curiosity piqued, he unfolded it to reveal a chilling message. "Our enemy is right outside the door," he read allowed. Instantly, Anil realized the gravity of the situation—the Sharma family not only knew their adversaries but also suspected Priya and him of being complicit in the scheme to steal the Heart of Kumari out from under them.

A hush fell over the group as the implication of the discovery sank in. The Sharma family had seen through their ruse; they had pieced together the family ties. They realized they could no longer trust Priya or Anil—and presumably Chief Bhaskar, by extension—leaving the Sharma family with nobody they could rely on.

Siddharth scanned the room, its chaotic state serving as a damning mirror reflecting their actions. Discomforting thoughts clawed their way into his mind. *We caused this. We drove this family to this point.* For a moment, guilt washed over him, a gut-wrenching wave of self-reproach. He pushed the emotion away just as quickly, barricading himself behind a wall of rationalization. Now was no time for remorse; they were too deep into whatever this had become. Yet, the room's disarray stood as a reminder of the ripple effects of their choices, and Siddharth couldn't completely shake his uneasy conscience.

Priya took in the unnerving scene of the room. Her disbelief was unmistakable. She knew she had to act quickly. *But what should I do?* The Sharmas had eluded her grasp, and Uncle Bhaskar's wrath would be unforgiving.

Priya turned to Siddharth and Raju, her gaze seeking a semblance of stability in a world suddenly filled with question marks. "I'll review the security footage," she declared, her statement saturated with newfound resolve. "Perhaps they saw Raju sleeping by their door and made a choice to exit quietly, desperate to sidestep any more complications or confrontations with us."

With that thought, Priya pivoted sharply, her stilettos clicking with increased urgency as she moved into the corridor. Each step felt like a tick on an invisible countdown clock, amplifying the critical nature of the moment. Her mind was a whirlpool of concerns and theories, each more unnerving than the last. The loud clacks of her heels followed her, pressing her to find answers before the unsettling quiet consumed them all.

Among the disturbing stillness of the room, the puzzling makeshift rope fashioned from the bedsheets seemed almost too obvious a clue. Unlike Priya, who had her own theories, Raju had reached a different conclusion: the family had likely discovered the secret door hidden within the closet.

Raju dashed to the closet, his heart pounding. He pulled the door open to see if the hidden exit was ajar. It was not.

As he straightened, a shaft of morning light angled through the window and spilled across the wall inside the closet. For an instant, dust motes shimmered into four faint letters—s s b t—before the air shifted and they dissolved. He blinked, uncertain if his tired eyes had imagined it, then turned away.

Despite the door being closed, Raju's chest swelled with assurance as he reflected on his observation. He was sure the Sharma family exited through the secret tunnel. *They would have awakened me if they had tried to escape through the main door. And they could never have made it down the three stories on a rope made from bedsheets.*

A tangle of thoughts filled his mind. *Had the Sharma family departed before or after the street boy arrived? Could it have been the street boy who led them through the hidden tunnel? If so, to what end? Did the street boy show up?*

The questions multiplied, but answers remained elusive.

Raju turned. "Let's go. They're not going to get far without their passports."

Priya's grip tightened on the gun. "They're not," she echoed. She never once wondered if the passports were still where she left them.

-24-
THE SEEKER'S TRIAL

अन्वेषकस्य परीक्षा

Beneath him, the water in the library suddenly began to recede, draining away with a powerful whirlpool. Harrison collapsed onto the cold stone floor, coughing and gasping for breath. He had a sudden, sinking feeling that he was now alone.

Slowly, he stood up. The once-prominent shelves, filled with ancient texts and manuscripts, dissolved like a vanishing hologram, leaving behind only an engulfing maw. Before him stretched a long, ominous tunnel, its depths swallowing any trace of the room he had just been in.

He spun around frantically, searching for his family, but they were nowhere to be seen. Panic clawed at his chest as he grappled with the sudden disappearance of everything he had known just moments before.

"Mom! Dad!" he called out.

There was no answer, only the silence pressing in around

him. Behind him was pitch black, and ahead, he could make out a tiny speck of light, beckoning him onward.

Harrison paused, willing his body to settle. "Stay calm," he whispered.

He strained his eyes, peering into the darkness. The walls of the tunnel were rough and cold, the stone damp and clammy against his fingertips as he edged forward. Water dripped from his soaked clothes, leaving a trail of droplets behind him. Each step felt like a defiant act against the consuming void. His legs trembled, and he had to summon all his willpower to keep moving forward.

His pulse thundered in the silence.

The dark pressed close as Harrison's mind raced with what might lie ahead. The light seemed impossibly distant, a pinprick of hope in a sea of uncertainty. *Was it an exit, or something more sinister?* The unknown gnawed at him, but he pressed on, driven by a flicker of hope.

Each footfall was audible, the darkness unrelenting from all sides. *The tunnel leading to the chapel had never felt this oppressive.* The air grew colder, biting at his skin, and an unnatural whisper seemed to drift through the tunnel, as if carried by an unseen wind.

As he walked deeper, the whispers grew louder, more insistent. They seemed to be calling his name, taunting him with his deepest fears and insecurities.

"You're all alone," they hissed. "You'll never find your way out. You'll fail, just like all the others."

Harrison's body resisted; he moved anyway.

Suddenly, the tunnel widened into a cavernous space, its walls weeping with moisture, the air thick with an unsettling stillness. A single flame hovered, painting the void in a flickering half-light. In the center stood a shadowy figure, its form shifting and writhing like smoke.

Harrison's lungs forgot the next breath. He felt the wrongness of it settle into his bones. His body answered before he could.

The figure's eyes glowed with a malevolent light, its mouth curling into a ghoulish smile that sent chills down his spine. Its fingers, long and gnarled, reached out, threatening to pull him into a suffocating darkness that felt all too real.

The figure spoke, its voice an unsettling whisper, "I have followed you throughout your life, through realms unseen. You cannot escape me."

Something tightened behind Harrison's ribs as he struggled to identify the shadowy figure—a presence his soul recognized but could not place. Dread surged, dragging something buried into the open.

"So…we finally meet face to face." Its voice scraped like metal on stone, a horrible, grating rasp that set Harrison's teeth on edge. "I've been waiting for this moment."

The flame moved violently as the figure spoke, fueled by its presence. It revealed fleeting glimpses of a face distorted in malevolent glee. Unsettling laughter echoed in the cavern, mingling with the distant sound of dripping water, creating a discord that filled him with fright.

Cold sweat prickled on Harrison's skin as he felt the weight of impending doom settle upon him. His voice trembled as he forced the words out. "Who are you?"

The figure's form rippled with dark amusement. "Who am I?" it repeated, its whispering tone dripping with mockery. "The real question is, who are you?"

Harrison stood frozen, his mind whirling. *It doesn't know who I am? What should I tell it?* The question lingered. *It must be a trick. Of course it knows who I am*, he supposed. *What should I say?* He searched deep within himself for the answer, shuddering as realization dawned. Without hesitation, the response emerged from the depths of his being, slipping past his lips with surprising ease. "I am the Seeker for the Heart of Kumari. Now, answer my question. Who are you?"

"Ha! Seeker for the Heart of Kumari?" it jeered. "The Kumari would never choose you!"

Harrison hesitated, contemplating its words. *Maybe it was right. Why would the Kumari choose me? But my name was written on the goatskin, which means I am the Seeker. Right? Pappa had said so. He wouldn't lie to me, would he?* Harrison's mind raced. *But what if he did?* Doubt crept in, gnawing at his resolve like a relentless tide. *What if the strange writing wasn't my name?* But then, he remembered the clues, the visions that had guided him, the soul-stirring pull that had led him here, and the text in the ancient tome.

"I am of the bloodline of the Shatranj Ke Sipahi, the chosen Seeker for the Heart of Kumari!" Harrison declared. "Now, give me a name."

The figure recoiled at Harrison's words, and its eyes widened in terror. A guttural hiss escaped its lips before it finally spoke. "Call me 'Malachi.'"

Harrison took a step back. The very mention of its name hit him like a physical blow. "What do you want from me, Malachi?" he demanded.

The figure's form regained its composure, sneering as it writhed with contemptuous laughter. "What do I want from you? Such a pathetic question. Do you think you're special, Seeker? Do you think you're worthy of the Heart of Kumari?"

"Yes! I am worthy!" Harrison said, his breath quickening. A mix of fear and anger bubbled within him. "Why do you taunt me?" he demanded.

Malachi's eyes flared with a wicked glow. "Why do I taunt you?" it echoed sardonically. "You fool, you have done this to yourself. You created me. I am what you carry. You stumble through life, oblivious to the world around you, clinging to your ignorance like a coward." Its gaze pierced through him like a dagger as it paused. "I want to break you. I want to see you unravel, piece by piece, until there's nothing left but your despair."

It moved closer.

"You're lying," Harrison shot back.

Malachi's smile widened. A chilling sight. "Lying? If only it were that simple," it hissed. "You can't even face your own fears, your own failures."

Tears welled in Harrison's eyes. "I don't understand," he choked out.

Malachi leaned closer, its presence suffocating. "Of course you don't," it scoffed. "You never do. You're too weak, too blind. But mark my words, Seeker, I will consume you. And when I do, you will beg for the darkness."

Harrison felt a gentle warmth on his shoulder, as if a comforting hand had been placed there. He glanced around but saw no one. In that instant, a memory of Raju's story, told while visiting the elephant nursery, rushed through his mind. A reassuring voice filled his thoughts. *'Courage is not the absence of fear, but the triumph over it. You have the strength within you, Harrison. Just as Amara's compassion healed wounds and Rohan's bravery overcame fears, you, too, possess this strength.'*

A sudden calm washed over him, as if the eye of the storm had passed over his soul. Amidst the chaos, a moment of clarity emerged. "I see now," he said softly, the trembling in his voice replaced with a quiet resolve. "You are not here to destroy me, but to challenge me. I don't need to defeat you," he said quietly. "I just need to stop believing you."

Malachi's laugh echoed through the darkness. "Oh, how touching." He sneered. "Love and courage? You think such sentimental nonsense can defeat me? Your fears, your insecurities—they are given form through your past, through those who have shaped you. I am every doubt, every belittling word, every failure that has ever haunted you. You cannot escape me by running, or by clinging to childish tales of bravery."

Determination rose through Harrison. "I'm not running anymore," he whispered, more to himself than to Malachi. "I understand now. I will stand up to you. I will confront my fears, accept them, and move beyond them."

Malachi's form flickered, a shadow of doubt crossing its eyes. "What foolishness."

Harrison took a deep breath, standing his ground. "Not foolishness. Strength. I will not let you control me. You may be part of me, but you do not define me."

In that moment, Harrison felt a shift within himself, a strong, growing resolve. The cavern seemed less oppressive, the shadows less menacing. The Heart of Kumari's power was within reach, not as a tool of conquest, but as a symbol of his journey to self-acceptance and mastery over his darkest fears.

"We will see about that." Malachi's malevolent laughter filled the cavern.

It's form began to shift and contort. Shadows writhed and coalesced, altering the dark figure into something more tangible, more familiar. The wicked glow in its eyes dimmed, replaced by a piercing, sneering gaze.

Something lurched in Harrison's chest as recognition dawned upon him. Before him stood his baseball coach, Coach Thompson, his face twisted with the same contempt that had haunted Harrison since he moved to Bahrain.

"You fool," Coach Thompson spat. "You always were worthless. You will never amount to anything!"

"I'm not afraid of you," Harrison shouted, his voice shaking but resolute. "You're not real. You're in my head!"

"I'm real," the coach bellowed.

Harrison turned away, but the coach's voice sliced through the air like a whip. "Look at me when I talk to you, boy! You think you're brave now? You're nothing but a coward, hiding behind your delusions. You've always been weak, always crumbling under pressure. Pathetic!"

Harrison flinched but stood his ground. "If you're real," he challenged, "then prove it. Hit me. Touch me. Do something!"

The coach's eyes gleamed with an evil light. "You want proof?" he roared.

In an instant, he lunged forward and grabbed Harrison by the ear, yanking him close. Pain shot through Harrison's head, but he gritted his teeth, refusing to show weakness.

"Feel that?" the coach hissed, his breath hot against Harrison's face. "I'm as real as your failures. You think you can stand up to me? You're nothing but a disappointment, a waste of potential."

Harrison's vision blurred with tears, but he met the coach's gaze with stern determination. "I'm not your puppet anymore," he said through gnashed teeth. "You don't control me."

The coach twisted his ear harder, but Harrison didn't wince. Instead, he reached up and grabbed the coach's wrist, his grip unyielding. "Let go," Harrison commanded.

For a moment, the coach's smirk faltered.

Harrison tightened his grip, using the pain as fuel for his resolve. "I said, let go!" he shouted, shoving the coach away.

Coach Thompson staggered back, his form wavering. "You think you're strong?" he challenged. "You'll always be a failure. You can't escape it."

The coach advanced, and Harrison felt the air thicken around him, pressing against his chest. He choked for breath. Fear rose within him, threatening to overwhelm him. He tried to suppress it, drawing on every ounce of courage he had.

He felt an onslaught of negative thoughts assailing him,

each one like a sharp dart aimed directly at his mind. They came in rapid succession, leaving no room for respite. The sensation was asphyxiating. Every unrelenting sting embedded itself deeper, compounding his despair.

"You never had what it takes, and you never will," Coach Thompson continued, his words filled with contempt. "Always failing, always blaming others for your mistakes. Pathetic."

Memories flooded back: the countless practice sessions where his coach berated him for every minor error, the relentless pressure to be perfect, the constant reminders that he was never good enough. He charged at the figure, his hatred growing stronger with each step.

"Come on, boy!" the coach taunted. "Put up your dukes! Fight like a man!"

Fueled by rage, Harrison swung his fist, landing a punch squarely on his jaw. The coach retaliated with a fierce uppercut, lifting Harrison off his feet and sending him crashing into the wall. Pain shot through his back as he slumped to the ground, but adrenaline kept him moving.

He got up and charged again, swinging his fists. But each blow felt heavier, less certain, as if he were fighting against an invisible force inside himself. A gnawing doubt whispered in the back of his mind. *Was this creature really the enemy, or was it a part of him all along?*

Coach Thompson swiped at him, and Harrison found himself slammed back against the wall. As he regained his composure, he looked up, and his breath caught in his throat. The coach's body began to distort and swell, muscles bulging unnaturally. Claws extended from his hands, fangs jutted from his mouth, and his eyes burned with a hellish fire.

Harrison's pulse faltered as he scrambled to his feet, torn between disbelief and terror. Every instinct screamed for him to run, but his anger flared, fueling his determination to fight.

Desperation gnawed at him as he glanced around the cavern. His eyes fell on a sword lying on the ground. *Where did that come from… It doesn't matter.* He lunged for it, his fingers curling around the hilt, knuckles whitening as the rough leather bit into his palm. He turned to face the monstrous coach, a new surge of resolve coursing through him.

Harrison swung wildly, his fury driving him to attack the beast with everything he had. He slashed at the beast with a fierce cry, but the more he fought, the larger his opponent grew. His blows seemed to have no effect, only feeding the creature's terrifying transformation. Harrison's anger was turning the coach into an unstoppable monster.

"Yes, Harrison!" the coach taunted, dodging another blow with a cruel smile. "Don't hold back! Keep fighting! Feed your rage!"

Harrison lunged, his grip tightening around the sword. "Why did you hit me over the head with my skateboard?" he demanded.

The coach laughed coldly, easily evading the blade. "To show you what strength is! Is it making sense now?"

Realizing the futility of his assault, Harrison became terrified. Each swing of the sword only made the beast more formidable, more horrifying. He knew he had to change his approach, but the question was how. He swung again, missing by inches. "Why were you always so hard on me? Why tear me down?" Each word spat through gritted teeth.

The coach dodged once more. "Because you needed to learn. The world doesn't go easy on you, so I couldn't either!"

Harrison's voice broke as he swung again, desperate for answers. "Why didn't you ever believe in me?"

The coach's smile wavered for a moment. "Who said I didn't?"

Exhausted, the coach's words struck a chord deep within

Harrison. A new thought pierced through the fog of anger and frustration. His doubts had never saved him. They had never protected him, never benefited his life in any meaningful way. The only thing his doubts had ever done was hold him back.

"Why stop now, Seeker?" the coach jeered. "Is that all you've got?"

Seeker? Just then, Harrison remembered this was his ego trying to undermine him, to exploit his deepest fears and insecurities. *I can overcome.*

The beast advanced, its eyes gleaming with malice, ready to pounce. Harrison's chest tightened as he braced himself for the attack. Desperation and determination clashed within him, a storm of emotions driving him to find a way to overcome his ego and transcend his inner self.

"I won't let you control me anymore," Harrison shouted. "I'm stronger than you think!"

The coach's sneer deepened, his eyes blazing with hatred. "Overcome me?" he mocked. "You think a few pretty words can change the truth? You're nothing but a weak, scared boy, hiding behind false bravado. You'll never escape your failures, because you *are* your failures."

Harrison's grip on the sword trembled as the monstrous coach advanced, towering with grotesque fury. He raised the blade again—then hesitated.

"Look at you, shaking like a leaf. You can barely stand, let alone fight. You'll never amount to anything. You'll always be the pathetic, sniveling failure who couldn't stand up to his own fears."

"This isn't the way," Harrison whispered.

"Too scared to fight? Pathetic."

"No," Harrison said softly. "I'm done fighting myself."

The air changed. A subtle shift. The beast faltered. He paused, its growls quieting. Harrison's fear and anger, once so powerful in their grasp over him, began to melt away, replaced by a deep, calm understanding. He could feel the malevolence within the creature ebbing, as if his newfound clarity was draining its power.

Slowly, Harrison released the hilt. The sword fell with a sharp clang. As it hit the ground, the monstrous form of the coach began to shrink—the claws retracting, the fangs disappearing. The darkness that had once pulsed within it faded away, dissolving into nothing, leaving only the human form of his coach.

Harrison stepped forward. "It wasn't your words that made me stronger. And it wasn't your cruelty," he said softly. "It was learning to stand up to my own doubts." He looked the coach in the eye, feeling a quiet resolve settle within him. "It was the moment I stopped believing your lies."

The creature looked at him—not with hatred, but something else. Its contempt had been replaced with understanding.

"I'm not afraid of you anymore," Harrison said.

And it was enough. The monster faded, then it was gone.

In its place, a soft, ethereal light filled the cavern. An angelic figure materialized, holding a radiant diamond. Her presence was majestic.

Harrison fell to his knees in reverence, overwhelmed by the sight before him. Awe struck him silent. He felt a profound sense of peace wash over him.

"Seeker for the Heart of Kumari, stand up," she intoned.

His eyes locked onto the diamond. Inside its facets, a brilliant emerald fire swirled, casting mesmerizing reflections through the deep crimson hues of its exterior. A tingling sensation coursed through him. *The fire—the answer to the riddle.* It stared back at him, living within the center of the gem. *This was the fire the ancient tome spoke of, the one that illuminated wisdom and understanding, revealing itself only to those who dared to endure.*

He looked up. "The diamond?"

"Yes," she chanted, her voice a melodic whisper. She held out the gem, its light pulsating. "Touch it, Harrison."

Harrison could see the emerald flame swirling and coalescing inside. He approached the Heart and gently placed his hands upon it. A surge of energy coursed through him, filling his entire being with a radiant warmth that seemed to reach deep into his soul.

The warmth ignited into fire—not burning, but coursing through his veins with a brilliance almost too much to bear. His knees buckled beneath the weight of it. Then came the visions—blinding, cascading. Memories not his own.

He saw his family scattered across a vast chessboard of stone—Sophie, Ravi, Kiran, Cyrus, Amma, Pappa—each standing motionless on a square while shadows closed in from every side. He tried to rush forward, but his own hand moved the pieces, pushing them toward danger as though he were the one placing them in harm's way. Horror seized him. *I brought them here. My choices put them at risk.* The thought nearly crushed his chest.

The Heart pulsed. Their fear was his fear. Yet beneath it, he felt their love for him, unwavering, binding him to them.

The Pattern whispered without a voice. *You are bound together. Their fate is tied to your courage.*

The vision shifted. A mountain rose, crowned in ice, its ridges aflame with moonlight. From its base poured a black tide, shadows flooding valleys, temples, markets, drowning the land.

Across the tide, the words THE WORLD ENDS NOW flared in burning script, vast as the sky. For an instant, the letters hung suspended in fire and mist, reflecting in Harrison's eyes—then dissolved, scattered into the darkness like ash on wind. At the summit the Heart glowed crimson, and when Harrison reached for it, it shattered, scattering fire into the void.

He cried out—until a second vision bloomed: emerald light threading through rivers, forests, prayer flags, through his own bloodline. Gopal Bhattarai stood before him, eyes filled with fierce devotion. He whispered words older than kingdoms. "Not power, but balance."

The light seared into Harrison's hands. A mark spiraled across his skin, a mandala alive, pulsing with his heartbeat. It was not scar but covenant.

The torrent of vision did not relent. Mountains, rivers, temples, shadows—past and future folding into one. The Pattern whispers, not in words but in pressure: *Everywhere is here, and every when is now.*

He gasps, the weight of it staggering him. Time is not a line but a circle. Place is depth. His family, his bloodline, the shadow tide—they are all present in this moment, bound inside the same breath.

Finally the visions receded, leaving him trembling, gasping. The cavern seemed smaller now, its shadows bent away from him. Something had claimed him, and he could feel its weight settling in his blood.

The diamond shimmered brilliantly for a moment, then vanished without a trace.

Startled, Harrison glanced down at his hands.

The glowing mark of a mandala still pulsed on his palm, a quiet reminder of what had passed—and what awaited him.

The angelic entity nodded solemnly. "The path to the Heart has revealed itself." She paused before continuing, her voice and visage taking a serious tone. "You will find the diamond in the Kanchenjunga Mountains. Go with Pasang; he will take you and your family to a Sherpa who will guide you. The journey is fraught with danger, and what it will demand of you has not yet been revealed."

Harrison nodded, feeling the weight of her words settle unevenly inside him.

The angelic figure smiled warmly. "Remember, Harrison, you already carry what you will need."

With that, the angelic figure slowly dissolved into the darkness.

***

"Get up, Harrison!"

The urgent cries of his family broke through the darkness.

He felt hands shaking him, trying to pull him back from unconsciousness. As he opened his eyes, the space around him came into focus, and Harrison found himself lying on the floor of the ancient library. He looked around and saw his family—Kiran, Cyrus, Amma, Pappa, Sophie, and Ravi—along with Pasang.

I must have fallen.

"Harrison!" Sophie cried. "We were so worried!" She knelt to embrace him. "We didn't drown. You wrote the answer to the riddle on the ceiling, and the water drained from the room."

Harrison's head throbbed.

"You were unconscious. You hit your head. You fell against the stone floor," Pappa explained.

Harrison winced, gripping his side where the pain flared, but he managed a weak smile. *Was it a dream?*

"I'm okay," he said, lifting his hand. Then, he stopped.

Across his palm, faint light shimmered—the outline of a mandala etched onto his skin. It pulsed once, in time with his heartbeat, then dimmed to a quiet glow.

"Kanchenjunga," he breathed out, the word escaping as if it had always been there, just waiting to be spoken.

"Kanchenjunga?" Pappa asked, his brow creased in confusion.

"The location of the diamond," Harrison explained, his eyes widening with the revelation. "An angelic figure, the Spirit of Kumari, came to me while I was unconscious." He paused, a look of awe crossing his face. "I touched something. It's real!"

"Then it can be found!" Sophie exclaimed, her eyes sparkling with excitement.

"Yes," Harrison confirmed.

"That's wonderful!" Amma said.

Cyrus looked around. "Is it over?"

Pasang turned to Harrison. "Your journey has shown that true strength lies not just in overcoming external challenges, but in mastering the inner demons that reside within us all. The Heart of Kumari is within reach, but remember, it is not just an artifact of power. It is a testament to the humility, accord, and wisdom you have demonstrated."

Pasang paused, then addressed them all with a solemn gaze. "You have endured the test set by the ancients for the true Seekers. The trials of fire and water were not merely obstacles but sacred rites of passage. You have emerged changed. What that change will cost you remains unseen."

They nodded, feeling a sense of the unknown wash over them.

Harrison looked around at his family, seeing the same resolve to keep moving reflected back at him.

Pappa drew a slow breath. "We'll go," he said. "Together, we will find the Heart of Kumari."

Sophie squeezed Harrison's shoulder, her grip both comforting and encouraging. "We've come this far because we've believed in each other. Let's keep moving." She extended her arm and helped him to his feet, her strength steadying him.

Amma stepped forward. "We are stronger together. The

Spirit of Kumari has bound us."

Pappa nodded, his expression unwavering. "We will honor that bond."

"Come. Follow me," Pasang said. He lifted his lantern, and the warm circle of light reached out, piercing the ancient shadows.

Sore, wet, and bruised, but alive—they gathered their belongings and stepped through the fifth door.

Kiran counted them as they went. "The fifth is safe," he whispered, mostly to himself.

The narrow passage ahead was damp and low, the air thick with the scent of stone and earth. The weight that had hung over them shifted—not lifted, just changed.

The Heart of Kumari was near, almost within their grasp.

As they moved forward, Harrison paused, letting the others drift a few steps ahead. In the quiet, he lifted his hand. With his finger, he traced the faint, luminous mark the diamond had left behind—a delicate tendril of light, still warm against his skin. It was proof of what he had always known. The path was real, and the summons could not be denied.

The trial had changed him; he could feel it in the steady beat of his heart, in the calm that steadied his breath. Yet even here, in the sacred shelter of stone and shadow, he sensed unseen forces stirring—ancient powers awakened by their quest, waiting beyond the world they knew.

The Heart had revealed only the beginning.

Beyond these walls, betrayal, darkness, and reckoning awaited.

Harrison closed his eyes for a moment, hearing the echo of water drip from unseen vaults, feeling the mountain's slow breath vibrating through the bones of the earth beneath his feet.

When he opened them, he was no longer the boy who

had stumbled into this hidden world by accident. Something had claimed him.

He was now the Seeker bound to the Heart of Kumari.

The Heart had been revealed.

None of them yet understood what it would demand.

The diamond waited—patient as death.

-25-
THE DEPARTURE

उपसंहारः प्रस्थानम्

NOVEMBER 15TH
KATHMANDU
7:00 A.M.

The Kumari Ghar did not wake. The night lamps had already been extinguished—pinched out by practiced fingers, their smoke thinned into the rafters, and gone. Water had been thrown across the courtyard stones, leaving them dark and clean, the faint smell of ash pressed into the damp. Bells rang from the nearby temples, not in unison, but in overlapping cycles that marked the morning as ordinary and correct.

The priest stood just inside the threshold of the girl's chamber, waiting for the final cue that would release him. For thirty-seven years, his mornings had followed this order. Rise before light. Prepare the offerings. Enter. Withdraw. Return before the city took notice. Today, the order held, but something beneath it resisted, like a floor that no longer answered the foot as it should

The Kumari sat where she always did, cross-legged near the window, red silk arranged with the precision of habit. Morning light touched her face without ceremony. She did not look at him. She did not need to.

He bowed, lower than required.

The carved door closed behind him with a sound that belonged to wood, not omen. Outside, an attendant passed, carrying a brass tray already cooling from incense. Another swept the edge of the courtyard, the broom's straw whispering across stone. No one stopped him. No one questioned why he left.

He crossed the courtyard alone. Prayer flags above hung slack, their colors dulled by sun, their mantras worn by persistence. A pigeon startled from the eaves, wing-beats sharp against the morning air. The city was already moving. It always was, by this hour.

At the gate, he paused. He could still return. The thought arrived cleanly, without urgency, and passed just as quickly.

The streets were wet—not from rain, but from washing. Water ran along the gutters carrying dust, yesterday's soot, scraps of flower stems. Near the curb, a fading chalk mark thinned beneath the runoff—W E N—before the current broke it apart and carried it into the drain. The smell of ash lingered low, mixed now with coffee.

He stepped out into Basantapur as shop shutters were being lifted and set back on their hooks. Brass caught the sun. Oil hissed in shallow pans. A line of schoolchildren moved past him in uneven pairs, their voices rising and breaking apart again. Somewhere a radio crackled to life, its signal thin but persistent.

He thought of her—not the girl in silk, but Her, the Kumari line stretching back beyond any living memory. He had served five. Each had been chosen, enthroned, then quietly replaced. Only once had he seen a Kumari's eyes widen in fear—early, and without warning.

She had sat on her crimson throne and spoken—briefly, without address—of a boy, a diamond, a road where the moon ran red.

The very next day, in the dust-shuttered vault beneath Dauber Square, he and the Chancellor had found themselves staring at an older prophecy—carved in a script that predated the Codex itself.

It spoke of a blood moon. That was before the Shatranj consolidated its power, before the chancellors rewrote the Codex to suit their own ends. They had closed the vault without speaking, but the words had followed him ever since.

That was fifteen days ago. Now those words returned without invitation, threading themselves between the rhythm of his steps.

Past the market gates, a street dog sat upon the low roof of a tea stall, watching him without movement. Its eyes caught the sunlight—gold rimmed in black—and did not follow him as he passed; they looked through him, as if measuring the space he left behind.

Somewhere deeper in the city, a bell rang. Vendors did not pause. A child laughed as it struck again. Only he felt the sound catch, hard and unfinished, and he walked faster.

He cut left at the end of a narrow lane where a prayer wheel the size of a milk drum stood chained to a brick wall. Someone had smeared fresh vermilion across the mantra letters—thick, clotted, almost brown. He did not spin it. His hand hovered, then dropped.

Today was not for blessings.

A tremor went through the street, too fine to be an earthquake—more like the city cleared its throat. He felt it in his knees. A shutter slammed two stories up. A baby cried once, then was soothed into silence with the practiced rhythm of a mother who had soothed many children before this one.

He passed beneath a tangle of low balconies where blue bulbs still glowed, stubborn and unnecessary. Laundry sagged in the damp, its edges darkening as the street woke. Water trembled in the dips of the stones, broken now by the rhythm of feet not his own.

Near the spice lane, the air changed—not in strength, but in source. It funneled between the stone walls and settled low, where plaster had cracked from the heat.

* * *

The alley. From the square, it was nothing—a seam between two buildings where plaster had peeled back to show older brick, older than the palace, older than the story that named it.

A vermilion handprint marked the entrance at shoulder height. No fresh garland. No incense. Only that breath, faint and damp, like something waiting behind the wall. He adjusted the strap of the cloth satchel across his chest and went in.

The alley narrowed until his shoulders nearly brushed both sides. At knee level, eleven oil cups stood guttering, their small flames staining the wet stones with yellow. No sunlight reached this place. The air held to itself—cool, stored, cellar-cold, as if the walls had learned how to keep what passed between them.

Halfway down, a shadow detached itself from the left-hand wall. "You shouldn't have come alone," it said.

"I couldn't come any other way," the priest answered.

The shadow tasted his voice, then moved fully into the light.

Meera Chandra appeared in a sari of deep ruby—dark as river stone in shadow, bright as a cut gem where the morning light slipped in from the lane behind him—and watched him with a steady amusement that never touched her mouth. Silver threaded through a thick, ebony braid that fell down her back. A ring set with black glass on her index finger. Not Queen by birth, but by appointment—and in the Shatranj that was the same thing.

"Vikrant is late."

"He is never late," she said. "He simply arrives at the moment that makes the rest of us look wrong."

A second figure eased from the dark along the opposite wall—broad through the chest, moving with the weight of a man too long at the tip of a spear. The priest knew him from the courtyard at Dharma Shanti: a face like weathered stone, hair falling in a silver spill down his back, and in the eyes, a small, startled kindness. They called him Neeraj Chandra, a king in the order; the mark burned into his arm made it certain.

"Pandit-ji," Neeraj said, inclining his head. "Why are you here and not with the girl?"

"The Kumari is fine," the priest replied. "But this could not wait."

Meera's eyes narrowed. "It must be grave indeed, to take you away from the Ghar."

"It is," he said. "Graver than you know."

Her gaze dropped to the satchel at his side. "You carry something," she said. "Something meant for no one's eyes."

He opened the flap. Not wide. Just enough to reveal the edge of something swaddled in ritual white—cloth spun thin as onion skin, layered until it became its own kind of armor. Inside: the written words of the Kumari. He did not take it out. Only let the alley breathe the faint scent of its ink. A promise they could see more—later.

From deeper in the alley came the slow cadence of boots. Not many. Enough. The flames in the oil cups leaned toward the sound, their thin bodies stretching as if pulled.

Vikrant stepped into the light, and the light dimmed without going out. He wore a black coat buttoned to the throat, no rings, no visible weapon. "Pandit," he said. "Why do you call us in the shadows?"

"I have something for you, my lord," the priest said. "A vow and something more."

Vikrant's smile was all mouth. "You and I have been weighing each other's vows since you were too short to see over your father's ledger of temple offerings. End this charade, old friend. You left the child—so whatever brought you here outweighs her."

"I have come to spare one," the priest said. "And condemn another."

That made Neeraj flinch. Meera's nostrils flared once, like a horse catching the first thread of smoke.

Vikrant's gaze did not waver. "Then say it," he murmured. "Don't keep the child waiting. Tell me—who do you mean to spare, and who do you damn?"

The priest shook his head, the hood's shadow cutting his face in half. "This isn't just about names, Vikrant. It is also about a location." He drew a folded sheet from his satchel, holding it so the light caught its creases. "The Kumari. She woke in vision and asked me to deliver this parchment to you."

"The diamond!" Neeraj said.

The priest studied him. "Yes, but there is more the goddess revealed. There is a cost to claiming it—one you cannot pay without consequence."

"Consequences," Meera murmured. "You came to admonish?"

The priest ignored her. His gaze held only Vikrant's, and his words came like a man untying a knot he had carried for years. "If the diamond is claimed without the Seeker, the Board itself will fracture. And when the Board breaks, the Pattern will fall with it."

Neeraj's breath caught. Meera's eyes flicked. Vikrant's smile went nowhere.

"You believe that?" Vikrant asked before demanding. "Where is the Heart of Kumari?"

"Before I tell you where the diamond is, you must be warned."

"What is your warning?" Vikrant's patience was waning thin.

"The Seeker must bring balance," the priest said. "And the Shatranj are found wanting."

Vikrant's laugh was short, sharp. "The diamond belongs to the Shatranj. We are its rightful keepers."

"She saw more than that."

The priest turned to Meera. "She saw your daughter holding the diamond...and a great darkness."

A tremor passed through the alley, though no wind stirred. Neeraj's gaze moved to the shadows behind the priest, gauging the escape.

Meera turned her ring once, black glass swallowing the light. "Children dream in symbols. Prophets polish their meanings. Show me a vision that is not just another mask for a threat."

"She did not speak," the priest said, "She watched. Your nephew was an outline cut from the sky—thin air showing through your form. And a boy, born for this purpose, carried what he could not hold."

It was too much truth for this small place. The alley seemed to crouch, as if bracing for a blow.

"You have given your warning," Meera said, the word edged with disdain. "Now, tell us the location so you can get back to the Ghar."

"Yes," the priest said. "But something in me resists—like a hand hesitating over the board. As if placing this piece will split the Pattern itself."

He had made his choice the moment he stepped into the alley. But choice did not make conviction. Not yet. Not while he could still feel the pull of obedience, of fear, of hope that maybe—just maybe—this didn't have to end in fire.

Vikrant stepped closer. "Give me the parchment, so we may claim the diamond before the Sharmas and set our legacy right."

The priest's hand hovered at his satchel. "You think restoration is won with possession? The Heart is not yours to command. The Kumari saw the Seeker—not your son—standing before it."

Meera's lips curved, cold. "Yet here you are, carrying her words to us. Do not dress obedience as defiance."

The priest faltered. The cloth at his side weighed like iron. "I serve the Kumari. Yet every step today cuts deeper into the Pattern." His breath caught. "If I set this piece…the Board itself may break."

Meera's fingers lifted slightly—a silent signal. A shadow shifted farther down the alley.

The priest drew the parchment at last. The alley seemed to lean closer, as if the stones themselves waited for his choice.

Vikrant's eyes burned. "Give it to me. Bhaskar commands it. With this, Raju will reach the chamber."

The words pierced him. Raju. Chamber. The very path the Kumari had shown—and the very crack in the Pattern he feared. Still, he placed the cloth bundle into Vikrant's waiting hand.

For a moment, he felt the Board tilt beneath his soul.

Vikrant held the prize, but his voice was cold as stone. "You have obeyed, Pandit. What happens now…is not on your hands."

The priest's face did not waver. "No. What happens now is mine to answer for. And that is why I must atone."

Before they could stop him, his other hand swept from his sleeve—the bone vial uncorked, the bitter almond stench sharp in the air. He drank as if sealing a vow, not ending a life.

Neeraj lurched forward, too late. "Why?"

The priest's knees buckled. His fingers slipped from the vial. The breath left him in a single, shuddering exhale. "Because I have—"

A bell rang beyond the alley—warped, delayed, as if the sound had chosen the wrong moment to arrive.

"…set—"

His body hit the ground. Unanswered.

Meera did not reach for him.

Neeraj inhaled—then chose not to speak.

Vikrant stood still, parchment in hand, gaze fixed not on the body, but on the space it had vacated—as if the Pattern had removed a piece and not yet told him why.

Above them, the prayer flags hung motionless.

Below, something vast registered—not as feeling, but as alignment.

THE LOST PROPHECY
नष्टः भविष्यवाणी

FROM THE SCROLL OF THE RED MOON

Preserved in the vault beneath Dauber Square, never spoken aloud.

When the blood moon climbs the
House of Stone,
And does not pass, but watches,
The Queen shall awaken,
The Rook shall rise,
And the Board shall break.

Only the Seeker may close the gate.
Only love may end the war.

BOOK THREE COMING SPRING 2027

A JOURNEY TO THE HEART OF KUMARI:
A TALE OF POWER & REDEMPTION

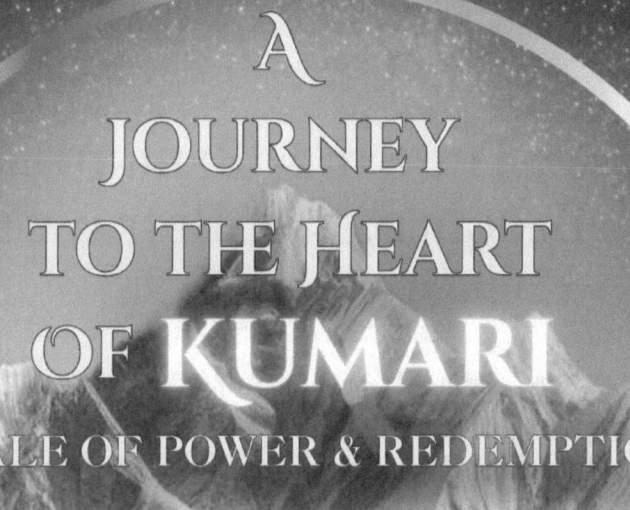

THE STORY BEHIND BLOODLINES & BETRAYALS

When I first began writing *A Journey to the Heart of Kumari*, I envisioned it as a single, sweeping manuscript. The story unfolded across Nepal, taking the Sharma family from Kathmandu and Chitwan to Pokhara and finally to the high Himalayas. It wasn't until I handed the draft to my developmental editor that I realized the challenge ahead. At over 150,000 words, the manuscript was simply too long for a debut novel.

My editor, a brilliant man with a knack for asking the right questions, gently posed one: "Have you considered breaking this into multiple books?"

Initially, I resisted. To me, the story was meant to be read as one cohesive journey, with all the threads converging in a grand conclusion. But as I wrestled with the idea, I realized it was an opportunity to give each segment of the journey its own identity. *Guardians of a Secret Legacy* could focus on the Sharma family's introduction to the mysteries of the Heart of Kumari in Kathmandu and Chitwan. *Bloodlines & Betrayals* would capture the tense, claustrophobic drama of their time in Pokhara at the Surya Chandra Inn. The third book would lead them to the high Himalayas for the ultimate confrontation.

Breaking the manuscript into separate books wasn't easy.

It meant reworking the structure and crafting not just one satisfying ending, but two more, each capable of standing on its own. When I decided to divide the story, the second section's conclusion felt incomplete—it lacked the depth and tension needed to function as a standalone novel. The challenge weighed on me until last summer, during a visit to my mother in the United States.

Over coffee, I shared my struggle, explaining how I needed to rework the ending of *Bloodlines & Betrayals*, as it felt flat and lacked a sense of urgency. As we talked, ideas began to take shape. Together, we brainstormed ways to transform the conclusion into something thrilling and memorable—an ending that not only stood strong on its own but left readers on the edge of their seats, eager for the next installment of the Sharma family's journey.

Around the same time, I had dinner with my son Harrison, who is now twenty-five and serving in the United States Air Force. We were planning a family vacation to Florida and discussing activities. The idea of visiting an escape room came up—our family loves the teamwork and problem-solving these challenges demand. That conversation sparked a new idea: *What if the climax of Bloodlines & Betrayals felt like an escape room?*

The original ending had Pasang leading the family to safety. *But what if Pasang tested them instead of simply being their guide? What if the Heart of Kumari itself tested their worthiness to wield its power?* I ran the idea past my mother, who loved it, and I began drafting. Then, the Chamber of Trials was born: a series of puzzles and challenges pushing the Sharma family to their limits. I added a water element to heighten the tension: an invisible clock ticking down as the chamber slowly flooded. This urgency brought the ending to life, turning it into a thrilling and fitting conclusion for *Bloodlines & Betrayals*.

The Shatranj Ke Sipahi: A Sinister Addition

Another critical element of *Bloodlines & Betrayals* emerged during a pivotal conversation with my editor. The book centers around the Sharma family's time at the Surya Chandra Inn in Pokhara, where Raju and Siddharth ostensibly protect them. However, the family soon realizes they're more captives than guests. At one point, my editor asked a simple, yet game-changing question: "Why don't they just call the police?"

It was an obvious question, but one I hadn't considered. Indeed, if the Sharmas were suspicious of their so-called protectors, they would turn to the authorities. But why wouldn't they? That night, I posed the question to my family. My son Kiran, sixteen at the time, had a ready answer: "Because the police are in on it." My husband Ravi agreed, adding, "They're corrupt and working with Raju and Siddharth."

This realization led to the creation of the *Shatranj Ke Sipahi*, a shadowy organization with roots in the Sharma family's own history. That evening, as we sat around the fire, Ravi glanced at our children playing chess and suggested the name: *Shatranj ke Sipahi*—chess warriors. It was perfect: strategic, sinister, and evocative. Over time, I wove their presence throughout the book, crafting their lineage and motivations. They became a powerful force, driven by their own dark ambitions for the Heart of Kumari.

A Tale of Tension and Betrayal

Unlike the expansive adventure of *Guardians of a Secret Legacy*, *Bloodlines & Betrayals* is a taut, suspenseful story that unfolds entirely at the Surya Chandra Inn. The inn becomes a pressure cooker of secrets and lies, with the Shatranj Ke Sipahi pulling the strings from the shadows. The story explores themes of trust, betrayal, and survival, pushing the Sharma family to their limits.

What began as part of a larger manuscript evolved into a standalone concept with its own identity. Crafting *Bloodlines & Betrayals* taught me to embrace change and listen to feedback, even when it meant rewriting or re-imagining key elements. The result is a story that stands on its own, setting the stage for the final chapter in the Sharma family's journey—a chase through the Himalayas.

In time, the trilogy will return to its original form—one complete volume, whole and unbroken. For now, I'm letting the story emerge as it must, piece by piece, allowing both the world and its readers to find their way into it gradually. Thank you for walking this path with me.

Glossary
नघिरा टुः

Aloo Parathas - Stuffed South Asian flatbreads filled with spiced potatoes and cooked on a griddle, often served with yogurt or pickles.

Annapurna - A Himalayan mountain massif in Nepal, sacred and famous among trekkers and climbers.

Babe Ruth - Famous American baseball player.

Banyan Tree - A sacred fig tree common across South Asia, associated with folklore, spirits, and ancient rituals.

Bansuri - A traditional bamboo flute used across Nepal and India. In this story, it resonates with otherworldly energy.

Bat Cave / Chamero Gufa - A well-known cave system near Pokhara, home to bat colonies.

"Careless Whisper" - A 1984 George Michael song.

Chitwan - A jungle region in southern Nepal known for wildlife reserves and ancient temples.

Deepika Padukone - Bollywood actress.

Dhaka Topi - Nepali hat made from Dhaka fabric.

Dharma Shanti Mandir Temple - A sacred temple located in the Mahendrapal Bazaar. A place associated with peace, ritual, and hidden truth.

"Every Breath you Take" - Song by the Police, 1983.

"Everybody Wants to Rule the World" - A 1985 Tears for Fears song tied to themes of power and destiny.

Fish Tail Mountain (Machhapuchhre) - A sacred, unclimbed peak in the Annapurna range, known for its fishtail-shaped summit.

Guggul - A resin burned as incense in South Asia.

Gunyu - Traditional Nepali wrap-dress worn by women in rural regions.

Gurung Ornaments - Traditional jewelry of the Gurung people, often crafted in coral and silver.

"Highway to the Danger Zone" - A 1986 Kenny Loggins.

Kali Raatri ("Dark Night") - a historical era of unrest in Nepal.

Kangchenjunga - The third-highest mountain in the world, rising on the border of Nepal and Sikkim. Revered as a sacred peak, it is often associated with guardianship, hidden realms, and ancient Himalayan lore.

Kathmandu Herald - A fictional newspaper referenced in the story.

Khukuri - A traditional curved Nepali knife.

Knight Sigil / Broken L - A symbolic mark representing the Knight's path.

Konkani - A coastal Indian language.

Kshatriya - Warrior-ruler class in traditional Hindu society.

Kumari Mandala - An ancient geometric symbol tied to the Heart of Kumari, marking hidden or sacred sites.

Mahendra Cave / Mahendra Gufa - A major cave system in Pokhara known for limestone formations.

Mahendrapal Bazaar - A bustling Nepali marketplace—a crossroads for merchants, street food, and hidden dealings.

Malachi - The name claimed by the wraith-like presence that confronts Harrison in the caverns.

Mandala - A sacred geometric pattern central to Hindu and Buddhist cosmology. The Kumari Mandala is a variant.

Mango Lassi - A chilled yogurt drink made with ripe mangoes, common across Nepal and India.

Masala Chai - Spiced tea brewed with milk, ginger, and aromatics. A staple across South Asia.

Mehbooba Mehbooba - A classic Bollywood song from the 1975 film *Sholay*.

Mohi - A noblewoman or consort in historic Nepali contexts.

Momo - Nepali and Tibetan dumplings, steamed or fried and served with chutney.

Naan - Soft leavened flatbread baked in a tandoor and eaten with curries.

Namaste - Traditional greeting meaning "I bow to you," spoken with palms pressed together.

Om Shanti Om - A 2007 Bollywood film starring Shah Rukh Khan and Deepika Padukone.

Pakoras - Crisp fritters of vegetables or meat coated in spiced gram flour and deep fried.

Pashmina / Dhaka - Traditional Nepali textiles. Dhaka is especially tied to national identity and craftsmanship.

Patuka - A long cloth belt worn with traditional Nepali dress.

Phewa Lake - Pokhara's iconic lake, known for mountain reflections and the Tal Barahi temple at its center.

Pokhara Museum - A cultural institution housing relics, maps, and tother historical artifacts.

Rickshaw - A common form of transport in South Asia.

Rook (Shatranj Ke Sipahi Brand) - A rank in the Order, known by a brand.

Sandalwood - Sacred aromatic wood often burned as incense.

Sanskrit - Ancient classical language of India.

Seti River - A glacial river running through Pokhara.

Shah Rukh Khan - Famous Bollywood actor.

Sheepy - Cyrus's stuffed lamb.

Shatranj Ke Sipahi - An ancient militant Order rooted in chess symbolism. Guardians and usurpers of the Heart of Kumari.

Singing Bowls - Himalayan metal bowls that produce resonant tones used for meditation and healing.

Spirit of Kumari - The divine presence connected to the living goddess.

Surya Chandra Inn - The Sharmas' guesthouse in Pokhara.

Tal Barahi - A temple on Phewa Lake's island dedicated to the goddess Barahi.

Taijitu - Symbol of yin and yang.

"Tainted Love" - A 1981 Soft Cell song.

Tandoori - A style of cooking in a clay oven, producing smoky, charred flavors.

Talwar - A type of curved sabre used historically across South Asia.

"The Greatest American Hero" - An American sitcom from the early 1980s.

The Heart of Kumari - A legendary red diamond tied to the living goddess.

The Seti Gorge - A deep canyon formed by the Seti River.

Thangka - A traditional Tibetan Buddhist painting on cloth depicting deities or mandalas.

Thorong La - A high pass in the Annapurna region.

Tibetan Prayer Wheel - A ritual wheel inscribed with mantras.

Vastu Shastra - Meaning "science of dwelling/architecture," it is the ancient Indian system of spatial harmony, alignment, and energetic balance used in building homes, temples, and cities.

Vermilion - Red powder used in Hindu and Nepali rituals.

About the Author
लेखकपरिचय

Ever the storyteller, Kimberly Ann Nayampalli takes readers on unforgettable journeys to vivid settings and into the very depths of adventure. With every narrative, she immerses you in the pulse of discovery, the triumph of overcoming challenges, and the wonder of each moment. Kimberly invites readers to explore the world and its mysteries through her tales, embarking on adventures alongside her characters.

Born and raised on Long Island, New York, Kimberly's innate curiosity has been a driving force on her journey into the world of writing.

With a bachelor's degree in Classical Archaeology and Mesoamerican Anthropology from the University of Albany, Kimberly's academic background has provided her with a deep appreciation for history and culture. This knowledge enriches her storytelling, infusing her work with historical depth and authenticity.

Before embarking on her writing career, Kimberly spent a decade as a flight attendant, allowing her to explore various corners of the globe. During this time, she met her husband, who shares her passion for travel. Their adventures together have not only created cherished memories, they have also inspired her writing.

Kimberly's life journey has taken her to different parts of the world, including a five-year stay in Bahrain. Currently living in Stuttgart, Germany, where her husband is employed by the U.S. Department of Defense, Kimberly's international experiences have broadened her horizons, deepened her appreciation for diverse cultures, and provided a wealth of material for her writing.

As a mother of four children, Kimberly also finds inspiration in her family life. She believes in the importance of sharing the world's wonders with her children, instilling in them a sense of curiosity and adventure.

With this same passion, Kimberly created The Nayampalli House as an imprint with purpose—where every book carries a deeper meaning. Rooted in her love for adventure and belief in the power of giving, its mission is to inspire others and forge connections across cultures and generations. A portion of every sale supports children in remote villages of Nepal, providing education, clothing, and essential supplies. In partnership with Treveda and the Northern Trekking Team, The Nayampalli House extends its reach beyond the page, uniting readers with communities around the world. For Kimberly, each book is a gift, and each reader a fellow traveler on a journey that braids adventure, compassion, and hope.

Above all, Kimberly writes to spark curiosity—to encourage readers to look closer, wander further, and believe in the hidden mysteries of the world. She invites you to step into her pages, lose yourself in the journey, and perhaps even find a few secrets meant just for you.

When she isn't writing, Kimberly can often be found exploring a new city's hidden corners, wandering through museums, or sketching story ideas in a well-worn travel journal. She treasures quiet mornings with a strong cup of coffee, evenings filled with lively family conversations, and moments when the ordinary invites her to look for more than what is seen. Whether traveling abroad or simply walking her local streets, she is always collecting details, snippets of dialogue, and fragments of history—the raw materials that become the beating heart of her next adventure.

To learn more about Kimberly and her adventures, connect with her on Instagram and Facebook at @the_alchemists_quill, or email her at fans@thenayampallihouse.org. Subscribe to her stories and behind-the-scenes lore on Substack at kimberlynayampalli.substack.com, and visit TheNayampalliHouse.org for additional information and updates.

Kimberly Nayampalli and her husband, Ravi
(Venice, Italy, 2023)

TO THE SEEKER
अन्वेषकाय

Now that you have walked this path with me, know this: what you have read is only the surface.

A mystery lies beneath—one that cannot be told outright. Scattered within these pages are pieces of a Pattern. They may seem like chance, but together they form a key.

No map is given.
No index will help you.
Only those who notice will know.

When you hold the key, bring it to:

TheNayampalliHouse.org/DiamondChamber

There, the Chamber will open, and you will uncover what has been kept hidden: forgotten lore, a lost chapter or two, letters never sent, glimpses into the rest of the saga, and the private pages of a journal never meant to be found.

May your journey be guided by the Heart.

Namaste,
K.A. Nayampalli

Your journey continues...

SCAN TO CROSS THE THRESHOLD OF *THE NAYAMPALLI HOUSE*®

AWAKEN THE SECRETS OF THE HEART OF KUMARI

www.ingramcontent.com/pod-product-compliance
Lightning Source LLC
LaVergne TN
LVHW030312070526
838199LV00069B/6456